THE
TRUTH
ACCORDING
TO EMBER

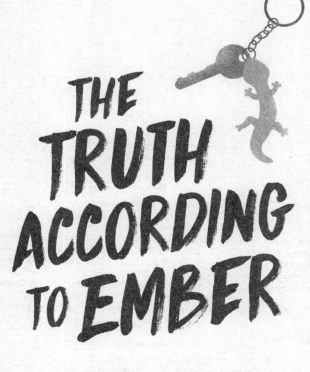

THE TRUTH ACCORDING TO EMBER

DANICA NAVA

BERKLEY ROMANCE

NEW YORK

BERKLEY ROMANCE
Published by Berkley
An imprint of Penguin Random House LLC
penguinrandomhouse.com

Copyright © 2024 by Danica Nava
Readers Guide copyright © 2024 by Danica Nava
Excerpt copyright © 2024 by Danica Nava

Library of Congress Cataloging-in-Publication Data

Names: Nava, Danica, author.
Title: The truth according to Ember / Danica Nava.
Description: First edition. | New York: Berkley Romance, 2024.
Identifiers: LCCN 2023051424 (print) | LCCN 2023051425 (ebook) |
ISBN 9780593642603 (trade paperback) | ISBN 9780593642610 (ebook)
Subjects: LCGFT: Humorous fiction. | Romance fiction. | Novels.
Classification: LCC PS3614.A923 T78 2024 (print) | LCC PS3614.A923 (ebook) |
DDC 813/.6—dc23/eng/20231117
LC record available at https://lccn.loc.gov/2023051424
LC ebook record available at https://lccn.loc.gov/2023051425

First Edition: August 2024

Printed in the United States of America
1st Printing

Book design by Daniel Brount

For every Indigenous woman who has ever felt invisible.
I see you. I am you.

THE TRUTH ACCORDING TO EMBER

One

I WAS NOT ALWAYS A LIAR. I MEAN, SURE, WHITE LIES WERE INevitable. I told them all the time. My habit of lying started with a simple "Yes, that beaded key chain *is* really pretty" to my best friend, Joanna, when we were fifteen. It was a vomit-green "lizard," and it was an insult to lizards everywhere. The key chain looked demented, all lumpy with gaps where beads should've been, but I lied through my teeth. What was I supposed to do? Tell her the truth and have her stop beading altogether? I couldn't do that to her. My little fib meant a lot to her, and I realized my words had an impact when she gifted the key chain to me that same Christmas with a little note that read, *Thank you for believing in me.*

That ugly little lizard, in all its garish glory, still lived on my key ring. It was so ugly, I was convinced that it could ward off evil; it was my little lucky charm and my most prized possession. Joanna ended up finding success with her beadwork. As the years went on, her ambitious designs served as a stable source of income, so I'd argue that my first white lie was a good one.

Sometimes, I lied because it was just easier. Who had time to get into the weeds of things? Just a teensy, tiny fib to save someone's feelings, or hide my own, did a lot to keep my sanity. I wasn't a pathological liar by any stretch of the imagination—it wasn't like I would lie and say I was someone that I wasn't, and not everything I said was a whopper. I wasn't a con artist trying to pull one over on people. I was just Ember Lee Cardinal, a sometimes liar, but mostly an overall good person.

But this lying business did get out of hand, I recognized that. I want to say for the record that if faced with the choice between plunging the toilets of an old and dingy (but well-loved) bowling alley for the rest of your life and the opportunity to dramatically change your circumstances with a few cleverly crafted lies, you would do it too. If an itty-bitty fabrication was the difference between barely keeping a roof over your head or having a stable career with growth—it was a no-brainer. I wasn't going to be slaving away disinfecting fifteen-year-old rental bowling shoes forever. Nope. I was changing my destiny.

I was going to be an accountant! Not like the "accountants" going viral on TikTok, but a real number-crunching, invoice-consolidating, checkbook-balancing accountant for a company—with a high salary! Not some job that paid $7.25 an hour but a *salary*. With benefits. No one in my family had ever had a salary before, and when we were sick, we would have to take a whole day off work and wait in line at the clinic, missing an entire day's pay. Private health insurance was on the table. Who was I? An accountant, that's who.

Kind of. Accountant adjacent? I took an intro to accounting class at the community college. It was enough to get an entry-level job, I knew that, and somehow, I still couldn't land any job interviews. I'd put in so many applications and gotten zilch in return. That was how I ended up here—desperation makes good people do bad things.

"Order nineteen," I yelled over the crashing sound of the bowling balls rolling down the freshly waxed pine lanes, knocking down pins.

"Not a single interview request?" Joanna, my best friend, roommate, and coworker, asked as she dumped a new jar of pickled jalapeños into the black Cambro for our patrons.

I handed the artificial-nacho-cheese-covered chips to two teenagers on a date. It smelled like burnt rubber; we probably should have stopped selling it today, but Bobby Dean was cheap.

"Not since you asked me this morning," I grumbled.

She meant well. Joanna was an artist, and this gig at Bobby Dean's Bowling Alley was perfect for her creative schedule. She made extra cash selling her jewelry, and she was so talented that sometimes people bought her stuff straight off her ears. It didn't hurt that she was smoking hot with her dark hair cropped to her shoulders, with vibrant purple ends standing out against her tanned skin. I, on the other hand, was not artistically inclined. My earning more money would take my leaving this place and getting a *real career*. I liked numbers and security, so accounting seemed like the best choice.

"How many rejections is that then? Twenty?" She wasn't looking at me as she wiped up some of the jalapeño brine off the counter.

"Thirty-seven," I corrected, and wished to Creator that I was kidding. I had a teacher once who told me if I applied myself, I could go far. I did apply myself. Quite literally, I applied to every job I could find online. I received thirty-seven rejections. All iterations of the same email: We regret to inform you that we have reviewed your application and decided to go with a candidate who would be a better fit.

What did that even mean? These were entry-level jobs that paid a few dollars more an hour than what I was making in the bowling alley. With every rejection, it was getting harder to believe they weren't auto-rejecting my application because I sounded like I came straight off the reservation . . .

Which I did.

My name was a pretty common Okie name. My high school was in Ada, right in the middle of Indian Country. But I felt like those shitasses hadn't even bothered reading my application or my cover letter. I was honest (mostly); I wanted to learn and grow. Did any of that matter? Not when you were "Indian," apparently. Something we could call ourselves but rubbed us the wrong way when non-Natives tried to foist the inaccurate label onto us.

"E!" Joanna cried. And there it was. The pity. The tone of *Why are you doing this?* The cry of outrage for putting myself in this type of situation.

I rolled my eyes, bracing myself for the same conversation I'd had a million times. "It's going to be fine," I said, and before she could try to convince me to give up, I walked off to start refilling the napkin dispensers. She followed me around the counter, dodging a few men and their beers.

I was shoving the tiny napkins into one of the silver dispensers when Joanna pushed the others away and invaded my space, leaning against the counter, casual confidence in all her Indigenous glory. Each of her fingers had a silver-and-gemstone ring, and her wrists were stacked with beaded bracelets that jingled as she tapped her chin in thought, drawing attention to her full lips. She was tall and commanding and didn't take shit from anybody. Including me.

"I believe you. You were always the smartest kid in our classes, and you've been dealt some shitty hands. Why don't you wait to apply for these jobs until you finish more of the accounting classes?" she asked.

"I need to be making more money now to pay for those classes." Sarcasm laced my voice as I mimicked her casual stance.

"I could give you a loan." Her exaggerated tone put mine to shame.

"No."

"It's not your fault that—"

"Stop."

Talking about the rejections, I could handle. I was not going to get into it again about my brother, Sage, and the reason I was broke. Joanna knew and I knew that he'd lost my money. Talking more about it wouldn't help me right now. I needed forward-moving action. I reached around her to grab one of the discarded napkin holders.

"Okay, I'm sorry. I just want to help you."

"I know," I sighed, and punched the napkins into their place harder than was needed. "All this would be easier if I was white."

"Why would you say something stupid like that?"

I said it to be flippant, but lights and bells went off in my head like a jackpot win at the slots in the casino. *Ding. Ding. Ding.* There was a possible solution to my problems.

"Joanna!"

"We have to be proud of who we are and where we come from. Don't buy into the colonizer's propaganda."

"Yeah, yeah, yeah." I grabbed her shoulders. "Listen to me." The napkins and customers around us were forgotten.

"Fucksake! What?"

"I'm just gonna be white."

"Your dad is white." She looked beyond confused.

"Exactly, so it's not *really* a lie. I'm just going to check the Caucasian box on the applications."

"Does that really matter?"

"Let's see."

"You also don't have any accounting experience on your résumé." She extracted my hands from her.

"So what? I do all the register balancing here, and I help you and my auntie with your online taxes."

Joanna's face brightened. She finally understood where my mind was at.

"I can be your reference." Her smile lit up my entire world.

"Some people have private bookkeepers to handle all their business stuff."

"You're hired. Now it's not technically a lie."

"This is brilliant! Why didn't I think of this before?"

"Because you were playing as if the game was fair. Everyone lies on their résumé. Play by everyone else's rules." Joanna was excited, and it was infectious. "You know," she continued, "we are the only ones who answer the phone around here. You can be the bookkeeper for Bobby Dean too. I can also be your reference here." With that last bit, she did her impression of Bobby Dean himself with his lazy Okie twang; it was a perfect match.

"So, I'm doing this then?"

"You're doing it." We squealed and hugged.

A rough and insistent tap on my shoulder reminded me that I was still at work. I turned around to see Bucky, one of our regulars. He played in the Little Big Horns bowling league of old retired Native men who thought Bobby Dean's, with the three-dollar beer, was the best place to spend most of their time. Their team name was totally a dick joke that no one but them thought was clever. None of them were Lakota.

"Toilet's backed up again." Bucky burped and used his thumb to point behind him toward the men's bathroom.

I watched Bucky make his way back to his buddies, dragging toilet paper that was stuck to the bottom of his shoe.

"It's your turn," Joanna said, and walked back around the counter.

I didn't care. With my new application strategy, this was going to be the last clogged toilet I was going to plunge at the bowling alley.

Two

I WAS ALWAYS EARLY TO EVERYTHING. AND NOT JUST A FEW minutes early. No matter what I did, I was always an hour or two early to things. Did I have a life? That was yet to be determined. There is a prevalent stereotype that Natives are always late to stuff, but it was physically impossible for me to be tardy for anything. It was written in my DNA that Ember Lee Cardinal was and always would be very early to everything. Especially if I was excited about something like, for example, an interview for an accounting assistant position.

That's right. I had an interview! My first application as the new and improved me was a smashing success. When they asked for my job history, I put *accountant* for Bobby Dean's Bowling Alley and Bar. For school I put that I was a graduate of the Oklahoma City Community College, with an associate's degree in business accounting / finance support. When I googled the school, they didn't offer just an accounting degree. News to me, and I took two classes there—English and algebra. Accounting / finance support sounded pretty fancy and qualified, so I put that down.

Then, when I got to the last question before submission, it read, "Check Your Ethnicity." The list included American Indian / Alaska Native (I steered clear of that one), Asian, Black or African American, Native Hawaiian or Pacific Islander, Hispanic or Latino, and then, lastly, White.

I clicked the box.

I submitted it and got an interview request back in a day. A one hundred percent success rate so far. The email in my inbox read, Dear Ms. Cardinal, we are very impressed with your application and would love a chance to learn more about you and discuss the position. Below are the times we are available for an interview. We are hoping to fill this position as soon as possible, so please let us know at your earliest convenience.

So here I was, loitering at a coffee place called Stellar Coffee Café, trying to calm my nerves. What made the coffee so stellar? It wasn't the price, but it had the best view of the prettiest building in downtown Oklahoma City—the First National Center. BancFirst Tower was taller by a few floors, but that building was an ugly rectangle. Devon Tower was super tall and new, and looked like aliens lived in it. The First National Center was stunning—it might as well have been the Empire State Building with its vintage art deco glamour. And I had an interview with a company that lived inside it. Things were really looking up.

I loved downtown. This was a metropolis, so much *more* than the mobile home I grew up in outside of Ada. The city center was beautiful and urban with green parks among the skyscrapers. There were cities with taller buildings, but I hadn't been to any. Sometimes, when I was downtown, I liked to pretend I was in New York City on my Okie-mind version of Park Avenue, with all the expensive shops and restaurants.

I breathed in the warm, earthy scent of my coffee and watched the street come alive with sophisticated commuters. People with what I liked to call dumb money. They drove expensive luxury cars that made no sense for a place like Oklahoma, where thirty minutes outside of downtown was flat rural land full of hay fields. The men and women hustled up and down the sidewalk looking at their phones, diamonds and gold winking in the morning sun. They were just like those people I'd grown up watching on television in *Sex and the City* and *Law and Order*. The high-powered lawyers with their briefcases and the bankers running late, needing to make their trades or whatever it was they did in there. I wanted to be just like them.

I stared down at my black skirt and blazer. Boring. And not even comfortable. I was much more at home in a pair of jeans, but rich businesswomen on TV always wore pencil skirts. I'd found this mismatched suit at Goodwill. I was like Goldilocks with a skirt that was a size too tight and a blazer two sizes too big. In my mirror this morning, I thought if I bunched the sleeves up, it looked intentional. It was the best I could come up with on a budget. In the light of my apartment, they looked like they matched pretty well, but with the morning sun streaming like a spotlight, the brightness showed that the skirt was slightly more faded than the blazer.

At least I had my freaky lizard key chain hung proudly on my tote bag. I didn't need shiny diamonds; I knew the lizard was winking at me and wishing me luck—at least it would if it had eyes, and I meant that in the literal sense. Joanna had forgotten to give it eyes.

I was going to nail this interview and get the job. It sounded really swanky to be in the accounting department for a startup company. The description on the website read, "Technix: A turnkey provider of excellence"—what the hell did that even mean?

I didn't care. Technix offered insurance, and I wanted it. Technix could be a cover for a Mafia money-laundering business, and I wouldn't care. Did the Mafia provide a 401(k) with matching contributions? If so, I'd look the other way.

I tipped back the last of my coffee. I was supposed to be rationing sips so it would last longer. The barista gave me the stank eye for taking one of the high-top aluminum tables for so long. I still had forty-five minutes until my interview.

I got up to get back in the long line, and within half a second, two men with laptops and books took my table. I now needed to find another place to prepare for my interview and calm down. My hands were slick with sweat, and the cheap material of my skirt showed the marks from where I kept wiping my hands. It looked like two landing strips on either side of my thighs.

I told myself not to be nervous, it was just an interview. No! It was the first office interview I'd ever had in my life. I told myself it wasn't like they were going to ask me to my face if I embellished a little on my résumé or ask me point-blank if I was really an Indian from the rez masquerading as an accomplished Waspy accountant. I've lied about little things before. So, this one itty-bitty truth-bending episode shouldn't matter, right? I just needed my foot in the door, and after that I would only tell the truth.

I wanted to feel bad about the lying, but really, I was more worried about getting caught in the lies. It was hard to feel bad about gaming a system that was designed to put people like me down. I was the first person in my family to attend college. It was just community college, and I hadn't finished—yet. But that still meant something. I was proud of it. If I could get this job, or one like it, then I could afford to pay for night school. I could live the truth then, proudly displaying my accounting / finance support associate's degree. How were people like me supposed to *honestly* get their feet over the corporate threshold when you had to have gone to the right schools, been a part of a sorority, and had at least three to five years' experience for an entry-level position? A real head-scratcher, that one.

Anyway, nothing I put was an overt lie . . . it was just not precisely the whole truth. My dad was white, and my mom was a Native mix of Chickasaw and Choctaw. That was just how it was now. We all were a mix of stuff. A real American melting pot, as my auntie said. My parents had me super young, and I don't remember a single holiday or birthday back then that didn't end with them shouting at each other. I was six when my brother, Sage, was born. Then my dad left.

My brother and I lived with our mom in a one-bedroom apartment for a while before she dropped us off at Auntie's house and never came back. I was thirteen and Sage was only seven. Auntie was technically her cousin, but they were close like sisters. At least that was what Auntie told me. It was hard at first, but I really loved living in that little mobile home with her. She took us to the library on the weekends and told me I was smart. No one had ever said that before.

So, yeah, checking that box felt like a big "fuck you" to the man. To every single gatekeeper trying to put people like me in a box with that stupid ethnicity question. What did that dumbass question ever accomplish? Some bullshit affirmative action quota? Something to save face and look like they really tried to hire diversely? Everyone likes to say it's so easy for minorities to get jobs now. That we have some sort of *advantage* after years of being treated as second-class citizens. Bull fucking shit. If that were the case, then why were all the good jobs still full of white people? Being hyped by Joanna in the bowling alley that night really fueled me.

The line still hadn't moved, and I was giving up. I had extra time to make it to my interview, and I wanted them to see me early and eager for the job. I turned on the balls of my feet, my orthopedic flats squeaked on the tile, and I collided with a wall.

It was a handsome, muscular wall, and I was going down, sideways. The wall had arms. They encircled me before I did a face-plant. They yanked me upright and pulled my eyeline to a chest with a soft, blue chambray button-up shirt.

I was mumbling my apologies and thanks all in one when the hulking wall bent down. His dark braids draped over his shoulders.

"This yours?" he asked me, looking up from his squatted position. His warm chocolate eyes were framed by strong brows. Smiling, he was holding a green thing.

My creepy key chain. It must have been knocked off my bag in my collision with this Native hunk. How did I know? We Natives have what is called "NAdar." Like we can sniff the rain or some shit—we laugh about it.

Okay, I was stereotyping based on my experience growing up in Ada.

"Chokma'shki', thank you," I said as I took the beaded thing from his outstretched hand. I wasn't testing him. It's what I always grew up saying. Our traditional word in Chikashshanompa', followed by the English translation. Auntie said it was the polite thing to do and helped reinforce the few words I did know to my memory.

"Gvlielitseha, you're welcome." He stood and smiled a handsome crooked smile. A smile that could get him in and out of trouble.

I didn't have time for trouble; I had an interview to get to, but I was rooted in that spot, and my face betrayed me because I was smiling a dumb, troublemaking smile back.

"Cherokee," he said, speaking with his chin, tilting it up toward me.

"No, I'm Chickasaw . . . er . . . an enrolled Chickasaw citizen. And Choctaw mix." The word vomit poured out of my mouth and I couldn't stop it. It would have been easier to just say how I was legally enrolled, rather than list my entire bloodline history. I could feel how red my face was.

"No, *I'm* Cherokee."

Duh.

"Cool." That was it, people. All I said to the hottest man to ever pay me any attention was *cool*. To make it worse, I waved goodbye and walked out the door, leaving Stellar Coffee and the most beautiful man in Oklahoma.

I made it to the corner and waited to cross the street, letting out a relieved breath. And I heard a throat clear. I turned to see the hot Native man standing next to me to my right. He smiled.

"You work around here?" he asked me.

"I do. I'm an accountant." I wouldn't call this a lie, per se. I was trying to speak it into existence, to let it be so. But also, I wanted to impress him even though I'd probably never see him again.

Before our conversation could go any further, a woman to my left pushed an empty stroller to the curb, wrestling a wiggly baby in her arms. She forgot to lock the brake, and the stroller started rolling into the street. I grabbed it before it could get hit by a car, tugging the stroller back onto the curb.

"Thank you so much," she said to me.

"No problem," I said. "Are you giving your mommy trouble?" I asked the cute baby, who was wearing gray, so I couldn't tell if it was a boy or a girl.

I received the most adorable smile, and then the baby's face contorted, and my life flashed before my eyes as a white explosion of spit-up erupted from the baby's mouth. I was in the line of fire. It was a direct hit all over my shoulder in a hot liquid stream.

I heard the rumblings of a throaty laugh behind me. I chose to ignore it.

"Oh my god! I'm so sorry." The mom was embarrassed. The light turned green, and it was our turn to walk. She pushed the stroller with one hand and rested her baby on her hip, looking at me as if I were a ticking time bomb about to go off on her.

The traitorous baby smiled happily, as if nothing happened.

It was fine. This was fine. I would just ask to use the bathroom when I got to the office. We made it to the other side of the street, and she dug through her diaper bag and pulled out a wad of baby wipes.

"Here!" She thrust them at me.

"Thanks." I gave her a tight smile. It wasn't her fault, nor even the baby's. I wasn't mad. Just embarrassed that I had a copious amount of spit-up on my interview outfit. We parted ways, and I walked into the First National Center, wiping away the worst of the mess. It was still pretty bad. I focused only on the stain and filed into the elevator with other workers.

I pushed the button for floor twelve at the same time as a larger tan finger moved in to hit it at the same time. I wasn't sure if it was the elevator button or the hand that sent an electric shock through me.

"It's not that bad," said the deep voice that rolled over me like thunder. I knew without looking that it was the gorgeous Native man who owned that finger. "Impressive reflexes back there."

I heard an exaggerated sniff, and that pissed me off. I stopped wiping and shot laser beams from my eyes into his face. I had to look up quite a bit to do it.

He laughed.

"Are you following me?" I asked.

"I work here. I've never seen you before, maybe you're following me?"

"You work at Technix?" My stomach dropped. This was karma in action. I'd lied, and now instead of impressing this guy, I had full-on embarrassed myself.

"I do. I've never seen you in accounting before." He curled up his eyebrow in skepticism, and his smirk was full of humor.

There was a beat of silence in the elevator. I was getting lost in his warm chocolate eyes. He narrowed them, and I saw the silent question there: *Are you gonna fess up?*

"Fine! I'm interviewing, but since I smell like spoiled milk, this is probably the last you will see of me."

"Nah, Technix is pretty chill. I'll corroborate your story that you were helping a baby. The HR ladies will love that shit."

"Yeah? Should we say the baby was in the stroller and I saved its life?" I joked.

He threw his head back and laughed. "I don't think we need to go that far."

The elevator stopped at each floor, and before long, it was just me and the handsome human lie detector riding the elevator to the twelfth floor.

"I'm Ember."

"Danuwoa." He presented his hand to me. I quickly concealed the wad of dirty wipes before I shook his hand. The electricity was most certainly not from the elevator. This man's energy zapped right through me. If he felt it too, he didn't let on.

The elevator stopped with a ding.

"We're here," he said, and stepped onto floor twelve.

Technix.

Three

THE DOORS OPENED UP TO A WORLD OF STERILE WHITE AND cool shades of gray. I took a deep breath and could still smell the fresh paint. A few feet from the elevator entrance was the reception area, with a curved wall that wrapped around the desk, hugging the cupboard behind it. It was the focal point of the room. The Technix logo was the only adornment, with the *T* and the *X* in large calligraphic letters.

Danuwoa leaned against the tall desk, sharing pleasantries with a young and petite Black woman with a twist-out updo and gold accessories that winked in the overhead lights. She looked up at me and gave me a cursory once-over, assessing me from top to bottom.

"Hi, I'm Ember Cardinal. I'm here for an interview with Monica Lewis." I smiled and hoped she couldn't smell me.

"You're kind of early," the receptionist said.

"Phoebe." Danuwoa's voice sounded like a reprimand, like he was accustomed to reminding her to be less judgmental.

"I had a bit of an accident. Could I use your restroom?" I

waved my hand, showcasing the wet stain as if it were the prize of the hour on *The Price Is Right*.

"Oh my, yeah, it's back there. Let me show you." She got up, but a frantic older woman approached the desk.

"Do you have extra stamps up here? We need stamps," the older woman said. Her thin gray hair was held up with a claw clip.

"Charlotte, it's okay. We have plenty of stamps." Phoebe looked at me apologetically and turned behind her into the cupboard.

"I'll show her to the bathrooms," Danuwoa said, pushing himself off the desk and heading toward the back of the room. "You comin'?" He didn't even bother looking behind as he asked me.

I ran a few steps to catch up. We walked through a maze of cubicles with half walls, so you could see over the top of everyone's heads. I'd never been in any office before, but I thought cubicles had walls that went to the ceiling or something and offered a little more privacy.

Danuwoa turned and looked at me and must have noticed my confused expression, because he said, "This is our new open floor plan. It's supposed to be more productive and equalizing." He motioned with his hand to a swinging door and led me through. To the left of the hall was an open kitchen and dining area. He stopped and pointed at the bathrooms to our right.

"Good luck, Ember Cardinal," he said with a wink before walking into the kitchen.

I pushed the door open, and the bathroom was empty. I sighed; I'd worked so hard to land this interview, I wasn't going to let this spit-up stop me. I set my tote bag behind the faucet on the sink and worked to pull out the twenty bobby pins digging into my skull. I had to shove that many into my hair to anchor my bun to my lower neck. I tried just sticking the pins in my mouth, but it quickly grew to be too much. I spat them out into the sink. Once I removed the last one, I ripped out the two elastic hair ties and uncoiled my long espresso-colored hair. It hurt so good letting it fall. I flipped my head over and massaged my scalp where the elastics and pins had pulled at my hair.

When I came up to check the damage, I was lucky. My hair was still damp from my shower this morning, so the tight bun gave it a little bend and wave. I raked my fingers as best I could through my long tangled tresses and pulled them all over to my left side, covering the stain. I could still smell my conditioner, and as long as this Monica Lewis wasn't a hugger and didn't invade my personal space, then she shouldn't be able to smell the vomit too much.

I dug through my bag and checked my phone. I had ten minutes until my interview. I also had a few questionably motivational texts from Joanna—they were all GIFs of Britney Spears with the words YOU BETTER WORK, BITCH in large flashing letters.

I took a mirror selfie showcasing the stain and sent it to Joanna. She texted back immediately, Eww what have you been doing??? 👟👟

I sent the eye roll emoji followed by the baby and vomit emoji, threw my phone back in my bag, and took out my lizard key chain. I squeezed it three times for luck and then headed back out into the corporate world of Technix.

More people were milling about in the break room, and I saw Danuwoa approach me, holding a Technix-branded mug full of coffee.

"You should've worn your hair like that from the beginning. It looks nice," he said, smiling.

"Smells good too. Come on." I curled my fingers in a come-hither way. "Have a whiff."

Danuwoa took one step forward and gave me another exaggerated sniff. After, he pursed his lips and shrugged. "Coconut baby vomit. You have refined taste."

I laughed at how completely ridiculous and confident this man was. Who the hell was he? I didn't have time to go down that rabbit hole. "I need to go to my interview."

"You got this." He lifted his coffee in a salute, and I went back through the maze to reception.

"Much better," Phoebe said with a nod. "You can have a seat. I already let Monica know you're here."

"Perfect, thanks." I sat down on the modern futon-looking couch in the corner next to a potted ficus. I crossed my legs at my ankles as Queen Clarisse Renaldi taught me when I was a kid. If dorky Mia Thermopolis could be a princess, then I could get hired here. I just needed one company to tell me yes. Technix was going to be that company.

A few minutes went by, possibly an eternity, and then I heard my name.

"Yes?" I looked up to see a mature-looking woman wearing a turquoise tunic, leggings, and a big chunky beaded necklace. It was an ugly outfit, but I was impressed we could wear leggings in the office. I said *we*, like I was already an employee. I was really great at this feigning confidence crap. Who was I kidding, my anxiety was through the roof.

"Hi, I'm Monica." She extended her hand; I took it in what I hoped was a just-firm-enough handshake. "Why don't you follow me back this way."

We snaked through the other side of the floor through another short gray cubicle jungle, similar to the one Danuwoa showed me, until we reached the farthest back wall and entered a glass-enclosed conference room. When I walked past her inside, she sniffed twice. In my nervous state, I opted to ignore it and pretended I didn't smell anything. Once I sat down facing the rest of the office, a few heads poked out from their workstations and stared at me.

I had never had an audience for an interview before. Unless you counted the one time I applied to Abercrombie & Fitch in high school, trying to find a weekend gig in the city. We had a group interview and the other girls laughed at me whenever I tried to answer a question. I was so embarrassed that I got up in the middle of it and left the food court. Yup, they had the interview in the mall food court.

But this time at least it was just Monica and me in this room with the thin piece of glass closing off the sounds of the employees typing and talking on their phones.

"Thank you so much for taking the time to speak with me today. It was a pleasure to read your application and cover letter." Monica placed a folder on the table and leaned back in her chair. "I prefer to do interviews a bit more informal than most. Why don't you tell me a little bit about yourself."

I tried to school my face to look like I was calm, but I was not calm. "Thank you so much for having me," I said with a smile to buy time to think. How to explain my background vaguely but detailed enough to show I was qualified for the position? "A little bit about me is that I am the first person in my family to attend college." That was a truthful statement. I just had to say what she wanted to hear. I sat in some classrooms, and now I could push all the paper you wanted me to.

"Yes, I noted on your application that it looks like you were working as a bookkeeper for Joanna Gates. Can you tell me about that role?"

I gulped. It was showtime. I had prepared for this. I started my spiel: "Joanna is a local jewelry designer with a small business. I have been keeping her books balanced and taxes filed for the last three years." Technically not a lie. Joanna dealt in mostly cash and never reported those earnings, so it wouldn't hold up in an audit, but that wasn't important. "It's a very think-on-your-feet type of environment, and every day is different from the last."

"That sounds exciting. Why the change into the more standard corporate accounting role now?"

This I could totally answer truthfully.

"I'm looking for stability. I want a schedule that is consistent and stable as I continue my education." She didn't need to know it was to complete the education I lied about and said I already had.

Monica smiled. I relaxed a little.

"I love that. Technix is a startup that is quickly expanding, and we have a desperate need for an accounting assistant to come in ready to roll their sleeves up. We are very well funded, and in our series C round of investors, so you can rest assured that a position here would be stable."

"That's encouraging to hear." I tucked my hair behind my ear, but then remembered I placed my hair perfectly to cover the stain, and moved it back out.

"So, what's your favorite thing about accounting?" she asked.

"I love numbers and how they balance with accounting. Same inputs and outputs." I prayed I hadn't said the last part like a question. I wasn't a savant. I just wanted the money.

"Okay, spoken like an accountant. What programs are you familiar with?"

Er. Right. Well, the job post mentioned something about SAP.

"I am very familiar with sap," I answered with a confident smile.

She looked confused. "Sap?"

"Yes, sap."

"S-A-P, you mean?"

Shit. "Right, sorry. With all the acronyms, I pronounce them like words to help me remember." I needed to cool it with my nervous chuckle.

"Ha ha! Hilarious. All right, why don't we do a round of rapid-fire questions?"

"Sure, hit me." I was doomed. I knew nothing about systems or computer programs other than my ancient version of Word.

"Favorite food?" If they were all like this, I was going to do great.

"Burritos."

"Musician?"

"Cyndi Lauper."

"Ooh, unexpected. Spirit animal?"

Cringe. I wished people would realize spirit animals were a thing for only a select few Indigenous cultures and not everyone had one. My smile wavered, but I answered anyway. "A squirrel." I chose the cutest, most random animal that popped into my head.

Monica threw her head back and laughed. "That's good. Okay, last one. Favorite formula?"

"Like in spreadsheets?"

"Uh-huh."

"Erm . . . the summation button."

"Ember, you are a riot." She wiped tears from her eyes as she wrapped up her chuckles. "Do you have any questions?"

"Yeah, I was wondering how many accountants this accounting assistant would support?"

"Great question." Monica leaned in and placed her elbows on the table. "There are five accountants, including Gary, who is the vice president of accounting, who you would be mostly assisting. Since we are in the middle of series C funding and have a few major things happening in the company, there are many projects someone like you would get to take part in. We are looking for someone with a can-do attitude who will think no task is too big or too small. We really like to feel like a family here. This is the perfect position for someone looking to learn on the job and grow with a company as we continue to scale up."

"I won't lie to you, Monica. What you have told me excites me, and I would really enjoy working at Technix. I'm a roll-your-sleeves-up kind of girl, and I am really hoping to grow somewhere long term."

Her smile was warm, and I felt so at ease in her presence. *Offer me the job!*

"Anything else from me?"

"I believe you've covered everything. The posting mentioned the company has great benefits. Could you explain a little about those?" My mind was blank. This job sounded perfect.

"We have company-sponsored outings, fully covered health insurance, and tuition assistance for those who qualify, to name a few."

"Oh wow, this all sounds so great." I was nearly salivating with excitement and want.

"I'm so glad you said that. I have a great feeling about you. Thank you so much for taking the time to come in, and I'll let you know our decision shortly."

That was it? I mean, sure, I was a pretty charming person, but that? Was I on acid? Did all that coffee do something to me? That was like a supersonic-speed interview.

As she led me to the elevator, Danuwoa sped by pushing a cart. It happened so fast, but he walked past me, and I caught a whiff of him. That sounds creepy, but it was not like I sniffed him, even though he sniffed me twice since I'd met him. I had to breathe, and in my totally casual inhale, I discovered that he smelled like a pure, clean man, with a hint of lavender. He nodded and kept going.

"That's Dan Colson, from IT," Monica said, giggling. "All the ladies love to look at him. Thank you so much again."

It was a goodbye and dismissal. I shook her hand and murmured another thank-you, then got into the elevator. Right before the doors closed, she winked at me.

I walked down Park Avenue and passed the county law library on my way to the parking garage where I'd left my car. I parked far away so no one immediately in my interview zone would see the junker 1996 rusty Ford Contour that I drove. It had been with me for a while, and I wish I could loyally say it was a reliable rig. It was not, but it got me from point A to point B on most days. Sage was great with it and usually fixed whatever popped up, so I didn't spend my entire paycheck at the mechanic, but he was currently sitting in jail and wouldn't be out for a couple of months. So . . .

Oh, Sage. I missed him and I wanted to strangle him for all the shit he put Auntie and me through. I took a deep breath to clear my head before my mind could linger too long on that. I had better things to think about, like spending my entire drive home wondering if I got the job. It was still early in the day, so I had plenty of time to overanalyze every part of my interview. Yay, me.

I-35 south was clear as I headed toward the community college where the apartment I shared with Joanna was. It was hot and humid. The sky was gray with heavy clouds. I hoped they would break on my drive and cleanse the air. I had no air-conditioning, so I manually lowered my window and let the wind blast my face. The air smelled like rain, earthy and wet as it masked the city smell that baked in the summer heat. The highway was all concrete and lined with thirsty grass. Gas stations peppered the drive, and the prettiest thing on my commute were the gold McDonald's arches. Was I only saying that because I was hungry? I'd never tell.

Don't get me wrong. I loved Oklahoma. Oklahoma was beautiful. Not the concrete and the sometimes stinky smell of the city, but the countryside. It was flat and expansive with endless plains, grass, and trees. We were at the tail end of tornado season, and the fresh smell that comes after the rain is something I wish I could buy in a bottle. There was nothing better than a thunderstorm in summer. I don't "rain dance," but I might send a prayer to Creator to encourage the clouds. The rain drove people into the bowling alley, and more people meant more tips.

Our apartment was—for lack of a better and more artsy word—ugly. Cheap was what cheap got. At least the locks worked, we were on the second story, and it had parking. Tandem parking. But Joanna made all her stuff at home in the living room and rarely drove her car, so it was fine by me to park behind her only slightly newer Honda Civic. The paint job on hers was still intact, and she had all four hubcaps, but I wasn't jealous or bitter or anything.

Stevie Nicks's raspy voice was blasting out of Joanna's room when I walked into our apartment. That meant Joanna was having a creative epiphany before our shift at Bobby Dean's started. My shoes flew in an arc across the living room floor as I kicked each one off.

"I'm home!" I yelled as I made my way to the small kitchen. After no food and lots of coffee this morning, my comedown from all that anxiety had left me famished. I raided the refrigerator, pushed aside two open cans of beer, and took out a can of refried beans with a plastic bag covering it. I had just opened them the night before, and sometimes I was too lazy to dirty a Tupperware container when I knew I would eat more of them soonish.

I grabbed the bag of corn tortillas and the shredded cheese and set up my workstation next to the electric stove. In a pan, I put a generous pour of canola oil and waited for it to heat. I rolled the little bean corn burritos and dropped them into the pan and listened to the satisfying sizzle, waiting for the comforting smell of fried tortilla to summon Joanna. She was a tortured, starving artist, and I had to make sure she was fed.

Like magic, she swooped into the kitchen, wearing her crocheted duster cardigan with long bell sleeves. Her quick steps made the long garment float in the air with the high drama she intended.

"Do I smell corn burritos?"

I turned them over to fry the other side. "Yup, but I'm not sure what you're gonna eat."

"Don't play me like that. I've been slaving away for hours."

"Hand me that plate." I motioned with my chin to the slightly dirty dish on the counter. It looked like it had been used only for toast, and it was fine.

Joanna brushed the leftover crumbs into the sink and lined the plate with a paper towel. Fried corn burritos were kind of our thing. They tasted good, they were cheap, and you could dip them in whatever you had. Salsa? Perfect. Guac? Even better. If you were a psycho like Joanna, you could even smother them in half a container of sour cream and nothing else. All that to say, we really loved our fried corn burritos, and we needed something to munch on while I recounted how I had met the hottest Native in OKC.

"His name is Danuwoa," I mumbled through a mouthful of beans and hot sauce as we sat on the small couch, our feet tucked under our legs.

"He sounds yummy." She licked stray sour cream off her fingers, the mini burritos now devoured. "Taken?"

"Probably, but that hair," I gushed.

"You and your hair fetish." Joanna reached for my plate; I gave it to her. Those who cooked didn't do the dishes here.

"It's not a fetish," I practically yelled so she could hear me over the running water. "I just love when a man has long hair. It's not creepy. I don't, like, collect hair and get off on it."

She came out of the kitchen and leaned against the wall. "I don't share a room with you. Maybe you do."

"Ha ha ha." I rolled my eyes.

She jumped back onto the couch next to me and swatted my arm. "Check your email."

"No way Monica would have sent me something this soon."

"You said she winked. That was basically her saying you got the job."

"Don't jinx it!" I pulled out my phone and opened the email app.

One unread message.

No. Way.

SENDER: Monica Lewis
SUBJECT: Technix Accounting Assistant Position

My stomach immediately dropped, and my heart started beating faster. Joanna leaned over my lap to look at my phone.

"Open it!" she commanded.

My thumb had a mind of its own as it tapped the screen to open the email.

Dear Ms. Cardinal,

We are pleased to offer you the position of Accounting Assistant reporting to Gary Horowitz in the downtown Oklahoma City office. Starting salary is $50,000 with a discretionary bonus. We are proud to offer full health benefits, including vision and dental, and eligibility starts immediately. We offer new employees 15 days of accrued PTO. Technix employees also receive free snacks daily and catered lunch once a month and membership to the building gym. The dress code is business casual. If this offer sounds exciting to you, please let me know at your earliest convenience. We are anxious to get this position filled, and we look forward to you joining the Technix team. If you accept, we would love your first day to be next Monday.

"Holy shit! Fifty thousand dollars a year?! You're rich, Ember! Rich!" Joanna jumped off the couch and gave a cry so loud there was no way our ancestors above missed it. "Yeeeeeeooooow!"

Tears blurred my vision as I set my phone down. I did it. Someone like *me* did it? I couldn't believe it. I jumped up and joined my best friend and danced around the living room.

I was officially an accountant!

Four

IT WAS GOING TO BE MY LAST SHIFT. I TRIED GIVING NOTICE THE rest of the week after my interview, and Bobby Dean avoided me like the plague. *Someone* got drunk and bragged to everyone I was going to leave that joint and be richer than them all. That someone was big-mouth Joanna. Who needed finesse? Tact? A plan for respectfully giving notice to your employer for the last three years? Not me when I had Joanna to broadcast my business for all to hear.

It was finally Sunday, and I started my real job the next day. No more smelly shoes. Goodbye, clogged toilets. I was moving on to the greener pastures of the corporate jungle. Sundays at the bowling alley were always a doozy. We had discounted beer pitchers and shoe rentals, so families came and spent all day here. The kids bowled, and parents drank with their buddies, taking bets on which kid would bowl a strike first.

I parked my car in the lot. Joanna refused to wear our uniform to or from work. She waited to change until the last possible moment. I had to give her props for her commitment to her style. I was lazy. I wore my uniform on our commute in and out. It was satisfying to peel it off at the end of the night and throw on pj's. I didn't want to change two times like Joanna when I was tired. But her style was her thing.

I popped my trunk and used a broken pool cue to prop it open. Joanna took out her fishing tackle case full of her latest beaded works and her uniform. I held up an old sheet, and it became Joanna's own personal changing room. She threw her cutoff shorts over my head, landing them perfectly in the trunk. Next came her vintage Dr. Martens boots, landing with hard thuds.

"All right, I'm ready!" she sang.

I lowered the sheet, and it was unfair that Joanna could make our cheap white baseball jersey–inspired uniform shirts look so good. The Bobby Dean's logo curved across our chests in rough screen-printed blue ink. Joanna filled hers out, her boobs peeking from her V-neck. Mine looked like I was wearing my brother's clothes, so big and baggy. Whatever, we would be covered in equal amounts of fake cheese and stale beer by the end of the night.

"Yeeooow!" A loud catcall came from the front of the bowling alley. I was walking behind Joanna and couldn't see who it was right away.

"What the hell are you doing here, Tito?" Joanna stopped and crossed her arms. I stepped from behind her to stare bloody daggers at my brother's best friend and worst influence. He was shorter than Sage by a lot. He was about my height, and what he lacked in size, he made up for by having a personality that filled the parking lot. He kept his dark hair cropped short, and today, he was sporting baggy shorts and Sage's favorite Metallica T-shirt.

"My queen," he said, placing his hands over his heart, one still holding a lit cigarette between his pointer and middle fingers. "You wound me. Can't I just chill and play some bowling?"

"Not this far from Ada you can't. The fuck you want, Tito?"
I asked. My patience had evaporated.

Two guys and a girl came out of the bowling alley laughing.
More of Sage's "friends." River and Skye were brothers, and Ricki
was Tito's on-again, off-again girlfriend. She came down the steps
and wrapped her arms around Tito's middle, taking the cigarette
and inhaling deeply.

"You do it yet?" she asked on a lazy exhale.

"'Bout to." Tito lifted his chin to me. "You've been dodging
Sage's calls from jail. That's fucked up."

"I don't see how that's any of your business." I wanted to
escape inside, but Native Tweedledee and Tweedledum were
blocking the entrance.

"He said you haven't even visited," Ricki said and took another drag, placing Tito's hand over her boob in her pink tank top.
I guessed they were on again at present.

"Been busy working. I know it's an unfamiliar concept to you."

"Ha ha, play nice, E. Sage wanted me to tell you that he needs
some money on his books."

"Why do you think I've been dodging his calls?"

"They don't feed him enough in there, ya know. It's mad
fucked his sister won't help him out."

Before I went to jail myself, Joanna stepped up, pulling me
back by the arm. "We got the message, Tito. We wouldn't want
Baby Sage going hungry. Now g'wan'n git, shitass."

"Don't shoot the messenger. I'm just looking out for our boy."
He blew a kiss as they brushed past us, heading to one of the
beater cars in the lot.

"Don't let them ruin your night, come on." Joanna looped her
free arm through mine, the other carrying her jewelry box.

"Tito doesn't fucking know all I have done to help Sage."

"Tito is an idiot who should be sitting in jail with Sage right now. It's your last night at the bowling alley. Don't think about all that. Let's live it up!" She kicked the door open.

I walked into the warm embrace of that plastic cheese and bowling alley floor wax smell. I wasn't an overly sentimental person, but a part of me would miss this musty old place. Bowling balls thundered along the lanes and collided with the dense maple pins; the sound of the impact ricocheted off the walls. Kids ran around screaming as adults milled about, drinking their beer from clear plastic cups. The dollar-a-song jukebox was blasting "Pour Some Sugar on Me" while some rowdy guys, clearly already drunk, rocked on, fists pumping in the air.

"Great, you two are here." Bobby Dean, the man, the myth, and the legend of the bowling alley himself, dared to acknowledge me. He wore his patched and overworn denim vest over a black T-shirt, his graying hair combed back in an Elvis-inspired pompadour.

"Hey, Bobby Dean, can I talk to you for a minute?" I asked, and he ignored me.

"Joanna," he started, pointing with his thumb behind him. "The bar needs help. Ember, the men's toilet is backed up and we have a full house."

He started walking away.

"Wait!" I called.

"Get to it," he threw over his shoulder, and he was gone.

"Rotten luck." Joanna gave me a salute and got to work.

If I didn't need the money, I would have just walked out, but as it stood, I was starting a new job, and I wouldn't have tips or anything holding me over until my first paycheck. This last shift was gas and food money for me. Stupid cheap-ass Bobby Dean and his shitty plumbing.

I grumbled on my way to the back, where the supply closet was nestled between the men's and women's bathrooms, to get the plunger and toilet auger. That's right. I was about to snake a goddamn toilet.

On my way, I spotted a tall Native man sporting one long braid down his back. My heart lurched, and I ducked behind a family with three kids picking out their bowling balls. It was irrational to assume that just because this man was tall and had a long braid, it was somehow Danuwoa, but I didn't want to stick around and confirm that it was him. The family finished grabbing their selections, and to my right was the Little Big Horns league on lane two. Like a cartoon thief, I hunched over on hurried feet.

Of the five retired men, Bucky was the slimmest. I turned over my shoulder and couldn't see the possible Danuwoa lookalike anywhere. I ducked down behind the bulky ball return hood.

I was met with curious looks.

"What're you doing down there, Ember?" Ron, the leader and former semiprofessional bowler, asked. He was sitting next to Bucky.

I ignored his question to ask my own. "Bucky, if I give you ten bucks, will you let me borrow your shirt?"

"Did you fall and hit your head?" He sounded bewildered. The rest of the men laughed.

"What do you care? Has a woman ever wanted to pay you to take your clothes off before?" Leroy quipped.

"Just your mom," Bucky said.

Damn, even I laughed out loud at that one.

"Yeah, she said she wants her money back. Don't waste your time with him," Leroy said to me as he moved his hat, which said NATIVE VETERAN on it, down over his face to hide his laugh.

I peeked over the hood and found, to my dismay, that it was definitely Danuwoa; I could not mistake his profile and jawline. He was at lane six with a group of girls, their ages unclear from this angle. I ducked down again before he could feel someone staring at him.

"I'll up it to fifteen dollars, please?" I hoped my puppy dog eyes would do the trick.

"Why?" They all leaned forward in their seats.

"Fifteen dollars and free beer, you don't need to know why."

Ron and Leroy screamed, "Done!" They began lifting Bucky's shirt off him, ignoring his protests and wiggles. Finally, the shirt was free, leaving poor old Bucky in a dingy tank. Leroy threw me Bucky's Little Big Horns shirt with his name embroidered on the right breast. Immediately, I threw it on over my work top and sniffed my underarms.

"Gross, Bucky! This smells like you haven't washed it in weeks."

"I haven't." He took a sip of his beer while the others laughed.

Was it worse to be caught working here or worse for Danuwoa to catch a whiff of me smelling like a drunk, dirty, sweaty old man? I stood up and saw that it was Danuwoa's turn. He was focused on the pins, and while his attention was diverted, I scurried over to the bar to inform Joanna of this unfortunate development.

"The fuck are you wearing? Did the toilet splash you again?" she asked me.

"No!" I ducked under the bar and pulled her to the small corner for the illusion of privacy.

"Ember, you stink! Did you fall into the toilet?" She held her nose.

"Danuwoa is here."

"The hot IT guy from your new job? That Danuwoa?"

"Do we know of another?"

"Chill. What's the problem?"

"He can't find out I work here. I lied on my application to get that job. If he let it slip that I worked here, it will all unravel."

"Is that why you stole Bucky's jersey?"

"I was desperate."

"Don't ever repeat that." Joanna ducked down under the cash register and opened her tackle box full of jewelry. She lifted the top tray full of earrings and dug around. "Aha! Here!" She thrust her old Victoria's Secret body spray at me.

"I hate Love Spell," I grumbled.

"Love Spell or poop. Which would you prefer to smell like?"

I groaned.

"Which would you prefer *Danuwoa* smell?"

I spritzed the spray from my head to my feet and gave two extra pumps under my arms. It was so strong and artificial smelling that it instantly gave me a pulsing headache behind my eyes. To my nose, I smelled worse.

"It's worse." Joanna coughed and gagged in confirmation.

Great. I turned around, and Danuwoa stood in front of me on the other side of the bar, leaning on his forearms. He looked just as surprised to see me.

"Danuwoa! Hi!"

"Ember? Do you work here?" He tilted his head in confusion.

"No, she doesn't!" Joanna pushed me under the counter.

"Danuwoa, this is my best friend, Joanna. *She* works here." I popped up from under the counter. Danuwoa took a step back away from me.

"Hey," he said, waving to her. "What's that smell?"

I laughed. I laughed the cringiest and fakest of laughs and changed the subject, because what could I say that would make any sense? I promised myself I would be honest after I landed that job, and here I was, lying again. "What brings you here?"

"I brought my sister and her friends to play. We're wrapping up. What about you?"

"I'm in a bowling league and we're playing."

"This I have to see. Which lane?"

"We were just taking a break."

"Is that so? I'd love to meet your teammates, *Bucky*." He read the name at my breast, saying the name like it was a dare. A challenge.

"Yeah, *Bucky*, go introduce Danuwoa to the gang," Joanna said, snickering.

"Um . . . well . . ." I was stalling, and in my indecisive state, I spotted Bobby Dean talking to a few regulars by the entrance. Shit! I hadn't fixed the men's toilet. "Sure. Let's go." I grabbed Danuwoa's arm and used him as my very large human shield to hide from Bobby Dean. Once we passed the line for food, I dropped his arm.

"Are you hiding from someone?"

"What? Me? No."

He lifted his eyebrow, and that said it all: *Why the hell are you acting so weird?*

I could only give a fake smile in response. This was a deep, deep grave I'd just dug.

"How did you get the nickname Bucky?"

"I really love deer."

"So, no buckteeth when you were a kid?"

Buckteeth! Damn, that was good. I should have thought of that. "Nope, never needed braces. Just love good ol' Bambi."

He stopped short. "What's really going on, *Bucky*?"

"My weekly bowling league game is all. Why?"

"You're acting weird, and you smell disgusting."

"What a rude thing to say to a lady you hardly know." I crossed my arms. We were surrounded by families and the loud crashes of pins falling.

"You're right. I'm sorry, *Bucky*, take me to your team." He kept saying Bucky like he was waiting for me to crack and admit the farce. I doubled down.

"Thank you, right this way." We walked to lane two, snaking through the crowd. The real Bucky was missing. What a blessing.

"Hey, hey!" Leroy exclaimed as he slammed his elbow into Ron's side.

"Hey, Bucky! We've been waiting. It's your turn." They all were laughing. Sure enough, Bucky's name was blinking on the screen. The real Bucky was going to hate me for this. These men were serious about their game and their points. I just hoped the free beer would smooth it over.

Working at a bowling alley for three years meant I was pretty good at bowling. But these men were semiprofessional, and all used their own heavy balls with huge finger holes. It was like the macho man contest of whose dick was bigger, but with who had the largest and heaviest bowling ball.

Bucky's was a shimmering green with his name engraved in cursive. I lifted it with my knees and slowly made my way to the top of the lane. It was so heavy, there was no way I could wind my arm back. I wasn't proud of it, but I used both hands and I granny-pushed that thing from between my legs and watched as the ball smoothly and slowly rolled its way straight into the pins.

Lucky Bucky! I got a strike! The men grumbled, clearly hoping I'd lose the game for him, but he was now in the lead.

"Shitass," Leroy cursed under his breath as I walked back to Danuwoa.

"Not bad, Bucky," he said, biting his lip.

"You can just call me Ember."

"No, I don't think I will."

I opened my mouth to protest, but the real Bucky hobbled over in his white tank.

"Hey, Ember, did you know the men's toilet is backed up again?" He took the empty seat next to Ron.

"Thanks for the TMI, man!" I yelled over my shoulder. "These guys are a hoot." I rolled my eyes at Danuwoa.

"Should we get the manager?" he asked.

"This place is a dump; they know about it."

He shook his head and smiled. "I need to get back to my sister. It looks like they're done. I'll catch you at the office, *Bucky*." He winked and went back to lane six.

I watched Danuwoa as he sexy-walked his fine ass over to the group of girls. They were changing their shoes. I pretended to be deep in conversation with the Little Big Horns as they left.

"Ember!" Bobby Dean barked as he found me. "Get over here."

I ripped Bucky's shirt over my head and threw it back at him. "Thanks, I'll get you another round of beer."

"Hey, Bobby—"

"Cut the shit. Why isn't the bathroom fixed?"

"There was a ball stuck in lane two that I just got out. I'm heading to clean up the men's room right now."

"Good, take this out back on your way." He handed me a full black trash bag and turned to leave.

"Wait! I have to tell you that tonight has to be my last shift. I'm starting a new job."

"All right. Get your shifts covered." He turned on his heel and headed to the bar.

Three years and not so much as a *Thank you for your efforts*. Whatever. After tonight I was done. No more late nights cleaning the bathrooms that college kids messed up while hooking up or getting high. No more dealing with entitled moms throwing birthday parties for their kids. And no more ass-grabby old men who loitered all day drinking three-dollar beer.

I dragged the trash out back, propping the door open with the mop bucket before swinging back the trash bag, preparing to launch it right into the dumpster.

Meow!

I screamed, releasing the trash bag too early—it missed by a mile. The orange tabby cat that haunted this dumpster rose on its haunches, hissing.

I hissed back.

"Fucking demon cat," I muttered. I bent to retrieve the trash, and the damn cat pounced. I only just managed to jump back before it could get its claws in my jeans. It had happened before. The mangy thing scared the shit out of me. My nose started tingling and my eyes watered. I was allergic, and this cat, in particular, was beyond demented.

I left the trash on the ground in front of the dumpster and retreated inside to relative safety.

I fucking hated cats.

I plunged and snaked the toilet, breathing through my mouth and wiping my runny nose on my sleeve. It was not glamorous work. After I washed my hands, the rest of my last shift passed by in a blur. It was time to close, and someone had put on "Okie from Muskogee," a Merle Haggard standard, and we all sang off-key as I started shutting down the bowling alley for the last time.

Five

FIRST-DAY JITTERS HAD THEIR GRIP ON MY STOMACH LIKE A vise as I made my way to the First National Center. My hands were like ice with excitement, but as long as no one planned to hold my hand, it didn't matter. My first-day-of-work outfit was the best in my closet, dark-wash skinny jeans that hugged my butt just right, a lacy tank top, and my new thrifted purple cashmere cardigan. It was like being a kid all over again, when we got new clothes but weren't allowed to wear them until school started. I had been waiting to wear this outfit for a few weeks to keep it fresh. What really set it off were my orthopedic flats. To quote a dumb Borat joke, *Not!* My arches were shit, so I had to wear them, but at least they were cuter than orthopedic tennis shoes. I wouldn't be caught dead in those.

There were so many things I wanted to do with my first paycheck: new clothes, new shoes, and a new car. I wanted to feel what it was like to say yes to my desire and splurge on some new outfits. But there was no use spending money in my head before it was in my hands. I had to actually work for two weeks before I could make plans.

The last time I had entered this building, I was hardly paying attention to anything. This time my eyes hungrily absorbed every detail, from the glass entrance to the marble walls and up to the people walking around on the mezzanine. It was loud and alive and exhilarating.

I filed into the gilded elevator, and most of the thirty-two floor buttons were lit up. We stopped at every floor until finally the doors opened to floor twelve, and I squeezed past the remaining riders to my new company.

Everything was exactly the same: cold, sterile, and modern. Phoebe was rifling through the cabinet behind her, and I cleared my throat to alert her of my presence.

"Hello!" she said when she saw me. She twirled around on her toe, pens and paper in her hand.

"It's my first day." I fiddled with my fingers.

"I remember you. Congrats and welcome. I was just gathering all your new-hire stuff." Phoebe put the contents in her hands into a navy-blue backpack that sat on top of her desk. "Here," she said and thrust the still-open backpack into my hands.

"Thanks! Will I need a backpack?"

"Every person gets a welcome gift on their first day. We all get a company-branded backpack, water bottle, T-shirt—sorry, we only had men's mediums left—notepad, and pens. I like the backpack because commuting with just a purse is hard. You end up becoming a bag lady with a purse, lunch bag, tote with extra shoes just in case."

"Great tip." I adjusted the strap of my very full tote bag.

"If you would come around and follow me this way, I'll show you to your desk." For someone so tiny, she took off like a rocket.

I felt like Shrek as I clambered my way after her, the echo of my steps going *thump, thump, thump.* I felt sorry for whoever was working on the floor beneath us.

"Over there," she said, indicating to the left, "is finance. The middle is HR, and this side"—she waved in the general vicinity to our right—"is all accounting. Through that door and hallway are the bathrooms and break room. C-suite is all on the seventeenth floor, so it's pretty chill here. IT has those desks outside of the conference room near finance."

She abruptly stopped, and I nearly plowed her down.

"And this is you. If you need anything, my extension is 505, and Dan should be over any minute with your laptop. All set?"

"Yeah, I think so. Thank you for the quick tour."

"Anytime. Did you bring lunch?"

"I did." Was that not cool? Oh my god, was I that nerd? I was broke. The bowling alley paid shit, and I had to stretch it. I was eating bologna, and it wasn't even fried. I was in a hurry this morning.

"Great, you can eat with me in the break room if you want. I know how awkward it can be starting at a new place."

She had no idea.

"I would love that." I gave her a genuine smile. Everyone was so nice here; I had no idea what people meant about women in offices being catty. Phoebe was an angel. I hoped she would stay that way after she saw my cheap-ass sandwich. It was just Wonder Bread, mayo, American cheese, and bologna. That was as broke as it got.

She tapped the top of my cubicle. "Great. See ya!"

Phoebe left, and I forced myself to take a calming breath. I could do this. I closed my eyes, and I pictured that fat paycheck and nearly drooled just thinking of the meat I could buy and slow-cook at home.

"Well, if it isn't strike-rolling Bucky?" Danuwoa's deep, throaty voice came from behind me. I spun around only to be left nearly breathless. He wore his hair down and straight. He was an ear tucker—his black tresses were endearingly tucked behind each ear. He was so good-looking it was almost too painful to stare at his perfection. The type of good-looking that sent men like him to Hollywood but then got them stuck doing historical reenactments because people like us were never romantic heroes. But Danuwoa the IT guy was definitely romantic hero–worthy. What the hell was he doing here and working in IT? I had to know.

"Danuwoa." I smiled and tried to keep a straight face to look down my nose, but I was a terrible actress, and I was starting to really like him. My face betrayed me and made a dumb dopey smile.

He placed a thin black laptop and charging cord on my sterile desk, accessorized only by more black cords, a phone, a monitor mounted on an arm, and a black block that I'd never seen before in my life.

"It's just Dan here." He gave me a smile back. "This snaps into place on the docking station"—he pointed to the black block—"so you can use the monitor. It's pretty easy. I'm sure you're used to it."

"Not really." I gave him a sheepish grin. A second monitor? My laptop was ancient. I got it at a pawn shop in high school, and it was damn near louder than my car if I had too many programs open at once.

"Here." He leaned across me, and my brain short-circuited from his closeness. He opened the laptop up and then clicked it into the docking station. "You hit this here"—he pointed to a button on the side—"and it will release it if you gotta be mobile." His hair fell over his shoulder and grazed my arm. The smell of lavender washed over me. I clenched my thighs together. I should not be reacting this way to a coworker. *He's just clean, Ember, get it together.* I scooted out my rolling office chair to give him more space while he worked.

He powered on the laptop and gave me a sheet of paper.

"This is your log-in and password. You can change it later, but go ahead and enter it now."

I did and waited for the profile to load and the company email platform to come up.

"So, how long have you been working here?" I asked him.

"It'll be two years in August," he said as he crossed his arms and leaned against the cubicle partition.

"Wow. You mentioned before that this place was chill?"

"Yeah, it's cool. The pay is good and never late, so that's all I care about. Well, that and I don't have to wear slacks."

I nodded and tried to sound nonchalant as I asked, "So, you and your sister go to the bowling alley often?"

"I'd never heard of it before. My sister's friend mentioned it. I think your settings are all set." He straightened. "Open Excel and I'll show you how to use a second monitor."

He had me drag a blank Excel workbook onto the big monitor that was attached to the desk. It was nerdy magic. For school, in the few classes I did take, I would window-hop when I needed to see things on another screen to put somewhere else. Or I would copy and paste a bunch of stuff into the document I was working on to make things a little easier, but man, a second monitor opened up a whole new world. My face must have mirrored my awe, because Danuwoa laughed at me.

"There was a study done that circulated around the company that said two monitors made all employees twenty percent more productive or something. So we all got two monitors."

"This is great! Thanks for showing me." I leaned back in my office chair to look up at him. "I'm not sure what I'm supposed to do now," I said as I picked my hangnail.

"You're Gary's new assistant?"

"Yup."

"He usually rolls in a little before nine." It seemed like Danuwoa was bored and wanted to stay and chat. "Ember is your given name, or did you pick it yourself?"

I snorted. "I was given an Okie name so that when I was in trouble, they had something fun to yell. Ember Lee has that good scolding flow to it, but I don't have a traditional name. Why Dan and not Danuwoa?"

"Because no one can pronounce it. Well . . . no one cares to learn how." It was a beautiful name and not that hard to pronounce; people were just lazy.

"*Dahnawa* means *warrior*, right?" I asked.

"Yeah, okay, I see you."

I rolled my eyes. "I don't gotta prove myself to you."

"But you just did." He raised and lowered his eyebrows. "My name is spelled a bit differently. *Dahnawa ditihi* means *warrior* officially. My grandpa was fluent in Tsalagi but spelled things phonetically. So my name is a bit confusing."

"It's not confusing. I've been to some intertribal dances in my day and come across a lot of interesting names. Shit, people just name their kids whatever nowadays." I laughed, blushing. Danuwoa, warrior. It really suited him. It was the kind of name I wanted to say out loud and often . . . which I most definitely should not do. I needed to quickly bring the conversation back to a safer topic—work. "So, tell me, IT Guy, what exactly *is* Technix? I couldn't figure it out based on the vague website full of smiling stock models. Are we a product or service company?"

"It's a little of both, I guess. I just handle the personnel technical problems. You should ask sales and product development what they do."

"There are only finance, HR, accounting, and IT on this floor. Who's in sales and product development?"

"The executives on floor seventeen and our team in Austin."

"You don't know what we do either," I accused him.

"Nope! Two years and haven't been able to figure it out."

"Then there's no hope for me."

"Doubtful, unless you change departments." Danuwoa folded his arms on top of the partition and rested his chin on them. It was like he was getting comfortable to stay awhile.

"No way, I only have the bandwidth to be an accountant."

"Ignorance is bliss." Suddenly he straightened and dropped his smile.

"Ember?" a loud male voice barked from behind me.

"Yes?" I smiled at whoever sounded so rough and angry, swiveling in my chair to greet them.

A short man with dark curly gray hair dropped a stack of folders onto my desk. "I'm Gary. Dan, is her computer all set up?"

"Yes, sir," Danuwoa answered politely.

"Good, and you"—he focused his attention on me—"Monica said you're familiar with accounting procedures?"

I could answer this. I had been up late into the night reading up on all things accounting. "Yes, I am very familiar with G-A-A-P."

Gary stood looking at me with his mouth open. "Gap. We say it like the word, not G-A-A-P. We might as well just say generally accepted accounting procedures then." He rolled his eyes, and I heard a light snicker.

I stole a glance at Danuwoa, my eyes cursing him for staying here and witnessing whatever this was. I couldn't believe I had made the same mistake from last week, but this time the opposite. I could not win with these stupid acronyms.

"Sorry, it's just how I remember," I said, giving him a sheepish smile.

"See ya around," Danuwoa said before he turned on his heel and left. Yeah, he had better leave. I barely knew the man, and he had seen me embarrassed too many times now. I needed to even the score.

Gary nodded toward the stack of files, moving on from my embarrassment and Danuwoa's departure. "These are your projects to get your feet wet and learn the lay of the land. Why don't you pull up QuickBooks and we'll get started."

I pushed the folders aside and started the program.

"You're familiar with how to upload invoices and print checks from this program?" His face was expectant and impatient.

"You bet." I gave Gary my biggest, most confident smile.

"Excellent. The folders are broken down by month. This is all from our Portland office that we are closing. Start with the month of April, and I'll have Lisa check on you when she gets in."

"Who's Lisa?" I asked.

"She's our senior accountant." He turned and left. His office was one of the small glass enclosures against the wall.

I closed QuickBooks and promptly opened a Google window and typed into the search bar **How to use QuickBooks beginners**. That lie didn't count, since I could figure it out easily enough with the help of the internet. I would become proficient in the program by the end of the day. I was determined.

Six

THE LUNCHROOM WAS ABUZZ WITH PLAYFUL CHATTER AND clanking dishes. Phoebe had invited me to sit with her, but I needed a moment to collect myself. The bathroom line was long, so I turned around and walked to the lunchroom clutching my plastic-wrapped bologna sandwich. Gary Horowitz scared me. What had I gotten myself into? He talked so fast that my hand was barely able to catch up as I took notes on a legal pad. They weren't decipherable. They were so messy it was like looking at the Zodiac Killer's letters.

Gary also gave me a stack of past-due bills, half-started department budgets, and a presentation that he needed to have turned around by tomorrow afternoon. I'd never done an executive presentation before! He said that I was supposed to take my laptop home with me and back as part of their security protocols. I interpreted that as I needed to work all night and figure out how to make a flashy executive presentation because this was a test. I was determined not to fail, but it was a lot to throw at me in four hours. Lisa, who came in shortly after Gary ditched me in the morning, was no help.

The break room was huge, and the back wall was lined entirely with windows. I spotted Phoebe in the crowd. She was sitting across from Danuwoa, and he looked like he was leaning. You know, like he was leaning into her. Perhaps Phoebe and Danuwoa had a thing? I walked up with as much confidence as I could muster, because no way was I going to be eating alone here. I swear Gary looked pissed that it was lunchtime, because he had to stop talking and adding to my to-do list. No doubt he would zero in on me if he caught me eating alone, and I needed a break.

"Hey, guys, is this seat taken?" Both shook their heads and inched their lunch bags over to give me more room at the table.

"How's your first day going?" Phoebe asked, all smiles.

"Does Gary always talk that much?"

"Pffft!" Danuwoa snickered and then started coughing. "Ahem, sorry. He hasn't been able to keep an assistant for longer than a month."

"For fuck's sake. Are you serious?"

"Shut up, Dan, you're gonna scare her away, and I like her." Phoebe threw a wadded-up napkin in his face.

"The devil himself couldn't scare me away. I need the money."

"From your lips to god's ears." Danuwoa scooped his yogurt into his mouth. "This is Oklahoma, we all need the money."

"Says the guy who was able to buy a house." Phoebe rolled her eyes.

"I don't waste my money on shoes and purses," he said, pointing his plastic spoon at Phoebe.

"Wow, do I detect a bit of sexism there?" I asked as I took a large bite of my sandwich, waiting to see what kind of guy Danuwoa really was.

"No, he's right. I can't resist a deal." She lifted her leg and plopped her ankle on the table, wiggling her foot to show off her cheetah-print mules. "I got these babies at the consignment store."

"Those are cute," I mumbled behind my hand as my tongue performed acrobatics. The white bread stuck to the roof of my mouth, and no way was I going to stick my finger in there to pry it off.

"Aren't they? I can show you the store one of these days if you want."

"I'd love that."

All the chatter and clanking of dishes ceased as the energy was completely sucked out of the room. I followed everyone's stares to a heavily pregnant woman on her cell phone opening a frozen dinner by the microwave.

Danuwoa rolled his eyes. "I gotta go hide." He grabbed the remainder of his food and darted out of the lunchroom.

"What was that all about?" I asked Phoebe. Did Danuwoa have beef with the pregnant lady?

"That's Natalie Sanchez, the executive assistant to our CEO, Mr. Stevenson. Also known as the Wicked Witch of Floor Seventeen."

Everyone in the lunchroom gave her a wide berth and avoided direct eye contact. What did she do to these people?

I guess I asked that out loud, because Phoebe answered me. "She has the eyes of a hawk and doesn't let anyone get away with shit. She can just tell if someone is using their work computer for social media or online shopping. She triple-checks every report or presentation before it can cross Mr. Stevenson's desk. If you want to move up in this company, then you have to kiss her ass and make sure you cross all your t's and dot all your i's. Oh, and never, ever slip up. She'll never forget it." Phoebe sent Natalie a glare and said under her breath, "Spiteful woman."

"What has she not let you forget—if it's not prying, of course?"

"She's going on maternity leave, and the company announced they were looking for a temporary replacement and anyone interested was encouraged to apply. I applied. She sat in on my interview. I never heard back, so I asked her about it in the bathroom, and she told me I wasn't right for the role. Can you believe that? I demanded she tell me what I was lacking, and she said she had observed me on several occasions abandoning my post and thought I was lazy and lacked attention to detail to keep our supplies stocked." Phoebe huffed and crossed her arms. "As if the reception desk was the check-in at the emergency room. I'm allowed to go to the bathroom or get coffee in the break room. She has standards that no one can live up to."

I recalled this morning when a frazzled Phoebe was throwing my welcome bag together at the last minute and only had men's shirts left, but I didn't want to judge her too harshly. "Is this your endgame career?" I asked, genuinely curious. How did other people who had been working in this corporate environment plan ahead? How did they advance?

"God no. I hope to meet a handsome man with money in this building, get pregnant right away, and become a stay-at-home mom."

We laughed together. That was some dream. Not my dream, but I got that it was what others aspired to. I never wanted to be in a position where someone controlled me and my money. No, thank you. Call it generational trauma and whatnot. No man was gonna keep my shit from me.

I finished my sandwich, and before long it was time for me to return to my desk. I walked through the door, and Monica waved me down from her cubicle.

"Ember! How's your first day going?"

"It's been busy." I sat in the seat she offered me across from her desk.

"I bet. I know Gary has a lot to do before we can close this month's books. Why don't you have a seat? I have a few things to give you."

Monica's cubicle was lived-in. Children's art was pinned to the gray fabric walls, and she had a family photo with her husband and four children. It was adorable. I was certain that it was weird that it was my dream to have a cubicle as lived-in as Monica's one day. Most people did not dream of pushing paper surrounded by fake walls, but I was not like most people. I was a recovering poor person, and a well-loved, decorated workspace meant stability, longevity, and steady income. I hungered for it. Cute family photos would be an added bonus.

Monica counted through a packet of papers. "This is everything. This small packet is Technix's electronic asset policy. I just need you to tear out and sign the last page saying that you acknowledge the laptop is company property and in the event of your termination or resignation, it will be returned promptly."

"You got it." I signed my name with a flourish and handed the torn page to her.

"Excellent. Next up is the employee handbook. It outlines our policies on dress code, communications, zero tolerance behavior, and interoffice dating."

"Interoffice dating?"

"To summarize—don't. We don't need the mess or headache. The policy outlines it all and the proper steps and disclosures." She gave me a no-nonsense look through her eyebrows, like she had said it before and people had not heeded her warning.

"Right, not worth the trouble. Noted." I was not going to be one of those people. I planned on keeping my job. Danuwoa was off-limits.

"I've already sent you a link to the mandatory training modules that you need to complete this week. It's all standard anti-discrimination and anti-harassment videos with short quizzes at the end. You need at least seventy percent on the quizzes, or you have to rewatch the videos."

"I'll pass them the first time, no problem."

"That's the spirit. I'm sure Gary has given you a million things to work on, so I'll let you go. If you need anything, my door is always open."

"Is that because you don't have a door?"

"Well, yeah, but I also care about everyone's well-being." Monica giggled.

I got back to my desk to look at the training videos, but my heart stopped. In my inbox was an invitation to my first-ever business meeting. The title just read Accounting All Hands. I clicked accept and smiled. I was about to do some really business-y things in thirty minutes in the CN conference room. I stood and looked over my desk. Lisa, the senior accountant, was sitting in her seat, looking at her computer screen and eating a sandwich.

"Hi." I got her attention.

"Hi?"

"What does CN conference room mean?"

"Chuck Norris conference room," she said through a full mouth. I could see her mashed-up egg salad sandwich. Gross.

"What?"

"It's the largest conference room on the other side of the break room."

"Why is it called Chuck Norris?"

"Because it's the largest conference room."

When I didn't say anything, she added, "It wasn't *my* dumb joke." Lisa rolled her eyes and went back to eating her sandwich.

Okies and our love for our own.

THE CONFERENCE ROOM WAS HUGE WITH TABLES PUT TOGETHER to form a large U shape in front of a projector screen. As with the rest of the office, it was bright white with tones of contrasting gray. I took a seat on the farthest side of the room and waited to see what *all hands* meant.

Lisa walked in and sat opposite me. We didn't say anything to each other as the minutes ticked by. Gary swooped in with a paper cup of coffee filled to the brim. On his heels, three young men followed. Gary set his closed laptop and coffee down on the table in front of the screen while the three men sat in the back next to each other, their backs to the wall of windows.

Gary kicked off the meeting. "Okay, everyone, thanks for coming on such short notice. I want to introduce you to our newest member on the accounting team, Ember."

This was an overly large room for just six people. My awkward wave was met with a lackluster response. One of the guys in the back, the one in the middle of two jock-looking guys, gave me a half smile. He was maybe thirty with black hair perfectly brushed over in a small swoop.

"Ember," Gary continued, "you've met Lisa. In the back, we have Martin, our director of accounts payable. In the middle is Nick, senior accounting manager for accounts receivable. And lastly, Ryan, our new staff accountant. He was promoted from your position not too long ago."

"Good luck," Ryan deadpanned. Only Martin and Nick chuckled.

"All right, great. With Ember, you now can give her the tasks you need help with, and we should be able to wrap up the month's end on time. Any questions?"

"Yeah, how much work can we give her? I'm really behind after we shut down Portland." Ryan was a little too eager to pass off his work to me.

"That's up to you. Her priority is to finish my tasks, and then you let Ember know what needs to be done and by when, and we can all work together to get it finished."

Ember is sitting right here. It took all my self-restraint to refrain from eye-rolling. Gary moved on from introductions and started talking about what was needed to wrap up the month and finalize everything related to the Portland closure. My notepad page was once again full of notes to myself like *Google bank reconciliation* and *What does provisioning for an audit mean?*

The meeting ended, with promises from Ryan, Martin, and Nick to send me things to "keep me busy." As if I needed the additional tasks with all Gary assigned to me.

The rest of the day was a blur. I finished inputting all the old invoices into the QuickBooks system and printed the checks and envelopes. Gary left early, so he hadn't been able to approve them, but I was proud of myself. I was packing up to leave when Danuwoa approached me.

"How was day one?" he asked.

"So far so good. I have a lot to do before tomorrow."

"The accounting bros started their hazing?"

"They described it as helping me stay busy. How was your day?" Relationships were against the rules, but I could be friends with Danuwoa. I could casually ask about his day, and it didn't have to mean anything.

"So far this has been the best part." Then Danuwoa had to go on and say that. He must have seen my panic, because he quickly added, "Because we get to leave."

"Oh." My half laugh was unconvincing. My nerves were shot through from being on high alert all day, and now being this close to him was not helping matters.

"Wanna head out together?"

"I have a few things I have to do before I can go," I lied. As much as I would like Danuwoa's company while heading to the employee parking structure, there was no way on Creator's given earth that I would let him see the state of my car.

"What part of town do you live in?"

Oof. I lived in the western part of the city, close to the airport and college, in a rough and sketchy area. It wasn't so bad, but my apartment was pretty ugly and run-down.

"Bricktown," I said, the lie rolling off my tongue. I wanted to live in Bricktown. It was historic and a convenient location with a really easy commute to this office.

"Oh, wow, I'm in the Fisher Square area. Well . . . see ya tomorrow then. Good night." He left.

Shit. Fisher Square was pretty nice. I felt bad that I'd lied—he probably wouldn't even care where I lived. I wanted to slam my forehead into the wall because I kept making dumb decision after dumb decision where Danuwoa was concerned.

I sat at my desk twiddling my thumbs for fifteen minutes to make sure he would be out of the parking garage by the time I got there.

Once I got home, I set up my laptop on the small table we used for meals and looked up some websites and videos for how to create amazing executive presentations. Gary had emailed me an old one and told me to just update the numbers, but it was really ugly, and I noticed there were a lot of misspellings. Either this was some sort of test and power play, or Gary did not give a shit about what was presented to the higher-ups. Or maybe no one even looked at the presentations and working as a corporate accountant was just going through the motions and checking off all the steps.

It was well after midnight before I went to bed, but I was proud of that presentation deck. I barely understood the content or any of the Technix-specific vernacular and acronyms, but I used all the old talking points and updated them, plus I thought the new template I created looked sexy as hell.

I woke up extra early and made it to the office to set up my workstation. I would be ready for Gary, and I was excited to have completed a task that at first seemed impossible. You know what was always said about expectations? Never expect anything and you'll never be disappointed. Was it wrong that I expected Gary to be proud of me since I completed his task?

Gary stormed by my desk, a travel thermos of coffee in his hand. "Send me that presentation, now."

"It's already in your inbox, sir."

"Great." That was it. He walked away to his glass office.

Seven

MONDAY. AFTER MY FIRST WEEK, IT WAS EVIDENT THAT GARY was the most pleasant on Mondays. Although, that wasn't saying much considering he was just as ornery and demanding as ever, but I observed these past two Mondays that he smiled more quietly to himself. It made me think Gary was probably an all right guy outside of the office.

Tuesday. By my second day, I got the hang of inputting invoices into QuickBooks. I still wanted to go back to school, but I was learning what I needed to for free now that I had specific things to look up required for my job. I learned that Martin, Nick, and Ryan all went to OU and were part of the same fraternity. They had a very strange bromance going. They did everything together—work, eat, bathroom breaks. It was a club I'd witnessed all my life and had never been invited to, nor did I have any desire to join their ranks. Lisa kept to herself and ate at her desk always.

Wednesday. I really loved Wednesdays. I ate lunch with Phoebe and Danuwoa every day, but on Wednesday, Phoebe had to eat quickly and run off, so it left Danuwoa and me to sit together. It was something I shouldn't have indulged in. His smile and singular attention for those thirty minutes left me giddy, but I regulated our conversations to simple, friendly topics. No flirting and no hint of romance. I felt like I was teetering on a very thin tightrope of what was friendly and what was romantic, but as long as we never crossed any physical lines, then we weren't breaking any of the company rules.

Thursday. I found our payroll specialist, Becky, crying in the bathroom. If she had been in a stall, I could have quietly backed out and left her undisturbed, but she was at the sink splashing water on her face and saw me. She fell prey to a phishing scheme. She really thought Natalie had emailed her asking to change Mr. Stevenson's bank account. Natalie did not email her and had confronted Becky in the lobby. That's what I gathered between her sobs. I didn't even know people could do that to companies. Auntie was always clicking suspicious links emailed to her, but I didn't realize there was a network of these kinds of scams cashing in on mistakes made at big corporations. I triple-checked every email in my inbox now.

Friday. Becky was not fired, but we all had to watch training videos on how to spot phishing schemes and avoid them. They were more interesting to watch since one of the videos was made by Danuwoa. His deep voice narrated one about spear phishing, which is what happened to Becky, who had thought an email came from a trusted source.

Lather. Rinse. Repeat.

Every day blurred together to be much the same, save for Becky falling victim to corporate phishing that one time. I had been at Technix for two weeks now, and this was what I had to say about all the red tape, gatekeepers, and requirements to get this job—all that was pointless. Anyone could do this job. Ember, who only graduated high school, could do this job. Joanna could learn to do this job. Hell, even boneheaded Sage could do this job. That thought made me bitter and a little resentful.

Years, tears, and beers were wasted over me getting to this point. This was boring. I mean, I liked the money, but I honestly didn't see how any of these people I worked with were better than me for having a four-year college degree. Had I sold myself short with this dream of being an accountant? Maybe I would take up bowling to have some sort of hobby outside of accounting. I was getting my first check today, so I would reserve judgment until I saw the amount—which was going to be a lot. Real money.

I was broke for years because there wasn't a single company that would hire me without the accounting classes. Then there was all the money I lost because Sage didn't show up to his hearing. That was some shit. Then there was the fee to get my car out of impound. But my brother was family, as my Auntie liked to remind me, and family was family. We stuck together. Even if my credit score was involved, then I'd like to say *To hell with family*, but I couldn't.

Even after everything he'd done, I still sent Sage money and a letter every month. I was practically a saint, I mean really. It was bad what he did, and I was still pissed at him. But there was nothing I could do about it now, and there was no use dwelling; I had things to do. Like errands for Gary.

Gary wanted me to pick up his wife's dry cleaning. Unbelievable. That was nowhere on the job description, and this woman who stayed at home all day couldn't handle this herself? Meanwhile, I had to drive my crappy car clear to the other side of town and back. Then I had to run several reports and dashboards for him when I returned to the office. So, what did a vice president of accounting actually do? From what I observed of Gary, he delegated everything and sat in his glass office and attended a lot of meetings.

I finished lunch and was accosted by Gary to immediately "zip out" and do a "quick favor" for him. I will forevermore be wary of any person who describes a task as zipping out for a quick favor. It would inevitably not be quick, and there would be no zipping with traffic downtown. I gathered my things and rushed to my car to get this rich white lady's clothes before Gary needed me for yet another thing.

There was a line out the door for the dry cleaner's, and it took me twenty minutes to get to the register. I would have to push my luck with my car and speed all the way back downtown.

"Thirty-two dollars," the young woman demanded.

"I was told this was paid for." I couldn't believe Gary would send me here with no money on a personal errand.

"No, these were thirty-two dollars, and Horowitz still owes for this. It's been here for two weeks." She put a plastic-wrapped suit on the counter. "Suits that are cleaned and pressed are fifteen."

"So, you need forty-seven dollars?"

"And the six-dollar storage fee."

"Storage fee?"

"I've had to hold on to this for two weeks. Does it look like I have extra space?" she asked me.

"Fifty-three dollars? For dresses and a suit? One moment please." I stepped aside so she could help the next person in line.

I called Gary's cell and grumbled when it went straight to voicemail. It was 1:50 p.m. and he needed my reports by 3:00 p.m. I was going to have to eat it. I got back in line, and when I made it back to the front, my hand shook as I gave the cashier all the cash in my wallet. I carefully folded the receipt and placed it in my purse. Gary had better reimburse me for this. I snatched the garments and ran out to my car.

The old bastard didn't start. This was *so* not the time for it to be acting up. I smacked the engine with my shoe once and tried the ignition. Nothing.

Twice, and tried again. Dead.

The third time I just kept hitting the engine over and over and over again, picturing Gary's smug face.

Fifty dollars was a lot of money for me, and I couldn't believe the thoughtlessness of my boss to send me on a personal errand while also expecting me to pay for his wife's clothes and the suit he forgot about. I was not raised that way. Auntie taught me never to expect any favors from anyone and to pay my own way. She even told me if I couldn't pay for a meal myself, then I had no business going on a date and relying on someone else to pay for me. She taught me that women had to protect themselves and men expected a lot for a twenty-dollar dinner. I still lived that way.

I slapped the hair out of my face and tried to calm my breathing. The other customers in the shitty strip mall stopped and stared at me. It was the nicest and cleanest strip mall I had ever been to, and that made my anger worse; it was like this neighborhood tried everything to make it seem wealthier and set apart from the rest of Oklahoma. I prayed my engine turned over. I slammed my door shut and took another breath. "Please work," I begged, and patted the dashboard and then turned my key in the ignition.

It roared to life. Thank fuck!

I never pulled out of a parking lot faster than I did from that one.

The cherry on top of the shit cake was that when I made it back to the office, my laptop would not power on. I snapped it into the dock that was supposed to charge this thing for me and pressed the button.

Could this day get any worse?

"Ember!" Gary's bark made me jump.

"Yes, sir?"

"Where's that presentation?"

"Working on it. I'm having computer problems."

"Well, get IT and fix it. I have to head into the conference room. My part is last on the agenda, so hurry up, then bring the computer to me."

"Of course."

I grabbed the desk phone and dialed Danuwoa's extension. This was the first opportunity I had ever had to call his direct line. The buzzy feeling in my stomach was from stress and nerves and totally not from the rich voice on the other end of the line.

"What can I do for you, Bucky?"

"Don't call me that," I groaned. "Can you come to my desk? I'm having a computer emergency."

"Sure, be right over."

The seconds stretched for an eternity, and my leg was bouncing a mile a minute as I waited for him to arrive.

"How can I be of service?" Danuwoa asked, casually leaning against the partition.

"My computer won't turn on, and I have to get this presentation for Gary ready for his meeting that is literally happening right now."

"Right, sit back, and I'll take a look. Try to take some deep breaths. It's all going to be fine; none of our jobs are life-or-death. They can wait a few minutes, or he can email the presentation out after the meeting and mention the technical error."

My feet pushed off from the carpet, and I wheeled back to give him some space. "With Gary, everything is urgent and a priority."

I watched as Danuwoa fiddled with my laptop and the docking station. Then he ducked under the desk. "Got it." He turned his head back to me. "Your foot must have unplugged the power supply. Your laptop is dead; it'll need a few minutes before it can boot up."

"The little people," I cursed under my breath. My leg was bouncing again. "I don't have time for this."

Danuwoa got up from his crouched position and sat on the desk, moving Gary's dry cleaning out of the way, his hands out like he was afraid to startle a skittish horse. "Yes. You. Do."

I looked at him from under my eyebrows. *Not. Helping.*

He crossed his arms. *I'm. Trying. To.*

We both jumped and looked at the screen as it loudly came back to life with the *ahh* noise. "Finally!"

"Shhh!" The angry sound came from Lisa's cubicle.

"Sorry!" I whispered loudly, and batted Danuwoa out of the way so I could log in to my laptop.

"Is everything there?" he asked me.

I double-clicked my folder, and the presentation was there and in order.

"Yes!" I went to eject my laptop from the dock, and Danuwoa's calloused warm hand covered mine, halting me.

"It's going to die again as soon as you lose power. You need to keep it plugged into the power source to use it."

"That's fine." I slipped under my desk and unplugged the power cord. Popping back up, I unplugged the top part of the charger from the docking station, took my laptop, and headed right for the conference room, thanking Danuwoa over my shoulder.

I waited outside the glass for an opportunity to knock. I didn't want to disturb the man talking. Gary knew I was there because he shot me a glare through the see-through door, and he motioned with his hand to get over there. I knocked anyway to be polite.

A blond man had his back to the door, but at my knock, he swiveled around in his chair and welcomed me in with a dashing smile.

You know, if Gary had a smile like that, I would gladly get his dry cleaning. I mean, wow. Unreal.

"Come in," the grump ordered. His voice was sharp. I fucking hated Gary.

I tiptoed my way across the conference room while one of the guys in finance was reporting to Mr. Stevenson and Natalie Sanchez. Oh god, I would have really liked to slip by my whole career and not garner her notice. I could feel her questioning gaze on me as I sat next to Gary and opened my laptop, then I dived under the conference desk to find the outlet hidden in the floor. Was it dignified? No. The man speaking paused for a moment but then resumed.

I popped back up and smiled at Gary. He tried to eviscerate me with his eyes. The feeling was mutual, man. I didn't want to be there, and I sure as shit didn't want to get his wife's dry cleaning, but here we were.

The older gentleman to the blond's right kept flipping through his slides as Gary asked me sharply under his breath, "Where the hell have you been?"

He couldn't be serious. "I was getting your dry clean—"

"Shut up. Open up the reports and don't say anything," he ordered in a hushed whisper.

I sat there absorbing everything that was said in the meeting, typing copious notes. I surmised based on the material and the slides that this was a joint finance-and-accounting meeting. The blond was Kyle Matthews, director of finance. He was upbeat and engaging, garnering everyone's attention as he provided a quick update on the forecast. I made a note to google *forecasting*. Then Mr. Stevenson took over talking. My fingers could barely keep up typing. I couldn't believe I was sitting in a meeting with the CEO of the company.

I glanced at Gary, who was sitting stone-faced. I was unsure how he could sit there doing nothing while the CEO was telling the finance and accounting teams the project he wanted completed for improving our systems and efficiency. I didn't understand all of it, but I did understand that if a directive came from the chief executive officer, then it was a big deal.

"Horowitz, you're up. Tell me how we're doing cleaning up the disaster that was our Portland office. What's going on with the accounts payable?"

Gary turned his head to face Mr. Stevenson. "I have my new assistant to help me comb through the documents, but it's a huge mess and it will take time."

I gave Gary some major side-eye—was he serious? All the files he dumped on my desk my first day were for Portland. I finished those. In fact, those were the reports I had pulled up on my laptop.

"Actually, I finished those. We reconciled one hundred twenty-five thousand dollars in accounts payable." I turned my laptop around on the table toward Mr. Stevenson and Natalie.

"It looks like you have no idea what's going on in your own department, Horowitz," Mr. Stevenson said as he stretched his arms overhead.

"She's new and we are still working on communication," my boss said, giving me the fakest smile. I had seen that predatory smile countless times in my life from various men. It promised retribution.

"Marvelous. Looks like we're done here." Mr. Stevenson stood up and walked out of the room, Gary on his heels. The older guy who was presenting, the vice president of finance, Grayson Adams, gave me a bewildered look and left.

Then it was just Kyle, Natalie, and me left in the room.

"That took balls, kid." Kyle shook his head to himself and gathered his things.

Kid? This was the first time I met with this man and he said that to me?

"Was that bad?" I asked. How could it be bad? I answered the CEO's question!

"You just made Gary your enemy. My advice? Don't talk unless you're spoken to. That was some unnecessary attention you just drew to yourself, and you're an accounting assistant. This was an executive meeting. You had no business saying anything. Good luck fixing that mess." He winked at Natalie with a wolfish grin and left.

Kyle was an ass. A beautiful, belittling ass, but could he be right? I mean, I *was* a nobody, but to have someone tell me so to my face? I had never been so embarrassed, and I'd just come from assaulting my car in a strip mall parking lot.

I put my head in my hands, trying to muster the courage to face Gary.

"Don't listen to Kyle," Natalie said. She had silently moved closer to me. I had forgotten she was there.

"He's right. I'm a big fat nobody who was lucky to land this job." I rested my cheek on my fist; my slouch over the table would put Quasimodo to shame. I wanted to curl into myself and disappear.

"From the looks of it, we were lucky to get you. When did you start?" She rested her crossed arms over her baby bump.

"Two weeks ago."

"In two weeks, you fixed the accounting mess that Gary had been putting off for four months. What are your goals?"

"My goals? Like in life?"

"For your career. Do you want to move up in accounting?"

"It would be nice to be an accountant and not just an accounting assistant."

"Where were you before you walked into this meeting?"

I wasn't sure if I should tell her I was running a personal errand for Gary and his wife, but seeing as how he was probably going to fire me for speaking up in this meeting, what did I have to lose?

"Mrs. Horowitz needed her dry cleaning picked up," I said, trying to mask the disdain in my voice, but my face was an open book.

Natalie laughed. Encouraged, I kept going. "The worst part was that he had a suit he forgot about, and no one bothered to pay the dry-cleaning lady!"

"No!"

"Yes! Gary never answered my calls."

"So, you paid for it?"

"Of course! Over fifty dollars!"

"What?! No way, why did you pay over fifty dollars in Oklahoma for dry cleaning?"

"That's what I thought. They were his wife's dresses and they looked expensive. I don't know. I just created a mess." I put my face in my hands.

"Hey, chin up. You're doing fine, trust me. And don't worry about Gary, okay?"

I lifted my head and watched as Natalie waddled out of the conference room before I rallied my courage to return to my desk.

Over the sea of gray cubicles, I could see Danuwoa's head as he walked along the opposite side of the floor. He smiled and waved as he navigated his way toward me. He pushed an IT cart full of miscellaneous electrical equipment. An old printer sat on top with cords and wires sticking out each way on the cart.

"Where did you find all that old junk?" I asked him, because this was a fairly modern office.

"This is all from the executive floor. Legacy stuff Mr. Stevenson wants gone. Could you use a printer? It works fine."

"Actually, I could. Thank you. Are you sure it's okay that I take it?"

"It's fine. It's either someone uses it, or we take it out to a field and *Office Space* its ass."

"Forget it, I've lived this long without a printer. I got a baseball bat in my trunk." I was serious; that was my weapon for when my piece-of-shit car broke down on the side of the road.

"Skoden." Danuwoa winked at me.

"Would it be an authentic *Office Space* printer ass-kicking since this particular printer has never done anything to me?"

"It does seem like an unjust fate for this beauty." Danuwoa rubbed the plastic side of the printer like it was a tame horse.

"I could use it, and if it acts up, then we can take it to a field and beat it to shit."

"Deal," he said with a laugh.

I had just scored a free printer.

"Ember!" Gary shouted and pointed to my desk.

"I'll catch up with you at the end of the day about the printer. Good luck with that." Danuwoa wheeled my new printer and the rest of the junk away. I ran to my cubicle.

"Mr. Horowitz, I—"

"Sit down."

I didn't want to obey his command, but the tone of his voice and red face had my ass in my seat in under two seconds. Angry men like Gary were a dime a dozen where I was from.

As soon as my butt hit my chair, his seething face was inches from mine.

"Never, and I mean *never*, embarrass me like that again. You know nothing. I looked up your résumé, and you have a basic accounting certificate from a crap community college. What makes your ignorant ass think you can understand anything that is going on at a tech company after two weeks?"

"Associate's degree," I mumbled. I knew what I made up on my résumé.

"Excuse me?" His eyes screamed murder. I should have shut up. A smart me would have looked down and not said anything, but I was not smart. I was a smart-*ass*, and there was a difference.

"I have an associate's degree from a 'crap community college.' Not a certificate." I didn't have either, but I had to defend my fake education. I didn't want any red flags with changes in my story.

"So, you're a smart-ass, huh?"

Obviously. I just went over this.

There was a very heavily pregnant pause. He took a deep breath, and then Gary's voice got lethally quiet. "You better wise up and shut up. Got it? You do as I say and never speak to executives like Mr. Stevenson without my permission again."

"I'm sorry, sir. It won't happen again." I wasn't good enough to talk in a meeting, but I never ghosted my dry-cleaning person. Granted, I have only ever dry-cleaned one thing in my life—it was my high school graduation dress, which I had found at the thrift store—but I picked it up and paid on time. So, what made these "executives" so special where normal people couldn't even talk to them?

Gary straightened to his full height, which was only slightly taller than my five feet six inches, but he was a stocky man that just took up space. I mean really, how could men just go about taking up space like that? In my cubicle no less! Why were women supposed to make themselves smaller when men like Gary got to puff up their chests and just invade spaces that weren't theirs? He made me so mad. I wanted my fifty-three dollars back, and I wanted a boss who didn't look at me like he promised death in my near future.

"Would now be a bad time to ask about reimbursing me for your dry cleaning?" I gave him a saccharine smile.

Gary's chest heaved as he took another huge breath. He snatched the plastic-wrapped garments off my desk and stormed away, glaring daggers at me.

I guess that was my penance. Had I known, I would have just left the dry cleaner's without his clothes. He was pissed regardless. I looked down at my hands, and they were shaking. I had to watch my back with Gary.

Eight

I KEPT MY HEAD DOWN FOR THE REST OF THE DAY; EVERY TIME
Gary came out of his glass office, I could feel him trying to
murder me with his eyes. I was never getting my fifty-three dollars back. On the bright side, I was getting a paycheck. A full-
time-salary paycheck. A $1,611 paycheck to be exact. I tried to
prepare myself. When I opened the envelope and saw the amount
on the pay stub, my breath caught. But as I sat in the bathroom,
locked in a stall, I cried happy tears. I had never in my life had
that much money at one time. This was mine. No one could take
it away from me.

I also cried because this might be the last time I ever saw that
kind of money again. Gary terrified me. Maybe I just wasn't cut
out for this kind of environment. I mean, I have dealt with abusive
jerks at work, but this guy could really keep me from having a career altogether. I was a fighter, but this seemed like an arena I was
outmatched and underprepared for.

I left the bathroom stall and splashed cold water from the sink on my face. I was dealt a shitty hand at various times in my life, but the one thing I could say was that I was very blessed that my face never bore the effects of a crying episode. Sure, my eyes were a little red, but they didn't get puffy. So I guess one could say I was a pretty crier. I'd take it, since I had to walk about out there.

After four on Fridays, upper management was gone. I could breathe easy knowing that I would have no more confrontations with Gary today. I really didn't have anything to do. I finished all my busywork from the rest of the accounting team, and now Gary didn't trust me to help him on any other projects. Even Lisa had gone for the day. Becky from HR was typing furiously at her computer. Our section felt empty and lonely.

Besides Danuwoa and Phoebe, I didn't really talk to anyone else here. After what Kyle said, I doubted anyone at his level would bother to talk to me either. It was like I finally crossed the line into the corporate world, but I was still *other*. I was still treated as less than. Even if I finished school and moved on to get a bachelor's degree, I didn't know how I would overcome that feeling. Was it in my head, or did people really treat me that way? I recalled the awful people at the bowling alley, and yup, I was definitely treated as a second-class citizen meant to serve, and then Kyle's words cracked through my mind like a whip.

It was stupid. His approval shouldn't mean anything to me. I didn't even know him. But having someone tell me to my face that I needed to know my place was beyond embarrassing. I just knew anytime I was happily doing any mundane task that the memory would come assaulting me left and right. I cringed with the anticipation of it.

"Hey, when are you headed home?" Danuwoa leaned against my cubicle wall, hands in his pockets with his ankles crossed. He looked so sure of himself, so comfortable in his own skin. Maybe I should have gone to school for IT.

"I don't have anything to do right now, and Gary is gone." I shrugged.

"Let's go." He pushed himself off the partition and motioned for me to follow him.

"I'm allowed to just leave?"

He turned his head over his shoulder and raised his eyebrow and kept walking to the front of the office.

I guess I could. Fuck it. If I was getting fired, then what did it matter? I popped my laptop into my bag and shuffled after Danuwoa.

He was waiting by the elevator chatting with Phoebe when I approached. The printer was resting on top of the IT cart.

He nodded at me and said to Phoebe, "Have a nice weekend."

I slowed to a casual, cool, and totally collected walk as Danuwoa pushed the button to call the elevator. I stood next to him, my orthopedic flats giving me maybe an extra inch of height so I came up to his shoulders.

The elevator dinged its arrival, and when the doors opened, we were confronted with a very pregnant Natalie.

She smiled and said, "Great, I caught you before you headed out." She said it directly to me. "Hey, Dan." She barely glanced his way before she grabbed my arm and pulled me into the elevator. "I only need you for a moment. You can come too, Dan. Mr. Stevenson's having problems with his laptop again." She rolled her eyes, and Danuwoa gave a heavy sigh before joining us.

"Is there something wrong?" I asked, still looking at her hand on my arm. She followed my line of vision and let go of me, giving me an apologetic smile, then pressed the floor seventeen button like a maniac. Pressing it more times does not move the elevator faster. People know that, right?

"No, the opposite. Some great news. I'll wait for Mr. Stevenson to tell you himself."

"Mr. Stevenson?" I thought I would throw up right then and there. For the rest of the day, if not my life, I was done talking to rich old white men with "executive" in their titles.

Danuwoa stepped closer to me; his presence was reassuring.

"He was very impressed with you today, and he just wants to tell you himself. You have nothing to worry about." Natalie smiled before hissing a breath and hunching over.

"Are you okay?" Danuwoa leaped forward, steadying Natalie.

"Braxton-Hicks contractions, I'll be fine." She rubbed her visibly tight stomach over her fitted dress.

As the elevator stopped at floor seventeen, Danuwoa and I looked with concern as she straightened and led us onto the executive floor.

This place was a glass castle. Everything was modern and shiny. Where floor twelve was kind of a cheap modern attempt, everything on floor seventeen screamed *money*. I felt as if my presence alone sullied this place. I've never been in any five-star hotels in my life, but this looked like the movies. It smelled exactly as I imagined, like clean leather. Shit, we couldn't afford leather. Not even for our regalia. I didn't have any besides some beaded jewelry my auntie and I made when I was younger.

I glanced over to Danuwoa to see if he was affected the same way I was. He appeared unfazed as he walked beside Natalie. She smiled over at him like they had done this walk thousands of times before, and they had.

"They've passed, no need to hover over me. I'm fine. You go

ahead and make sure his laptop is in working order for the weekend, I need a moment with Ember."

Danuwoa looked at me and raised his eyebrow, wordlessly asking, *This is weird, will you be okay?*

I silently nodded and faced Natalie.

"What you did in that meeting today took guts. Gary sucks.
Since I've been here, he has been awful, but Mr. Stevenson gets
attached to people, and he chooses to overlook a lot of things. I
don't condone it, but it's the way it is. I have a baby on the way,
and I need a paycheck."

I stood there awkwardly listening to her tell me these things. I
could see Danuwoa through the door.

Natalie continued, "I'm sure you've heard I'm looking for a
temporary replacement for me while I am on maternity leave?"

I did not like where this was going.

"I did hear some rumblings."

"Great, Mr. Stevenson is going to offer the role to you."

"I don't even know him!" I squeaked.

"It's fine; I still have a few weeks before my due date to train
you. You can call or text me anytime."

She made it sound so official, like I'd already agreed. I had not
agreed!

"You need to ask for at least a ten percent raise. He likes when
people negotiate. He'll respect you for it."

"But I just started." All my life, I had never asked for a raise.
I didn't even know that was allowed. I thought that was a reward
for doing a good job for a year or two: a raise was bestowed upon
you. In this world, you could just ask for more money?

"Being the executive assistant to the CEO has a lot of responsibility." I immediately took a step back, and she quickly added,

"It's not hard, but you will have to keep track of many things, and being 'executive facing,' you get a higher salary than just a typical admin. So, when he offers, just say you would love to and ask if he would be interested in increasing your pay by ten percent to cover the new role and responsibilities. Okay? Got it?"

I was wide-eyed, trying to absorb it all, but she was spraying everything at me like a hose on full blast.

"Great, let's go in." She waddle-marched her way into the office.

I had no choice but to follow.

"Why don't you go ahead and close the door?" Mr. Stevenson asked. I stood there like an idiot until Danuwoa and Natalie looked at me. He was talking to me. Mr. Stevenson wanted me to close his door.

I sprang into action and released the glass door; it made a low click as the magnet in the bottom activated. It was see-through. Rich people probably took a shit behind glass thinking that was enough privacy. I bet they wanted everyone to see their golden toilets.

Like magic, the glass turned opaque.

I faced everyone else in the room in awe. Mr. Stevenson, in his red sweater-vest, chuckled.

"I love doing that," he said as he waved a small white remote. "It's smart technology. I press this button, and it connects the door to electricity, and the crystals in the glass turn opaque. When I turn it off, the glass goes clear again. It never gets old."

Danuwoa snickered as he leaned over the desk, practically on top of Mr. Stevenson as he fiddled with the sleek computer.

I smiled as I crossed and uncrossed my ankles.

"Please have a seat." He pointed with his hand to the empty chair next to Natalie. I took three large steps to get to the seat, grateful this man took pity on my awkwardness. But by the side-eye I was getting from Natalie, my big ogre steps were only adding to it. I tried to take a calming breath, but with my luck, I probably looked like a gaping fish. I just wanted this over with. Clearly, they had the wrong person in mind for the job. I didn't even know where to start with being an executive assistant to the CEO. That sounded too fancy for my ass. I glanced at the corner, where the floor-to-ceiling windows connected, and in front of them was a bronze saddle sculpture. This may have been a new tech company, but in Oklahoma, people took cowboying seriously.

"Great work today," Mr. Stevenson began, leaning back in his chair. Danuwoa scooted himself and the laptop a few inches away to get some space. "Gary has been a loyal employee, but he can be lazy. Natalie told me you've only been here two weeks, and in that time, you were able to go through the old invoices from the Portland office. I need someone like you. Sharp, with great attention to detail, and a real go-getter. Natalie said you'd be perfect to fill in for her, and I agree. How about it?" He brought his arm down and looked at his watch.

He offered me the job so casually, as if he were ordering a meal. Natalie nudged my foot with her own.

"Thank you so much for considering me. I don't have any executive assistant experience. I don't want to fall short of your expectations." I gave a genuine smile to Natalie, because I was being honest—unlike how I landed at Technix in the first place.

"You don't have to worry about that," Natalie spoke up. "I'll train you myself and leave very detailed instructions. I'll make sure everything runs smoothly, and I think you'll enjoy yourself." She wiggled her eyebrows, and I knew she was prompting me to haggle a pay increase.

"If I were to take this position, er, that is to say, I would be happy to consider this position; however, it seems like it's a job that has a lot more responsibilities. Would it be possible to increase my compensation to match . . . those new responsibilities?"

Mr. Stevenson's face lit up with a smile. "What would be fair to you?" he asked me.

I looked at Natalie, who smiled encouragingly, and then I caught Danuwoa's eyes when I glanced back toward Mr. Stevenson. What was he thinking of all this? It was kind of absurd to be talking about a job offer and money with an IT guy in the room. And not just any IT guy, but Danuwoa, the hottest guy on the planet.

"Ten percent?" I asked, internally cringing at how high my voice sounded. I should have sounded more confident, but what the hell did I know about any of this? I was in too deep.

"Perfect! We'll have you start shadowing Natalie on Monday. You almost done with that, Dan the Man? I have dinner reservations with my wife."

"What about Mr. Horowitz?" I asked.

"You don't have to worry about him," Natalie said, beaming as she stood. She motioned me to follow her out. I got up and looked back at Danuwoa. It felt like a century had passed since he asked me to skip out early and take the printer.

"You're all set," Danuwoa said, and relinquished the laptop back to the CEO.

"Wonderful!" He slammed it shut. "I hope you all have a great weekend." He started packing his briefcase, the three of us forgotten.

"Come on," Natalie whispered. Outside the white opaque glass, a new Ember emerged, a richer and more reassured me. The kind of person I had always dreamed I would become. Gary wasn't going to fire me, and now he had no power to ever fire me!

I never had aspirations to be anything other than an accountant, but this new job, temporary as it was, was a huge break for me. I could be anything.

"Congrats! Stealing the show and not even a month in." Danuwoa nudged me as we walked to the elevator.

"Thank you, Natalie," I said, and turned and hugged her around her belly. "You didn't have to do that, but thank you."

"You earned it. I look forward to training you on Monday. Now get going. I have some things to wrap up before I can kick these shoes off."

The doors to the elevator shut, and I grabbed Danuwoa's toned arm. "That just happened, right?"

"Yup, you just got a raise and a new job. With all that new money, you can buy a new printer, ya know?"

"No way, I want that dinosaur."

Nine

PHOEBE WAS PACKING UP HER DESK WHEN DANUWOA AND I got back to the twelfth floor to pick up the printer.

"Guess who has a date?" She sang her question as she twirled on her foot.

"Ember, do you have a date?" Danuwoa asked me, and I caught on.

"No, Dan, do you have a date?"

"Afraid not." He shoved his hands in his jean pockets and turned to face me, Phoebe completely forgotten as we locked eyes.

"You guys are the worst." Phoebe slammed her lunch bag into her backpack and continued, "I have a date with someone with a real career path. My plan is already coming together."

"You can't plan to marry a guy just based on his salary and title," Danuwoa lectured. "He could be abusive, or a serial cheater."

"Who cares? I need a starter husband." She winked and headed to the elevator.

"How about you focus on just having fun on this date?" I asked her.

"Oh, making men fall in love with me is the fun part."

"You're ruthless and would really get along with my best friend." I laughed. If Phoebe and Joanna were ever together, the world would combust with all the badass feminine energy.

"Bring her to our next happy hour," Phoebe said.

The door to the elevator opened, and I went to the cart with the printer and started pushing it toward the door.

"Hold up—the cart doesn't leave the building." Danuwoa picked up the bulky printer and entered the waiting elevator.

I followed.

"Can I help? I can carry that."

"Nah, it's fine. You park in the employee lot, right?"

"I do," I answered as I fidgeted with a stray thread on my tote bag. Oh, crap on a cracker. He was going to see my car.

Danuwoa walked to the back of the elevator and balanced the edge of the printer on the gold handrail. I watched his look of concentration in his brassy reflection out of the corner of my eye. Phoebe caught me looking and smirked.

"Who's the lucky guy?" I asked to change the subject. In my experience, getting people to talk about themselves was easy, and I had no desire for her to make assumptions about Danuwoa and me. I wanted no trouble for either of us. We were here to work.

"That's a secret for now. I don't want to jinx it."

We all fell silent going down. Once the elevator made it past floor five, Danuwoa asked me, "Do you have any fun plans this weekend?"

"Joanna and I are going to celebrate getting my first paycheck." And the fact that I was just promoted and given a raise. I could not wait to tell her when I got home. I looked at Phoebe, who appeared to be in la-la land. Probably planning her starter wedding. My gut told me not to mention the promotion to her; I didn't want to kill her buzz before her big date, and I hoped it wouldn't ruin our budding friendship. She had really wanted the job. Danuwoa must have caught my hesitation and lack of mention of the promotion, because he flashed me a reassuring smile that awoke the butterflies in the pit of my stomach.

I'd never had a serious boyfriend or anything. I usually just had elaborate crushes on guys I had hardly ever talked to and created a false reality in my head about why the relationship never worked out. It was safer that way. Easier. I didn't experience the heartbreak and headache of someone letting me down. If I never depended on anyone or opened up to anyone, then I never had my expectations squashed.

The beginning of one of these crushes was exciting for me. The anticipation of not knowing when a brief interaction would be. Me in my head daydreaming of that interaction later and letting my imagination play out different what-if scenarios. What if I said something flirty after I said hi? What if I was bold and just kissed him in the elevator? The last one had just popped into my head, and my cheeks felt hot. Phoebe was here, for god's sake, but my romantic imagination couldn't care less.

What was great about these what-if scenarios was that they weren't real. I was safe. But right then in that elevator, my heart lurched, and this fake scenario was starting to feel not so fake. My brain did a what-if scenario of its own. What if I let someone in? What would it be like to have romantic plans on a weekend? My palms grew slick as my mind spiraled in a panic. I was not ready for any of this, and Danuwoa was completely off-limits. I basically had my dream job at Technix. Nothing could jeopardize that. Not even Danuwoa.

I hoped Joanna remembered we had plans later tonight. She was always going on spontaneous dates or hooking up with someone from an app. Some mornings I'd find an older guy in our bathroom, and others I'd find a younger woman. Joanna had no specific type. She loved love. She was addicted to the rush of it. She had more heartbreaks than I could count, and I lived through each one with her.

I was the stable one. I made sure our apartment was clean. I made sure there was food in the refrigerator, and I was always there to pick up the pieces of Joanna's broken heart. It was the same way with Sage and me. I was always there to fix whatever Sage broke and help Auntie move on from whatever disappointment Sage dealt her.

There was no one to help them if I ever broke down. I had to be everything for everyone, and as exhausting as that was, it also defined me. I wasn't an artist. I wasn't a great cook. But I was dependable, and I showed up for those I loved. That had to count for something in this life.

Sometimes I just wished I could be the one to try and fail. The type of person to take risks. I mean, I did lie on my job application, and now I had more money in a single paycheck than I got for a month working at the bowling alley. Maybe there was something to this risk-taking adventure. At least there was with the little fibs that helped me along the way.

"What do you have planned for the weekend?" I asked Danuwoa.

The elevator doors opened to the main floor lobby. He let Phoebe and me out first and then followed behind with the behemoth of a printer in his arms as he answered, "Just going home to my baby."

Phoebe cackled and said, "Bye, guys, I hope you have fun doing whatever you plan on doing with that thing." She winked as she skipped to the front entrance.

The world stopped spinning and my brain short-circuited. I had no idea how many seconds or minutes passed, but I forced the words out of my mouth. "Oh, a baby . . . how nice."

"Yup, my little rescue cat, Patches. She's my baby."

He was looking at me, teasing me.

A cat was worse than a baby. I hated cats.

"Oh, I love cats," I said. I wanted to slap my palm to my forehead. There was no reason for me to lie. He wasn't my boyfriend, so it didn't matter. Only, I felt like it really mattered to Danuwoa, and I didn't want to tell him that cats freaked me out and made me sneeze like crazy. "So, it's just you and your cat hanging out all weekend?"

"I lead a pretty quiet life. I have a few things to do for my sister and that's about it."

"Oh."

Danuwoa and I walked to the side door that led to our parking lot.

It was an awkward silence. I barely knew Danuwoa, and here he was carrying a heavy-ass printer for me, helping me. Were men nice for the sake of it? Or did they do things because they expected something for it? In my limited experience, it had always been the latter.

"How old is your sister?" I asked as we walked to the curb and waited for the light to allow us to cross.

"Twenty-three."

"I have a younger brother. He's nineteen."

"Does he raise hell?"

"Hell is child's play for Sage."

Danuwoa barked a laugh, and the feeling of making him do that felt so good. I wanted to do it again. At least I could honestly relate to him in being the eldest sibling. We crossed toward the

parking lot, and my nerves were having a rave in my body. I was
wired and tingly, embarrassed that this guy would see that before
I had this job, I was pretty much at rock bottom. At least the car
was clean, not that you could tell a dirty rusted car from a clean
rusted car, but the interior didn't look like I lived in it.

"Walela is an angel," he said, smiling to himself.

"Sisters usually are. It's the boys that get fucked up."

"Ha ha, very funny. Which way?"

I led him to the very far corner of the parking garage.

"Ta-da! My junker ride. I'm borrowing this car. Mine is in the
shop." It came out superfast, the lie. I don't even know why I said
this one. Danuwoa had been nothing but a sweetheart who teased
me a lot. If he teased me about my poverty, I'd probably retreat
into myself and never come out again.

He just looked at me with that one quirky eyebrow raised in
confusion, while he balanced the ancient printer in his arms.

"I don't think this will fit in your trunk. Does the passenger
seat fold down?"

He didn't react or care at all. If Joanna were here, she would
remind me that men don't care about things like what kind of car
you drive. I rolled my eyes at the imaginary Joanna in my head.
"It does, but then it won't go back up." I smiled sheepishly.

"Bricktown isn't far." He started walking away with my printer,
presumably to his own car.

Oof. That. Shit.

"I'm not in Bricktown . . . anymore . . ."

This man just smiled with fire in his eyes. "Oh yeah? Move
recently, did ya?"

"Yes, I did."

"And no mention you were moving during lunch at all in these
two weeks?"

"It must have just slipped my mind."

"Where did you move to?" He knew I'd lied, but I couldn't come clean. I wouldn't. It would be too embarrassing.

"I'm southwest of the city, near the airport."

Danuwoa turned swiftly on his heel, a feat that seemed impossible given the sheer weight of the printer. "I'll follow you home and drop it off for you."

"You really don't have to do that. We can fold my seat down. No one ever wants to drive with me in my crap car anyway."

He stopped and turned. "I thought you were borrowing the car."

I forced my face to stay neutral and not give anything away, but I wanted the parking garage cement to open up beneath my feet and swallow me whole.

"I am. It's an extended loan because I needed money to fix my car."

"Uh-huh." He wasn't buying it, but he continued walking.

He was four parking spots away and stopped at the bed of an old hunter-green Chevy truck and opened the tailgate. He slid the bulky gray printer onto the bed. I stood in awe as he began strapping bungee cables to it. So we were doing this then. I was taking him to my apartment, and Joanna would never let me live it down for the rest of my days. Henceforth, this Friday shall be referred to as the day I, Ember Lee Cardinal, brought home the world's hottest man.

He slammed the tailgate closed and said, "Let's go."

Safe in my car I breathed deep. "Please start. Please start. Please start," I prayed to Creator as I turned over the key. There was a pause, and my heart sank to my stomach, but mercifully the engine turned over. I tried to calm my nerves as I inched the car to the exit, waiting for Danuwoa.

When he was behind me and the road was clear, I pressed the

gas a little too fast. On a loud scream, the tires of my car burned out of the parking lot, leaving skid marks on the asphalt. I had twenty minutes to get my ass together. Immediately I dialed Joanna.

She picked up on the first ring. "You on your way, bitch? I got the pregame started, ow-ow!"

Drunk Joanna was basically useless for the task I had for her. "Put the drink down and listen. I have our IT guy following me home—"

"Shit! Are you in trouble? What the fuck? A stalker?"

"No, I am bringing him home—"

"You're bringing a boy home! Is this that good-looking guy, Daaannn?" She sang his name.

"Yes. His looks are irrelevant. He's bringing a printer from the office."

"Oh, boo."

"Listen, please. I need you to get all the bras that are hang-drying out of the bathroom. Throw them somewhere out of sight. Then I need you to just tidy up as quickly as you can. Can you do that for me? Pretty please? And don't make that face."

"You can't see my face," she huffed.

"I know the face you make when I mention cleaning of any kind."

"You worry too much. I'll make sure your bras are out of sight, but know that the man has already noticed your membership in the itty-bitty titty committee." Joanna laughed and hung up on me.

I threw my cell into my tote bag on the passenger seat and flipped it off. Joanna couldn't see it, but it felt good anyway. My boobs were *not* that small.

When we pulled up to the apartment complex, I wished it

weren't daylight saving time. It was still bright out after five in the evening, and the sun illuminated everything wrong and ugly with the building. But hey, $875 a month for two bedrooms was a steal. And now with my check easily covering my portion, that new car fund was stacking!

I parked behind Joanna and rushed to the street to meet Danuwoa. My phone began ringing. He was probably confused. **Oklahoma County Detention Center** popped up on my phone screen. Nope. Not today. I declined the call. Sage was probably calling to ask for more money on his commissary account or something again. He could wait a day or two. I threw my cell back in my tote and waved Danuwoa to park on the street.

Printer in tow, I led him up to our second-floor apartment. It was such a drag when hauling groceries or laundry, but at least we didn't have to hear anyone above us.

"You can go ahead and drop it over there." I pointed to the corner of our sparsely furnished living room. There was no way it would fit in my bedroom, and we had no desk or anything to place the printer on top of.

I heard Danuwoa's grunt as he put it down, bending his knees and back. I felt really guilty making him lug that around for me. He opened his backpack and took out cords. "Do you know how to set this up?"

Joanna came bursting out of her room like a bat from hell. "Where's this guy at?"

Poor Danuwoa looked absolutely terrified, frozen with the cords lifted in midair.

"*Hello* again, want a drink?"

"Joanna, we are all in the six-hundred-square-foot apartment. You do not need to yell."

"Sorry, you know when I drink I can't gauge my volume at all. Is this better?" Her whisper was over-the-top.

"Much." I rolled my eyes and gave my attention back to the ever-helpful and ridiculously patient Danuwoa. "I have no idea how to set it up, but I can probably find a video online. You have done more than enough for me today."

"I'll take a beer," he said over my head to a waiting Joanna.

"My kinda man," she said, her tone appreciative and seductive. That bothered me. My body reacted as if I had heard nails on a chalkboard. I'd have to examine my reaction to that later, because Danuwoa was sitting on our old nasty brown carpet and plugging in wires.

"How many computers need to be hooked up to this?" he asked.

"Just two laptops, but if you don't mind showing me how on one, I can figure out the other."

He paused what he was doing and leveled a look at me. I was fairly certain I couldn't read minds, but with Danuwoa, his eyes were so open. I could see exactly what he was thinking without him having to say a word.

His eyes said, *Shut up already.*

I narrowed mine in response. *Don't tell me what to do. I'm trying to be nice and respectful of your time.*

He curled up a single eyebrow and won the silent exchange. *You think you could make me do anything I didn't want to do?*

The hiss of the cracked beer can cleared the mounting tension.

"Order up!" Joanna handed the beer to Danuwoa. "E, can I steal you for a moment?" She overexaggerated her blinks. I thought she was trying to wink. She was three sheets to the wind, and Danuwoa chuckled.

I walked to my room, Joanna on my heels.

"I remember him being good-looking."

"He *is* good-looking." I threw my hands up.

"Wrong. He is the Native Daddy of our girly fantasies," Joanna said, then burped.

"You are being so loud right now." My index fingers were drilling holes into my temples with how much I was rubbing them out of mortification.

"Pfft, he can't hear us." She pushed me aside and headed straight to my closet. "We need to get you into something cute. You're inviting him out, aren't you?"

"I'm sure he has better things to do." And he would probably say no since it wasn't allowed. This would not be a company-sanctioned outing.

"Right now, he is in our living room hooking up the oldest fucking piece of machinery I've ever seen—voluntarily. I think he would be down to go out."

"Joanna," I warned.

"What's the problem? You like him."

"I could get fired and I just got this job."

"It's not a date and nobody has to know."

She threw my best sundress onto my perfectly made bed. It was white with a square neckline, fitted waist, and a slight flair to the A-line skirt that went just below my knees.

"Put it on and shake out your hair. We'll see you out there in five minutes. I need to get laid tonight, and I can't do that if I am worrying about you being alone in a bar. So, entice him to say yes."

Ten

I DID WHAT JOANNA SAID. I PUT THE DRESS ON AND EVEN AC-
cessorized it with my favorite pair of fringe earrings, which
Joanna had beaded for me. They were made with several different
shades of green, and I was pretty sure she gifted them to me so I
would stop carrying around the lizard. These were a better representation of her work and skill, but I would take that lizard with
me to the grave. I shook out my hair at the roots, really getting in
there with my fingers to bring some more life into it after a day at
the office. Looking at myself in the mirror, I was almost ready, I
just needed a little dab of blush on my cheeks to brighten my face.
There. I looked great. But I couldn't get myself to walk out my
bedroom door. A part of me wanted to put my other clothes back
on because *this* was asking for trouble. I had enough lies to keep
track of, and I did not want Danuwoa to become one of them.

I had my big-girl panties on. This didn't have to mean anything. He could say no. That would not define my night. We were
celebrating me and this new job. I twisted the doorknob and
stepped into the unknown. If Danuwoa had plans, who cared? So

what if I thoroughly embarrassed myself? Didn't matter. I was now an interim executive assistant to the chief executive officer of our company. I had no idea what I was supposed to do for a CEO, but I did know my bank account would be better for it. It made me untouchable to Gary, and Danuwoa got to witness this triumph. So, if he didn't want to go out drinking, that didn't really matter, because I was moving up.

Joanna said I had five minutes, and I had underestimated how badly a tipsy Joanna could make a mess of things. She had Danuwoa sitting on our couch, both laptops open next to him, and Joanna was modeling her wig collection.

"This one is my champagne wig. It only comes out on special occasions," she explained as she tenderly wrapped the platinum synthetic hair in wrapping paper and placed it back in its designated ziplock bag. That was her expensive wig—it cost fifty dollars—so she refused to wear it in any dirty dive bar. She had only let me wear it once, and that was just a quick moment to see what I would look like with platinum blonde hair. It looked bad. I was a brunette for life.

Danuwoa was giving her his polite attention, but as soon as he noticed me, Joanna was forgotten. He took me in from head to toe like he wanted to devour me. After he looked his fill, his eyes met mine and he smiled. Never in my life had I been so earnestly checked out. It was silly, but I wanted him to always look at me this way. He scrambled up off the couch. "Everything is all set. I don't want to keep you from your night out."

"Thank you for doing that," I said and paused, wringing my hands together. "Would you want to come out with us? I'd love to buy you a drink as a proper thank-you."

"I had a beer," he said and shoved his hands into his pockets and looked down.

"I promise to get you something better than Milwaukee's Best."

"It's the best Milwaukee has to offer." We smiled like dumb teenagers.

"God, I can't listen to this. Are we going? I have our ride outside." Joanna packed her wigs into their storage bin and closed the lid.

"I can't stay out too late, but I could stand another drink."

"Skoden!" Joanna marched to the front door and threw it open, disappearing into the now dusky evening.

Danuwoa sat in the passenger seat of the silver sedan Lyft while Joanna and I sat in the back. The car smelled like stale Pringles, the sour-cream-and-onion kind, and cigarettes.

It wasn't a long drive to our favorite bar, the Moonshine Pub. It was run-down, the sign was ridiculous, and the LARPing nerds frequented the place on Thursday nights. There were no Renaissance-costumed people on Fridays. Abe, the Friday bartender, had a generous pour.

Danuwoa was silently taking it all in as Joanna and I made our way to the bar.

"My chicas are here!" Abe sang as he set down our usual orders. Joanna drank whiskey, straight, like a cowboy who had seen some shit. I was a child. I had a Dirty Shirley. I liked my cocktails so sweet that I couldn't taste the alcohol and I had always limited myself to one.

I patted the empty bar stool to my right and yelled over the music, "Tell Abe what you want."

"Whatever beer on tap is good." Danuwoa sat next to me and inched his chair closer than it originally had been. I tried not to read too much into it, but those butterflies in my stomach had other plans.

Abe set the overflowing pint on the bar and was off to fulfill other orders.

Joanna raised her glass. "Cheers to Ember and her new rich-person job! Hopefully she remembers us little people when she gets a house and 401(k)!"

My red drink was still up in the air with Danuwoa's beer when Joanna kicked back the entire contents of her whiskey and let out a "Yow!"

We were celebrating, so I didn't warn her to slow down. It was Friday night, and I'd seen Joanna way drunker than this.

I took a sip through the black straw of my drink and announced my promotion. She slapped my arm in disbelief when I laid out the events of that afternoon. She looked to Danuwoa to corroborate.

"Shit, what the fuck? I always knew you were meant for bigger and better things." She caught the eye of a woman leaning over the pool table in cutoff shorts and a Guns N' Roses T-shirt. "You two good? I am going to make myself known to the hottie in the bad-girl number."

"I'm fine, do you want me to wait for you to go home together?"

We all three stared as the girl exaggeratedly bent over, her butt cheeks peeking out from the shorts.

"I don't think I'll be home tonight. You make sure E gets in an Uber or something, safely. Got it?"

"You have my word," he promised, then Joanna floated over to the hot chick. "Is she real?" Danuwoa asked me, bemused. I couldn't blame him. Joanna had that effect on everyone.

"Joanna is one of a kind. Does her being openly bi offend you?"

"Hell nah, she is just so energetic. Sorry if I'm a boring companion in comparison."

"Not at all." I looked down at my drink, unsure of how to proceed. This wasn't a date, and I didn't want to start playing twenty questions. I doubted he would appreciate an interview. My mind was spiraling trying to come up with something to say when he broke the silence between us.

"How do you feel about your new promotion?"

"Nervous. I know it doesn't seem like a lot of money, but I've never made so much before. I'm afraid I'll screw it up and lose my job."

"No way! Technix is easy. Great pay, benefits, and schedule. Just watch out for Mr. Stevenson and his moods."

"I can handle old white men," I lied. I mean, if one were being inappropriate with me right then, I would tell him off, but I was pretty sure you couldn't just go and tell off your boss. Not when you needed the money. "What about you? Did you always want to work in IT?"

"I like computers and the pay is good."

"You don't have any lofty ambitions?"

"I work to live and that's it. I like my free time. Not everyone wants to be some executive with all the stress and ego. I deal with that plenty if I can't fix a problem fast enough."

The beers must have loosened his lips, because he continued: "You know more than half the IT problems are their own damn fault? They never turn off or update their laptops, and then things freeze and crash. You really can tell what kind of person someone is when they are pissed about technology not working."

"Is there anything worse than slow internet? When I was growing up, we couldn't even afford to have the internet, but fast Wi-Fi is such a game changer." I giggled behind my hand.

"Am I gonna have problems with you, Ember?" He leaned his upper body closer to me. I really hoped there would be absolutely zero problems from me, but if he kept looking at me like that, then we were in for a whole lot of problems at Technix.

"With a moody executive and technical problems bound to arise, I daresay you will." My voice was husky. Emboldened by the Dirty Shirley, I twisted on my bar stool, and my legs were tangled in his. There was a warning siren going off in my head, but I didn't care. Danuwoa was right here, and his undivided attention was more intoxicating than the alcohol.

"I'm pretty sure this is a bad idea." He finished his beer, then angled his head within inches of mine. If I leaned forward, our lips would touch.

"What exactly?" If this was just hanging out as friends, then it wasn't a problem. I really wanted to hear him spell out why we'd be a problem. That he felt something between us too.

"Romantic entanglements with coworkers go against the rules."

"Is that what this is? I thought I was just buying you a thank-you drink for the printer," I said, challenging him by licking my lips.

His heated eyes tracked the movement. No one had to know what happened in a dark bar. One kiss would scratch the itch, and if it was a bad kiss, then that would be the end of that. We could just be friends and blame the booze for a momentary lapse of judgment.

I leaned forward at the same time he did. His smooth, warm lips barely grazed mine, and it was electric. I wanted more—

"You guys!" Joanna yelled.

Danuwoa and I broke apart, the moment gone and lost.

Joanna came bouncing back, dragging the girl from the pool table by the hand. "This is Donna."

"Hi," Donna sang in her southern drawl.

"We're leaving, but you two have fun, okay?" Joanna hugged me and winked, and then she was off.

Danuwoa and I sat at the bar, me nursing my red fizzy drink and him looking anywhere but at me. I knew we should not have crossed this line. Now it was awkward. We'd almost kissed. Our lips barely touched, but now he looked very much like he regretted it and was miserably stuck with me.

I slurped down my drink so I could call an Uber and die of mortification in the comfort of my own home.

"Would you lookie here, we got ourselves a real Indian," a drunk man's voice slurred behind me. I thought he was talking about me, but when I turned, two frat boys wearing solid-colored polos and boat shoes were staring at Danuwoa. One stood behind Danuwoa, and the other was on his right side, leaning an arm against the bar.

"Tell us, Indian man, can you go outside and do a rain dance? It's getting hot out there," the one wearing the blue polo said as his friend in the white polo snickered. They looked the same, like generic rich white boys from OU. Their buddies at a high-top behind us were egging them on.

"You had your laugh. Can you please leave me alone?" Danuwoa rolled his eyes and turned toward me.

The blue polo guy behind us started talking in that Hollywood Injun speak, deep with broken English. "The stoic Indian, me wise man, leave alone." I still hadn't forgiven Johnny Depp for doing it in *The Lone Ranger*.

"Just ignore them and hopefully they'll go away." I threw the last part over my shoulder, making sure the frat twins heard me.

"How long did it take you to grow this braid?" Blue Shirt held Danuwoa's braid in his disgustingly racist hands. I felt incensed. No one—and I mean no one—but family touched our hair.

Danuwoa saw the steam coming from my ears as I stood up, ready to engage these dicks.

Before I could move more than an inch, Danuwoa's arm snaked around my waist, and he pulled me in close. I was practically in his lap. "It's not worth it." His whisper sent a shiver down my neck.

"Can we go?" I whispered back, my mouth inches from his. I couldn't be here anymore. These assholes had violated our safest bar. As single women, Joanna and I didn't have many safe places. This was the first time I'd ever encountered anything like this here.

Danuwoa stood and our bodies were pressed together. His hulking form blocked me from the drunk idiots, and he placed his hand on the small of my back, steering me toward the exit.

"What? We were just having fun! Didn't know you were on a date with an Indian princess." They started chanting and moving their hands to their mouths. Sometimes, I really hated Oklahoma.

I lost control of my body. I whirled on the idiots and launched a fat loogie at the leader of the pack in the blue shirt, who dared touch Danuwoa's hair. It flew in an arc and landed right in the center of his forehead.

"Fuck! Nasty bitch."

Danuwoa stalked over to the blue shirt guy and socked him in the gut. The man keeled over. "Time to go," Danuwoa said. He tucked me under his arm and whisked me to the door.

"Get him," I heard from behind us.

"I wouldn't do that if I were you. If you want to keep drinking, settle the fuck down," Abe yelled over the noise.

The frat guys stopped following us.

Outside, Danuwoa had his phone out, ordering a ride home.

His shoulders were tightly wound, like he was ready for a fight if those jerks came out looking for one.

We didn't say anything for several moments; he just showed me his phone, and our ride was three minutes away.

"I'm so sorry, Danuwoa. Joanna and I have never experienced anything like that here. Had I known, I would never have suggested it."

"You can't protect us from shit like that. Racist assholes will always make themselves known. I had fun."

I looked at him skeptically and crossed my arms.

"I had fun up until that point. Your spitting skills are . . . impressive."

"I shouldn't have done that. It was impulsive."

"I probably shouldn't have punched the guy. I don't feel bad about it."

"What a pair we make. Escalating a situation with our rash decisions."

"We're friends, Ember. I'm not going to let drunk assholes get away with calling you names. Let's get you home and you can forget all about it."

Friends. He didn't mention the almost kiss, and I wasn't going to bring it up. Being friends with Danuwoa was better than being nothing to him. I didn't want to forget everything about this evening, especially not the half second when his lips brushed mine. That I wanted to replay in my head a few times before I slept.

The car ride was quiet, both of us subdued after a long day at work and dealing with jerks at the bar. We had become friends. My heart fluttered as I recalled the feel of his muscular arms around me for those brief moments.

Danuwoa broke the silence. "So, uh . . . Native Daddy, huh?"

"You heard?!" I was beyond mortified.

"Every word," he said with a laugh.

"For the record, I don't have daddy issues."

It was dark, but the streetlights illuminated him enough. He wiggled his eyebrows. "Wanna start?"

I pushed his chest, laughing at his dumb bravado. "Shut up before I jump out of this car."

This was bad. A romance with a coworker was doomed. I wanted to keep my job, and I really wanted to spend more time with Danuwoa. There was a way I could have both, but it would mean more lies, and I wasn't sure if Danuwoa would be open to starting a fling and having to hide it. He wasn't a dirty thing. I didn't want to hide him. I was starting to think that he might be the coolest person I had ever met. This was tricky and messy and exhilarating.

We parted ways outside my apartment complex. He waited in his truck and watched me until I got in my front door. Then I heard his old truck drive off.

Eleven

TODAY WAS THE DAY. I WAS GOING TO START MY TRAINING with Natalie on the executive floor. I didn't need to stop off at my old desk since I never stored anything personal there. My laptop was in my bag, so I rode the elevator up to floor seventeen with a smile on my face.

Natalie was already there, clearing the desk directly in front of Mr. Stevenson's office. The glass walls were opaque, so I couldn't tell if he was in or not.

"Happy Monday!" She beamed at me. "I hope you're ready to get started. Mr. Stevenson is already here." That answered that.

"Is he usually this early?"

"Sometimes. It depends on his schedule for the day. Today he had a haircut, so he was here early in the morning. He gets his hair trimmed once a month and has to have the first appointment of the day with Tiffany at Poise—actually, why don't you set your stuff down and grab a notepad."

I'd brought my company backpack today, and I hung it on the back of the desk chair.

"The best way to learn is to just get immersed in the job. I'm going to show you things as we go, but it will be you who is going to do everything, cool?"

"Yeah, totally."

"Great, first things first, we have a brief morning meeting with coffee. Mr. Stevenson brings his own thermos full of his specialty blend and has a professional setup at home, so you never have to worry about that. He has his own fridge, and you will have to stock it. Go ahead and set up your laptop."

I took my laptop out of my backpack and plopped it onto the docking station.

"Go to our server. I had IT give you access to my folder." She pointed to the little yellow folder icon with the label "GE."

"It stands for general executive. I'm the only executive assistant for our C-suite, so it's just you and me who go in that folder. In there is a subfolder labeled 'Admin' with instruction lists about anything you could possibly need: vendor information, Mr. Stevenson's company credit card and personal cards, et cetera. This folder will be your bible."

"You really thought of everything," I said in awe. I loved organization, but this was another level.

"I didn't come up with this system. I've added to it and made my own adjustments and improvements, but this is from decades of assistants who have worked with Mr. Stevenson over the years. He is a very particular man."

"Should that worry me?"

"No. I don't mind it, at least—it's a job, right? We get paid to be here and be of service. I've worked for a couple CEOs in the past, and Mr. Stevenson is by far the most straightforward. You don't have to guess what he means or feels, because he is very direct. He's getting older, so he might say some things that are questionable, but in my experience, he doesn't have any malice. He's just from that generation."

I remembered Danuwoa's racist experience over the weekend, and I didn't care what generation a person was from—if Mr. Stevenson said fucked-up shit, I didn't know that I would be able to stay. Couldn't people just be normal and kind?

"It looks like I scared you. I promise this job is fine and has perks for some of the not-so-glamorous stuff," Natalie assured me.

"I just want to do a good job."

"I know you will because you care. You remind me of myself a bit."

"I'm not pregnant," I teased.

"Gosh, no, and be glad you aren't. I've developed a hemorrhoid, and it sucks."

"Is another unpleasant side effect of pregnancy TMI?"

"You lose all sense of modesty."

We giggled and then heard a curt "Natalie" come from Mr. Stevenson's office.

Natalie stopped laughing, straightened her posture, and motioned for me to follow her into his office. I had a sense of déjà vu as we all three sat in the same positions as last Friday. All that was missing was Danuwoa.

"Welcome, Ember, I look forward to getting to know you. Has Natalie brought you up to speed on our company off-site meeting?"

"It's barely eight thirty-five in the morning, I was getting to it." Natalie rolled her eyes. She must have a really familiar relationship with this man, because I would never blatantly roll my eyes in front of my boss.

"I hope you enjoy California, Ember." He leaned back in his swivel chair and laced his hands over his middle.

"California?" I asked.

"We host quarterly meetings off-site for directors and above from all our locations. We discuss our revenue targets and improvements to the product," Natalie explained. I couldn't help but wonder what our product even was. She continued, "We have dinners, guest speakers, team-building exercises, and some free time to enjoy where we are before flying back. It's usually a three-night stay at a five-star hotel or resort."

That sounded fancy as hell.

"It's all planned, except we will have to update the room list and reservations to add you to everything. It won't be a problem."

"I give the keynote address, and then we have someone fun give an inspirational talk or a comedian to entertain us. Tell her the theme, Natalie," Mr. Stevenson said, winking.

"Spiritual awakening." Natalie gave a tight smile.

There was an awkward pause. They wanted me to say something. Mr. Stevenson leaned in.

"Oh, how interesting," I said. It sounded like some new age shit.

"Anyway." Natalie changed the subject. "Dan has your last PowerPoint, so I'll show Ember how to get that ready and introduce her to your head pilot."

"What's on my schedule for today?" he asked.

Natalie folded over her skinny laptop, and it transformed into a tablet. With her finger, she scrolled and said, "You have a call at nine with Gary." She shot me a look. I guess that was supposed to explain my new position. "The company newsletter goes live at nine thirty, you have lunch with your wife at the club, and this afternoon you have golf with your investment partners."

"Busy day. Well, Ember, you're in great hands. I'll call you if I need anything."

We were dismissed. Back at the desk we now shared, I turned to Natalie. "Is he out of the office most days?"

"In the summer, he's usually out doing things. I finished all the prep work for the off-site, so we have some downtime, and I can really train you in detail. When he is out of the office, it's easier to wrap up all the projects. I won't lie to you—when it's busy, you will have to work long nights. It's not every night though, you just need to practice your time management."

"That's doable."

"Let's call our contact at the hotel, and I'll e-introduce you to all the important contacts."

"E-introduce me?"

"Yeah, through email."

"Oh . . . so, where in California are we going?"

"Y'all are going to Santa Barbara. There's a small airport Mr. Stevenson flies into and has a friend with a hangar park his plane for the stay. We usually go there once a year. When Mr. Stevenson and his family travel abroad, they fly commercial. Getting an international license for his jet is expensive. There is a 'Travel' subfolder with everything you should need, but he has no vacation on his master calendar coming up while I'm away."

I was at ease. I mean, I had no idea what I was doing, but Natalie's confidence rubbed off on me. She had instructions and tutorials for everything. This was such a happy accident and the best thing to ever happen to me. All I had ever wanted was to be an accountant, but that was before I knew a job like this even existed.

My phone started buzzing in my backpack. I took it out. **Auntie** popped up on my screen. I silenced the phone and let it go to voicemail.

"Let's put your phone number in Mr. Stevenson's cell before he heads out for his lunch. Now, I have already updated the spreadsheet with your name for the travel plans, and you don't have to worry about a plane ticket or anything."

No plane ticket? I spoke too soon—this job was flashy, but accountants got to stay at their desk and not have to drive a piece-of-shit car across state lines. Most of those states were all desert. It would break down before I even made it halfway through New Mexico. Was it too late to grovel to Gary for my old job back?

"Then how am I getting to California? I don't know if I can drive all the way there."

"You fly private with Mr. Stevenson, silly. You and Dan. Sometimes a couple of other executives unless they have plans and it's easier for them to fly commercial. You look like you're going to be sick. This is one of the perks I was talking about." Natalie set her tablet down and rubbed her belly to give me her full undivided attention.

"I've never been on a *private* plane before. I think it will ruin me for future travel." I just wanted to impress Natalie. She was so experienced and nice to me. It was such a stupid lie. I'd never been on any plane, period. But it just rolled off the tongue a little too easily, pretending I'd experienced more things than just what Oklahoma had to offer.

"Oh, it will—you don't have to go through security, and to get to the hangar with Mr. Stevenson, you drive right on the tarmac. It's bizarre being so close to planes, but you get used to it."

"Nah, that's some rich people nonsense. I don't think I would get used to flying on private jets."

"Fair enough. I'm sending the updated list and cc'ing you now."

The rest of the morning was a blur. My email inbox had never been so full, what with all the necessary introductions and then— bam. At nine thirty on the dot, the company newsletter dropped in my inbox. This was the first one I had seen since I started a lifetime ago—okay, a little over two weeks, but a lot had happened in that time.

Meet Natalie's Maternity Leave Replacement!

They'd ripped the photo off my barely used social media. It was hardly professional. Joanna had snapped the photograph when we were at the park last summer. I was happy and smiling under the shade of a tree. This was not how I wanted Phoebe to find out I had gotten the job she wanted and was rejected for.

I needed friends, and this felt like I just threw her kindness in her face. I prayed Danuwoa would help me explain the crazy circumstances around how I was thrust into this position.

Beside my photograph was a short paragraph.

Ember Cardinal takes the reins of Interim Executive Assistant to the CEO while Natalie is on maternity leave. Ember is new to Technix but has already made a lasting impression. Her background is in accounting.

The newsletter moved on to the social activities for the summer and an **Ask the CEO Anything** link. I knew a handful of people at this company, and now every single employee had my name and photo in their inbox.

"Who writes the newsletter?" I asked Natalie as she was feeding documents into the scanner behind the desk.

"I do. Well, I guess you will now. But don't worry, there's—"

"A folder labeled 'Newsletter'?" I finished her sentence.

"Ha ha. No, it's called 'Company Communications,' but in that folder is a 'Newsletter' subfolder. I'm glad you're catching on. There is a schedule for when we publish, and what we will publish for the year that's already been approved. It should be easy. You only have to send one while I'm out, and I've already written it."

Natalie was incredible. I wanted to be like her when I grew up. Polished. Poised. Put together. Prepared for anything. Not to mention she was the cutest pregnant lady.

"Why do people call you the Wicked Witch of Floor Seventeen?" I blurted out. She was so nice to me, and I had not witnessed her be rude or mean to anyone in my presence.

She winced and sat in the adjacent chair and rubbed her stomach.

"Braxton-Hicks again, give me a minute."

I should not have asked that. What was I thinking? It didn't matter what people called her behind her back. She sat with her eyes closed, breathing deep. I'm sure people called me far worse at the bowling alley, and I would not have appreciated some new chick asking me point-blank about it.

"Okay, that's over. I know people call me that and worse. Prepare yourself. Now that you have the ear of the CEO, everyone will want something from you. Everyone in corporate America wants to get ahead and will use any means or person necessary to do that. Mr. Stevenson is better at sniffing out the users than most CEOs I've worked with, but there are snakes everywhere. People will ask for extensions for deliverables or be flat-out sexist and try to send you out of a meeting to get coffee. As the executive assistant to Mr. Stevenson, you are his right hand. You are a strategic partner. Don't let anyone try to walk all over you or treat you as less than. It took me years to grow a backbone, and that is why people call me the Wicked Witch. I have learned to say no and say it often."

Natalie Sanchez was a passionate woman. Chills ran down my arms from the fire in her as she gave that speech. I had googled

How to be an executive assistant, and the top results told me to be a yes person and have coffee ready in advance, but how Natalie described the role, it sounded powerful. It sounded like the word *executive* in the title meant that you were an extension of the executive too. You were not an admin making copies and ordering coffee. Natalie didn't do those things. She had lists and Gantt charts for every project. My eyes glazed over as she taught me her system. She didn't care that I didn't know how to do any of the stuff she was showing me. I wasn't expected to. I had been plopped here from accounting, and she understood that there would be a learning curve for me.

Natalie was wasted as an executive assistant. She could run a company. I didn't fear her. I wanted to be her. She was the most incredible person I had ever met.

Twelve

LUNCH WAS WEIRD.

Natalie had a personal call, so I ventured into the break room on my own. I was nervous to see Phoebe. I really wanted to be her friend. I stopped at the bulletin board outside the break room to rally my courage. There was a sign-up sheet for Cake Day. There were twelve spots, one for each month to celebrate all the birthdays in that month. October was blank. I picked up the pen that was hanging from the board by a piece of blue yarn, and signed my name with a flourish.

"Coming through, EA!" Martin bumped me out of his way with his hip. He took a clear tack and stabbed it through his flyer. FANTASY FOOTBALL DRAFT. It was a save-the-date for Labor Day weekend. The pool entry fee was one hundred dollars. "Better save up, kid—everyone enters the fantasy draft here. Kyle won last year. He got two grand," Martin said, looking down at me from his height.

"I don't watch football."

"What? Too good for accounting and football?" He clutched his chest like he was wounded.

"No, never, I just don't really care about football, and this EA gig was totally random."

"Hmm . . ." I wasn't sure if he was buying it, but he added, "What about basketball?"

"Thunder up." I pointed my chin at him. A true Okie test I passed, as I really was an OKC Thunder fan. Had to be in this state.

"That's what's up," he said as he gave me knuckles. "We do March Madness here too. Some big money to be made there."

"Uh . . . yeah . . . I'm not doing all that."

"Better learn if you want to keep working your way up here. It's all about who you know."

"Hey! Ready?" Nick yelled from down the hall.

"Yeah!" He nodded to Nick. "Congrats though. Gary's pissed, but I think you'll fit right in." Then Martin was gone.

As soon as I entered the lunchroom, the energy died. A few people lifted their hands as a greeting. Phoebe and Danuwoa sat at their usual table, and I sat down to join them. Today I had left-over beef enchiladas. I couldn't tell you how great it was to have hot leftovers with flavor and not spongy bologna.

Phoebe refused to look at me.

"Happy Monday," Danuwoa said, giving me a knowing smile. A smile that promised more and knew too much. I couldn't stop the blush from blooming on my cheeks. Thankfully it was private, since Phoebe was so mad at me, she ignored my presence.

"Did you have a nice date on Friday night?" I asked her as a peace offering. I didn't set out to stab her in the back to get this position.

"I did. Thanks." Her tone was curt.

"*Phoebe,*" Danuwoa chided.

"I'm done. You want to grab coffee from across the street?" she asked him.

"I have to finish this and then set up the new TV in the executive conference room."

"Can I bring you back anything?" Again, she looked only at Danuwoa's face as she stood up and cleared her place.

"Nah, I'm good."

"Catch you later." She turned on her heel and stormed out of the room, chucking her trash in the bin on her way out.

"She'll come around." Danuwoa sounded sure.

I was skeptical. I had heard that there was drama and conflict in the corporate world, and it seemed like Phoebe went from friend to foe with the flip of a switch. "I really pissed her off," I said as I dug my fork into my meal. "I'm now down to knowing only two friendly people."

"It's quality over quantity." He smirked.

"When Natalie is gone, I'll just cling to you."

His brows rose in surprise.

"I didn't mean it like that," I said, panicked. "I mean like as friends and stuff because it can be boring not talking to anyone." When he still didn't say anything to make me more comfortable, I gave up. "Oh, let me eat in peace."

He laughed, but there was fire behind the mirth in his eyes. I looked away, stabbing my food, when he said, "I very much look forward to you *clinging* to me."

My cheeks were on fire. The way he said "clinging" had my brain conjuring images of our tangled limbs in bed, my hands clinging to his back, digging my nails into his flesh while he rode me hard.

His throaty chuckle was proof enough that this was exactly

where he wanted my mind to go. "Well, if you ever are bored talking to no one on that lonely floor, you can always ping me. I'll be happy to entertain you."

The subject change was what I needed. My pulse was racing from my entirely inappropriate arousal.

"I'll take you up on that." I wiped my mouth and excused myself to get some much-needed distance to cool down and face the rest of the day.

I made it to the elevator when I heard, "Hey, Ember! Wait up!"

I turned and saw Kyle jogging to catch up to me. His golden mane flowed in his created breeze. He looked like he could be in a shampoo ad; all the commercial people had to do was have him run in slow motion. That was not fair. His smile was devastating.

Phoebe sat at her desk in front of the elevator and rolled her eyes.

"Yes?" I schooled my features into nonchalance since I was a big fat nobody to him.

"Congratulations on your promotion." He stopped and ran his hand through his hair.

"Thanks, it looks like speaking up is a good thing here."

He gave me an awkward laugh. "Point taken. I was only looking out for you."

"Yeah."

Ladies and gentlemen, this was stupid awkward. With the corner of my eye, I tried to see what Phoebe was doing. Having an audience for this made it extra painful. I pushed the button to call the elevator as an escape.

"Yeah. Cool. Well, if you need anything, let me know. I know we have the conference coming up, and Mr. Stevenson does wait until the last minute to finalize his presentations. Whatever you need, I'm your guy."

Ding. My salvation arrived.

"Will do." I saluted a quick farewell and hopped into the elevator.

The executive level was a welcome quiet. Natalie had not come back yet, so I had a few minutes to center myself. I went to my backpack and pulled out my cell phone. I had three missed calls from Auntie and a text message.

AUNTIE: I need u 2 come home this wknd 2 help me. Call l8r. <3

My aunt still had a flip phone that was ten years old, and she texted like she was in an AIM chatroom with all the abbreviations. When I'd lived with her, she would sit and watch *The Price Is Right*, typing out texts to her friends, counting to the letter or number she needed. Sage and I bought her a smartphone for Christmas two years ago. She gave it away. She liked her old phone, with a worn and faded WWJD sticker on the back.

I felt immediate guilt. I hadn't tried to call Sage at the jail, and I hadn't been home to visit Auntie in over a month. I could only focus on so much at a time, and this job needed all my attention. It was already changing my life for the better. I know, I know. *Money isn't everything.* Well, when you had no money and then got some, it was everything. It made all the difference.

I typed a note to myself to call and add more money to Sage's commissary account later.

Natalie waddled in, hand on her back and a smile on her face.

"Had a good lunch?" I asked her.

"Food always makes me happy." She sat down next to me.

"Same."

"All right, you ready to go over expenses?"

"Yup, whatchu got?"

"Everything comes through our email, and I like to print the reports to review. Mr. Stevenson has to sign approval, and that's when you use his signature stamp. All this is standard, so I go ahead and approve on his behalf." She stood and opened the drawer attached to the bottom of the desk. She bent down slightly and took out a file and a retractable stamp, then paused. Her face contorted, and she dropped the stamp and folder with the loose sheets of paper and let out a groan.

"Another Braxton-Hicks?" I asked her as I jumped up with my hands raised. I didn't know how to help a pregnant woman, but sitting while she looked like she was in so much pain seemed wrong.

"Oh no." Natalie looked down.

My eyesight followed hers. She was leaking. Based on her horrified expression, she'd either peed her pants, or her water broke.

I grabbed her arm and she looked at me. "It's going to be okay. Who can I call for you?"

"I'm not ready!"

"You're going to be a great mom!"

"What? I know that. But I'm not ready for her to come out. We have more to go over for the off-site."

All I could do was blink in shock. This woman was about to push out a baby and she was thinking about a meeting? "You don't have to worry about that. Can you walk? Let's get you to the hospital."

"My partner is a few hours away picking up a handmade rocking chair."

"Okay, can you call him? I can take you to the hospital."

"Her," she corrected.

"Sorry to assume. Can you call her?"

Natalie's breathing was tense, and she just kept nodding as I led her to the elevator.

"Wait! My bag."

I left her by the elevator and sprinted back to get her purse, and just as I returned, the elevator opened.

"What the hell is going on?" Danuwoa asked as he held the elevator door.

"My water broke."

"I'm taking her to the hospital."

"Do you need help?" He guided Natalie in as I pressed the ground floor button a million times.

"You have to get Mr. Stevenson's upgraded conference system installed, or he'll have a field day. It was delayed twice already," Natalie said to Danuwoa.

"Manufacturing delays are not my fault."

"Who cares? Natalie, stop talking about work. You need to focus on meeting your little one. And you"—I looked up into Danuwoa's eyes—"you need to help me get her to my car. Sound like a plan?"

They grumbled their acquiescence.

I liked this new take-charge version of me.

We slowly made it to the parking lot. Natalie stopped to breathe through a contraction, but we made it to my car.

"Is this thing even safe?" she asked.

"It's better than walking or pulling up in an ambulance," I deadpanned as I opened the door. Danuwoa ushered her in.

"You good?" he asked me.

I closed the passenger door and strode to the driver's side.

"Never better. Good luck installing that phone system." I wiggled my fingers goodbye.

My piece-of-shit car took three tries to start. I would have been mad and embarrassed had Natalie's laughing not eased some of the tension. Laughing was better than shouting in pain.

"I'm going to be getting a new car." I rolled my eyes, but my smile contradicted my annoyed look.

This beat-up piece of junk *was* funny. On the way to the hospital, I told Natalie about the different times my car had stalled or refused to start. She had another contraction, but my stupid stories were a welcome distraction.

I drove up to the labor and delivery wing and threw my car into park.

"Stay here," I ordered, and I ran into the hospital to find someone to help me get Natalie inside.

"Can I help you?" a middle-aged woman asked me warmly.

"My coworker is in labor." I pointed out the door. An orderly with red-and-green buzzed hair grabbed a wheelchair and followed me out.

Natalie was already out of the car and pacing along the curb on her cell phone.

"I don't care. I need you at the hospital now!" She looked up and giggled at me and the young man as she waved her cell phone. "My mom will be here soon."

"I'm Tej. If you could take a seat, I can wheel you in and we can get you admitted," the colorful orderly said.

Natalie hobbled to the wheelchair and sat down. "This shouldn't take too long. I'll check in on you tomorrow to make sure everything is going smoothly with Mr. Stevenson." She craned her neck as Tej started pushing her away.

"You focus on getting that baby girl out. I have everything handled at the office!" I called after her.

Thirteen 🖋

I DID NOT HAVE EVERYTHING HANDLED. THIS WEEK WAS A MESS. I prayed and prayed for Friday to come, and it was finally here and off to an even worse start. I had double-booked Mr. Stevenson for two very important meetings, one with finance and one with legal. I refused to bother Natalie, who was now home with her baby girl. She sent me a photo to include in the company newsletter to announce her daughter's birth at the end of the month.

This role was a lot of pressure and stress for being bored most of the time. I dialed Kyle's extension. He answered on the first ring.

"Ember, what can I do for you?" He had a voice that always sounded flirty.

"Hey, so something came up and I'm gonna have to push your meeting back until Monday."

"No can do, kiddo, I need these numbers approved." I hated when men called me kiddo. He was maybe twenty-nine or thirty at the most. Patronizing ass.

"Do they have to be approved on a Friday? Monday morning first thing, I promise."

"I really hope this doesn't become a habit. Mr. Stevenson and I have a very close working relationship, and he likes to be heavily involved in all things finance."

I rolled my eyes. What executive didn't like being involved in "all things finance"? It was money. Give me a break.

"Okay, thanks. Bye!" I hung up the phone and fixed Mr. Stevenson's calendar. I crossed my fingers in hopes that he had not seen the mistake yet.

My favorite task of the day was finalizing the menu for the conference dinners at the hotel. Steak, steak, and more steak. There were fish and veggie options too, but all I cared about were the free steak fillets and barbecue sandwiches I had planned. Planning events was a lot of fun when you didn't have to pay for any of it yourself.

I heard stomping down the hall and looked up to see Mr. Stevenson with his head down barreling his way to his office, leather briefcase in one hand and his oversized thermos of coffee in the other.

"Good morning, Mr. Stevenson," I greeted.

"In my office, now." He sped past me.

Inside his domain, he threw his briefcase down on his desk. I believed I was about to experience one of Mr. Stevenson's infamous foul moods. I grabbed my laptop and headed in, bracing myself for whatever was about to be thrown my way.

"Happy Friday," I said with as much cheerfulness as I could muster. It was a lot.

"Sit down." He steepled his fingers together as he leaned over his desk.

I sat down and plastered a fake smile on my face.

"Why was my calendar a mess this morning?"

My stomach dropped and my heart skipped a beat. He had noticed my mistake. Great.

"I apologize, there was a double-booking, but I fixed it."

"Why do I now have a meeting with our legal counsel instead of the finance team, who is now pushed to Monday? I received a call from my nephew."

Nephew? What? No one here looked like they could be related to Mr. Stevenson . . . apart from all the white people. Shit, Technix could employ most of his family then. I remembered Kyle had wanted that meeting with Mr. Stevenson, but it wouldn't fit. I guess I knew Kyle and Mr. Stevenson's "close working relationship."

"Kyle is your nephew?"

Mr. Stevenson leveled a glare at me through his bushy eyebrows for interrupting him. A close working relationship indeed.

"As I said, I got a call from my nephew. I need the month end to wrap up and get finalized before our conference. That was a poor lapse in judgment from you. Jacqueline Wethers is our legal counsel, and I'll have to listen to her whine about the current litigation and the legal bills on a Friday. Never, and I truly mean *never*, do this to me again. Natalie should have explained the hierarchy of importance to you. Write this down: finance, marketing, everything else, then legal, and lastly HR and personnel problems. Got it?"

"Noted. I promise it won't happen again."

"Good. You're dismissed." He stabbed the number pad on the new conference phone on his desk as I walked out of the office. I closed the door and immediately it turned opaque.

I made a mistake. People made mistakes. Was it so bad that I deserved that kind of treatment? You would think I lost thousands of dollars or something.

Jacqueline's email said it was extremely urgent and could not wait. Had she lied to me? I hardly knew these people well enough to understand the nuance of electronic correspondence and the actual urgency.

I pressed send on the email with the final menu options and then had nothing to do but replay the scolding I just got and panic about the worst-case scenarios. *Does Mr. Stevenson hate me? Will he fire me?*

I opened Teams, typed in Danuwoa's name, and wrote him a message.

EMBER CARDINAL: Heyy

The two *y*'s made it casual. Totally could not be misconstrued as flirty. One *y* would have been too professional, in my opinion.

DAN COLSON: Heyyy

Oh my god. A third *y*? Was that flirty? I felt like that was totally flirty.

EMBER CARDINAL: Why don't you have your full name on here?

DAN COLSON: Bc I'm IT and I can program it how I want.

EMBER CARDINAL: Can you do that for every device?

There was a pause, but my anxiety was abating already. I was smiling and more relaxed.

NATIVE DADDY: I am the master of this universe.

EMBER CARDINAL: What the hell? Does it say that for the entire company?!

My face was bright red, but I was laughing out loud.

NATIVE DADDY: Just for our chat.

Great. I was going to have to convince him to change it back. I wouldn't survive if someone walked by and saw his username on my laptop screen.

EMBER CARDINAL: I'm not sure I am comfortable with you fetishizing yourself like this.

NATIVE DADDY: I believe it was you and your roommate doing the fetishizing . . .

EMBER CARDINAL: JOANNA NOT ME!

NATIVE DADDY: Gotta run.

He sent one final message.

NATIVE DADDY: Have a great weekend if I don't see you.

Mr. Stevenson's conference call must have wrapped up, because the office wall turned clear in my peripheral vision. I was starting to think that this smart glass, while cool, was fucking weird. Like, just have normal walls. I didn't want to stress about him going from clear to opaque and back again while I was picking my nose or something. There was also something really Big

Brother about how he sat behind me. Granted, his desk was at the end of his large office, but it was facing the back of my head. The only privacy I had was from the short cabinet that ran the length of the wall. Maybe I could find a big, full plant to put on top directly behind my head. Just in case I had more of these instant message exchanges with Danuwoa before he changed his contact name back again.

My desk phone lit up. **Thomas Stevenson** appeared on the caller ID.

"Hello?"

"Please come in." His voice was much calmer than before. Could I get a neck injury from this personality whiplash?

I wasted no time grabbing my laptop and heading in.

"Great news! Our patent litigation matter has settled. This is great. Great! The investors will be really happy. I'm going to head home. You should too. Enjoy your weekend." Mr. Stevenson grabbed his briefcase and thermos and headed out of the office, pausing at the door to let me out first.

He went from menacing Bond villain to friendly and chivalrous southern boy in an hour.

Natalie and Danuwoa were not kidding about his moods. He swung back and forth like a pendulum. Could I trust that he really meant I could leave early? I breathed deep and took my time as I packed my things to head home, giving my mercurial boss time to change his mind.

Fourteen

THE FIRST FEW WEEKENDS NOT AT THE BOWLING ALLEY WERE a nice break, but when Joanna was busy working, I had nothing to do. I was conditioned to wake up early and had already brought my laundry back from the laundromat. My pent-up energy needed a release before driving down to my auntie's home. My home. She was a late riser on the weekends.

I was dreading this visit. I knew she would ask me about Sage, and I just didn't have the mental or emotional capacity to be understanding. Sage had burned her time and again, and yet her doors were always open to him. But that bail money was my college fund. I'd scrimped for years to save enough for school, and him skipping out on his hearing meant my money was forfeit. The wound was still too raw.

I bleached the tub and toilet, vacuumed and dusted all six hundred square feet of the apartment. I couldn't delay the inevitable any longer. I hopped in my car and got on I-40 East. It was hot and perfectly clear. Not a single cloud floated in the sky.

I loved driving out to the country. Honestly, I missed living in the country. There was a lot of criticism about Oklahoma. I'd heard it all my life. It was flat. There were tornadoes. There was nothing here. Yes, it was flat, but driving on these country roads, you could see the expanse of the plains. The tall grass, the wheels of hay for cattle. The red earth wet from the rain. It smelled fresh and clean. It was quiet and peaceful. This was what Oklahoma really was. Beautiful.

It would be nice to one day buy a big house out here. Maybe even get a pet, like a goat or something. When I couldn't sleep, I loved watching videos of baby goats in pajamas hopping around.

I zoomed on 3 West, as fast as my car could go, toward Ada. I was pushing my luck with the car, but I wanted to get to Auntie's house as fast as I could. The drive was nice, and I was beginning to relax when a loud, fizzy sound started coming from the engine. That couldn't be good. Then—*pop!*—smoke started spewing from the hood.

I was hacking and couldn't see shit as I swerved my car to the shoulder along the side of the highway.

This was probably the worst-case scenario. The car itself was trash, but getting out of it to check what was going on under my hood could be life or death. I would be an open target. Easy for someone to grab and drive off. I could end up as one of the missing and murdered. I rolled my windows up to offer myself some protection, but I was already coated in sweat from the summer heat. My cell phone had half a bar of reception out here. Most people I had encountered were friendly, but girls like me didn't know who we could trust. Anyone could stop and offer help, but then grab me the next second. I'd grown up hearing so many stories about this exact situation.

I tried to calm my breathing, but the car was too hot. I rolled the driver's side window down another half an inch. Any potential murderer would have to have very skinny fingers and arms to get through the gap and unlock the door.

I hadn't even wanted to come, and now I would either have to die of heatstroke or take my chances walking to the gas station that I knew was a mile up ahead.

I slammed the wheel. The impact made my ugly freaky lizard key chain swing back and forth. I ripped my keys from the dead ignition and screamed at the thing. "You were supposed to be good luck! Fuck. Fuck. Fuck!" That felt good, but I needed to take action and save myself. Joanna didn't answer her phone, but I sent her a pin of my location. If anything did happen to me, someone had better know exactly where I was when I stopped and where I was going.

I called my auntie. "Sweet girl, you on your way?" she asked me.

"I am close . . . ish, but my car broke down. Could you come get me?"

"Shit, Sage is running an errand in my car. Let me call him and have him come get you."

Sage. My brain froze. As if this day couldn't get any worse.

"Sage is out of jail?"

"Yeah, he was let out early for good behavior and overcrowding. That's what I have been trying to tell you." I ignored her tone. I was in no mood for a lecture.

Sage was better than being left stranded. "Okay, I am like a mile or so from the gas station on Highway 3."

With my auntie on the line, I braved getting out and opened the hood.

"Fucksake!" The hood was so hot, it was a miracle I was able to take the stand and lock the hood up. The poor car hacked and coughed as it spit out gray smoke.

"You think maybe it's time to buy a new car?" She laughed. "No weirdos have stopped, have they?"

I suddenly heard honking that grew louder by the second.

"No, but I think one is about to." I ran to my trunk to get my emergency baseball bat.

"Stay on the line with me." Her voice grew scared, and my stomach was in knots.

I waved the smoke away from my face with the bat to see what I was in for, and a familiar hunter-green Chevy slowed down and pulled over in front of my car.

Danuwoa hopped out, squinting against the sun.

"What the hell are you doing?"

I pointed at my phone lodged between my shoulder and cheek with the bat and said, "Calling for help."

"Can I give you a lift?"

Creator was testing me, tempting me to break the stupid Technix no-dating policy. But I could really use a ride, and it was almost fate that Danuwoa had happened upon me. And it was better than being stuck in a car with my brother.

"Yes!" I beamed at him. Into the phone I breathed, "Don't bother Sage. My friend was driving by and is giving me a ride. I'll see you soon." I ran to my passenger door and grabbed my stuff. "Thank you so much. It's dead. It died a horrible and painful death," I told Danuwoa as he approached me.

"It lived a long and fulfilling life. A valiant effort that should be commended. The Ford Contour is no more." He placed his hand over his heart, and with his other sent a kiss up to Creator. At my laugh he gave the smoking car a small bow.

More laughter bubbled out of me once my body realized I was safe.

"It might be a tight squeeze. Walela is with me, and she's in her regalia." He pointed, and I followed his thumb. Poking out of the window was the smiling face of a young woman wearing thick black glasses, with a tin crown on her head reflecting the bright sun like a safety beacon. Relief washed over me.

"Heading to a pageant?" I asked.

"I'll let her tell you." He opened the passenger door and said, "Walela, meet my coworker and friend Ember. Ember, this is my sister, Walela."

"Hi, Ember! Are you okay?" Her infectious smile morphed into a concerned frown with her question. Walela's robin's-egg blue dress was trimmed in red ribbons, and she carried a hawk feather smudge fan. The sash across her chest read MISS INDIAN OKLAHOMA.

Danuwoa answered for me. "She is now. Hop out so Ember can squeeze in and we can drop her off."

"Are you coming to the ribbon-cutting ceremony too?" Walela pushed her glasses up her nose as I climbed into the truck.

"I wish! I'm going to visit my aunt. She lives outside of Ada."

Walela followed behind me and closed the door. She adjusted her crown and arranged her dress to avoid any wrinkles.

"You look very pretty. That color looks great on you."

"Thank you! It's my favorite color. I'm the first girl with Down syndrome to win the title." She nodded with much-deserved pride.

Danuwoa's weight shook the cab as he slid into his seat. "Ready?"

The bench seat in the truck felt very small as my bare thigh pressed against Danuwoa's denim-covered leg. My tank top was wet from my sweating buckets in my car, and even though the deodorant was advertised as extra strength and lasted forty-eight hours, I could smell that it had lied. Was this penance for all the tiny fibs I told around Danuwoa?

I was wet and stinky sitting next to this gorgeous man and his sweet sister in her beautiful regalia. I really hoped my smell didn't rub off on her.

This was really too much. I was brought to Ada under vague and false pretenses so my aunt could facilitate some sort of reconciliation. Ha! Sage would have to apologize and admit to his wrongdoings before I could even consider that. Knowing him all my life, I was sure that it was an impossibility. He was too self-centered and reckless to ever show remorse.

"Whoa, careful. Your thoughts look like they are physically causing you pain. How do you get your eyebrows so close together like that? Walela, look. Ember gave herself a unibrow!"

She giggled while I tried to rub the tension out of my forehead.

"What's the ribbon-cutting ceremony for?" I asked her, to change the subject.

"A new tribal youth building is opening, and the newspaper will be there. I get to cut the ribbon with the other Indian princesses."

"Do you get to use those jumbo scissors?" I asked.

"Yes! But they only have one pair, and we all have to try to hold them. It's annoying."

"Do you elbow them out of the way so you can be the only one holding the scissors?" I asked her.

"No, I sometimes make them uncomfortable by mentioning that I have Down syndrome and *really* love holding the scissors. They usually give them up real quick." She laughed, mischief twinkling in her eyes.

My kind of girl. I was impressed. I loved a good guilt trip.

"*Walela*," Danuwoa warned. "You aren't supposed to do that." He rubbed his face to hide his smile and kept one hand on the wheel. He looked sexy driving this old truck with the window down and his hair floating along in the wind. His knowing eyes met mine, catching me as I was appreciating him. Then he flexed his bicep, subtly tightening his muscle as he casually held on to the steering wheel. I couldn't contain the cackle that erupted from me. It was so ridiculous. I was a mess with my hair plastered to my face and neck, and he was flirting with me.

I loved it, and that terrified me. This was not supposed to happen. Danuwoa and I were supposed to maintain our distance outside of the office. After the bar and now this, my feelings were all levels of confusion.

We continued to drive, and I was silent, waiting for my exit to get out of this truck and calm my racing brain. I was carless, on my way to my aunt's house. My convict brother was home, and it was all too much. Just pile after pile of shit. And here I was in between Danuwoa, who had never been anything but kind to me, and his sister. I was this wet, smelly mess. I felt tainted and unworthy of whatever this kindness was. If I had met Danuwoa at the bowling alley before Technix, none of this would have been a problem. I would have felt like his equal. Just two Natives in Oklahoma having fun. But what made me feel icky was that I had lied to even be in the same stratosphere as Danuwoa at Technix. He didn't have to lie to get his job or keep it. Then there was the no-dating policy at work. This was a tug and pull between Danuwoa and me.

He had been my lifeline at the office since I joined, so kind and helpful. He was always sending me jokes on Teams. After the almost kiss at the bar, I stayed up late at night imagining what it would be like to belong to him, to really kiss him, and I think he wondered the same. The way he waited for me to get on the elevator or offered to get me coffee made me feel like he cared about me as a lot more than just his coworker. But I couldn't trust that.

Danuwoa could have anyone, and he was so good at flirting, it was probably just a casual thing for him that I built up in my head. There had been a few cute guys at work at the bowling alley over the years, and Joanna and I would get "work crushes." And that was all they ever were, just fun distractions to flirt with to make the shift go faster.

Whatever this was with Danuwoa and me was all it would ever be. A distraction.

He mentioned he supported his sister, and after meeting her, there was no way I could allow Danuwoa to straddle the line with me. He could get in trouble or fired if people thought we were dating. I couldn't allow that. I was resolved. Danuwoa would stay a friendly coworker.

That's how it had to be.

Finally, my exit. I was a few minutes from home. I would be walking into a shit show, but that was normal. Bringing a man like Danuwoa home was not normal. Further, I couldn't allow Danuwoa anywhere near my family when they could very much mention the fact that I had lied about a *few* things. I wanted to trust that if he discovered I had insufficient education or experience and blatantly lied to get this job, he wouldn't throw me under the bus and shun me for being a fraud. But this was me, and I didn't have a track record for good luck.

"Pull off here," I said, pointing. I navigated the rest of the way as Walela told Danuwoa everything she was excited about doing at this ribbon-cutting ceremony.

Auntie's mobile home was old and dirty on the outside. She said it was yellow when she got it, but it looked kind of dingy brown now. The outside did not reflect the care and order she kept inside. "We're here."

Danuwoa slowed down to a stop and parked.

"We grew up in a house like this," Walela said.

"Yes, we did." Danuwoa smiled. "Hop out."

I turned to crawl after her, but he caught the bottom edge of my tank top to stop me.

"Can I help you?" I asked with mock outrage.

"Wait a minute. Are you okay?"

"I'm fine."

"The last twenty minutes you were wound tight like a ball. What's going on?"

"Just family drama, you know?"

He leveled that narrowed expression with one eyebrow raised that silently said, *Clearly, I don't.*

I gave him my own look and made sure my eyes said, *It's none of your damn business.*

He rolled his eyes, and I looked down at where he still held my shirt. He let go and threw his hands up.

"I just want to help." That was the problem. I didn't need help. I had managed everything for everyone on my own, and I couldn't get used to someone helping me, or I'd never be able to shoulder these burdens on my own again when that someone inevitably left.

I needed to keep my job and my lies under wraps, and I needed to stay away from a man like Danuwoa. He could do better than my messy ass. There was someone out there softer, easier. He needed that. That was what was different about us. He *needed*, and I couldn't give any more parts of myself away. I had Sage, Auntie, and Joanna, and the small part of me left had to finish school and build a stable life for myself. I could not afford distractions. But he did help me today, in a huge way. It may seem dramatic, but had I been left on the side of that road, sure, maybe Sage would have made it. Maybe a tow company would have eventually come. But there was a very real possibility that I could've been in danger.

"Thank you for stopping when you saw me."

"It was a happy coincidence. Do you need a ride home later? The pageant should only take a couple hours."

I should have said no. I should have kept my distance for every thought I just had, but I was selfish. I needed an out so I would not be stuck here overnight or in the car with Sage. Having a timer and a ride was my perfect escape.

"Actually, that would be great—if you really don't mind. Whenever you're able to get me is totally fine."

"Great. I'll text you when we're on our way."

I got out and hugged Walela. I hoped the other girls gave her the scissors.

I waved them off and saw my aunt standing in the doorway, hands on her hips. I braced myself.

Fifteen 🪶

"WHY DIDN'T YOU INVITE THEM IN? THEY LOOKED NICE!" MY aunt chided me as I walked past her into the living room.

"They're busy." I set my tote bag on the floor next to the couch. I remembered the day she got this couch. We were kids and were so excited that we immediately threw ourselves on the soft brown corduroy. The corduroy was worn in places on the armrest and seat, but it was still the best couch to melt into and smelled like the sweetgrass she burned every night when she prayed.

This small home seemed huge when Sage and I moved into it. We each had our own room instead of a cramped one-bedroom with our mom. Compared to that old apartment, this was palatial. Now, after spending time on the executive floor at work and ordering sushi lunches that cost more than what Auntie spent on groceries in a month, I could see the effect time had had on this little place. The small wrinkles in the patched plaster walls matched the growing lines on my auntie's face. She smiled and plopped down next to me.

"It's so good to have you home. Sage went out to grab some ground beef. I'm making Indian tacos."

"You sent him with your car and money?" I couldn't be bothered to mask my disapproval.

She tsked. "Sage is young, but he's trying to do better. Give him a chance."

I ignored her and crossed my arms over my chest.

"Who was that man?" I know she asked to change the subject, and she was the town's biggest gossip. I had yet to bring any person home apart from Joanna, and that was because she lived down the street with her mom when we were growing up.

"I told you, he's a friend."

"I never had friends that were that good-looking. He looked like a fine young man. I saw that smile. He likes you."

"He likes me because I'm his friend."

"With benefits? Isn't that what you young kids do nowadays?"

"Auntie! No! We aren't talking about this. Can I help make the dough while we wait for Sage to get back from the store?"

"I hoped you would ask. Come on, I have everything laid out."

Where the outside was a sad, dingy yellow, the kitchen was cheerful and bright. The walls were lined with white ceramic tile, and the linoleum had little pink bows in a pattern. It was home.

The flour, Crisco, salt, and baking powder were already out.

"Wash your hands, you look like you have seen better days."

"It was hot as hell out there." I turned on the faucet, and the water sputtered out at first until it got a good flow going—same as always. After drying my hands on the embroidered kitchen towel, I grabbed my favorite apron. It was made of a faded red-checkered fabric, so soft from years of running it through the laundry.

This was a dish I had made so many times that I never used any measurements other than my hands. I scooped handfuls of flour into a bowl while Auntie warmed up the milk in the microwave. I threw in a generous pinch of salt and some baking powder, and she came and poured in the warm milk. I mixed the ingredients with my hands, forming the sticky mixture into a mound that was starting to resemble dough. I began kneading it, punching out my frustration.

"Whoa, careful there. We don't want tough fry bread. We want it light and tasty."

"Sorry," I mumbled and broke off a piece, rolled it into a ball, and then squished it flat. With the palms of my hands, I slapped the dough back and forth, rotating it slightly to keep it round.

Auntie started whistling as she spooned some Crisco into the pan and moved it around with the metal spoon to make it melt faster. Once she was satisfied the pan was getting hot enough, she joined me and broke off a piece of dough, working it in the same way she taught me, except hers always turned into a perfect circle, all the same thickness throughout. Mine were always a little lopsided and wonky, but they tasted just as good.

"Let's test it," she said, giving me a mischievous smile and dropping her dough into the pan. It fit perfectly into the bottom. The bubbles rose quickly, and with her fork she flipped the dough over, revealing the perfectly golden-brown bottom. Only a few minutes, and it was done. She popped it out and I threw mine into the oil, letting the satisfying sizzle and warm smell of frying dough settle me. I felt like the old me again. Not anxious. Not mad and resentful. Just Auntie and me doing what we loved.

Once mine was done, she placed it on the paper towel and sprinkled sugar and cinnamon, the oil catching the sweet crystals and spice.

We liked to test our batch first, purely for quality's sake. The warm fry bread was sweet and exactly what I needed. The spicy cinnamon with the sugar, it was like our own Indian cinnamon roll . . . except without all the butter, and it was flat and bumpy with the air bubbles.

"Ah, it's perfect." She kissed her fingers like an Italian chef, and we smiled, munching on our sweet snack.

The front door closed, and I hunched my shoulders, bracing myself for my first meeting with my brother in almost a year.

"Yo, Auntie! I'm back!" Sage carried a white plastic bag into the kitchen, holding it up like a prized catch of the day. He was wearing black sunglasses, and his hair was buzzed. He had cut his hair in jail. That broke my heart. Was he forced to, or did he choose to do it?

My stomach dropped. Tito sauntered in after him. He had buzzed his head since the last time I saw him. Probably to copy Sage or some poor attempt at solidarity. Of course Sage would be out of jail and immediately hanging out with his old crew again.

Sage saw me. "Hey, hey! Big sis! I didn't know you were here yet. I didn't see your car outside."

"That's because it's dead on the side of the highway."

"What's good, E?" Tito asked me as he kissed Auntie on the cheek. I ignored him.

"It had a good run," Sage said with a laugh.

"You mean when you used it and got your DUI?" I dead-panned.

"Okay, enough. Are either of you boys hungry, or you want some of this sweet bread?" Auntie took the grocery bag from Sage and started emptying it on the counter. "What's this?" She held up scratchers and a pack of cigarettes.

"Oh, I used the change, let's scratch 'em for old times' sake. Maybe we'll win enough for a new car," he said through a mouthful of our sweet before-meal treat.

"Sage, did Auntie say you could have her change from the grocery money?" I swear he was nineteen, but I had to talk to him like a six-year-old.

She made a zip-it sound and shook her head.

"Relax, E, we're here to have a good time," Tito said and leaned against the wall.

I was trying to be respectful. Auntie invited me here and welcomed Sage home with open arms, but his casual disregard for anyone other than himself was triggering. Not to mention the fact that they allowed Tito to waltz back into their lives.

"If you want me to stay, then Tito has to go," I declared.

"What? No way. He's my best friend and I've only just seen him."

"Sage, it's for the best. I want peace. Tito can come to dinner another day," Auntie said, smoothing it over like she'd done ever since we came to live with her.

"It's for the best, man. E, I'll catch you later." Tito winked and left.

Sage sat down at the worn wood table with a huff. I could barely believe we sat and did homework together at this very table a few short years ago. Ate our family meals at this table. Where we cried when Auntie sat us down to tell us that Mom was never coming back and she had full legal custody of us, then promised to always be there for us. Sage was so small then. She and I both tried our best to shield Sage, and watching him ruin his life and mine made me feel like we made a huge mistake. I never wanted Sage to shoulder any burden, but as he got into mess after mess and spent our aunt's limited money, I resented the lack of responsibility he had.

I was just as much to blame as Auntie. Sage was spoiled and always would be.

"I love scratchers—thank you, Sage. But you really shouldn't smoke. It's bad for you," she said from the counter. "Let's all scratch one."

She brought us teaspoons and the scratchers. Sage went to town scratching all the boxes, looking for matching numbers. It came up empty and he threw the busted card in the air.

"Whoo! Five dollars! I'm a winner!" Auntie cheered.

I took the edge of the spoon and scratched away. I hated these. No matter how many times I had tried and failed to win, my heart always lurched with the hope that maybe this would be my lucky ticket. It could be the solution to all our troubles. But as I revealed box after box without a match, I deflated. That was the problem with hope. It created expectations, and when they weren't met, you were left feeling crushed.

But my lucky break *did* happen. I had a new job that paid real money. I needed to train myself to expect nothing more.

"So, tell Sage about your new job," Auntie nudged as she swept up the scratched-off foil.

"No more Bobby Dean's?" he asked as he leaned back in the old oak dining chair.

"Nope!"

"She's an accountant!" Auntie's pride was like a warm balm to my soul.

"No shit."

"Actually," I said and rubbed my palms together, "I was promoted."

"What? Already! Oh, this is great news!" Auntie went to the fridge and got out her favorite strawberry-flavored wine coolers. "We have to celebrate!"

"What do you do now?" Sage asked, though he sounded bored.

"I am the interim executive assistant to the CEO of the

company." I smiled and maybe gloated a little. Hard work does pay off. Not that Sage would know.

"What the hell is that?"

I used the buzzwords Natalie taught me in my training. "It's a strategic position directly supporting a one-hundred-million-dollar organization." The words were buzzy, so buzzy that they buzzed right over Sage's head, and I could tell I'd completely lost his attention. "I help the big boss and got a raise."

"Sick! I have some news too, wait a sec." He shot up from his seat and ran to his room. The thing with mobile homes was that the bottom was hollow, so you could hear every step.

He came bumbling back, waving a white envelope like it held the answers to all of life's questions.

"This is for you." He extended the envelope and I read my name in all caps. The handwriting was neat and even. On the top left corner, the sender's name was written: *Mitch Cardinal*.

No wonder Sage was so happy. In his head, this was the answer to all of our life's problems.

Dad.

Somehow Sage came in contact with Dad. After nearly twenty years, this was the first time I had seen that name on anything. I never received a birthday card. Nothing. Neither did Sage, but the smile on his face made it seem like all of that was forgiven and forgotten.

"Take it, it's from Dad."

I refused to accept it. "No."

"Don't you want to know what he has to say? Why he left?"

"He left. I don't need to know anything else or whatever excuse he has."

"But he's changed. When he gets out of jail, he said he wants to be a family again."

"I don't care what kind of heart-to-heart you had while in jail, Sage. He only talked to you in there because he clearly had nothing better to do and nowhere else to hide. What was he even in there for?"

"Stupid drug stuff, but he's a good guy. He found god and—"

"And you can save it. Can we start dinner? My friend will be on his way soon to take me back to the city."

"Ember, I think you should read the letter." Auntie sounded quiet and subdued.

"Why are you siding with him? You're always siding with him. I don't want the letter, and you can't make me take it." I stormed out of the kitchen. Anger rose within me, and my vision blurred. I hated it. I kept walking until I was out the door. I went to the back of the house, to the old black walnut tree. The tattered rope that once hung a tire swing was dangling limp; not even a slight breeze blew on this hot day.

I squeezed my eyes shut and held my breath. I tried to settle my anger. Mitch Cardinal was a glorified sperm donor. He wasn't worth any more of my tears. Couldn't my life just be normal? Couldn't Sage just be normal? Reconnecting while in jail with a dad who couldn't give a shit about you wasn't my first choice for bonding.

"You've gotta let go of this anger and resentment, Ember. You should be happy," my aunt said as I heard her steps approach me. I still had my eyes squeezed shut as I breathed in and out. The country air was the best. It was clean, and even in the oppressive summer heat, it was calming. I gave myself five more seconds before I opened my eyes to face my aunt.

"He's so selfish," I whined.

"Sage or your dad?"

"Both! I am just trying to live my life and do good. Why is it so much harder for me to be happy? Sage can burn bridges and make mistakes, and he gets a pass." I kicked the red dirt with the toe of my sneaker. I was still wearing the red-checkered apron, and this visit was turning into a melodrama.

"Sage chooses to be happy. He makes mistakes, but he's jealous of you."

"He wouldn't have to be if he had graduated high school," I said, rolling my eyes.

"Ember Lee." She used my full name. She was pissed. "I didn't graduate high school. Why do you sound so judgy? Sage will find his path. There are construction jobs. Not everyone is quick to leave and forget this life." Her voice was sharp, and the lecture stung worse than a slap in the face.

I didn't think I was better than my aunt, nor did I think I was better than Sage because I wanted to continue with school. It just wasn't in my nature to accept things as they were. Was that bad? Was I the wrong one?

I didn't think so, but I wanted to keep the peace. I could avoid another encounter with Sage for a while, but I had to survive this one, so I apologized. "I'm sorry. I just want what's best for him."

"Only Creator knows, and He has a plan for all of us. Now, do you want to start those tacos? Maybe they'll be ready by the time your handsome friend without benefits picks you up."

"Ugh, don't say that to him."

She turned to go inside, extending her arm to invite me in close. I went to her, wrapped my arm around her sturdy waist, and went back inside with the only person who had ever truly given a damn about me. I never wanted to disappoint her.

Sixteen

THE SMELL OF CHILI POWDER AND CUMIN FROM THE KITCHEN made my mouth water. I was hungry, and tired of fighting and being mad. Auntie did so much for us, and the least I could do was play nice with Sage for a couple of hours. Even if that entailed listening to his "funny" stories about jail. I didn't think the fights he witnessed were all that funny. Auntie must have talked to him, because he didn't mention our dad or the letter again.

My phone buzzed in my back pocket.

DAN IT: Be there in a few.

I knew it was boring to have him as "Dan IT" in my phone, but I was practical and didn't want to chance anyone at work thinking he and I were anything more than what we were, which was strictly friendly coworkers. Also, seeing his contact as "Native Daddy" on Teams at work was more than enough to deal with at the moment.

ME: I hope you both are hungry. Auntie is insisting she feed you for giving me a ride.

DAN IT: Starved

"Sage, grab the extra chairs and extend the table. We have two more joining us," I yelled from the couch.

He came out of his room and opened the closet where the extra dining chairs were stacked on top of each other.

"Is Joanna coming by?" My brother looked hopeful and dumbstruck. He'd had a crush on Joanna since forever. Poor kid, the woman would break him—mentally and, knowing her repertoire of kinks, probably physically.

"No, my friend from work and his sister are giving me a ride back into the city."

"A'ight then." He went to work setting up the table.

"Ember, come in and help me fry this bread. I made more dough," my aunt said.

On my way back to the kitchen, I stopped next to Sage and grabbed his arm. Under my breath, I warned, "Do not do or say anything rude to scare off my friends."

He shook his arm out of my grip, and I saw the little shit's smile. "Is a boy coming for dinner, E?" He was loud enough for our aunt to overhear.

"It's not like that," I huffed.

"They're friends without benefits," she said, pointing with the spatula she used to brown the meat.

"Don't say that," Sage and I said in unison. And then cringed that we still were able to jinx ourselves even having been apart for so long.

"What? That's what you told me!"

"You told her that?" Sage asked, bewildered.

"No, she asked if we were hooking up, and I said no and told her to stop talking about it." I rolled my eyes and went to beat the dough into submission. This dinner was going to kill me.

"Remind me never to talk to her about my love life." He sat down at the now extended table with enough room for six people.

"You would need a girl to actually be interested in you to have a love life," Auntie said with a cackle.

"Sick burn," I said. I missed this. The silly family comfort. This was what it was like before Sage went to jail. My heart broke a little more remembering how things had changed, but some things always stayed the same. Sage's love life was as dismal as mine. But that was Ada. We knew these people all our lives, and while some had high school sweethearts and married early, others, like us, never found our soulmates next door.

The doorbell sang through the house. Sage and I locked eyes and sprang into action. He beat me. He always did.

He threw the front door open, his hand palming my face to keep me away. I heard him say, "Whoa."

"You okay there?" I knew Danuwoa was asking me, because he was always so damn nice.

I swatted Sage's hand away and pulled him from the door to let Danuwoa and Walela inside. "I'm great. This is my brother, Sage. Sage, this is Danuwoa and his sister, Walela."

"Sup."

"Hi!" Walela's bright smile erased the awkwardness that followed my brother and me everywhere. She had left her crown and smudge fan behind, but her sash was worn proudly.

"Pretty dress," Sage complimented her. It earned him a bright red blush and shy smile.

"I made it," she said.

"I've always wanted to learn to sew," he said.

"It's easy," she said with a shrug.

"This is our aunt's home, welcome," I said as the sound of the dough sizzling in the pan gave me an out from awkward introductions. "I hope you're hungry."

"Come on in. Can I get you anything to drink?" Sage asked, unprompted, so I guess he was going to be on his best behavior.

"Water would be great, thank you," Walela said to Sage.

"It would be my pleasure, Your Highness." He looked to Danuwoa for his order.

"Water is great, thanks."

Sage nodded and headed to the kitchen, and the rest of us followed him.

"Howdy! Have a seat. I'm so glad you both could join us." My aunt was flipping the last of the dough over in the pan.

"It smells great!" Walela announced.

"I'm Ruthie," Auntie introduced herself as she placed the last hot piece of fry bread on the counter. "Go ahead and serve yourselves."

Sage placed cups of water on the table as I directed our visitors to the assembly line, handing them Auntie's favorite mismatched plastic plates she'd had since Sage and I got to pick them out from the thrift store when we first moved in. She had said she wanted her home to feel like ours, so we got to pick out all our own stuff.

I gave Danuwoa my favorite *Rugrats* one. He smirked and under his breath asked me, "You doing better?"

"Much," I said through my teeth, hoping he got the hint to drop it. He nodded and started scooping the chili mixture on top of his fry bread and layered it with lettuce, cheese, tomatoes, all the goods.

I was a weirdo. I liked all that, plus cayenne pepper hot sauce and canned black olives.

Loaded plates in tow, we all sat at the table. I sat in the middle of Auntie and Danuwoa. She grabbed my hand and nudged me to take Danuwoa's and bowed her head to pray. The funny thing was . . . we never prayed over our meals. My aunt was a religious woman who went to church sometimes, always made it for the major holidays, but Sundays we were busy catching up on chores when we all worked on the weekends. We thanked Creator regularly, and Auntie was better about her before-bed ritual of burning braided sweetgrass she got from her friend living in South Dakota and showing gratitude for the day's blessings. But I saw her shit-eating grin as she glanced at Sage. She was orchestrating this whole thing just so I could hold Danuwoa's large, perfectly calloused, and entirely too nice hand.

"Dear Creator, blessed Lord, please bless this meal and everyone at this table. We humbly thank you for keeping Ember safe after her car broke down and making it so that her handsome friend and his lovely sister were able to rescue her."

"All right," I mumbled and squeezed Auntie's hand with as much force as I could muster.

"Ehack!" She coughed her surprise and started wrapping up. "And all god's men said?"

"Amen," we all said in unison. Walela was the only enthusiastic one.

I loaded my fork with the perfect bite. The ratio of fry bread to meat, cheese, and iceberg lettuce was perfect with one olive and a drizzle of the hot sauce. As soon as my mouth was full, Sage asked, "So, Dan, you Ember's boyfriend? Ow!"

My mouth may have been too full to say anything, but my foot reached his shin just fine under the table.

Danuwoa swallowed his bite, both elbows on the table, his fork hanging from his hand, and looked Sage in the eye. "We're friends." The boys had a staring contest. Sage lost and looked down at his plate first, smiling to himself.

"For now," Sage said, because he refused to allow Danuwoa to have the last word.

"As Ember's friend, I hope you can convince her to finally buy a new car. She is so cheap," Auntie said, laughing.

"So that *is* Ember's car on the side of the road?" Danuwoa asked.

Shit. I knew he saw through my lies, but to confront it like this . . .

"Yes, that's my shitty car, okay? Can we drop it? I'll get a newer car." I threw myself back against my chair, arms crossed.

Danuwoa looked at me, then to my aunt. "Walela and I were talking about it on the way here actually." Walela smiled at me from the end of the table. "We wanted to offer to give you a ride to a car dealership and keep you company while you looked for something." He blushed and cut into his meal. "Only if you want."

"That's a great idea." Auntie slapped my arm. "She'd love to," she answered for me.

"Excellent! I am a great negotiator," Walela said matter-of-factly.

"No one would dare offer a bad deal to Miss Indian Oklahoma. She's definitely going," Sage said.

"It's settled. We'll pick you up tomorrow morning." Danuwoa took a large bite as if the matter was closed. It most certainly wasn't. All it would take would be one person from Technix to see us out together before the rumor mill started. Neither of us could afford to lose our jobs.

"I—" I started to protest.

This time it was Sage who kicked me under the table.

"Thank you," I said as I glared daggers at Sage, rubbing my shin. "Can we eat in peace now that you two are done meddling?"

Danuwoa's rough-denim-clad leg bumped mine. Through my lashes, I saw a hint of a smile. He was enjoying my discomfort. They all were. Traitors, the lot of them. It made me smile too.

The rest of dinner was comfortable. I had not forgiven Sage, but with Danuwoa and Walela there to take the majority of my aunt's attention, I could breathe and relax. When it was time to go, I hugged Auntie tight and waved to Sage from afar. He waved and went back to looking at his phone. I hoped something would push him to grow up and finally be responsible.

We piled in the truck and headed back to the city. It was still a little light out and the heat had finally broken, so going to pick up my piece-of-trash car off the side of the road wouldn't be too difficult.

Danuwoa drove around, pulled up in front of my car, and backed up until he was a couple feet away. He got out, and instead of forcing Walela out, I exited from the driver's side to help. He took the tow bar and a toolbox out of the bed of his truck.

"You just happened to have a towing kit in your trunk?" I asked as I followed him to the hood of my car. He set the triangular tow bar on the ground and began setting up to attach the bracket, sitting on his knees in the dry dirt.

"Nah, I borrowed this from my buddy." He took a look under the front of my car.

"Does your buddy live close by?"

"Eh." He came up and twisted his long hair into a bun at the nape of his neck.

"Just eh?"

"I gotta get this done if we want to make it back tonight."

"How far out of your way did you guys go?"

He set down the tools and braced his hands on his thighs. "God, you're relentless. Can't you just say thank you?"

"I was just asking."

"Do you want to tell me why you lied about where you lived and your car?"

"What? No. I . . ." I trailed off, unable to finish.

"Didn't think so. Go wait in the car with Walela."

"No, I want to help."

"You can help me by dropping it."

"Fine." I glared.

"Fine." He rolled his eyes and got under my car and flexed the muscles of his arm. He totally did that on purpose. Macho man bullshit.

It was dark, but my car was successfully being towed along the highway as we made our way into the city. The lights made everything look pretty. The darkness blanketed the dust and run-down parts of town. After our little tiff, neither Danuwoa nor I said a word. Walela seemed tired, so we just drove along for a bit in silence.

Walela finally spoke up. "I like your family."

"Yeah, they can be pretty great," I said with a smile I didn't fully mean.

"It's just me and Danuwoa. Been that way for a long time."

"I didn't know that." I looked at Danuwoa. He gripped the steering wheel tighter. We were similar in that we did not like talking about our personal issues. Mine seemed so trivial compared to this man single-handedly taking care of his sister. I needed therapy. Lots and lots of therapy. "It sounds like you have an amazing big brother who looks after you."

"He's the best! But he sucks at laundry." She stuck out her tongue.

"I ruined one dress, Walela." He sounded like this was an ongoing argument.

"My best dress. I do all the laundry now. I like it. No more wrinkles or bleach stains," she said with a giggle.

"I'll tell you a secret. I just wash all my clothes at once . . . on cold." I laughed.

"What about your whites!" Walela gasped.

"I'm too busy to do separates. Maybe when I slow down, I can give it a try."

"Yes, you should. It'll change your life."

Danuwoa barked out a laugh. I laughed too as he pulled his truck up to the curb, my apartment yards away. He got out and I followed him, waving my goodbyes to Walela. Outside, I walked around the front of his truck to the sidewalk. I didn't know what to do with my hands. Everything felt like it was too much.

I did what was safe and deserved. "Thank you."

He pushed his hands into his jean pockets and shrugged. "Don't worry about it."

"I was grilling you and you were only helping me. I'm sorry."

He leaned against the grill of his truck and nodded. "Sulphur."

"What?"

"My buddy drove up and met me. He came from Sulphur and lent me the tow bar and toolbox."

"Oh, that's really awesome."

"It's what we do. We help each other. No questions asked."

"And I ask a lot of questions. I know." I played with my fingernails, a nervous habit.

"You just make a list of the stuff you want in a new car. We'll see you in the morning."

"Yup, been making the list for years." I pointed to my head. "Are you sure this is a good idea? Going shopping together, I mean?"

He rolled his eyes and headed back to the driver's side of the truck.

"Okay, good night." I headed toward my complex, feeling Danuwoa's eyes watching me the entire way.

Seventeen 🖋

T HE DAY WAS ALREADY HOT, AND THE BLACK ASPHALT RE-
flected the heat back up, making me sweaty. We walked up
and down the used car lot, looking at the parked cars. I had made
a list of must-haves:

1. All four hubcaps. (I was vain.)
2. All one color with a nice paint job. (Vain, remember?)
3. Working AC. (Practical!)
4. Automatic. (Easy to drive.)
5. Less than 60,000 miles. (I wanted to drive this one into
   the ground.)
6. Cost less than $16,000. (I wanted a cheap car payment.)

So I had my list. Sedans were the most practical choice, as they
were the cheapest on gas. But I kept eyeing a cute compact SUV.
It was white and in my price range, but had seventy thousand
miles, and with gas prices going up, my brain was saying no.

Walela liked the navy-blue Chevy Malibu. It was newer and under budget, but it was like sitting in a tin can. I would likely buy that one, but I kept looking at that cute white compact SUV.

"Why don't you test-drive it?" Danuwoa suggested.

"What if I love it?" I asked.

"Isn't the point of getting a new car to get one you love?" He liked to answer me with more questions. It was infuriating.

"It has ten thousand miles more than my target mileage."

"So?"

"And it will cost me more on gas."

"You live close to the office. I don't think it would cost that much more."

"It's cute." I looked down at my list and crumpled it into a ball. "Yeah, let's just test-drive it. It might drive like shit, and then I'll just get the Malibu."

"There you go, Walela," Danuwoa called. She was talking to the sales rep who insisted on following us around. "You want to test-drive this one with us?"

"No, I'm hot! I want water," she called back as she brought the sales rep to us.

Danuwoa explained we wanted to test-drive it, and the salesman headed inside to get us the keys, taking Walela with him.

It was just going to be Danuwoa and me in the SUV. I needed Walela as the buffer to keep things PG. Danuwoa showed up today wearing a fitted T-shirt that had no business being that tight. The hussy within me wanted to test-drive more than just cars today, and I didn't know if we could help ourselves from just completely going at it in a pretty spacious SUV. If I crashed the car in the process, then I'd definitely have to buy it. If we didn't also get arrested for public indecency.

My mind was whirling from inappropriate arousal, and out of

nowhere, Danuwoa asked, "You looking forward to going to California?"

"I've never been on a plane before."

"My first time flying was two years ago for my first work trip. The private plane is pretty nice."

"I bet. It's crazy how the other half lives," I said just to say something. I looked at the entrance of the used car dealership, waiting for those keys.

"One percent," Danuwoa corrected me.

"What?"

"How the other one percent live. Half the population does not fly on private jets."

"It was just an expression," I grumbled.

"And I was just teasing." He crossed his arms and smiled.

"Stop doing that."

"Teasing you?"

"That and smiling and being likable in general."

He took a step toward me and lowered his voice. "I promise to try to hate this car for you. Is that better?"

"Much." I gulped, because he was so close, and just under that lavender soap scent, I could smell his sweat. I was cringing internally for thinking that too, but human biology was making me like that masculine smell. I needed help. Divine intervention and maybe a bucket of ice water to douse the flames burning in my core from Danuwoa's stare.

"All right!" The cheerful salesman's arrival broke the mounting tension. "You're all set. Just bring the car around to the front when you are done."

I got into the front seat, and my butt was happy. Wow, there was a lot of cushion. The tan cloth seats were clean and soft, and the matching steering wheel was smooth and sturdy in my hands.

It was a terrible sign—I liked it already. I turned the key over, and it purred to life instantly. No stalling. No sputtering. It worked great. The best part? As I pressed on the gas, we smoothly entered traffic. I cranked the AC dial and let the cool air blow my hair wild like I was in a Shakira music video.

"This car sucks. It's too nice." Danuwoa's laughter was infectious as I drove in a large square around the dealership, a big smile plastered on my face. "Why would you want working air-conditioning? Get me out of here." He must have pulled the lever to recline the seat, because it fell back, then promptly sprang up straight. "Hey, the passenger seat works. Unacceptable!" His laugh floated around me, and I couldn't help but join him.

"Okay, okay. I'm buying it."

He rolled the power window down, stuck his head out, and howled. I pushed my window button and did the same.

Inside the dealership, it was ice cold from the air-conditioning, and I loved it. I also loved that I was getting a cute new compact sports utility vehicle.

"Please follow me. My office is just over yonder." The salesman led the way.

We all three piled into the small enclosure. His nameplate read JEFF. Man, I felt bad I didn't remember his name from earlier. I was too excited looking at all the cars.

An hour into the process I was wilting, painfully hungry. "Does it usually take this long?" Jeff left a third time to ask his boss about the payments to try to get them lower.

"Yeah, probably three hours." Dan shook his head.

"Y'all can leave! This is ridiculous. You've both done so much to help me already."

"Relax, this is fun." Walela patted my hand.

"He's going to come back and offer you gap insurance,"

Danuwoa leaned over and whispered. "Don't take it. It's just another way the dealership makes more money."

"What the hell is gap insurance?"

"Oh, he'll tell you."

I was about to make him explain, but Jeff came in shaking his head. "I'm sorry, Miss Cardinal. That's the lowest we can go, but I hope the fact that we accepted your car as a trade-in worth five hundred dollars eases things. The monthly payments of two hundred seventy-seven are the best we can do."

"Jeff, you've been more than fair to me." Truly, Danuwoa lugged my hunk of junk to his place last night and brought it to the dealership to get it off our hands. We probably would have been turned away and pointed to a junkyard, but Walela worked her charm. They would sell the Contour for parts. The fact that they offered me a $500 trade-in value made me think they were going to make a lot more than that off it.

"Great, now for six dollars more a month, we can tack on gap insurance. You know about gap insurance, right?"

"Why don't you tell me." Danuwoa and Walela snickered next to me.

"If you were to drive out of this lot and the car is totaled, your insurance company might not cover what you still owe. Gap insurance will pay you the gap between what your car insurance deems your car is worth totaled and what you still owe on the car loan. It's the smart thing to do."

"I can say no?"

"Well . . . er . . . technically," Jeff stretched the collar around his neck.

"Great, no thank you. I'm very hungry. Can we speed this process up?"

"You're a little bossy one, aren't you?" To Danuwoa he said,

"How do you keep her in line?" He chuckled like he'd cracked the world's funniest joke.

If I didn't so desperately need this car, I would have walked out. That's the way it was for women. We had to suck it up and accept misogyny and sexism so we could get through our business.

Danuwoa crossed his arms and glared at Jeff. Jeff got the hint and began typing away on his computer to process my car loan.

"The stoic Indian, huh?" Jeff let out a nervous chuckle. I swear saying nothing was always better than filling the silence just to fill it. Especially when you didn't contribute anything and offended those around you.

"I get hangry, so can we quit the chitchat?" I asked, because if this guy said one more ass-backward thing, we were going to walk out of there without a car, but with our dignity intact. I would like both a car and my dignity. Sometimes that seemed like too much to hope for.

Finally, an hour and a half later, I had my new keys in hand, and I felt like a new woman.

"Walela, you riding with me?" I asked.

"Heck yeah!" She fist-bumped me.

"Come on then—Danuwoa, see you at my place."

"I wouldn't miss the world's best corn burritos for anything."

I had promised to feed the Colson siblings. It was the least I could do. I swear, if either needed a kidney, I'd give it. Without them, I'd have bought the sedan and been stuck with higher payments with the damn gap insurance and probably still chitchatting with racist and sexist Jeff.

Joanna was sunbathing on a plastic folding chair on our "balcony." It was the railed walkway that led to our apartment door and the four others down the way. She was in cutoffs and a lime-green bikini top. I honked my horn like crazy and she flipped me off. I don't think she could tell it was me driving—I hadn't told her what I was getting, because I wanted to surprise her. I pulled along the curb and got out. "Fuck you too!"

"Oh, what? You got *that*? What happened to my cheap and cautious friend?" She stood, hands on the rail, and laughed.

"I'm still getting groceries from the dollar store, but this baby drives like a dream. You eat yet?" I yelled up to her.

"Nah, I was waiting for you!"

"My buddy and his sister will be joining us. I'm making corn burritos!"

"My girl, let's go!"

I got back in the car and turned to Walela. "Brace yourself. Joanna is my best friend, but she is wild."

"I can be wild." She stuck out her chin.

"I bet." I giggled. "I hope you like wigs."

"I LIKE THE PURPLE WIG THE BEST. DANUWOA, CAN I DYE MY HAIR purple?" Walela asked as she flipped the purple cropped synthetic wig's hair off her shoulders.

"Maybe after your reign," he countered as he sipped his beer from the couch after our meal. I was impressed; he ate six of my little fried corn burritos.

That appeased her as she continued digging through Joanna's beads, the wig still on her head.

I got up from my spot on the floor and went to the bathroom. Once I came out, Joanna was leaning against the wall, waiting for me. She nodded to my room, and I followed her in.

"You like him." She crossed her arms.

"Of course I like him. He's my friend." To distract myself from Joanna's piercing gaze, I emptied my tote bag onto my bed.

I lifted my crumpled sweater, and a white rectangle floated down.

"Ugh, Sage," I groaned, and chucked my sweater harder than was necessary into the plastic laundry basket I kept by my dresser.

"What is that?"

"Sage bullshit." I took it and shoved it into the top drawer, right under all my socks and undies.

"When we go back out there, actually sit next to your *friend*. He isn't a leper."

"No, what he *is* is trouble and off-limits."

"Nobody's gotta know," she sang.

On the one hand, I was grateful Joanna didn't dig deeper into the envelope; on the other, I wished she would stop trying to get me to seduce the IT guy from work.

"Will you promise not to embarrass me?"

"No," she said with a deceptively sweet smile.

I rolled my eyes, and with confidence I didn't feel, I went back out to the living room and sat next to Danuwoa on our worn couch. He nudged my knee with his. I smiled at him. It was nice. But nice things never lasted for me, so I looked away.

"I like what you've done to the place," he said, and pointed with the beer bottle's neck at the old cardboard box we used as an end table.

I feigned offense. "We covered it with a pretty textile."

"Ember once bought the cutest coffee table for thirty bucks at a garage sale," Joanna offered. "It was painted green and was the perfect size."

"Where is it?" Walela asked.

Joanna looked at Walela conspiratorially. "She felt so guilty spending the money that she sold it on Craigslist for forty bucks."

"I made a profit at least."

"Walela, tell Ember she is allowed to have nice things," Joanna ordered.

"Ember, you're allowed to have nice things," Walela said.

"I've had to get over my poor pride," Danuwoa said, taking a swig of his beer.

Poor pride was what my family and I flaunted instead of Ben Franklins. We didn't need money or fancy shit. We didn't need anything. We had each other. All our friends and family were poor, and we looked down on those who had money. Like they weren't as tough as us. It was backward, but it was just how it was for us.

"How'd you get over it?" I asked quietly.

"Walela needed new shoes. Then one day at Walmart, a flat-screen TV was on sale. I kept walking past it, probably three times before Walela demanded I get it. It's easier to spend money on her than myself. I love that TV."

"I love my new car."

Danuwoa gave me a crooked smile as his eyes melted me into the couch. I was no longer Ember; I was a puddle of molten lusty girl lava.

My hand was resting on the couch between us. Danuwoa took my hand in his and squeezed it.

Then he sighed. "We should head out."

"Aw, I want to stay," Walela said.

"Yeah, you guys can stay," I offered.

"Really? Don't you have your bowling league tonight? If I'm not mistaken, you told me you played with your team every week.

It's Sunday night; did you think I forgot?" His smile was border-line vicious. I did think he forgot. Hell, *I* even forgot! Shitass. He was daring me to admit to my lie. That was not going to happen.

"Leroy is sick tonight, so practice was canceled." I batted my eyelashes incessantly, staring up into Danuwoa's warm chocolate eyes, sending a message: *Nice try*.

His deep laugh and eye roll said, *You can't fool me*.

I needed to drape my T-shirt over the fan in my room to cool down. I was sweating and slightly aroused. Not good, not good at all.

The Colson siblings got up to go, and I walked them both out to their truck.

"Thank you for keeping me company while car shopping. I didn't know it would be such a chore."

"I liked it! Danuwoa, you should buy a new car so we can go back." Walela's happy enthusiasm was contagious. Danuwoa gave her the keys and sent her ahead.

It was just Danuwoa and me in front of my apartment complex. He opened his mouth to say something, and I refused to hear it. I wasn't ready for anything to change. I had enough to worry about at the office, and I didn't want Danuwoa caught up in it. I tackled him in a hug and whispered another thank-you, before I kissed him on the cheek. It took all my self-control to break away and run back up the stairs.

"See you at the office!" he called after me.

"What just happened?" Joanna asked me.

I was flushed and out of breath from my sprint. "Nothing."

"Mm-hmm. You have that look about you."

"It's buyer's remorse. I just signed up for five years of car payments."

"You can't lie to yourself forever, you know." Joanna headed back to her room, to escape into her beadwork no doubt. I was still reeling. I didn't want to be a liar. Not to myself and most certainly not to Danuwoa. Nothing and everything happened. Danuwoa was stealing my heart, and if I didn't distance myself, I'd never get it back. If we both lost our jobs, he wouldn't look at me the way he did tonight.

My life was a mess.

Eighteen

HAD TO GET A CREDIT CARD. I DIDN'T WANT TO, BUT IT WAS unavoidable. If my auntie knew, she would cluck her tongue and warn me that I was going to start making bad financial decisions, because once you got used to spending money you didn't have, it was hard to stop.

The plastic card was cold in my hand. It had a limit of $1,000. Practically nothing, but if I maxed it out, I'd be screwed.

The car loan was a necessity, and I wiped out my bank account with the small down payment I was able to scrape together. I needed money to get by, and without tips from the bowling alley, I was in a bad spot. I was not going to ask Auntie to help when she had Sage living with her again, and I couldn't let Joanna know. She'd try to lend me money, and not only could I not do that to her, but it would look bad. Here I finally had a dream job, and I couldn't even afford lunch money.

I was resolved. I would sparingly use the credit card, and then when it was finally payday, I would pay off the balance and never touch the thing again. That was until Phoebe decided one fine day to start talking to me again. I was sitting with Danuwoa at our usual lunch table when she plopped down with a smile on her face.

"Hey, friends, whatchu eating?" She strained her neck to appreciatively look at what Danuwoa had on his plate. I was salivating for the saucy-looking meat and noodle dish. It smelled like garlic.

She made a face at my Wonder Bread sandwich. Same. But I had splurged on deli ham, so it wasn't bologna this time. She opened a container of sad salad greens. Danuwoa had the best lunch. The shitass.

"Are you guys excited you get to go to California? I had hoped I could go," she said, glancing at me with a pinched look, as if the reason she couldn't go to California was that I was Natalie's replacement and not her.

"It's gonna be a lot of work," Danuwoa said before he took a huge bite of his food.

The reminder helped, since Phoebe was instantly happy again. "What are you going to wear? I've heard people say the dinners are so elegant and fun."

"Probably just a dress in my closet," I said with a shrug.

"What?" She was aghast. "You cannot wear some old thing. You will be with anyone who is anyone at the resort. What if DiCaprio was vacationing there!"

Danuwoa laughed.

I smiled. "If on the off chance Leonardo DiCaprio were to somehow notice me while vacationing at a resort with a twenty-year-old Brazilian model, then he would see me looking comfortable."

Phoebe stabbed at her lettuce with a fork. "What a wasted opportunity. At least come shopping with me."

"That consignment shop you mentioned?"

"Yeah, it's not too far from here. Even a dress and new shoes would do wonders."

I supposed one used outfit wouldn't be that great of an expense, and Phoebe was trying to be nice to me. I didn't want to ruin it. I needed more friends in this office than just Danuwoa. What better way to bond than over clothes? "Okay, let's go," I said.

"Great! You have to wear something nice. That's what Kyle always tells me—you have to dress for the job you want, not the one you have."

"Oh, is that what *Kyle* says?" Danuwoa teased.

"He tells me a lot of things. He mentioned Gary is still pretty pissed at you, Ember."

I'd managed to avoid Gary like the plague.

Danuwoa's cell phone rang, and Phoebe leaned toward me. "Word of advice, watch your back. Gary apparently said he would love to see you put in your place in front of Mr. Stevenson."

"Well, no one has to worry about that. If I make so much as a typo in an email, Mr. Stevenson puts me in my place. He misses nothing and doesn't let anything go." I rolled my eyes. I just wanted to be an accountant. I didn't want Natalie's job. I wanted the pay, but if these people knew what it was like to cater to the whims of a CEO day in and day out, they wouldn't want this job. When my performance was judged more on the mood of the person than my actual work, it was like stepping on eggshells. It was emotional whiplash, and no matter how I tried to prepare for every possible scenario, Mr. Stevenson's response was never what I expected it to be.

One day, he was really nice when I tripped and fell in his office. Like in that one instance he was reminded of my humanity and that I wasn't a walking punching bag. But other times he demanded perfection.

Danuwoa hung up his phone. "I gotta run and fix the copier for HR. I'll catch you later."

"See ya," I said through a tight smile.

He looked at me with raised eyebrows. *You okay?*

I nodded.

He nodded back and was gone.

"I'm sorry," Phoebe whispered. "I've worked for people like that. It's not easy."

"No, it's not."

"It's nothing a little retail therapy can't fix though." Phoebe's mischievous smile made me chuckle.

I supposed not.

I MET PHOEBE AT THE CONSIGNMENT STORE SHE HAD RAVED about.

It was a small store, but everything was pristine. It wasn't like the thrift stores I frequented with stuff thrown on the ground by kids and racks picked over by the regulars who visited daily to get the best stuff first. It didn't smell musty from carpets that were never vacuumed.

Phoebe was already inside, sliding hangers quickly across a rack while she assessed what was available.

"Aha! This is perfect," she exclaimed and quickly thrust the hanger in front of my shoulders to lay out the dress against me. It was sexy. Too sexy. There was no way I'd even try it on—who did she think I was? It was bloodred, with tight ruching along the sides.

"My arm wouldn't even fit in that." It was the width of a Slinky.

"It stretches! It's BCBG and only sixty dollars—come on, that's a steal!"

"I don't even know what that means, but four letters in the alphabet shouldn't cost sixty dollars. Nope, not happening."

"What do you hope to look like then? This is your chance to dress up and play the part of sophisticated executive assistant at a world-class resort. Live a little." Phoebe pushed the dress to me again.

"I just want to look like me, but with nicer clothes."

"That dress is very nice. Hold on to it and let's keep looking."

Phoebe moved on to another rack and I followed, going through the motions. When she finally spoke again, it made me jump.

"So, you have your eye on anyone cute at Technix or in the building?"

"Uh . . . no. That's not even allowed." I tried to brush her off, looking at an ugly beaded dress from the eighties.

"Looking is fine. Besides, no one follows that rule," Phoebe said as she rolled her eyes. "You and Dan seem to be getting close."

"We're just work friends." My laugh was hollow, and my heartbeat was picking up. This conversation was too stressful for a leisurely activity. "Besides, I have a boyfriend."

I lied. What the fuck was wrong with me? Why did I say that? There were a million better excuses than making up a boyfriend.

"That was fast. Who?"

"Oh, just a guy I've known all my life. His name is . . . Ron." Internally I slapped my forehead. Another lie that I definitely did not want to get to Danuwoa. He had met Ron and the bowling gang, and he very much remembered them all. "It's on-again, off-again, so maybe don't mention it for a while?"

"Oh." For once, Phoebe was shocked into silence. "Yeah, okay."

I went to the back of the store under the guise of looking at the wall full of shoes. If I was looking, I might as well look at something I liked. My orthopedic flats were really comfortable to wear all day, but I could get away with a heel or something for one evening.

Every single pair of nice shoes had the skinniest stiletto heel. I was trying to be adventurous, but I wasn't going to try to balance on those things. I'd be teetering all night.

One pair of shoes caught my eye. They were strappy and shiny and, just like the dress Phoebe picked out, entirely way too flashy for me. The heel was clear and stacked, so they would be easier to walk in compared to the stilettos, but the straps would crisscross around my ankles and looked long enough to go up my calves. They were sexy Cinderella shoes. I picked up the right one and nearly dropped it.

They were my size and made by some designer I'd never heard of before. They were also eighty dollars. What kind of second-hand store didn't have anything below fifty dollars? It couldn't hurt to at least try them on. It wasn't like the dress; I could easily slip my shoes on and off.

Four inches taller, I stood in front of the mirror on the wall, and I loved them so much. I posed each and every way, turning and craning to see myself at every angle. They made my ass look great.

Phoebe popped out of nowhere. "Ember! You *have* to buy those. They'll look great with the dress too."

"I'm on a budget, so I should only get one thing."

"This is Santa Barbara, not an OKC bar. Get both. You'll wear them again, so it's a sound investment."

"Oh, what the hell, I'll get them."

"You won't be sorry!" she squealed.

AFTER I HUGGED PHOEBE GOODBYE, I TOOK MY TIME STARTING UP my car, and Phoebe kept looking at me weirdly from her car across from me. So I left the parking lot behind her. Except, when I should have turned left, I turned right and circled around the block back to the consignment store. I hated the dress and was going to return it with Phoebe none the wiser.

"Back again already?" the white-haired shop assistant asked.

"I changed my mind about the dress. Can I return it?"

"Oh, no can do. I'm sorry, but all purchases are final," she said as she pointed to a handwritten notice on the wall behind her.

"I only just bought it. Can you please make an exception?" I needed that money for food, not a dress I'd never be caught dead in.

"If I make an exception for you, then I have to make one for everybody."

"There's no one else here." Steam was coming out of my ears.

"I'm sorry, I can't help you."

I wanted to scream. It was my own damn fault. I turned out of the store on my heel in a huff.

Nineteen

"Y OU PAID HOW MUCH FOR THIS?" JOANNA PICKED UP THE RED dress with two fingers.

"Sixty dollars," I groaned, throwing my face into my pillow.

"I'm trying it on."

I turned around to watch Joanna strip down to her undies and try to squeeze into the dress.

"Fucksake!" She flung herself onto the edge of my bed for better leverage to wiggle the dress over her curvy hips.

I laughed.

"Fuck you, shitass. You said it was stretchy."

"It is!"

She lifted her pelvis up, and the dress popped over her hips and slid home. She launched herself to her feet. "Success!"

"Ugh, no. It looks hot on you."

"Bitch, you mean *hell yeah* it looks hot on me. Someone has to benefit from your dumb purchase. I look amazing." Joanna smoothed her hands down her stomach, admiring her curves, which the dress hugged.

"Keep it." My head hit the pillow again. There was a dip in the mattress, and then Joanna's head joined mine on the pillow. The two of us lay there on my full-sized bed, looking up at the cottage cheese ceiling.

"I'll buy it off you."

"Pfft, no. But you can buy groceries for the week."

"Deal. I'm *so* gonna get laid wearing this thing," she hissed and wiggled next to me.

"You could be wearing a trash bag and not have a problem in that department."

"Oh, I have."

"Shut up!" I pushed her off the bed, laughing.

"I swear!"

"No, I don't want to hear about your sex games."

"Prude." Joanna stuck her tongue out. "You're just depressed and in a bad mood because you haven't been laid. Just hook up with Danuwoa already. Put the rest of us out of our misery."

I threw my pillow at her face. "I can't and you know that."

"I know you're twenty-five. When you look back on your life, you're gonna regret not snagging that fine ass when you had the chance."

"All right, let's not objectify the man."

"But it's so fun."

"I just need to keep my head down and focus on my goals. I want to start school again, and I want both Danuwoa and me to keep our jobs. So, he's off-limits."

"You're still going back to school?"

"Of course."

"But you already have a job better than you wanted with the degree. Why waste the money and time?"

"School isn't a waste to me."

"You're so weird! You won't fuck the guy, and you want to go back to school when you have everything you want." Joanna got up from the floor and started pushing the dress down.

"I only have this job because of the lies I told. Any moment I can be found out and fired. Or if I kiss Danuwoa like I want to, I can lose my job. My life couldn't be more complicated."

Joanna pulled her shirt over her head and stepped back into her jeans.

"I love my not complicated life. I miss working at Bobby Dean's with you," she said.

"Who does he have snaking the toilet now?"

"Uh, people." She waved her hand vaguely, not meeting my eyes.

"Who?"

"Everyone has to do it. I should get going."

"Why are you being cagey?"

"I don't want to upset you."

"Spill."

"Bobby Dean hired Tito when you left."

"I can't control that, why did you think I would be mad?"

She hissed a breath and said, "Well, Sage has been coming around too."

Just like Sage to be messing around with Tito and not looking for work or anything. Some shady people hung out at the bowling alley late at night.

"What kind of trouble is Sage getting into?"

"Not much, but just being a shitass and drinking and smoking with Tito at the end of the night in the parking lot."

"Is he driving? You know what? No. I can't worry about Sage. I can't control him. He has to figure it out."

"So, you aren't mad I didn't tell you sooner?"

"No, but if he gets into real trouble, you'll tell me?"

"E, besides drinking with Tito, he isn't a bad kid. He's looking for work."

"Underage drinking, you mean."

"We all did it."

"That's not the point."

"Relax, you get to go to California. You get to be there with Danuwoa." She sang his name, and it made my stomach flip.

"It's a work trip. Strictly business."

"Mm-hmm. He looks like he could get right down to business if you let him."

I threw my pillow at her face.

"That's the spirit. Live a little! What are you doing on this business trip anyway? Sitting in boring meetings?"

Er. That. I had looked at the itinerary, and it was going to be a corny appropriating mess.

"It's bad."

"What do you mean bad?"

"It's a spiritual awakening trip."

"Don't say it."

"The special guest who Natalie booked is someone named Sasha Storm Cloud."

Joanna's eyebrows scrunched. "An Indian?"

"More like pretendian. Her website is a bunch of nonsense about being adopted by a rotating list of tribes."

"Oh."

"Yeah."

"Well, shit. At least the trip is free."

We laughed. Pretendians were a thing we encountered a lot outside of Indian Country. We weren't here to question people and bring up blood quantum bullshit, but if you claim to be Native, you should know who your people are and help the community you've claimed, not make a profit from a fake identity.

"Have you told Danuwoa?"

I smiled my most mischievous smile. "No. I want to see his face."

"You're cruel to that man, and all he ever did was like you."

"He teases me just as much, if not worse. He still won't change his name on my company computer. It still says 'Native Daddy.' I have to hide my laptop whenever he messages me."

"Marry the man, Ember. Men of that quality do not grow on trees."

"Don't you have a shift you should be getting ready for?" I rolled my eyes.

"Fine, but don't think I won't sneak condoms into your duffel bag," she warned and then was gone.

Twenty

NO, NO, NO. THIS IS ALL WRONG. HOW AM I SUPPOSED TO INspire the company with this? Get me a photo of that Tim Tebow guy praying on the football field," Mr. Stevenson demanded.

Danuwoa and I exchanged glances. The photo Mr. Stevenson hated currently in the deck was Colin Kaepernick kneeling on the football field, essentially the same thing Tim Tebow did, but one meant a lot more than the other. One was a white man praying, and the other was making a stand against systemic oppression. Danuwoa and I knew which one was more inspirational, but we had to make Mr. Stevenson happy. He then muttered, "It's a shame he's busy and we couldn't book him for California."

Natalie had booked Sasha Storm Cloud, a self-proclaimed medicine woman and spiritual leader, as our special guest and speaker, and while the content was also questionable, it was better than being evangelized by an ex–football player.

"How about like this?" Danuwoa turned his laptop around to show us the requested Tim Tebow photo.

"Excellent. I'm going to finish my remarks on the plane.

You"—he pointed at me—"call the pilot and tell them we'll be leaving now." I jumped up from my seat and ran to my desk, leaving Danuwoa behind to finish packing up. We were cutting it close to the schedule. I still needed to make it to the hotel for my meeting with the event coordinator and make sure the stage and configuration of the space were correct. Then there was the audio and visual testing to make sure Danuwoa's computer could connect and project the corresponding slideshows with the speaker, and the microphone and everything were working. It was going to be a long night.

I was panicking a little. Okay, rather, I was panicking a lot. This would be my first time on a plane, and if it went down, I didn't think I wanted my last moments to be with Mr. Stevenson. With my luck and his attitude, he would blame me for the problems with the plane before we plummeted to our fiery deaths. That was my anxious brain thinking of the worst-case scenario, but it was hard not to when I wanted everything to go right.

"Hello?" Justin, Mr. Stevenson's head pilot, answered on the first ring. I sat down in my chair and stuffed the event binder into my backpack.

"We're on our way. Wheels up in twenty." Never in my life did I think I would ever say something like that. Tom Cruise said things like that, not me. What was this life? It was exhilarating and I couldn't remove the smile from my face if I tried.

"Ten-four." The line disconnected. Everyone who worked for Mr. Stevenson was efficient. We got the job done and did not make time for small talk. Was Justin married? Did he have kids? Who cared? I didn't. He had a current piloting license from the top school in the country, and that was all that mattered to me. I was putting my life in his hands getting on this tiny private plane.

"Let's go." Mr. Stevenson sped past my desk, his momentum

cutting through the air, blowing my hair back. How an old man carrying a briefcase could move that fast beat me.

I hiked my backpack over my shoulders and grabbed my duffel bag. It had been my travel bag since I was a little girl. It was highlighter pink and made out of that crinkly, scratchy waterproof material that everything from the nineties was made out of. I'd never gone anywhere longer than a sleepover party, so I owned no luggage. With my superfluous and stupid purchase of that dress, I was not about to run up my credit card more for a suitcase I would be using once. But the second Danuwoa glanced down at my duffel, he smirked. I regretted not going to a thrift store or Ross to find a cheap carry-on.

He followed Mr. Stevenson to the elevator; his black backpack matched his sleek carry-on suitcase with four wheels on the bottom, which he pushed. When I made it onto the elevator with the two of them, Danuwoa spun his suitcase in a circle.

"Show-off," I said under my breath, and I patted my duffel bag like it was my prized pet cat.

Danuwoa snorted and covered his nose. Mr. Stevenson was oblivious, scrolling through his phone. I had ordered a car service to take us to Will Rogers World Airport, and it was waiting right on the curb. I would never get used to this A-list treatment.

The driver opened the door to the back seat for us. We parked our luggage on the curb. Before I could put my duffel on the ground, Danuwoa took it from me and put it on top of his suitcase. It was a mindless gesture for him, but it made my heart constrict. This was not good. He gave me a quick, small smile, but the chivalry was something I'd never get used to.

Mr. Stevenson walked to the door, pulled the lever on the seat, and folded it down, and then, phone in hand, pointed for Danuwoa and me to file into the very back. We shared a look and wordlessly climbed through. Had I known I was going to crawl into the very back of an SUV, I would not have worn a pencil skirt. Since I was significantly smaller than Danuwoa, I opted to climb in first, and was embarrassed my ass was on full display. I righted myself and sat in my seat, pulling the fabric down as much as I could to look respectable and modest. The cheap polyester did not budge a centimeter.

Danuwoa looked unaffected, and I didn't know which was worse—the fact that I had to demean myself and crawl into the back like the help that I was with way too much leg showing, or the fact that when I did so Danuwoa didn't care at all. Whatever. I put my backpack on my lap and took out my event binder, flipping to the schedule divider to take my mind off it.

We would still get there in plenty of time to check into the hotel and for me to make my meeting with the event coordinator. VIP private travel had its advantages. Before I Ubered to the office, Joanna asked me to text her a photo of the bathroom in the private plane. She said she had seen plenty of influencers posting photos of private cabins, but no one ever shared the "deets" of the bathroom situation. Bathrooms were the equalizer of humanity. It didn't matter how rich you were or where you were. Everyone had to shit. Really, if you were shitting in a bucket or in a gilded toilet, did it matter? The act was the same.

What could I say? She was weird, but was she wrong?

"Penny for your thoughts?" Danuwoa asked me, and I snorted.

I covered my mouth to try to contain the sound. If he only knew where my thoughts were.

"What?" He looked so confused. I had a fit of giggles. "There's some joke I'm not getting here."

"Nope," I choked out. And he wasn't gonna. There was no way I was telling him about the bathroom thing.

We pulled up to the private entrance gate as it parted, and we rolled through, stopping next to the shiny white plane. It was small. I'm not sure if size really matters in a plane in terms of safety, but this was no Airbus. Mr. Stevenson got out and made a call. Thankfully, Danuwoa folded down the front seat so we could get out.

The air was hot, but not yet suffocating. I turned to get a good look at the death trap—I mean airplane—we would be flying in. The stairs were set up and led to the open door. I glanced at our boss, who was whispering sweet nothings on the phone to who I assumed was his wife. He caught my look and nodded for us to go ahead onto the plane.

Danuwoa let me go first, and I ascended into what I would describe as a motor home with wings. It had that distinct motor-home smell: plastic and polyester and upholstered carpet. There was a small sink and refrigerator that looked like your run-of-the-mill RV setup, only from nicer brands. The seats were light tan genuine leather, but it didn't feel all that much different from sitting in a nice RV. There was no flight attendant. The entrance area to my left led to the cockpit, and inside, one of the pilots was tinkering away with the dashboard. I'm sure he was doing a lot more than tinkering, but I didn't know what. The other pilot was outside loading our luggage into what I assumed was a plane's equivalent of a trunk. I took it all in and almost forgot Danuwoa was directly behind me.

"Head down to the table with the four seats. Mr. Stevenson and his wife, if she travels with us, sit in the seats up front," he said.

"Okay." I shuffled my way to said table and parked myself in one of the window seats. I was sitting on a private plane, about to fly above the ground and travel like fifteen hundred miles or so. "Do you think we'll fly over the Grand Canyon?" I asked Danuwoa.

"We usually do when we go to California." He was unpacking his laptop.

"That's cool." I tried to sound chill and not excited. That was something I had always wanted to visit, and seeing the canyon from above—that sounded amazing. I could handle flying in this tiny flying motor home, if only to see the Grand Canyon. "You're going to work on the plane?"

"IT problems never rest. I installed Wi-Fi on here. He expects us to at least look busy while traveling with him."

I'd never gotten my laptop out and booted it so fast. Danuwoa just chuckled at my awkward, rushed fumbling.

"All right, who's excited to go to California?" Mr. Stevenson sang as he set his briefcase down next to his seat, then made his way over to us. "Good, you're working. Ever been on a private plane before?" he asked me.

"Yes, sir. All the time." It was a joke, so the lie didn't count against my no-more-lying rule.

He laughed. "Well, you're in for a treat. No need to buckle up or anything." He tapped the headrest of Danuwoa's seat, then continued to the back.

"The bathroom is back there." Danuwoa answered my un-asked question.

I nodded.

"I would give it a while before going in there after Mr. Steven-son though." He smiled to himself as he started typing away on the keyboard.

"Gross."

"Don't shoot the messenger. I'm just trying to spare you." He raised his hands in surrender.

"My hero Danuwoa," I said, tone laced with sarcasm, though I was actually grateful. Joanna's bathroom pic could definitely wait. Before long, Mr. Stevenson whistled his way to his seat.

"Ready?" Justin, the head pilot who seemed a little too young to hold such a position, stood with his arms braced against the walls of the small pass-through to the cockpit.

"Let's roll," Mr. Stevenson ordered as he shook out his newspaper and began reading.

The engines started spinning and were louder than I thought they'd be. Things were moving beneath us. I could hear things going up and down, opening and closing. Then we started rolling along the tarmac. I took my lizard key chain out of my backpack and gave the ugly head a kiss for luck, then sat back in the chair.

Across from me, Danuwoa seemed unfazed. I couldn't look out the window. I was plastered against the chair; my hands squeezed the armrests at my sides. I could feel us turning slowly but smoothly. There was a pause. Then the plane started going, rolling forward and picking up speed. Faster and faster, then suddenly I couldn't feel the wheels on the ground. We were elevated and rising higher and higher. My stomach was against my back, and I was pinned to my seat. It felt like I was on a roller coaster, going up and up before the drop. Except the drop never came. Soon we flattened out and Justin announced our elevation.

My ears popped.

Inside the cabin, it was quiet except for the hum of the engines from outside. I did it. I was in the middle of the sky. Danuwoa was oblivious to the transformation and experience my body went through, but I was more relaxed.

I looked at Mr. Stevenson; he was dead asleep, mouth open and everything. It made sense he would be serene. This was his plane. It was only a two-and-a-half-hour flight, but I should have brought snacks.

"Psst," I whispered, and kicked Danuwoa's leg too, just to make sure he knew it was me trying to get his attention.

"What?" he whispered back.

"Do you have any food?"

"No. Are you hungry already?"

I nodded. I was too nervous to eat a big breakfast, and we'd worked on that presentation through lunch, but now that we were just cruising, I felt fine. And I was ravenous.

"Come on." Danuwoa got up and motioned me to follow him toward the bathroom.

"No funny business. I'm not interested in joining the Mile High Club," I teased.

"That's too bad. I'm already a member." He kept walking.

I felt my mouth drop to the floor. He had said his first time on a plane was with Mr. Stevenson for work. Who did he hook up with? He turned back to see if I was following him and started laughing. He returned and grabbed my hand to lead me to the back. "I was kidding." He rolled his eyes.

We stopped at a cabinet on the opposite side of the lavatory.

"I knew that. I was acting shocked for the comedic effect." I crossed my arms.

"Hmm."

I couldn't be thinking about Danuwoa and the Mile High Club when we were flying a mile high in a tin can and he was looking sinfully delicious with his mischievous smile.

"You going to open this then?" I pointed at the cabinet with my thumb.

He obliged. Inside were shelves full of granola, fruit snacks, chips, and chocolate. "Bon appétit." He grabbed a yellow bag of potato chips.

The plane lurched—we were going to plummet and die! I launched myself into Danuwoa's arms. He dropped his chips and held me. Our faces were inches apart, and my adrenaline was coursing through me. The terror made my mouth dry, and I licked my lips. His eyes watched my tongue. I wasn't sure who moved first, but our lips were seconds from touching when the plane lurched again.

I clutched at his shirt, panic erasing any lusty feelings. We stayed there in front of the cabinet, Danuwoa holding me for several moments, but the plane stayed level. He let me go.

"It was only some slight turbulence. You okay?"

"You call that slight? The whole plane jerked up and down! We are in a metal can in the sky!"

"Your freak-outs are kind of cute."

I pushed out of his arms. "I had a *slight*"—to use his word—"moment of panic. I'm fine." I cleared my throat.

He picked up his basic-ass flavor of chips off the floor, winked, and sauntered back to our seats.

I rolled my eyes and focused on real matters. Food. I raided that cabinet and got one of everything and brought my haul back to my seat. Danuwoa smiled, and I ignored him as I went to town munching on my snacks.

Hours went by, and I was bored. I should have brought a book or something. Danuwoa was typing away, and it was so warm in the plane I was nodding off. I shook myself awake.

Mr. Stevenson was still asleep with his mouth open wide enough to catch flies. My bladder pulsed, and it was as good a time as any to relieve myself and take a photo of the bathroom for Joanna.

Private plane bathrooms were exactly like small motor-home toilets. Really, I couldn't get over this. I pushed the button with my foot to flush, and the drain in the toilet opened with a loud hiss. Did it go in a tank or fall straight down from the sky? There had to be a tank, because I feel like I would have heard about human waste falling from the sky.

I washed my hands in the small motor home–like sink. I know I should stop obsessing over it, but people liked to pretend these private planes were so luxurious! I snapped a selfie in the mirror for Joanna, then jiggled the lock to leave.

It was stuck.

I pushed the lock over and over again, leveraging all my strength. It wouldn't budge. I was locked in a tiny bathroom.

I didn't do well with being trapped in small, enclosed spaces. My cell phone had no service, so I couldn't call Danuwoa. I should have connected it to Wi-Fi too, but I couldn't remember the long string of letters and numbers that served as the password.

I did not want to bang on the door and yell and wake up Mr. Stevenson. How embarrassing. I lightly knocked, and prayed Danuwoa could hear me. "Dan, help please."

I waited. And waited. And waited.

I looked at my phone, and only three minutes had passed. I started fiddling with the lock again, and its toggle popped off into my hand. It was never going to open.

Fuck.

I threw myself at the door using all my weight. It still didn't budge. I rubbed my shoulder but didn't let it deter me. I had to get out, and it had to be now.

Like a battering ram, I ran into it again and grunted. It hurt like hell and didn't do anything. Again and again, I banged the door, trying to knock it down. I was stuck in a dumb airplane bathroom, and no one could hear me or help me. My hands started shaking, and I tried taking a breath to calm down.

I had tears in my eyes. I was about to start kicking and screaming.

"Ember, are you okay in there?" Danuwoa asked from behind the door, knocking softly.

He came for me! Relief unlike any I had ever felt rushed within me. I would not be left in here. I was saved.

"Danuwoa, no. I'm stuck!"

"In the toilet?"

My cheeks heated in embarrassment. "No, not the toilet! The lock is stuck, and I can't get out."

"Oh shit, okay, turn the lock and I'll pull from this side?"

I croaked a sob, barely getting out the words. "The lock broke off."

"Hey, it's gonna be okay. I'm gonna kick the door down. I won't leave you stuck. Got it?"

"Got it."

"All right, stand back."

I closed the toilet seat cover and stood on top; it was the farthest I could get in the tiny bathroom.

"Okay, I'm out of the way."

Boom! The door swung open with such force, it hit the wall and closed again, only for Danuwoa to slowly open it.

I jumped off the toilet and fell into Danuwoa's solid chest.

"Oh my god," I nearly cried.

"Shh, kawolade'dv," he soothed, rubbing my head and pushing my hair back.

"I don't speak Cherokee," I sniffed.

"Breathe," he whispered.

The plane started descending.

"Oh my god, why is the plane going down?" I tried to get out of his arms.

"Bucky," he said.

"Don't call me that." Hearing that awful nickname grated my nerves, and I glared at him.

"We're preparing to land. That's why I came to check on you."

"Is Mr. Stevenson still sleeping?"

"Yeah." He looked confused by my subject change.

"That's why I didn't yell for help. I didn't want to wake him." Danuwoa grabbed me by my shoulders and crouched so we were eye to eye. "The next time you are ever scared or trapped anywhere, you yell, okay? Fuck Mr. Stevenson and his nap. Got it?"

I wiped the few fearful tears that escaped my eyes from my cheeks. "Yup."

"That's my girl, let's sit down and look at the ocean."

Twenty-One

SANTA BARBARA WAS BEAUTIFUL. I LET DANUWOA HOLD MY hand as we flew over the Pacific Ocean and a tiny island right off the coast before we landed. It was strictly platonic, and it did *not* make my frazzled mind even more confused. I did not like the way his hand encompassed mine. I was totally not lying . . .

The day was clear and sunny—that stereotypical California weather I'd grown up hearing about. The sea air was light, and a warm reprieve from Oklahoma's humid summer.

A black SUV was waiting for us outside the hangar. Right then, the soundtrack to my biopic would have been "We Fly High," because it was obvious and cheesy. The shot would be slo-mo and dramatic, the wind would catch my hair just right, and I would look at something by lowering my sunglasses a tad down my nose. In reality, no music played. Mr. Stevenson had a fire under his butt or something, because he snapped, "Hurry up," and sped down the stairs.

I forgot my sunglasses, so I squinted in the bright sun, trying to hold on to the rail with one hand and shield my eyes with the other. I could feel Danuwoa's hand hovering behind me, making sure I didn't eat shit down the stairs and onto the tarmac.

Safely on the ground, I walked to get my pink duffel bag, but Danuwoa quickly looped it over the handle of his luggage and rolled it away to the car. We were relegated to the very back again, and this time I attempted a crab crawl to get in sideways without sticking my butt in Danuwoa's face. Was it more dignified? Either way, I felt more embarrassed, since the way my thighs opened and closed as I moved over shimmied the fabric higher than what was polite. What could I say? I was a train wreck.

Danuwoa snickered and gave me a look that said, *Really?*

My eyes zeroed in on my kill: *Come hither.* For good measure, I snapped my hand like a crab claw.

He shook his head and laughed as he climbed in after me.

We drove away from the hangar along a field toward the freeway. The resort was only a few minutes away, and I was soaking it all in from my window. Mr. Stevenson was barking orders to someone on the phone, and I was grateful I wasn't needed for small talk to keep him entertained.

The driver turned in to a cobblestone driveway and slowed around a huge three-tiered fountain full of succulents, not water. I guessed the drought really was bad here. It was breathtaking nonetheless. The Spanish hacienda–style facade was grand and elegant. The valets in their red vests came up to help with our luggage. I grabbed my duffel—I knew our contract included porter fees, but this looked like the kind of place you tipped for everything. Did the concierge send you in the right direction? Cash tip. Did the valet smile? Cash tip. I was low on funds, so I could handle getting my duffel to my own room for free.

"I have a meeting with the coordinator in fifteen minutes. I'm going to check in and drop this off. I have my cell if you need me."

"Great," Mr. Stevenson said with a nod. "Dan, I need you to help me with my phone. My emails aren't syncing."

I waved my goodbyes and walked inside the most palatial building I had ever been in. There were fuchsia orchids floating in water in long glass vases. It smelled clean and briny.

Key in hand, I walked down the corridor to the elevator. Floor three was just as beautiful as the lobby. The inside of my room was incredible. It was larger than both Joanna's and my rooms back home combined. A large white cloud was the centerpiece of the room. It was a huge bed that looked so fluffy, all I wanted to do was get a running start and fling myself into its embrace.

I had no time. I freshened up in the bathroom, grabbed my backpack, and ran back downstairs. I was meeting Vivian, the on-site event coordinator, in the lobby for a tour and review of the final details.

I slowed my roll and took a calming breath before exiting the elevator. I didn't want Vivian's first impression of me to be a huffing and sweaty linebacker.

A tall Black woman stood in a navy suit; her locs were coiled into a chic bun on the top of her head.

"Hi." I waved to her. "I'm Ember. Are you Vivian?"

"I am," she said, her smile warm as she extended her hand to shake.

"It's a pleasure to meet you." I hoped my handshake exuded the right amount of strength to show confidence. I did not want to give anyone a dead fish.

"If you would follow me this way, I'll show you the event space and where you'll be having dinner."

We exited the building and walked around the property, past the gorgeous pool, to the Esparza Ballroom. Inside was the classroom setup Natalie had ordered with a stage and podium. Tables lined up in rows facing the stage, covered in long black tablecloths.

"Everything should be all set," Vivian said, holding her clipboard.

I walked through the aisle breaking up the rows and double-checked the settings.

"Do you have more outlets? I think one extension cord won't be enough for each row. I know how it is in class. Everyone uses their computers plugged in the whole time, and I don't want anyone fighting for a plug."

"I'll have to double-check with our team to see what we have available. We have two weddings and another conference this week, so it's busy."

"I'd appreciate it."

"Over here, we have the boxes that were delivered. The beach balls and books."

Right. Those things. Mr. Stevenson wanted company-branded beach balls and a business book to be given away to each person as party favors.

"Perfect. Where will you have the coffee, water, and snacks set up in here?" I asked.

"Catering will bring those in tomorrow morning, but we usually do it by the door here so they don't disrupt a meeting in progress."

"I know in the contract the food and beverage order we have for breakfast is requested at eight a.m. I want to make sure the refreshment setup is done before we start at eight thirty a.m. Then have the snacks delivered before our first morning break at ten thirty."

"It's all handled. If we run into any problems, I'll let you know, but this isn't our first event." She smiled in reassurance.

"This is my first event," I admitted. "And I'm worried that a million things could go wrong."

"Take my advice—worrying makes you suffer twice. And the things you usually anticipate going wrong are never the ones that do. It's always something random. You just gotta roll with the punches. I'll be here to help."

"Thank you." I was so grateful to have someone helping me so that I wasn't alone. "We have a scheduled dinner tonight. Is that close by?" I asked.

"We have you on the terrace with the ocean view. The cocktail reception is at five p.m. and then dinner at six p.m. I can show you now if you'd like?"

"Yes, please." The ocean breeze hit me in the face as we stepped outside into the sunshine. I would never get used to this, because this was just a temporary gift. I wanted to kick my orthopedic flats into the shrubs and take off running straight to the beach. Unfortunately, that would have to wait until we had our free evening.

The terrace was stunning, but nothing was ready.

"Do you think everything will be arranged by five? My boss is never late, and if I am messing up something, then he is sure to be early to see it." I clutched the binder to my chest.

"I'm going to make a call to catering. The tables should have been brought out by now. It's going to be fine," Vivian reassured me, practically oozing calmness.

Natalie had selected a custom, themed cocktail for the evening. I was looking forward to taste testing it, but the bartender wasn't here yet. We had an hour before everything had to be prepared and I could go back to my room to change.

I sat on the bench and waited for Vivian to get off the phone. Judging from her expression, it wasn't good news.

"So, I have the tables and chairs being brought now. There was a slight snafu with one of the other events. I'm going to stay and help set up."

"I'm staying too." I got up from my seat, took my backpack off, and threw my hair into a bun.

"You don't have to. I promise I can get it ready for you in time." She placed her clipboard and blazer next to my backpack on the bench.

"It'll be faster with another set of hands."

A maintenance guy pushed a cart full of folded tables and chairs. We got to work arranging everything. I was sweating and aching from lifting the tables.

"Is housekeeping bringing those linens?" I asked.

"They should be on their way. It's four twenty-five. Why don't you freshen up? I have it handled here."

"No way, I can't leave."

"You're going to attend the dinner like that?" Vivian asked. I must have looked worse than I felt, but what choice did I have? I wasn't a participant in this event. I was here to make sure it went off without a hitch, and this seemed like a big hitch. These tables were ugly and needed something to cover them.

The bartender wheeled his supplies up the ramp to set up. Hey, at least I could test this cocktail. Purely for quality's sake. I hoped whatever was in it was strong.

Finally, two housekeepers wheeled carts carrying white linens folded in plastic bags. I took my cue from Vivian and ripped open a bag and shook out the tablecloths, throwing them on the tables, while the housekeepers stayed to straighten them.

There were 120 people arriving in minutes, and the flowers were nowhere to be found.

"I thought you had an on-site florist?"

"Weddings," Vivian huffed.

"We need something to go on these tables. They look plain."

"Ladies?" Vivian asked the housekeepers. "Can you grab a few of the vases of orchids from the lobby? Start with the ones atop the fireplace first. If we need more, we can take from the centerpiece."

The two young women set off with their empty carts. "Quickly, please!" Vivian called after them.

"I have some drinks ready," the bartender called over.

"Great!" Vivian headed to the bar and started sipping an Ocean Breeze.

"Thank you," I said as I lifted the cold glass to my lips. It looked like blue Kool-Aid, packed with ice and an orange slice and tiny decorative umbrella peeking out. It was disgusting, but the young bartender looked so hopeful. I hid my grimace and stole a glance at Vivian. Her face said it all. It was nasty.

Maybe a pregnant woman, such as Natalie, with questionable cravings was not the best person to pick out a custom cocktail. Thankfully there was surf and turf for dinner. I'd never had lobster tail before, and I couldn't wait to try it. Hopefully the rest of the company was as forgiving of the foul drink.

The housekeepers returned with enough of the orchids to make the terrace look beautiful.

Vivian led me back to the bench. "I am so sorry about the flowers and the cocktail. I won't charge you for the use of the lobby flowers, and I can ask Devin to mix something else."

"A new drink would be great, or can he simplify that mix? Remove a few flavors?"

"I'll handle it—"

"Ember!" Mr. Stevenson's voice boomed through the terrace. I had run out of time. I couldn't even put my hair down. I stuck a smile on my face and turned around, hoping he was in a good mood. "Hi, Mr. Stevenson."

"This looks great. Excellent work. Point me to the bar." He snapped his fingers, pointing at me like they were guns. Danuwoa trailed behind him, still rolling his suitcase and hiking his backpack higher on his shoulders.

"Right this way." I ushered Mr. Stevenson to Devin and hoped the toned-down cocktail tasted better. I stepped beside Danuwoa and shouldered him. "You didn't get to check in?"

"I haven't even had time to use the bathroom."

I took the handle of his suitcase, my hand brushing his. I ignored the little flutter in my stomach at the contact. "Go, go. I got this."

He nodded with a grateful smile and went down the corridor to the bathroom.

I wheeled his luggage over to the bench that housed my backpack. I squatted down, pretending to get something from my pocket, and did a little sniff test of my pits. Creator had mercy, for I was stink-free.

People started arriving. I recognized only a handful; the rest were complete strangers from different office locations. I wanted to shrink within myself and escape. I didn't want to be here. I was not a schmoozer. I liked numbers. Basic cost and profit equations. I never wanted to do this.

"Hey, Ember!" Kyle waved to me; he was standing with Jacqueline. I had only seen our legal counsel's tiny photograph on her email profile. In person, even from several yards away across the terrace, she was stunning. The typical southern belle debutante, big golden curls and a perfect smile. Kyle excused himself and approached me.

"Excellent work on the venue."

"Natalie planned mostly everything before she had the baby."

"Well, it's you here, take the credit." He laughed and gently nudged my arm with his fist.

Taking the credit for someone else's planning and work did not sit right with me. Without knowing what to say and not wanting to be alone in a crowd of colleagues, I just nodded.

"Thanks for looking after that." Danuwoa returned, smiling at me. "Want to get in line and grab a drink?"

"Some firewater, as your people say, right? Light me up!" Kyle answered as if he had been the one asked. "Glad you're here, Dan—my laptop is bugging. If I have more than two spreadsheets open, it freezes. Can you look it over tonight?"

Danuwoa answered, "Yeah sure." But I could feel the tension in his chest. He looked exhausted and hungry, and as the only company IT person on-site, he would have his hands full.

"Let's get that drink." I tugged Danuwoa's hand and walked to the queue, waiting for Devin's blue concoction. Kyle was behind us, but he was already shaking hands and slapping chests with his office bros.

Seating was not assigned for our plated meal, but it was obvious that Danuwoa and I were the odd ones out. Everyone formed their cliques, chatting and laughing. We hung back, sipping the much-improved blue drink.

"Why don't you go mingle?" he asked me.

"Why don't you? You actually know these people," I countered.

"Ah, I know them, so I avoid them."

I snorted. "Are they that bad?"

"Nah, in the office everyone's fine. It's when people drink and throw their phones or computers at me nonstop that gets tiring."

"Can we sneak out and get ready for tomorrow?"

"Hell nah, Mr. Stevenson will be looking for us. We have to finalize this PowerPoint. He changes everything the night before."

I was dead tired. The time difference was only two hours, but this dinner felt like it was dragging on toward 10:00 p.m., when it was getting closer to 8:00 p.m. Pacific time.

"It'll be fine. He just likes company while he writes his notes. I mostly search for free images to put on the screen."

"I still have to blow up all the beach balls. And fill the goody bags and stuff the name-tag lanyards with everyone's printed name cards." The to-do list was never-ending.

Cocktail hour was wrapping up as servers started bringing out plates of food. Everyone saw the cue and began heading over to the tables. Danuwoa and I snagged a round table toward the back.

The food looked magical. The melted butter and garlic reached my nose, and my mouth was salivating. I couldn't wait to dive in. I cut off a piece of the lobster on my plate and eagerly shoved it in my mouth. I started chewing and chewing and chewing. It was not what I was expecting, and I forced myself to swallow it.

"You like the lobster tail?" Danuwoa asked me as he cut into his steak. It grounded me, reminding me to be in the moment.

"Is it ungrateful to say no?" It was kind of chewy and fishy. I know—this from a girl who loved fish sticks and ketchup.

Danuwoa just laughed, the sound like music that floated along with the ocean waves. It gave me chills, and I lied, telling myself it was from the cool air.

Tomorrow was an early day. I got a three-dollar face mask from the grocery store to put on before bed. I couldn't wait to sink into that squishy bed and relax. There was a full bathroom, and I could even take a bath. This thought was the only thing keeping me going while dinner wrapped up and people started breaking off for bed.

Mr. Stevenson stood from his table and looked at Danuwoa and me. We got the hint. It was time to get to work. We grabbed our stuff to meet our boss, who was looking at the pool. Young women were hanging out in pink bikinis, except one in all white. A bachelorette party. It was creepy he was just standing there in the night watching them. It was a five-star resort, and that's what people did at the pool. They wore bikinis. But there was something cringey about an older man in his khakis and button-down just standing there on the path full-on gawking.

"Ready, Mr. Stevenson?" I was really glad it was Danuwoa to alert him of our presence.

The cheeky guy turned around and winked at Danuwoa. I was so ready for the night to be over. Creepy fucking men. It never mattered if they were old, young, rich, poor. You could count on them being creepy. But Danuwoa was different. He didn't spare a glance at the bachelorettes at the pool. He kept walking toward the ballroom, our event space. Maybe there was hope for men after all.

Danuwoa and Mr. Stevenson huddled together at one of the tables, murmuring about the presentation.

I, in my pencil skirt, sat on the floor blowing up fifty beach balls. The name tags were done and laid out. Each seat had the *Ask for Forgiveness Later* business book, and vouchers. If they finished reading it, Mr. Stevenson would pay them fifty dollars. I guessed that was a sign that he loved the book and believed everyone had to read it? I was wary of self-help books, especially ones that touted taking advantage of situations. My people were historically always the ones getting taken advantage of for individual, corporate, and government monetary gain.

It was ten local time, so my body was slowing down. I pumped the last rainbow beach ball and felt my energy levels deflate to the lowest they had been in a very long time.

"Get to bed, Ember," Mr. Stevenson said gruffly.

"No, I'm okay. I can help."

"Dan and I are almost done. See you in the morning." Mr. Stevenson went back to reviewing his notes.

Danuwoa looked less tired after dinner, like the meal had revived him. But I could see the long day was having an effect on his demeanor. He was slouched and hid a yawn behind the back of his hand before waving me off.

I bid my farewells and trudged my way back to my hotel room at last.

Twenty-Two

I HATED ELEVATORS WITH MIRRORS. I GET THAT THEY WERE there to make the small space feel larger, but I looked haggard as fuck.

I forgot to ever take my hair out of the haphazard bun I threw it in before the cocktail reception and dinner. At some point, it slid down to the side of my head like a deformed unicorn horn. I had been working around Mr. Stevenson all night like this. Walking through the hall to my room, I shook out my hair, rubbing my scalp to ease the tension and pain the tight elastic caused.

In my customary Ember-not-giving-a-fuck fashion, I kicked my flats off my feet and high into the air. Where did each land? I didn't know. That was future Ember's problem. I let my bare feet sink into the soft carpet as I slipped my arms inside my shirt, freeing myself of my bra. I threaded it out through the armhole of my shirt and flung it in an arc, already forgotten. Braless and shoeless, I stepped into the bathroom, the white marble a cold shock to my tired feet.

I started the bath, dumping the full bottle of the gardenia-

and-citrus-scented shower gel into the tub. I wanted to get lost in the bubbles. And that was what I did. I sank beneath those suds, the hot water like a warm caress telling me I did a good job. I stayed there until I was pruney. My eyelids were droopy, and before I could fall asleep in the tub, I mustered the last of my strength to get out. I wrapped myself in the white plush hotel-branded towel. I braided my hair back and put the three-dollar sheet mask on my face.

As I crawled into bed, I hoped the mask would make me look refreshed tomorrow. The bed was heaven. The pillows were ecstasy. I let my eyes close and welcomed the darkness and oblivion of sleep.

A LARGE WEIGHT SLAMMED ON TOP OF ME. I ERUPTED INTO screaming and flailing.

There was someone on top of me. This was how I was going to die.

A man shouted, "What the hell?"

I barely registered it as he rolled off me onto the bed, curled into himself as he felt the full force of my vengeance. I wouldn't go down without a fight.

I may have screamed, "Die, motherfucker!" as I threw punches at my assailant with everything I had.

"It was a mistake! I'm not here to hurt you! Stop, please!"

The adrenaline was leaving my body. Logic was slowly returning. The man was retreating from me as my attack slowed. He didn't try to touch me or fight back.

"I'm going to turn the light on. I think the hotel accidentally double-booked this room."

I knew that deep voice.

"Danuwoa?" I asked.

The room was suddenly illuminated, and I had to squint my eyes and blink repeatedly to adjust to the light.

"What the hell is on your face, Ember?" Danuwoa, now standing by the light switch, laughed. He had the audacity to laugh!

"I thought you were here to rape and murder me! Don't laugh at my mask!"

He rubbed his face, clearly exhausted.

"What time is it?" I asked.

"It's almost two."

"In the morning?"

He just leveled me with a look of pure impatience, then he blushed.

I peeled the dried sheet mask off my face. Note to self, never sleep in these again. I looked down at the crumpled mask in my hand, and it was then that I noticed my left nipple was exposed, peaked from the air-conditioned room and just flaunting itself for Danuwoa to see. I was naked in nothing more than the hotel robe that, in my sleep, had come untied, and now Danuwoa was in my room, and I was just sitting there dumbfounded. I covered myself and jumped out of bed.

"Grab your stuff," I said as I marched to the door.

Still in shock at seeing my boob or my beating the shit out of him, he silently complied and followed me all the way to the lobby.

There was a lone worker standing at the front desk. He looked relaxed, listening to his music with one bud in his ear, his head bobbing to the beat.

I rested my arms on the counter, still in my now traitorous robe. "Hi."

"Hello, how can I help you?" He ripped the white bud out of his ear.

"There appears to be a huge mistake. You see, there I was sleeping my good, deep sleep when I was awoken, most violently, by this man," I said, motioning to Danuwoa next to me with my thumb.

"Ignoring the dramatics," Danuwoa said, rolling his eyes, "it appears we were booked in the same room."

We gave the receptionist the room number, and he began typing away making "mmm" sounds.

After the fifth one, I glanced at his name tag. "What's going on, Raj? Those *mmm*s aren't giving me any confidence."

"I apologize, ma'am." Did he just fucking call me *ma'am*? That cheap-ass face mask didn't do shit. I was hoping to be called *miss* until I was in my early forties. He continued, "This was a mistake on our end, and I was looking for alternatives, but we are completely booked."

"You don't have a single open room?" Danuwoa groaned.

"I'm so sorry. With the weddings and conferences, there are no vacancies this week." Raj looked apologetic.

"There isn't a supply closet we can throw a cot in for the night?" I asked. My exhaustion made my voice sound harsh.

"A cot?" Danuwoa questioned me. He looked pissed.

"I'm sorry, ma'am, it goes against hotel policy to allow a guest to stay in a closet."

"Quit calling me ma'am, Raj. Is there anything you can do?"

"I can call surrounding hotels to book you or Mr. Colson a room there for the night. Then we can look tomorrow to see if anyone checks out early," Raj offered.

Danuwoa sighed. At this rate, he wasn't going to get any sleep and make it for all the early setup tomorrow.

"No, he can stay in my room," I grumbled.

"Excellent. I'll put you as our top priority for a free room. We will also comp you any room service for your stay for the inconvenience."

Without another word, I trudged back to our hotel room, Danuwoa silently following. The poor man couldn't catch a break.

Inside the room, I went to the mini-fridge and took out a cold water bottle and handed it to him. I was going to make sure these charges were comped too.

"I didn't hurt you too badly, did I?" I sat on the edge of the bed while he sat in the chair.

"Besides my eardrums from all your screaming? Nah, I'll probably have a bruise or two from where you kicked me, but you missed my family jewels, thankfully."

"In my defense, I didn't know it was you."

"It was so dark, I just saw the bed and jumped in."

"Well, the bed is mine." I threw him the thin throw blanket that was falling off the bed. "You can sleep there."

"This chair? Are you serious?"

"The floor is another option."

"Ember." He glared. I glared too. We had an Indian standoff. Finally, he caved and huffed, "Fine."

I climbed into bed and watched as he kicked his shoes off and took off his pants and shirt.

"What are you doing?" I shrieked.

"Getting ready for bed." He turned to face me. Danuwoa wore boxer briefs and had abs. Chiseled eight-pack abs.

"You don't wear clothes?" I clutched my metaphorical pearls to my chest. This man would be the death of me.

"I'm a furnace." He sat in the chair, arranging the thin blue blanket around his legs. It didn't even cover his full torso.

"Okay, well. Good night." I reached for the light switch, and we were encased in the dark. I knew I was bone tired. I should have gone back to sleep, but I was wired. I was aware of Danuwoa being only a few feet away from me, half-naked.

It didn't sound like he was having any better luck. I heard him shift in that leather chair, his skin peeling off the material as he moved from sitting up to, I assumed, slouching. He grumbled again, and I heard him get up and lie on the floor.

"Oh my god, okay. You can sleep on the bed. I can't sleep with you moving around all over." I lied. I couldn't sleep because he was in the room, period, but I did feel guilty he was relegated to the floor and overworked, no less.

"Great!" I heard him jump up and then felt the weight of him shift the bed as he hopped in.

"Over the sheets," I warned.

It was dark, but I knew he rolled his eyes as he peeled back the down duvet and respected my wishes.

We lay there on our backs, arms across our chests. Inches apart. He *was* a furnace. He radiated heat, and now I knew he looked like a ripped god under all his clothes.

My thick robe was too scratchy. I was too hot. I was too aware. I curled my toes and clenched my core.

I made a huge mistake inviting him into my bed. We were forbidden work colleagues.

"You okay?" His deep voice was raspy from drowsiness.

"Perfect," I hissed through my teeth.

At some point he dozed off as I lay there, listening to his even breathing. Calming my body from his proximity. The sky was starting to wake up when I finally gave in to sleep.

Twenty-Three

MY ALARM PIERCED THROUGH MY SLUMBER, AND I WAS awake. At some point during those early hours, Danuwoa had turned over. His toned arm was heavy across my waist.

We were cuddling.

This was bad. We were here working. We were not dating. There was this insane chemistry, but it was wrong, so, *so* wrong. If someone were to see us . . . Sirens went off in my head. You were not supposed to mix business with pleasure, it said it clearly in black and white, and I signed that I acknowledged the policy. And yet here I was on my first work trip sharing a room with the hottest man employed by Technix. Fuckboy Kyle was a plastic Ken doll compared to all that was Danuwoa. From his hair to his muscles and tanned skin . . . I had to stop looking at him before he caught me.

Too late. He caught me staring. I made sure my robe was closed tight, and grabbed the collar with my hand.

"Good morning," he said as he rolled over to get out of bed. I averted my eyes as he adjusted his morning wood. How could someone be so confident in front of the opposite sex? He was just casually walking around in his underwear as if it were so natural and normal. This was the farthest thing from normal.

He went to the coffee maker, yawning, and popped in a pod. We had a limited amount of time to get downstairs to do a quick tech rehearsal and grab breakfast with the rest of the company. I went through my duffel to get out my dress and blazer for the day.

"Dibs on the shower," I said.

"I think you'll need this." Danuwoa handed me my discarded bra from last night. I snatched it from his hand. My face was hot. He smirked and went to grab his freshly brewed coffee.

I wish I could say it was a sexy bra, but I didn't own a sexy bra. It was a cheap basic nude underwire bra from Walmart that was worn in but comfortable. It was my trusty, sturdy bra. The one I knew would not show under anything, and the straps never slipped.

As I stood with the shower streaming down my back, I cringed remembering my bare boob was just hanging out last night. Which was worse? My ugly old bra or a boob flash? The worst part was the ache that lingered from lying next to Danuwoa all night. Now was *so* not the time to get all hot and bothered—in a shower with him in his underwear on the other side of the wall. I got out and tried to center myself. I could worry about whatever was going on with him later. All I had to do was make sure everything happened on schedule and without a hitch.

I took my hair out of the braid I slept in, letting the waves fall around me. I was wearing my white dress again, this time with my black blazer. I put some tinted lip balm and mascara on and went out to face Danuwoa.

"All yours," I said as I watched him stretch on the floor. Was

I in a porno? Who just hangs out in their underwear stretching when sharing a room (and bed!) with a coworker?

"Great, there's some coffee for you." He pointed as he got up and headed for the shower.

A smart Ember would have just left the room and headed down to the event space right then. But smart Ember was unavailable. She was leaving an out-of-the-office automatic reply in my brain. I was left horny, curious, and dumb. Exactly how all my crushes left me. The difference? This crush was currently very naked in the shower, and I thought he was crushing on me back. This was not how I operated.

What was wrong with me?

I gathered my backpack, made sure I had everything, and looked for my shoes. Past Ember sucked. She left me hanging here searching for where my left shoe could possibly have been flung last night. I got on my hands and knees, looking under the dresser and chair.

"We gotta stop meeting like this." Danuwoa laughed.

I craned my head and of fucking course! He was dripping wet with a towel wrapped low on his hips. Water droplets fell down the V that pointed to his you-know-what region. The room grew about twenty degrees hotter in the span of a second.

"Stop drooling; you're objectifying me."

I gave him the bird and continued my search for my shoe, this time making sure my butt wasn't sticking up too much—an impossible feat in this sundress.

"You gotta stop walking around in nothing. Have some modesty," I grumbled and hit my head on the desk.

"Looking for this?" He tossed my missing shoe. It landed with a thud by my side.

"Where did you find that?" Thankfully, he was wearing socks

and underwear, and was starting to button his dress shirt when I was brave enough to spare him a glance.

"Under the bed." He pulled his pants on.

"Thanks."

"Why don't you wear those?"

I followed his finger to the sparkly, strappy shoes I brought just in case I wanted to feel fancy.

"I'm not going to wear those all day," I said, rolling my eyes.

"They're pretty sexy." He blew out a whistle. "They look like they strap *all* the way up your legs."

His voice was doing things to me. "They do." I gulped.

"Maybe you can put them on tonight?" He said it like it was a promise of indulgence and sin. If I put those on, it would be.

"If I feel like it," I said, mustering up the bravado I didn't feel, playing coy in a game I wanted to give in to.

I watched from the corner of my eye as he finished getting ready. His hair was wet and loose. One day, I wanted to braid that hair. Oooh, that was a stupid thought! What was I thinking? We hadn't even kissed or had any sort of arrangement to work around the Technix dating policy. That was a million steps from where we were, and yet, my fingers twitched, itching as he started braiding his hair into his signature beautiful long braid.

"Shall we go down?" he asked.

"What? Together?"

"How else?" He slung his backpack straps over his shoulders.

"No way! Anyone could see us!"

"So?"

"So? Do you want us to lose our jobs?!"

"We are the earliest people up. Everyone else is still sleeping right now."

I grabbed my backpack and walked to the door. "I'm leaving

first. Wait five minutes before you follow me, got it?" I opened the door just a smidge and peeked out. The coast looked clear. "See you down there."

I slipped out and headed down the hall toward the elevator. I heard another door close, and I jumped. I was scared out of my mind. On the wall hung a long mirror, and I casually stole a glance to see if I recognized the person behind me. I did.

I stopped short. "Didn't you hear what I said?" I angry whispered, which was always louder than my normal talking voice, but mad me was not rational.

Danuwoa laughed and kept walking to the elevator. Nothing pissed me off more when I was already angry than someone laughing me off.

The elevator opened. We stepped in but I was seething.

"Relax. No one is around."

I stepped right up to him. Directly in his space. "How hard would it have been to just listen to me?"

We were sharing air and it was electric. Charged. As if a spark would be set off at any moment.

He took a step closer to me. Our chests were now inches apart, and he whispered in my face, his breath smelling like the toothpaste he just used. "About as hard as it was for me to lay in that bed next to you, knowing you wore nothing under that robe."

"So, you decided to flaunt yourself in your underwear all morning?"

"Did that bother you?"

I tried to take a step back, but his hands grabbed the straps of my backpack, keeping me in place.

"Yes," I gulped.

"Why?"

"You know why." I looked down for a moment, but his hand

released one of my straps, and he used it to tilt my chin up so I was looking into his eyes.

He kissed me. Right there in an elevator of a hotel full of our coworkers, Danuwoa eviscerated my soul. He was forbidden, and the spark that set my body aflame. His lips moved over mine, coaxing my stunned mouth to respond to him. To stop fighting and enjoy. It was sweet and sexy. So tender and sensual.

I wanted him to back me up and press me against the mirrored wall, but before we could go further, the elevator stopped on the floor beneath us. I was barely coming to my senses and didn't pull away fast enough. A man whistled.

Not just any man, but Kyle.

He stepped onto the elevator in the clothes he'd worn the night before, his hair disheveled. "Please, don't let me stop you on my account."

Danuwoa stepped away, and I felt ice cold, shock seeping through my body. Being caught kissing him in front of the CEO's nephew was the absolute worst thing that could ever happen. My fight-or-flight response was kicking in, and I couldn't wait for the elevator door to open so I could flee the scene. Danuwoa tried to touch my hand, but I moved it away. I was pissed and wanted to throw up. What the fuck did Danuwoa do? I told him to listen to me.

I exited the elevator and clocked that Danuwoa grabbed Kyle's arm and held him back. On autopilot, I fled toward the ballroom on quick feet to make sure everything was ready. I paused only once before I turned the corner to see that Danuwoa and Kyle were having an intense, hushed conversation. A part of me knew that whatever Danuwoa was saying was not going to help.

Twenty-Four

"WHAT DO YOU MEAN THERE ARE NO MORE ROOMS AVAILable?" I screeched at Denise, the daytime receptionist. I had skipped out of the conference to check the status of room availability. I had stayed for Mr. Stevenson's opening remarks. He was a terrible speaker. It was beyond boring, but I paid my dues before I slipped out of the conference right as Mr. Adams started speaking on the quarterly numbers, under the guise of "checking on things." Now, I sat in the lobby running different scenarios in my head.

There was no way I could share a room with Danuwoa again, especially not after *that* kiss. And I *especially* couldn't now that Kyle had seen the kiss. I'd never been kissed like that before in all my life. That was the kind of kiss that people fantasize about, and it never should have happened.

Would Kyle tell Mr. Stevenson?

I wandered the grounds for fresh air, trying to get my thoughts under control. It was foggy and cold this morning, and I could barely see the ocean from the path. I roamed for what felt like hours. My sole saving grace was that I was only needed behind the scenes, really. Mr. Stevenson was busy being fangirled over by everyone from all the offices and listening to the speakers. Natalie planned everything down to the minute, and since the cocktail fiasco, everything else had been running like a well-oiled machine. The team-building activity didn't start until after lunch.

What if Danuwoa kissed me again? What if we shared the room? What if we kept things casual? What if Kyle gossiped to the whole company? Or worse, what if he told his uncle and got me fired? I was going back and forth; would it be so bad if people found out? We were adults. It was a silly rule anyway. But I remembered Walela, and Danuwoa needed to take care of her, just like I needed my job. The last thing either of us needed was to be job-hunting. That sounded like a horrible start to a relationship— if that was even what he wanted. If it was just sex, that was almost worse. Danuwoa was special, and my romantic heart wanted to be special to him.

This all started because I just wanted to be an accountant, damn it. How did my life get so complicated?

I obsessed over these thoughts repeatedly as I walked back to the conference. Back in the ballroom, the buffet lunch was ready to be served. I crumpled my blazer into my backpack and quickly scanned the room to see where Danuwoa was, to avoid him. He wasn't here. Slightly relieved, I got in line for food. I reached for a corn muffin at the same time as the man in front of me. It was Gary.

"Sorry about that," I said.

He just stared at me with annoyance. He took the muffin and continued piling his plate. I lost my appetite following Gary through the line. I went outside to eat my food, where I found Danuwoa in deep conversation with Sasha Storm Cloud.

She was stunningly beautiful. Her brown hair was giving way to gray, and she wore regalia, a purple jingle dress usually reserved for powwows. It was like Danuwoa could feel my eyes on him, because he looked up at me. His eyes screamed, *Help me!*

I took my plate over to them.

"*Aho*, daughter." She inclined her head to me.

"Uh, hi."

"I'm Sasha Storm Cloud. This fine warrior was telling me he is Cherokee. I too am Cherokee, from a line of strong Cherokee princesses."

So I was right. I wished Joanna were here.

"Oh wow, really? What clan?" I asked.

"My poor family was displaced with the Great Removal. We lost our records. I was fortunate enough to be adopted by the Sioux when I was a wandering little girl."

"Cherokee to Sioux, wow."

Danuwoa snickered behind his hand. I wasn't Lakota, but it was known that *Sioux* was a derogatory name, and generally those from that tribal nation did not refer to themselves as just *Sioux*. It wasn't a law, and every person from every tribal community was different. But the red flags were popping up nonetheless.

"I am also Navajo from my father's side," Sasha added. It was people like her who made us look bad. Could she be a descendant? Sure. But the story was weird. It was not my job to interrogate her and ask for proof.

"How nice," was all I could say. I wanted the interaction over with.

"If you'll excuse me, I have to set up for our activity. It was nice meeting you." She put her fingers to her forehead and brought them out toward us in a salute that looked vaguely familiar.

As soon as Sasha Storm Cloud was out of earshot, Danuwoa

folded over laughing. I was glad she was gone, and she was rather silly, but the laughing seemed excessive.

"She did the *Avatar* 'I see you' thing," he said between laughs.

"Shut up, I thought I'd seen that before." I couldn't help but start laughing too.

"Did you know about her?" he asked me as he straightened, his chest still spasming with laughter.

"I saw that Natalie booked a spiritual leader." I chuckled.

"I'm not staying for this. Let's ditch."

"We can't ditch. We'll be missed."

"Nah, they don't need any computers for whatever shit Sasha Storm Cloud has planned."

"I'll bet she has some peace pipe thing planned," I said with a laugh.

"I'll take that bet—what are the stakes?" He leaned toward me.

"Uh . . . twenty bucks?" I took a step back.

"Ember . . ." his voice warned. His eyes pierced me, and I was starting to feel like goo inside.

"What would you want?" My voice had a mind of its own; it dropped an octave to a husky whisper.

"You in those strappy shoes from earlier."

Oh my.

I let out a breath. I could do that. "No peace pipe and I wear the shoes."

"Only the shoes." His voice was deep, and the rumbling did wicked things to my stomach.

"What do I get if I win?" I gulped. I couldn't answer that right away. It was scandalous. Danuwoa was inches away from me. We were outside the conference room by the bushes, and it was just us, the only two people in the world in our own little sexually charged bubble.

"Would an earth-shattering orgasm do?" He whispered so low I could feel it in my core.

I throbbed. I knew I should still be mad at him for kissing me and compromising our jobs, but it was impossible to stay mad at Danuwoa. He was kind and happy with the most infectious smile that felt so safe. But boy was he frustrating with his forbidden sexual pursuit.

"Shut up." I shoved my plate of food into his chest. It was as if I dumped a bucket of ice on myself. What were we doing? We were at work surrounded by colleagues. Monica from HR was inside chatting with Jacqueline from legal.

He laughed and grabbed my hand. "Come on."

I glanced around to make sure no one was looking at us, and we took off sprinting down the path.

I was in California for the first time, in a five-star resort, and had a free evening to explore with a man who had just promised me an earth-shattering orgasm. I needed a dip in the ocean to cool off.

"To the beach!" I announced to get the heck out of there. What he said was daring and left me off-kilter, and I had to do something to get us back on an even playing field.

"Let's go," he said, leading me.

With everyone in the workshop with Sasha, there wasn't a single Technix employee in sight. The walking path around the hotel grounds turned into a sandy path that led to the beach. It was afternoon, and the only people we encountered were couples on romantic walks.

Danuwoa had discarded my plate of food in a nearby trash can. I let my eyes wander from his profile, down his neck, to his arms. He had rolled the sleeves of his button-down a quarter of the way up, exposing his tanned, toned arms. That should be a sin. In dress codes, where it states women must wear skirts at or below their knees, there should be a clause in the policy stating men are not allowed to roll their sleeves up like that. I lazily looked back to his face and caught him admiring me. I knew it in just the same way I could tell what he thought when he looked at me. He had the most expressive face.

I looked away, smoothing out the white skirt of my dress. I could not have Danuwoa giving me puppy eyes. No, worse—he was giving me the cute Puss in Boots eyes, and I was fumbling Shrek taking up too much space, saying the wrong things, and walking around a five-star resort in orthopedic flats.

Once we got down the hill, Danuwoa grabbed my hand again, and I let him. Fingers laced, we kept walking in silence. The waves crashing against the shore and the wind whipping about our hair were our only companions as we walked south.

The beach was empty, our own private world. I liked Danuwoa. More than a coworker and more than a friend. I couldn't lie to myself about it anymore. Not out in nature, with the ocean bearing witness to our joined hands. The fight-or-flight response I was having after our kiss in the elevator evaporated, and I was left feeling content and hopeful.

It was romantic and casual all at once. There was a small dune, and Danuwoa let go of my hand and plopped down, patting the golden sand next to him. I smoothed my dress down to cover my bottom as best I could and attempted to sit as elegantly and sexily as possible. I arranged my dress around my knees, but Danuwoa wasn't watching. He was unlacing his shoes and rolling up the bottoms of his pants. When he finished, he pointed to my feet, and I slid off my flats. I buried my feet in the warm sand and wiggled my toes as I watched the grains of sand slide off my feet.

I'd grown up barefoot in the red earth of Sulphur and Ada and the silt from the rivers and creeks, but I'd never felt ocean beach sand before.

"It's hot," I said, smiling.

"Wanna stick your toes in the Pacific?" He was already getting up and brushing the sand off his pants.

"Yes." Before I could try to maneuver my way up, he reached out a hand and pulled me up with more force than was truly necessary. He pulled me close to his chest as I swung up. Then he promptly pushed me away to get a running start toward the water.

I chased him. We ran into the waves, and I screamed. It was shocking how cold the water was. I expected it to be warm based on movies, but it was freezing. I had to jump up and down to alleviate the pain in my feet as my body got used to the water. Danuwoa kept running and then circled back to me. He kicked up his leg and showered me in the seawater.

Not to be outdone, I kicked my feet, and I never knew I could have such perfect aim. My splash nailed him square in the face.

He took his hand and wiped the salty water away. He narrowed his eyes, black with determination. "Big mistake." He charged after me, and I was too slow to react. He grabbed me in a bear hug and twirled me around the water. My feet sprayed us both with all the splashing and waves. I was screaming and laughing with Danuwoa and then, suddenly, we both stopped. He held me up by the waist, and I looked down at his face, never seeing something so gorgeous. His high cheekbones and proud nose were framed by thick black eyebrows and full lips.

I lowered my face, and I kissed him, his lips wet and salty from the ocean. I drank it all in, digging my hands into his hair. He responded by tightening his grip around my waist and plunging his tongue into my mouth. I welcomed the invasion and greeted his tongue with my own. We stood there in the ocean as we kissed each other like we were the last gulp of air we would ever breathe.

I moaned, and in response, he groaned and deepened the kiss.

My eyes were closed as I explored what it was to be consumed by Danuwoa. My hands roamed as he lowered me down, dragging my body against his chest. As I stood pressed against him, I felt his attraction to me through my dress.

He began leading us back up to the dune where we left our shoes, peppering my lips with more kisses like if we stopped, we would never begin again. I knew I didn't have the power to resist kissing Danuwoa anymore and I was a fool to fight it. This was what I had been missing, what our chemistry had been building up to.

I tripped over my own shoe and tried to slip it on my foot while still clutching Danuwoa, but it was hopeless. I peeled myself away from him and sat down on the ground, not caring that my dress was drenched and I would be coated in sand. Danuwoa plopped down next to me and smiled that perfect white smile.

I abandoned my shoes and launched myself at him. He landed on his back, accepting my kiss and weight. Never had I felt such desire and power. I climbed over him, straddling his legs as I kissed him more, grinding against the promise in his pants. He groaned as his hands explored me before they wrapped around my arms, pushing me away.

"I love where you're headed, but we have to stop," he panted.

My chest heaved as I looked at his kiss-swollen lips. I shivered as the cool wind blew across my wet skin and clothes. It broke the spell. We were on a public beach. Anyone could happen upon us. Mr. Stevenson could happen upon us.

"Oh my god," I whispered, embarrassed. I slid off him in a sandy, wet heap. "What have I done?"

"Something I hope we continue once we get back to our room."
He sat up and kissed the spot on my neck below my ear. It sent a
bolt down straight to my core. I curled my dirty toes in the sand.
"What if tonight we just had fun? No thinking of what-ifs or the
future?"

It should have unnerved me how well he knew my mind. I
never told him about the constant what-if scenarios I overplayed
in my head, and I was panicking about our make-out session out
in the open on a work trip. I really wanted us to keep our jobs.
Maybe just one what-if scenario: What if we just had fun? No one
could see what we did in the room behind closed doors, and
Danuwoa was professional. Besides, Kyle seeing us kiss wasn't
that big a deal. Kyle had been flirting with Jacqueline all through
dinner last night. He probably didn't care. Probably no one at
Technix actually cared. I was just following the rule because I was
new to working in the corporate world. Danuwoa and I were
adults. We could be mature, and bone as mature people did.

"We can get to know each other," he said and kissed my neck,
drifting lower as he continued, "watch a movie. Order room service." He ended his persuasion with a kiss on my shoulder.

"A movie sounds nice," I whispered, allowing myself to smile,
to bask in his attention. I could forget about all the tomorrows and
just be with Danuwoa tonight. There need be no pressure to it,
and if we timed our elevator ride right, we could get by unseen by
anyone we may know.

"Great!" He slammed his feet into his shoes while I did the
same. We dusted ourselves off and ran along the beach, back to
the trail that led to our hotel and our room.

Twenty-Five

I WENT UP FIRST, AND THIS TIME DANUWOA LISTENED TO ME and waited ten minutes before following me up to our room. I was possibly having sex tonight. Not just any sex, but earth-shattering sex with Danuwoa. My heart was racing. I hadn't had sex in more than a year, and he seemed to be the kind of guy who liked surprising moves and sexy talk. I was not well-versed in any of that. I was flushed the entire ride up the elevator, looking at my beet red, rumpled reflection.

The head start gave me time to peel my soiled dress off and lock myself in the bathroom, warming my body in the hot shower and cleaning my lady bits well just in case. I wore my pajamas this time and didn't wash my hair. It was the fastest I had ever show-ered, but I knew Danuwoa would be just as cold and sandy, and we weren't there yet with sharing a shower. I would combust and die but, oh, what a way to go.

When I got out of the bathroom, he was already there, sitting on the bed in just his underwear.

"Do you never wear clothes at home?" I asked, my face warm.

"Not if I can help it." He winked as he got up and walked right to me. We were inches apart, and I craved his lips on mine. He read my thoughts and kissed my cheek. "No peeking at me while I shower," he whispered.

I stood rooted in that spot. I heard the door close over the sound of my own blood roaring in my ears. I was in way over my head. The sound of the water running broke my lusty trance, and I scurried to the bed.

I ordered minestrone soup and pizza from room service. Was it a weird combo? Yes. Was it a sexy food pairing? No. But I was starving, and the cold from the ocean lingered. My hot shower was too short to fully thaw me.

Danuwoa took his sweet time in the bathroom. I didn't want to imagine what he was doing in there for so long, but my mind wandered there anyway, to all the possibilities. I tried very hard not to imagine the frothy washcloth spreading soap along his arms, up and down his abs, and lower. I no longer needed the minestrone; thinking about Danuwoa washing was warming me up from my core down to my toes.

The water stopped, and I fanned my face.

This time, when Danuwoa exited the steamy bathroom, he was wearing a faded Peter Gabriel concert T-shirt. His hair was dry and freshly wound in two shining braids.

"Peter Gabriel?" I asked him, skepticism coating my voice.

"He's an unparalleled genius." He walked to his suitcase and folded his soiled clothes and placed them in a drawstring bag. I was starting to understand that Danuwoa was a neat freak, but after living with Sage and now Joanna, I appreciated his order.

"Can't say that I've heard much of his stuff." I picked at a loose thread on my joggers.

"That can and will be fixed." He closed his suitcase and jumped onto the end of the bed. "Did you order food yet?"

"Yeah, I have some pepperoni pizza and soup coming."

"Soup?" He teased me with his smile as he rolled onto his side, his head propped on his hand.

"I'm cold."

With his free arm, he tapped his chest. "Come here."

He was inviting me to cuddle with him. I kicked him with my foot, and he rolled off the bed. It was a fight-or-flight response from my wild nerves.

"Hey!" His face looked bewildered at my betrayal.

"Be careful, Danuwoa, I wouldn't want to ruin you," I said, laughing.

He sat up and rested his arms on the bed. "It's funny. I woke up this morning thinking, 'I hope this girl destroys me.'"

That earned him a pillow square in the face. I wanted to get to know Danuwoa. I loved kissing him, but sleeping with him could complicate things. My brain was doing it again . . . What if we were incompatible? I didn't think he was exaggerating about the earth-shattering orgasm, but the first time sleeping with someone never culminated in an orgasm for me—ever. It would make things awkward at work if this was a failure. Eating in the lunchroom and avoiding eye contact because I would have intimate knowledge of what his penis looked like. That was a unique and uncomfortable experience I wanted to avoid. I mean, I did want that knowledge. It might take multiple sessions to really get a full grasp of the *situation*, but I did not want to crash and burn and be left with my heart in tatters and still have to take care of everyone—Auntie, Sage, Joanna.

"You're blushing, so I know you like me," he said smugly. He threw the pillow back at me, and I caught it in my arms, hugging it close to my chest.

"You mentioned a movie. What do you have in mind?" I rolled my eyes.

He got to work navigating the guide on the hotel TV. We had limited options with what was free. "We have *Babe: Pig in the City* and *Unsolved Mysteries*. What are you in the mood for?"

There was a knock on the door. Remote in hand, Danuwoa opened the door for the room service food cart. Once the waiter left, Danuwoa opened the metal covers.

"What will it be? I love eating while watching something," he urged.

"Do I want nightmares of strange deaths, or do I want to watch a cute pig roam around?" I tapped my chin.

He clicked over to the pig movie, and we dug into our meal. I smiled to myself because he just got me. He was down to watch a children's movie about a pig with me so I wouldn't have nightmares. Granted, he wanted in my pants and I was gonna let him. We sat back on the fluffy bed, me slurping my soup and Danuwoa eating his pizza slices like tacos, folded in half and sideways. He moaned as if that pizza was the best thing he had ever tasted, and it made my core throb remembering his moans from the beach. I cleared my throat and continued eating. Once we had our fill, I moved our plates to the cart and pushed it away from the bed, turning off the lights for a cinema experience with the large flat-screen TV.

Back in bed, Danuwoa had shifted closer to the middle. I situated myself with the covers pulled up to my chest, arms crossed at my waist. He nudged my shoulder. Smirking, I nudged him back with my bony elbow. He thwarted my attempts at wiggling away by wrapping his right arm around me and pulling me into his side.

We were cuddling. We were watching a children's movie. We

were never going to end up as just friends. From the moment he knelt and handed me my ugly key chain, I knew Danuwoa was special.

I lay there against Danuwoa's warm body, my leg curled over his as his hand rested on my hip. When the credits rolled, we stayed in each other's embrace. Danuwoa brought his other arm around and lazily stroked from my hip down to my thigh. The hand that had been on my hip the entire movie slowly circled my ass. The warmth his hands left on me through the duvet melted the last of my walls.

I would let him kiss me again, because if he didn't, then I would kiss him. Either way, we weren't going to sleep tonight without a repeat performance of what we tasted at the beach. I glanced up to find Danuwoa staring down at me, a small smile on his lips. He bent his head and kissed me lightly, but that small touch unlocked the carnal hunger I had developed for him. The sound of whatever programming started after our movie faded. All I could focus on was Danuwoa's lips on mine. His hand moved from my hip to my ass, and, emboldened, I clutched his shirt. He pulled away, and I gasped in outrage that he would separate from me after only the smallest taste.

"I don't want to stretch it out," he said and whipped the old shirt over his head and chucked it across the room. My hands found his bare chest more enticing than the material of any shirt could ever be.

"Shut up and kiss me," I demanded.

And boy did he. Our showers and hot food energized our desire. Our passion on the beach was only a sampling of what Danuwoa could do. Being on a bed made it that much more intense. He sucked on my bottom lip, and my back arched to a degree I didn't think was humanly possible.

I stopped my hands from wandering his chest to lift the hem of my shirt up and over my head. We were bare from the waist up. He kissed me with a groan before peeling his lips away from my mouth to trail kisses along my neck and down to my collarbone.

"Is this okay?" he whispered.

My "yes" sounded like a cross between a growl and a moan that was quickly silenced as he cupped my breasts, squeezing, appreciating their weight and softness. I had to give the guy credit: he made my little boobs feel full and desirable, even as one hand engulfed each entirely.

He put his mouth on my breast. The wet heat of his sucking drove me to insanity. I curled my toes and pressed my thighs tight around his leg as I clawed at his biceps. His tongue circled my exposed, hardened peak, and I was on fire. He played and nipped, his tongue trailing along between my breasts. His warm breath on my sensitive skin sent shivers throughout my body. I was near the edge of begging him to end my torment. Then he switched to my other breast. I whimpered, feeling his smile and chuckle as he bit down gently, and I bucked. It was not graceful, but I no longer had control of my body or my responses to his touch. Danuwoa was in control. My body, my pleasure, all of it at this moment belonged solely to Danuwoa and his tongue.

I was impatient, my hips grinding my core along his leg. It did nothing to ease the ache, and I was soaked through to my sweatpants. My primal instincts were in charge. With his lips on mine, I couldn't remember why I hesitated at all, delaying this, because this felt more right than anything else in my life.

Danuwoa's hands left my breasts and dragged down my torso, his calluses leaving a wake of goose bumps before they wrapped around my ass, giving me a tight squeeze. He yanked the waist of my pants down and stripped me bare, flinging my clothes in one swoop. The subtle bluish glow from the television illuminated our bodies, and in his eyes, I saw the hunger I felt reflected back at me.

His mouth trailed reverent kisses along my body, caressing every inch of skin before he nudged my knees apart, opening me for him. God, I had not shaved. I did not anticipate *this* when I left Oklahoma. His thumb rubbed my slit.

"Yes," he said in a way that appreciated my slickness, that body hair or no, this was all for him. "You gonna share this pussy with me?"

Oh.

Danuwoa was a dirty talker. My core burned as hot as my cheeks. I had never been with a man like this. I'd never heard anyone speak like this. I loved it. It was hot and his mouth was filthy, and I needed it. I needed him.

"Yes," I panted.

He threw his braids over his shoulder, and I watched as he slowly, so fucking slowly, lowered his head to my pussy. He licked it from bottom to top. His moan of pure approval and satisfaction sent my head back and my body arching. I was not Ember; I was a goddess, and this bed was my altar and Danuwoa my most devoted worshipper.

He licked and sucked, and I went wild, searching for the release that was building. He brought his large hand down onto my stomach to hold me in place as he continued to feast, and my muscles went taut as my orgasm ignited and my entire body shook. I came with his name on my lips.

Oh yeah, Danuwoa Colson was the Native Daddy of my dreams. Holy shit. That was the promised earth-shattering orgasm.

I was panting and never craved anything in my life as much as I craved more of Danuwoa. He kicked his boxers off, and his cock jutted free and proud. I grabbed him, my hand circling his river-rock smooth fullness, and when I gave him a firm squeeze, it throbbed in response. He growled before swatting my hand away and jumping out of bed.

"What the fuck?" I cried in outrage. I was *not* done with him.

He knelt before his backpack, and I admired his braids falling on his naked back, long dark arrows pointing down to his perfect bare ass.

"Got it!" He turned around, shaking a condom foil back and forth in his hand, his smile still glistening from my arousal.

He stood and ripped the foil open. "Close your mouth," he chuckled.

I was nearly drooling, watching as he rolled the condom over his hardness. The foil was discarded behind him, and like a predator, he stalked toward the bed, crawling on his hands and knees, pushing aside the fluffy duvet until he was above me.

I let my legs fall open even wider, inviting him to settle his full weight on top of me. Creator, did we fit perfectly. He settled between my hips, rubbing his cock up and down and side to side on my slick slit. The anticipation was killing me. He did his job. I was a Slip 'n Slide down there. I hooked my ankles around his ass, using my strength to nudge him to give me what I wanted.

He kissed me then. Deeply. As he speared my mouth with his tongue, I felt myself stretch to accommodate his fullness and length. He slid farther and farther until he was at the hilt. Danuwoa released my lips and hissed a satisfied breath.

He slid out and back in, nature guiding our rhythm as we explored each other. He was languid, savoring the feel of me. I kissed where his neck met his shoulder, and he slammed home hard. *Yes.* Just yes. I needed more of that. I bit him right where I had just kissed, and it unleashed Danuwoa. In and out, it was a frenzy. I clawed his back and licked his neck, taking all he gave me.

When it was over and we were both spent and covered in sweat, we lay there, our pinkies entwined.

THE RAYS OF DAWN FILTERED IN THROUGH THE FILMY WHITE drapes, and I woke up as content as a cat lying next to Danuwoa. He was a stomach sleeper. I was a drooler. What a pair we made. I turned to my side to face him, his arm and a wayward braid draped over me.

Today we would go home. Would things go back to how they were? Would they continue to grow into something more? Or were we friends with benefits? God, Auntie would gloat in my face.

Danuwoa's finger pressed the scrunched-up space between my eyebrows. "Shh. It's too early to be thinking that hard."

I swatted away his finger, but he grabbed my hand, playfully biting me before placing a kiss.

I giggled because after last night, I was surprised it wasn't all a very vivid dream.

"So?" he asked me.

"So what?"

"Care to share what has you up so early, worrying?"

"I was just thinking about what happened last night . . ." I let my voice trail off. He had to be thinking the same thing as me, right?

"What about last night?" He grabbed me from behind my waist and pulled me closer to him.

He was going to make me say it. "If we would be having repeats in the future."

"I think you can feel that a repeat performance is a definite possibility." He shook his hips to illustrate the fact that he was rock-hard.

"That was not what I meant! I meant when we get home, how would things continue?"

"We just keep seeing each other until we don't want to see each other. That's usually how these things work."

"Without seeing anyone else?"

"No one else." His expression was serious.

"What about work?"

He kissed me before answering, "Work has nothing to do with us. We can keep things professional around the office."

And that was the last of the conversation before we lost ourselves in each other's bodies again, tangled limbs, the duvet and pillows on the floor. We had a few hours before the final meeting started and we flew back home to reality, and I was going to make the most of it.

Twenty-Six 🪶

"HOW!" MR. STEVENSON SAID AS HE BEGAN HIS CLOSING RE-marks on the stage, wearing a fake war bonnet made of dyed chicken feathers. A gift from Sasha Storm Cloud.

It was beyond offensive using this "Hollywood Injun" greeting and wearing this costume. It was a caricature of a Great Plains chief.

He continued, "Our quarterly sales are through the roof, and I couldn't be more proud of this team. This has been our most successful and productive quarterly meeting. With your copies of *Ask for Forgiveness Later*, I know this second half of the year is going to be the best in Technix history!" I zoned out, not listening to the rest of what he had to say.

What had we missed at Sasha Storm Cloud's spiritual awakening class? Danuwoa was sitting in front of the stage with all the sound equipment, but he looked over his shoulder at me: *What the fuck?*

I was sitting next to the area sales manager from our Austin office, Tina. I leaned over and asked, "Was there a peace pipe ceremony yesterday too?"

Tina giggled. "No, but we did do a lot of chanting and burning sage, and we wrote down the things we wanted to let go of on tiny pieces of paper."

Damn, I was gonna have to wear those heels for Danuwoa. Oh no, poor me.

Apart from having to share a room with Danuwoa, which, after last night and early this morning, I didn't mind at all, this meeting was a success. My first ever business trip and big conference was done. Danuwoa had to pack up all of his computer equipment, so I stepped outside to say goodbye to this magical place. A place I never would have been able to afford to come to in my life if it were not for this job. I walked along the sandy path to get one last glimpse of the ocean and the beach that changed everything for Danuwoa and me.

"Hey, hey, EA!" Kyle's singsongy voice floated to me over the breeze. I turned around, bracing myself for an innuendo or something about that elevator kiss he witnessed.

"Hi," I said, and lifted my hand in a small wave. I hoped my smile didn't look too fake or annoyed.

"Great work this week." Kyle leaned against the wood of the fence, propping his elbows behind him. His stance was casual and nonchalant. My intuition was sounding the alarm. I didn't trust whatever camaraderie he was trying to develop with me.

"Thanks, I should head back inside and do a final check before the flight back home." I stepped away from the fence, turning from him and the beautiful ocean.

The sound of Kyle's laugh followed me as I went to prepare for our departure.

Things went from bad to worse when Danuwoa and I piled into the back of the SUV taking us to the hangar with Mr. Stevenson. Kyle hopped in next to our boss and threw me a wink. Danuwoa was busy on his cell phone filtering through his help desk tickets to send to colleagues in the office by priority.

I pretended to be very interested in my event binder. Was it too late to go into the career of acting? Because I thought I nailed it. On the plane, Danuwoa and I claimed the same seats we had on the way here. Kyle sat up front with Mr. Stevenson, and I thought that would be the end of our interactions. But ten minutes after takeoff, Mr. Stevenson barked for Danuwoa to fix the Wi-Fi and his laptop.

I was left alone in my window seat when Kyle plopped down next to me. I glanced up at Danuwoa, who gave me a small shrug before looking back down at Mr. Stevenson's computer.

"Got any work to do on the flight?" Kyle asked me.

"I have some emails to catch up on once Dan gets the Wi-Fi back up."

"Cool, cool. I have an assignment for you since you have an accounting background and great attention to detail." He smiled and winked. I was sure he thought it was charming, but it made me want to ignore what he had to say.

The part about accounting was intriguing, as I still very much wanted to learn more about it before I could reenroll in school. I missed the mundanity of straight accounting work. Being on a private jet was a novelty, but I really enjoyed having a job that was predictable.

"Flattery will get you everywhere—what is it?"

"We have all the executive expenses that need to be coded and looked at. We wouldn't want to be audited, and right now things are a bit of a mess. It shouldn't take too long."

"I can review expenses." I smiled, relieved he had not once tried to bring up Danuwoa and me kissing.

"Excellent. When we get back, I'll send you all the deets." He drummed his hands on the table before hopping up and heading back up front.

Before long, Danuwoa folded himself into his seat, breathing a long exhale.

"We will not be having Wi-Fi on this flight," he said as he rubbed his face.

"Is he pissed?" I asked.

"Definitely."

"It's not like we can just land the plane to figure it out," I offered.

"I felt like he half expected me to offer to climb out of the plane like Tom Cruise to fix something," he whispered and leaned toward me over the table.

I giggled and said, "Hopefully he falls asleep soon."

"Ember!" Mr. Stevenson barked from his seat at the front of the plane. I spoke too soon. The man was awake and alert and . . . in a mood.

"Yes, sir?" I asked when I approached his seat.

He lifted himself up slightly and leaned back into the seat, digging his hand into his pocket. "Here." He handed me a handful of wadded pieces of paper. "My receipts. Don't lose them."

"Okay," I said and stood there, waiting to see if he needed anything else, and my presence must have irritated him.

"That's all." He snapped open his copy of the *Wall Street Journal* from the hotel, and I was dismissed.

I gingerly opened each crumpled receipt to flatten and sort. Just how was I supposed to explain new headphones as a business expense? I was going to have to review the expense policy again, because I was certain we did not cover alcoholic beverages for employees unless at a catered event like what Natalie planned. I paper-clipped and filed them away in my binder for safekeeping.

THE ADRENALINE HIGH FROM THE LONGEST AND MOST EXCITING three days of my life crashed and burned. Danuwoa's energy was subdued too as he gave me a ride back home. He said we would see each other exclusively, but did he mean it? Men in Oklahoma said a lot of things and made a lot of promises in the comfort of a bed, but with real-life pressures, were these promises real?

The butterflies that never seemed to go away in his presence fluttered in my stomach. They had me hoping that Danuwoa's words truly meant something. That Danuwoa was someone I could actually count on.

He parked around the corner from my complex on the street, away from the streetlight. With the time zone difference, it had been dark when we had finally landed. I opened the door to get out, but he yanked the hem of my shirt and pulled me back. "Get over here," he said before he conquered my mouth. I sighed. It had been a long day and nearly ten hours since his last kiss. My body had quickly grown addicted to it.

Under the cover of night and the intimacy of being alone in the tight quarters of his truck, I gave him a kiss that promised more. Danuwoa's expert hands slid up my thigh and under my skirt, sweeping a teasing caress over my underwear.

I pulled away from his lips. "Inside. Now."

We were running up the street, my hot pink duffel bag strapped across Danuwoa's chest like a fluorescent bandolier bouncing up and down from his quick steps. Before I could climb up the stairs, he stopped and pulled me into his embrace for another kiss that I felt down to my toes. Even tearing ourselves apart for a few minutes to get inside, on a bed, and behind four walls was physically painful. We needed each other's kiss like we needed the air to breathe. We were insatiable lust incarnate, and I didn't care.

In a passionate haze, we made it to my front door. I fumbled for my keys, Danuwoa's hands wrapped around my lower waist, pressing me close to feel his arousal.

"I love that key chain, some might even say it introduced us," he whispered against my neck.

I giggled and opened the door.

What I saw made me drop my keys. It was like a bucket of ice water hit me. My mood and thoughts about the things I wanted to do to Danuwoa in my bedroom evaporated. Because sprawled out on our couch was Sage. To further add to my annoyance, he was wrapped up in my favorite fleece blanket, which he had taken from my bed.

"Just friends my ass. Auntie and I were right! You were lying about that. I can't wait to tell her." Sage laughed as a lit cigarette hung from his mouth.

"What are you doing in my house?" I marched up to him, yanking the cigarette away from him.

"Hey!" he yelled in outrage, sitting up to reveal he was lounging in just his boxers.

"We don't smoke in the house." I coughed for the dramatic effect. The smell of the smoke was nasty. I ran to the kitchen, past a confused and awkwardly standing Danuwoa, who was using my pink duffel bag to hide his hard-on, which no doubt was quickly deflating after this episode. I ran the cigarette under the water in the faucet since we didn't own an ashtray. What a clusterfuck.

"Where's Joanna?" I yelled over the sound of the running water.

"She said she'd be back soon," Sage yelled, attitude coating his tone. As if he had anything to be put out by. Family drama was not something I wanted to deal with tonight, and I especially didn't want to do it with Danuwoa as our audience. As much as it pained me, I had to send him home so I could deal with Sage.

"Can I talk to you for a moment?" I asked Danuwoa. He nodded, setting my duffel on the floor before following me to my bedroom, where I closed the door to shut us away from Sage.

I looked longingly at my full-sized bed. It was probably better to pump the brakes tonight anyway. There was no way Danuwoa would fit in my bed. His feet would hang off it. I remembered our night at the hotel. Could it really have been only last night? So much had happened in such a short span of time.

"I'm sorry," I whispered, looking at the center of his chest. I was unable to meet his eyes, worried I'd find only disappointment there. I felt like all I did was disappoint people.

His hand lifted my chin. "Why are you sorry? Family comes first, Ember. I don't care, because I know I'll have you in this bed and mine. It doesn't matter if it's tonight, tomorrow, or a month from now."

"I really hope we don't have to wait a month," I said, smiling.

He laughed and kissed me. It was a sweet, tender kiss. This one was meant to reassure me and give me strength to face whatever drama Sage brought into my life.

The front door slammed, and Joanna's loud voice boomed, "Wear some damn clothes in our home!"

"I better clear out," Danuwoa whispered as he caressed my cheek.

"Yeah." I stood there, rooted in the same spot.

"Yeah," Danuwoa answered. I swear we had hearts in our eyes, and I didn't hate it.

I stood up on my tiptoes and kissed him again, a sweet good-bye, but my lady bits were screaming in protest. They too wanted Danuwoa on my bed doing all the things.

Before I could act on those wants, I pulled away and opened my door. Danuwoa lightly swatted my butt and winked at my glare.

I walked into my living room arena, getting ready to fight and kick Sage out of my home. Why he was here and for how long I didn't know, but I knew Joanna had something to do with it. The feeling of betrayal fueled my anger.

Danuwoa waved to Joanna and escaped out the door. He was lucky; I too wanted to escape this showdown, but I had to participate.

"Just what exactly are you doing on our couch?" I asked Sage, but I looked directly at Joanna eating her McDonald's fries dipped in ranch.

"He said he needed a place to crash for a few nights while he gets a job," she answered me, mouth full of mashed fries.

"I got a lead on some construction work, and Joanna is gonna pay me to help her at the jewelry show at the fairgrounds this weekend," Sage said, stretching out on the couch, arms behind his head. At least he had put a shirt on.

I looked back at Joanna and rolled my eyes.

"I'm not going to let you live with me, Sage. I have boundaries." I stomped to my forgotten duffel bag and took it to my room.

Sage followed me.

"I didn't say anything about living with you. I just need some help until I'm on my feet. Jobs pay better in the city, and there isn't much going on in Ada right now."

"Whatever." I refused to look at him. I yanked my dirty clothes out of the bag. Sand escaped the folds of my wadded-up white dress, leaving a small pile on my comforter. It was a reminder of all that had happened between Danuwoa and me. That's what I wanted to be doing right now, exploring more of what we could be—not babysitting my delinquent brother as he used me and my friend for the hundredth time.

I nudged Sage with my shoulder to get him out of my way. He moved a quarter of an inch, and I wanted to scream.

"Did you read Dad's letter yet?" he asked me as he crossed his arms, judgment coloring his face.

Now that made me scream. "God! Of course not, and I'll never read it. I don't care what he has to say. Unless there is a check in there that can cover all my school expenses, then I want nothing to do with it or him."

Sage had the decency to look embarrassed. He looked down in shame and muttered, "I told you I was sorry."

"Saying sorry while in jail so that Auntie and I paid the commissary isn't a real apology, Sage."

"I meant it. I mean, I still mean it! Why are you like this? You think you're better than me. You always have because you graduated high school and now have a fancy job," he scoffed, escaping back to the living room.

"Fancy job?" I followed him on his heels. "Let's get this straight. Yes, I did finish high school, but it's not like we went to some fancy private school, or I got the best grades. I worked hard, Sage. Something you're too scared to do. You give up when things get hard."

"Shut up," he said, pulling his pants over his boxers.

"You'll listen. Without college I couldn't get a job to call me back or interview me. I sacrificed so much to save that money for school, and you skipping out on your bail was a slap in my face. I have never had delusions of grandeur or lofty ambitions. I just want to be comfortable and stop struggling." Tears started pouring down my face as I watched Sage shove his feet into his sneakers, once again too afraid to listen to a hard conversation.

I pushed through, continuing to drive my points home. This was a conversation 365 days in the making. "We cried for you, Sage. When Auntie and I got the call that you had been arrested for drunk driving, we were scared out of our minds. Auntie didn't have the money, and it wasn't for her to pay. You're *my* baby brother, and I didn't think twice about paying the bail. I knew—I thought—you wouldn't betray me and that I would get it back. I was so stupidly wrong. You didn't show up to your hearing and we couldn't find you for two days and I wept again. I wept because my brother cared more about having fun and partying with Tito than me and all I sacrificed and worked for."

Sage rubbed his fists in his eye sockets, as if he was forcing the unpleasant memory away. "I made a mistake. I'm not the same person. I just want to get a job and pay you back, E."

"I'll believe that when I see it. So go ahead, sleep on our couch and get a job. Help Joanna at the fair. But don't ask me for any more favors and don't ask Auntie for any more help."

He left without another word, escaping into the night to cool off. His stuff was still here, so he would be back. He always came back when he had nowhere else to go.

"That was a lot," Joanna said from our tiny dining table.

"Too much?" I asked, sitting down to join her. The energy I used to say all that I had pent up left me depleted. I wiped the tears off my cheeks.

"No. It had to be said, but it still doesn't feel good. It's baby Sage." She squeezed my hand.

"It's baby Sage," I conceded, bitterness rolling off my tongue. We always called him that. He had a baby face and was the cutest kid you'd ever meet. He could charm his way out of anything, and we laughed at his fumbling mistakes growing up, writing it off as baby Sage being baby Sage. "You really offered to pay him to help you?"

"I said I would pay him, but he didn't ask about the currency. He can pick one of my creations as payment. Any money he makes should be going to paying you back. I wouldn't do you like that," she said as she got up to throw away her take-out trash. "Now, forget about Sage. You had IT Guy Danuwoa in your room. What exactly happened on this work trip?" She opened the fridge and took out two cans of beer, placing one in front of me before sitting down, head resting in her hand, eager for the tea.

"Some things . . ." I felt my cheeks heat.

"You fucked the IT guy!"

"Why do you have to be so crass?"

"Oh, so you made long, languorous love to the IT guy?" She rolled her head, exaggerating her voice like an audiobook narrator of the dirtiest romance novels.

I took a swig of the beer, hiding my smile. It tasted like piss, but it was cheap and had alcohol. I took another gulp for this conversation.

"Tell me, is our Native Daddy packing down there? What's his technique? I must know!"

I kicked Joanna's leg under the table. "Oh my god, stop. We had sex and that was that."

"No, your face tells it all. You had a lot of sex. A lot of *good* sex."

"I'm going to bed." I stood and chugged the beer, needing the alcohol to erase the remaining tension from my confrontation with Sage.

"What about the no-dating-colleagues rule at work?"

"It's as you said, we're adults and can keep things professional."

Twenty-Seven

W E WERE NOT PROFESSIONAL. IN FACT, WE WERE THE FUR-
thest thing from professional. I had no idea what it was
about being with Danuwoa, but he unlocked this carefree, joyous
side of me that threw caution to the wind. On Monday, we tried
to keep things PG. We ate lunch in the break room and kept our
hands above the table. We waited until we made it to the parking
lot after work before we started making out in his truck.

By Tuesday, I was ravenous for Danuwoa. It was his fault—his
rumbly voice in my ear before bed inspired sinful dreams. With
Sage still on the couch, we had no repeat performance of our sex
marathon in California. Something had to give to relieve me from
the aching desire for Danuwoa.

This morning was perfect, sunny, and wonderful. Moody Mr.
Stevenson was tolerable, staying behind his foggy glass office until he
left for a meeting. And I had an opportunity. I was alone and it was
my chance to get some much-needed and very legitimate IT help.

My fingers shot off a message.

EMBER CARDINAL: I am having a technical issue on floor 17.

DAN COLSON: Hardware or software?

My heart sank a little that he had changed his name back from Native Daddy without telling me, but my mischievous and emboldened side perked up.

EMBER CARDINAL: Definitely hardware.

DAN COLSON: All right, I'll come up.

I undid the top three buttons of my shirt. My cleavage wasn't much, but it was all for him. Minutes passed by and I tapped my fingers along my desk, impatient to taste his lips. I twisted back and forth in my office chair until Danuwoa finally strode out of the elevator and down the hall toward me.

"Good morning," he said, his knowing look making the butterflies in my stomach flutter. I knew my cheeks were pink.

"Morning," I said and stood up, hesitating over whether I should do what I was planning on doing. I was not the most versed in seduction. I mean, I read a few naughty romance books, so how hard could pulling off a clandestine rendezvous in a supply closet really be? He approached me, his fingers lightly brushing mine. My mind was made up; I wanted to try this. The thrill made me feel powerful, desirable. "There is something wrong with the shredder in the closet."

I slowly walked toward the closet that housed the shredder and extra office supplies, making sure to give Danuwoa a show behind me with the exaggerated sway of my hips. Once he walked in, I closed the door.

If he was shocked at my boldness, he didn't show it. He just stuck his hands into his pockets and looked at me through his eyelashes. Then he bit his lip and grinned. "Hardware? A bit on the nose," he teased.

"And here I thought I was being *very* creative."

"The moment you got this promotion, I fantasized about *this* exact situation. Though you were always wearing fewer clothes, but oh, the dirty things I would do to you." I was in his arms, lightly biting his earlobe. The way he talked nearly made me come undone.

"What about what I would do to you?" I snaked my arms around his neck and kissed him.

Whatever control I thought I had of this situation was gone. Danuwoa pushed me up against the closed door. His hands slithered down my body, sending ripples of electric current in their wake. My nipples hardened and strained against my bra. His large hands cupped my ass and lifted me. I wrapped my legs around his waist. My stretchy skirt rolled up my thighs, exposing more of myself.

Danuwoa's possessive hands gripped my thighs, holding me in place as he ground his hardened length against my core. Our layers of clothes were a torturous barrier.

I took his face in my hands, deepening the kiss. His right hand moved up my leg and came around my thigh, and then I felt his thumb brush my clit.

I bucked and bit his lip.

"Fuck yeah," he groaned. He kissed my neck before he whispered in my ear, "I've thought about nothing but getting back in this pussy since we checked out of the hotel room in California."

I whimpered and shivered. Danuwoa made me *feel*. His finger moved my panties to the side of my slick slit. He groaned in approval. "So wet for me, god, gvgeyui, Ember. You drive me crazy." His finger filled me, but it wasn't enough. I demanded he give me his mouth again, and our tongues danced as he continued to circle my clit with his thumb and pump his finger in and out.

"Danuwoa," I breathed. I was getting close.

"I want my name on your tongue when you come," he growled.

"I want you to come on my tongue." I kissed him from his jaw down to where the collar of his shirt met his neck. What I said unleashed an animal. Danuwoa was relentless as he pinned me to that door, one hand working me as his other desperately grabbed my breast.

There was a distant ding outside the door.

"Did you hear—Danuwoa!" I shattered against his hand. I bit into his shoulder to silence the uncontrollable ecstasy.

"Ember!" There was no mistaking who that voice belonged to. There was no time to savor the moment.

"Is that—"

"Put me down," I whispered, cutting Danuwoa off.

He gently lowered me, and thank goodness for the door, because my legs were like jelly after that. I pushed my skirt down and buttoned up my shirt all the way. I looked to Danuwoa for approval, but he was adjusting his hard-on.

He looked like he had just fucked in the closet, which meant I looked like I had just been fucked.

Fuck!

"He wasn't supposed to be back for at least an hour," I whispered, already panicking.

Danuwoa got down on the floor on his hands and knees.

"What are you doing? We are about to be caught," I hissed.

"No, we're not." He held up the black cord to the shredder. He had unplugged it. Genius.

"Is my hair okay?" I asked, self-conscious and a little scared that this was the end of our Technix careers.

Danuwoa stood and took my hair and put it all in front of my shoulders. "That should be fine."

"Ember?!" Mr. Stevenson's voice boomed with impatience.

I took a breath to steady myself and then I opened the door. "Yes, Mr. Stevenson?"

"Oh, there you are! Have you seen my thermos?"

"No, sir. I didn't see you bring it today."

"Oh, that would explain it. Well, let's get to it," he said, looking past me. I turned my head, and Mr. Adams was waiting by the elevator.

Then Danuwoa exited the supply closet. "Good morning, Mr. Stevenson, Mr. Adams." He nodded his greeting.

"Dan, what are you doing up here?" Mr. Stevenson asked.

"Oh, I had problems with the shredder, and he fixed them," I jumped in. "Thank you," I said to Danuwoa.

"It's my pleasure." He waved his goodbyes and escaped toward the elevator.

Mr. Stevenson waved Mr. Adams to his office. The door closed, and the glass walls turned opaque. My heart was hammering, and my blood was rushing in my ears.

That was too close.

Danuwoa smiled and gave a small wave as he stood in the elevator waiting for the doors to close. His eyes said, *This isn't over.*

I wished I had a flirty comeback, but I'm sure the last thing Danuwoa saw before the doors closed him in was me looking like a deer in the headlights.

What the hell had I done? We were moments away from being

caught. It was stupid and could never happen again. I had a car payment now and needed to keep this job. If I was fired after less than three months, who would hire me? My track record would be shit, on top of the fact I had to lie to get my foot in the door. Joanna couldn't keep pretending to be my past employers.

I sat down at my desk, my head in my hands. There was an ache of unsatisfied lust, and now my brain was in overdrive. I had to tell Danuwoa that we could only see each other away from Technix, like miles away and hours after work and on the weekends. No more secret sexy hookups in the office.

I worked on autopilot, coding receipts to create a travel and expense report, highlighting the ones I needed more details on. I would get to see Danuwoa again during lunch in the break room. We shared this dirty little secret, and I was going to have to find a way to break it to Danuwoa that he needed to lower his expectations. I didn't think he would mind, but how could he not fantasize about what we would do next? My dirty mind fantasized about him bending me over this exact desk.

Lunch. I needed lunch.

Phoebe was still at her desk when I exited the elevator with my lunch to head to the break room.

"Hi, Phoebe." I smiled and waved.

"Hi, *Ember*," she said, drawing out my name. Her tone was overly nice, like those fake friendly voices people have as they try to ruin your life. I braced myself for what was coming next. "How was the conference trip? I heard you and Dan got *friendly*. How does Ron feel about that?"

"What?"

"A little birdie told me you were seen getting cozy in Santa Barbara. Is it over with your boyfriend, Ron?"

Shit. Right. My boyfriend.

"No, Ron and I are very much going strong. I'm not sure what you heard, but it must have been vastly exaggerated."

I added fake boyfriend Ron to my ever-growing list of little white lies. That one was harmless, and I doubted Danuwoa would care. Now that we were dating, I'd have to come clean and tell him that I didn't actually play in the Little Big Horns league. I'm sure he was just gonna love that.

Phoebe held up her lunch pail. "Let's go eat," she said, smiling as if she were letting me off the hook easily about the Dan thing just this once.

Danuwoa was sitting at our usual table, spooning soup into his mouth and scrolling on his phone. Phoebe swooped in and took the seat next to him. I sat across from them with a hint of a smile on my lips, and his smile mirrored mine. We shared a dirty little secret. One that couldn't be repeated, but sharing our private rendezvous was a thrill.

"We need to do another happy hour. It's not fair y'all got to go party in California," Phoebe lamented as she licked the strawberry yogurt off her spoon.

"Sure, where do you want to go? O'Connell's?" Danuwoa asked.

"No, it's boring. I don't want to watch the guys play darts or pool and wait forever for a turn. We need something fun and exciting."

"What about bowling?" Danuwoa asked, giving me the most mischievous look.

"I love bowling! You have a place in mind?"

"I do—a fun place with cheap beer."

I kicked his shin under the table, and he tried to hide his grimace and continued anyway, "Bobby Dean's Bowling Alley and Bar."

"Sounds perfect. I'm gonna send an email. Let's all go tomorrow. Ember, you should bring your boyfriend."

Danuwoa's chest puffed up.

"I want to meet this Ron fella," she finished before floating happily away.

"What now?" His face looked like he'd sucked a very sour lemon.

"Nothing," I said, wadding up my napkin.

"What the fuck, Ember?" He looked concerned.

"Not here and not now. I'll explain . . . later."

A hand clamped down my shoulder. It made me jump, and I turned around to see who it was and why they thought it was okay to just come up and touch someone like that. It was Kyle. Of course it was Kyle.

"Done with lunch?" he asked me.

I nodded, pointedly looking at his hand, waiting for him to release me.

"Great, follow me and we can discuss that project I mentioned." He massaged my shoulder as he said it, and it had my hackles rising.

I looked at Danuwoa from the side of my eye. He was frozen, glaring at Kyle's offensive hand on my shoulder. Before he could do anything to add further speculation that we were in a relationship, I shot out of my seat, and Kyle had no choice but to release me.

Kyle smiled and carried on as if nothing uncomfortable or awkward had just happened. "California was a blast, wasn't it?" It was a pointed question at Danuwoa.

"Let's go. I have to do some work for Mr. Stevenson and don't want him missing me for too long." I ushered Kyle toward the exit, giving Danuwoa an apologetic look.

His return glare said, *You have some explaining to do.*

I rolled my eyes. *Yeah, yeah, yeah.*

Phoebe strode in, carrying a pack of paper towels, and winked at Kyle. "Happy hour tomorrow?" she asked.

"Hell yeah, first round is on me," he said as he left the kitchen.

Kyle led me to the glass conference room. He held the door open, ushering me in before shutting it to join me at the table. He leaned back in the swivel chair, arms behind his head, and he flexed his biceps. There was only one man on this planet who could do that and have it not be totally cringe, and he was currently sitting in the break room very confused.

"You know the history of Technix, right?" Kyle said, beginning the conversation.

"Uh, no." I was thrown off.

"I appreciate your honesty," he said with a laugh. "The website is vague, and that was intentional."

"Okay . . ."

"Mr. Stevenson is my uncle. My mom's brother," Kyle clarified, moving to lean forward in his chair, as if we were co-conspirators.

"That must be nice." I mean, what was I supposed to say? Yeah, I got it. He was rich and smart. Did he need a nepotism plaque?

"Our CFO was fired before you came on—he got on my uncle's bad side. You know from cleaning up the accounting with the Portland office closing that it was a nightmare. Things weren't adding up on the accounting side, and the situation was hush-hush."

I had no idea why he thought I would care about this.

He continued, "Uncle Dearest keeps his cards close to his chest, but without Natalie here, all the expense approvals have been piling up, and we need to recode the expenses for the executives."

Ah, okay, now we were back on track with what was relevant to me. "So, this is the expense project?"

"Yup. I need you to go in and approve some expenses. I'll send you receipts and what department to bill them to, then you can just approve on Mr. Stevenson's behalf so we don't have to bother him with it."

"Did Natalie do that?" That was one thing we hadn't gone over in my quick training. She showed me where to submit expenses and what program to use, but we never went over the hierarchy. I'm sure there was a subfolder about it.

"Yeah, all the time. It's summer and he's a busy guy. Plus, the fact that a lot of these are old will piss him off. It's better this way."

I already did all of Mr. Stevenson's expenses, so adding Kyle's wasn't that much more work. He was a total creep, but accounting was something I actually enjoyed, so I liked getting more opportunities to do it. Plus, Natalie was a rock star and had been with Mr. Stevenson since the beginning of Technix, and if she did it, then I would too. I really didn't want to bother her while she was on maternity leave to ask for dumb advice.

"All right, that sounds fine. When does this need to be completed?"

"Before the end of the week would be great for me and the team. Thanks, Ember. I knew I could count on you being a team player."

I rode the elevator back to floor seventeen, wondering if being a team player in this environment really meant just doing a lot of shit work for other people to look good. I glanced at the supply closet and blushed. Had that really only been this morning?

As promised, my inbox was full of forwarded emails with scanned attachments from Kyle. I opened the first one. A $1,700 restaurant bill. Those sales guys really liked to schmooze clients. I immediately closed the window and wrote back, What was the purpose of this dinner and who else joined you?

My desk phone rang, making me jump. **Kyle Matthews.**

"Hi—"

"Listen, it's best if you only call me to discuss this or come down to my desk. I don't like my email being cluttered when it's a simple question. Got it?" His voice, which was overly nice in the conference room, now sounded annoyed and entitled. I was doing him the favor, and he was giving *me* attitude? "I don't have time to go over each expense line by line. Just know finance and sales have a lot of team dinners to discuss corporate strategy and to meet with clients. So all of these expenses are related to that. Uncle Tom and I talk about it all the time, you don't need to worry, just flex that creative accounting muscle. Got it?"

The line went dead before I had a chance to respond. Creative accounting? All righty then, Kyle.

I began filling out the travel and expense documents. How I missed working with numbers. Even though this was a mind-numbingly boring task that included no formulas, I missed using a spreadsheet the way it was supposed to be used. We had department codes for the C-suite: general executive (GE), accounting (ACCT), finance (FIN), sales (SALES), information technology (IT), human resources (HR), and legal (LEGAL). It was fairly straightforward.

There were liquor store receipts, fancy restaurants (I had to look them up online, since never in my life had I heard of them), and sports tickets. This was a headache. I started compiling the charges in chronological order, but I did not feel right submitting a receipt for a new laptop computer without knowing the reason for the purchase. I hesitated for only a moment before I called Kyle's extension again.

"What?" he snapped.

"Did you mean to include the laptop receipt? Is that a personal one that got mixed in? I just know IT hands out laptops—"

"Why don't you ask our good friend Dan? I have a meeting to get to. This is a simple task that needs to get done."

The line went dead, and my blood ran cold. Kyle mentioned Danuwoa too casually, probably to get me to shut up, and that was what I was going to do. No way was I going to drag Danuwoa into this mess. We couldn't afford to draw more attention to ourselves, and I needed this target off my back with Kyle, the fucking prick.

As the interim executive assistant to the CEO, I had access to Mr. Stevenson's signature stamp for approvals or letters, but I'd never used it. I saw Natalie use it one time for a contract she printed out. She didn't even show it to Mr. Stevenson, just slammed that stamp onto the page, then scanned and sent back the contract within five minutes. So that was what I did. I printed the expense report and stamped Mr. Stevenson's signature on the approval line. The ink was thick and blurred on the edges, but the signature was unmistakable. I then scanned and submitted it to the accounting department. Task done.

My phone buzzed.

DAN IT: Ready for round 2?

Just seeing his name on my phone made me forget all about Kyle and the expenses. They were behind me and it was already five. I turned off my laptop, giddy with excitement. I shot off a quick response: Your place or mine?

I was in the elevator when his message came in. Is your brother still on the couch?

My fingers fired off, I'll meet you at your place.

Pack a toothbrush, he reminded me. I guess I would be sleeping over then.

What if I want to share? I cackled as it sent.

DAN IT: **Is that where we are?**

ME: **You tell me.**

I had to put my phone away in my bag as I drove home, clenching my thighs together.

Twenty-Eight

EVEN THOUGH I HAD MY NEW CAR, I WAS STILL PARKING TANdem behind Joanna. It would be nice if I got to park inside to protect the white paint from the elements, and by *elements* I meant the mourning dove shit that rained down from their nests in the carport. But I was about to see Danuwoa's home for the first time, and Mama wanted to get laid. Nothing, not even bird shit, could sour my mood.

I walked through the front door, confronted with the smell of fried bologna and a "Shit!" Sage was cooking. There was one thing that could indeed sour my mood.

I looked in the kitchen to make sure he didn't start a grease fire. He was sucking his finger.

"Hey, welcome home," he said with a huge grin. "I'm making sandwiches." He pointed with the spatula at one complete sandwich on a paper plate, white bread spread with mustard and a few slices of fried bologna. It smelled good, so I nodded and took a fat bite, taking the plate with me to the little café table.

He joined me and we ate in awkward silence. Sage was overly polite and happy. It wasn't that I hated him being here. I loved my brother, and before everything happened, I enjoyed his company. And if I were being honest, having him in my home and next to me meant I could keep an eye on him and that I knew he wasn't getting into trouble. But he was nineteen. I couldn't babysit him forever.

I ate my last bite, wiped mustard from the corners of my mouth, and tried to get up to pack for the night. Sage grabbed my hand. "Hey, wait."

"What?" I sighed, sitting back in the chair. I was tired of fighting.

"I have some exciting news." He let go of my hand and leaned back into his chair like a cocky bastard.

"Did you win the lottery today?"

"No."

"Okay." I got up and walked away.

"Wait," he whined at my heels, following me into my bedroom. I went straight to my closet to get my trusty pink duffel.

"I got a job," he told me. His cocky demeanor was gone, replaced with appropriate humility.

"That's great." My tone was flat, bored. Old me would have been extremely excited and supportive that my baby brother got a job. That was before he screwed me over. Sure, he apologized to me for skipping bail, but what was an apology with no actions to fix what he did? I slammed a pair of sweats into my bag.

"Are you staying at Dan's?" he asked me, as if he had a right to know where I was going.

"Yeah," I said, my tone sharp. It meant the discussion was over.

Sage scratched his head and powered through. "It's getting

pretty serious then? You should bring him to Joanna's jewelry show. Make him buy you something nice," he said with a smile, nodding his head like he had just given the best brotherly advice in the world.

"What is it you want, Sage? I haven't kicked you out on the street or sent you back to Auntie's, so why are you in my room?"

"I'm just trying to get things back to how they were. I messed up, but I want to fix it."

"What's this job then? What's your plan?" I stood, hands on my hips, my duffel forgotten.

"I'm not going to tell you. You'll get all judgy, but I'm gonna get my own place here in the city and work to pay you back."

"I've heard this before. I'll believe it when I see it."

I didn't need his money from his secret, probably shady job. I had a great job now. I needed a brother I could trust to not take advantage of me and, more importantly, Auntie. Auntie, who took us in and needed her social security income to live off, not give to Sage, who refused to be serious and keep a job.

"Sage, go back to school. Get your GED. You have so much potential. You're amazing at art, and you could go to college to learn more and get a job in it. You don't have to hustle or struggle. You don't have to keep making bad decisions. That's what I want for you."

"Fuck, Ember! I'm here saying I have a job that pays a shit ton and plan to start paying you back. You think you're better than me because you finished school and know accounting. Not everyone is good at school or wants to go to college. My life is different, and it's mine to live."

"What kind of life is that? What does this shit ton–paying job have you do? Is it even legal? Are you going to end up back in jail? Don't you want a family and kids someday?"

"I'm not having kids, are you crazy? Stop picking on me and everything I do wrong. You just avoid everything. Sure, you can do math, but when life gets hard, you shut down and pretend it's not happening."

"Hmm, like when you just fucked all and took off, skipping on your bail?" I threw my hands in the air.

"I said I was sorry! Maybe it's a good thing you didn't read Dad's letter. I don't know if I even want you in our life!"

"What life together? You think when he gets out, you're gonna have some magical happy family? Did he promise to play catch? Grow up, Sage. You know what, forget the GED or school. Give me twenty dollars of every paycheck until you pay me back, and then we can both be out of each other's lives."

I snatched my duffel bag and escaped from my room and my apartment. Maybe Sage was right. I did run away to avoid tough things, but I couldn't stand fighting with Sage anymore. I needed my own life to live and enjoy.

As I pulled up to Danuwoa's town house, I pushed all thoughts of Sage and my dad's letter from my mind. Only when my breathing was calm did I remember I forgot my toothbrush.

I turned off the street and into a townhome development tract. Each house was connected and looked exactly the same. There were so many units there was no way I'd be able to remember which one was Danuwoa's by memory. With my luck I'd walk up to the wrong door. Everything about the residential tract was neat and orderly. The light blue paint was fresh on all the units. It was a stark contrast to the shitty brown apartment I lived in.

I walked along the curved cement path, following the numbers until I came upon unit seventeen and knocked on the door.

Danuwoa opened it wearing a fitted white T-shirt, his biceps straining against the fabric. His hair was loose from the braids he wore earlier, and his dark-wash jeans trailed down to his bare feet. This was Danuwoa in the comfort of his own home.

"Meow!" A black-and-white cat wove possessively through Danuwoa's legs. It was staking its claim. I schooled my face into a smile.

"Hi, kitty." I bent to let it sniff my hand. It hissed and took off running up the stairs behind Danuwoa.

"Patches!" he called after his beloved. "Sorry, she's usually more friendly."

"That's okay. I'm just new."

He grabbed my bag and pulled me into him. I crashed into his chest as his mouth gave me the warmest welcome.

"Come in," he murmured against my lips.

The inside of his home was heaven. It felt like a home. Whereas my apartment was furnished with the cheapest, simplest furniture I could find. That table Joanna and I ate on was found next to a dumpster. Danuwoa's home had art on the walls, photographs of him and Walela through the years. It was a movie set of the most perfect, cozy home.

He had a plush gray sectional in front of a large flat-screen television and a rug on the wood floors. I had never known a single man to own a rug before the age of thirty.

"Wow." My brain didn't work. That one word said it all. It was the nicest home I'd ever stepped foot in.

Then I sneezed. And sneezed. And sneezed.

On top of forgetting my toothbrush, I also forgot to take an antihistamine before showing up here.

"You okay there?"

Between sniffles, I asked for a tissue. He showed me to his small bathroom under the stairs. To my horror, it was also the cat's bathroom, which housed her litter box.

I used an obscene amount of toilet paper to wipe up my leaky nose. Danuwoa was a gentleman and left me to my privacy. I hadn't been enclosed in a house with a cat since I was a little girl.

I left the bathroom with a neatly folded square of toilet paper to my nose. "Just some allergies bothering me. Do you have any Benadryl?" I asked through watery eyes. Unless I left his home, I would not be able to escape the cat dander, but my need for Danuwoa was too great. I would suffer through the creepy possessive cat and the allergies it gave me to get another taste of this man.

"Yeah, but it's an old bottle of children's Benadryl."

"That's fine."

He opened the cabinet above his coffee maker, taking out a bottle of thick purple salvation.

"I don't know if you should take this. It probably won't even work. I can run out and get you some pills."

I took the bottle from his hand and chugged it. "It's fine." I gagged. It tasted foul, but I figured since it was for kids of who knew how many years old, taking that much would make it like a normal dose.

Danuwoa's face looked horrified. "Right . . . okay . . . so . . . want a tour?"

"You're offering to let me snoop? Heck yes!" I gave him back the empty bottle of medicine and took a look around his kitchen.

"I didn't say anything about snooping."

It was too late. I'd already opened every cupboard and drawer to see what he had. You could tell a lot about a person by how they kept their kitchen. Everything had a place, and it was clear he bought the entire Threshold line at Target. I could respect that. If I weren't a miser, I'd shell out the money on that brand too. But Walmart, thrift stores, and garage sales did fine for me.

"Mmm, what is that smell?" I sniffed. My nose was clearing up already.

"Dinner. I have corn chowder cooking in the Crock-Pot. Are you hungry?" He was leaning against the fridge, and he looked so damn sexy in his navy-blue kitchen. Blue house, blue kitchen, blue plates. I believed he let Walela pick out most everything.

"Corn chowder sounds good," I said, and sauntered up to him, wrapping my arms around his neck. I had scarfed down the bologna sandwich, unsure if I should expect a meal. This was all new to me, but the smell coming from the Crock-Pot made my mouth water. I could force myself to eat a bowl, happily.

He threaded his arms around me, setting his hands on the top of my ass.

"You're staying the night, right?" he asked me and kissed that delicious spot where my ear and neck met.

"That depends," I said with a shiver.

"On?"

"What state your bedroom is in."

"Take a look around. I'm a neat freak. I assure you my room is spotless."

I kissed his Adam's apple and whispered, "Not for long."

"This way." He spun me around, slapping my bottom to get us moving out of the kitchen and toward the stairs. The wall had frames in all shapes, sizes, and colors documenting Danuwoa and Walela's family. A perfect example of a nineties family portrait was the focal photo. I stopped to look at it. In it was a middle-aged couple, Danuwoa's mom and dad. His mom had poufy teased bangs, and his dad had a gray braid about half as long as Danuwoa's now. They were sitting down with a baby Walela in their arms. She was wearing a white frilly dress with lace and ribbons.

Kneeling in front was Danuwoa—his hair was short, and he was missing his two front teeth. They looked happy.

"I love this photograph." I touched the glass.

"Me too," he whispered.

"What happened to them?" I asked.

Danuwoa took a deep breath. "My mom died two years after this photo . . . complications from diabetes."

"I'm so sorry." I turned around, wrapping my arms around his waist. So many of our people suffer from the affliction and have left the world too soon.

"Dad died almost four years ago of a heart attack." He gently rubbed my back.

"So, it's just been you taking care of everything for some time now."

"Yeah, but Walela and I make a great team." He kissed the top of my head. "Let's see my room."

I didn't ask anything else. He would share more about his parents and taking care of Walela on his own when he was ready. I turned to head up the stairs the rest of the way, feeling my heart grow three sizes bigger.

He rested his hand on the small of my back and reached around me to open his bedroom door. I was no poet, but I was beginning to think Danuwoa had a poet's soul. The room was masculine in a refined way. Greens and natural wood. At the foot of his king-sized bed was a woven thunderbird blanket. In the corner of the room by the window was a hanging spider plant, meshing the contemporary with nature in an intentional way. Like his bedroom was his own curated museum meant to be his escape and oasis from life. I was really regretting how cheap I'd been.

"This room is beautiful." My smile was shy. What had I ever

done in my life to deserve the attention and affection of a man like Danuwoa?

"Watch this," he said, and pressed the light switch. The shades were automated and began to close. At the same time, on the wall opposite his bed, a projector screen lowered.

"You created your own cinema in your bedroom?"

"I like my comforts." He watched me as I walked around the room.

"Do you have an old-timey popcorn machine hiding in your closet?" I slid the door open to check just in case. His clothes were neatly hung, and his shoes lined the floor.

"And make my fresh linens smell like fake butter? No, thank you." He just smiled at me as I made my way to his connecting bathroom, then I set my duffel on the ground outside the door.

It was just as I expected. It was white. Clean. You would never in a million years think a bachelor lived here. I left the bathroom, surveying the bed. "So, you just created the perfect Neflix-and-chill room?"

His laugh sent goose bumps up my arms as he came and circled his arms around my waist. "Netflix is the furthest thing from my mind."

Danuwoa slowly brought his face to mine and nuzzled the place behind my ear. It was at once endearing and sexy as he nipped my earlobe, and I let out a small yelp that he silenced as he captured my mouth. We were tangled limbs. "Wait," I panted as I pushed him away.

"Sorry, too fast?"

"What? No." I smiled. "I need to change real quick."

"Unnecessary, as I want you naked." He licked my neck as his hands trailed down my curves.

"You'll like this." I extracted myself from his arms and locked myself in the bathroom.

Now was the time to make good on the bet. I slipped out of my orthopedic flats and slid my skirt down. Without my cardigan, I was in a white tank top and my hot-pink panties—the sexiest ones I owned. If I was going to keep this up with Danuwoa, and I seriously hoped I would, I needed to invest in better lingerie.

I sat down on the closed toilet and began the process of lacing up my sparkly heels, weaving the straps up and around my calves and tying them in a bow at the crease of my knee. Task complete, I stood and yawned. I had to be quick about this before the Benadryl knocked me on my ass.

The room was still dim, and Danuwoa was fiddling with his phone right where I had left him. He looked up at me and gulped. His eyes devoured me from head to toe.

He put his phone away in his pocket.

"Walela is babysitting, so we have the house to ourselves for a few hours," he whispered, his voice husky and an octave lower than before.

"Great." I bit my lip and walked what I hoped was a sexy walk. I went slowly because I hadn't worn heels in forever. I was back in his arms kissing his lips, taking my time to taste him.

Seconds or minutes later, I couldn't tell, the kiss turned fierce and hungry. We ripped at each other's clothes, stumbling our way to the end of the bed. We reached our destination and Danuwoa fell back effortlessly, while I crashed down on top of him. The awkwardness did nothing to slow down his kisses and nips.

Danuwoa's ocean of a bed would be tangled sheets by the time we were through. I would never tire of exploring his body. His touch seared my soul and had ruined me for all others. He was a drug, and I was waiting for my next fix.

Our clothes were gone, and I was left in only the strappy, sparkly heels. He stared at my face, his eyes saying everything we didn't dare utter out loud. I closed my eyes and kissed him again.

I couldn't acknowledge it. Not yet. It was like if I voiced it, it could be ripped from me. I'd never had a real relationship before. I'd never experienced love, and I didn't want to examine this feeling too closely just yet. My heart was so full in my chest. Before my brain could start analyzing my feelings, Danuwoa flipped me onto my stomach, lifted my hips, and kissed me on my core.

I waited there, bare ass up, as I heard the telltale sound of the condom foil ripping open. There were only a few seconds before Danuwoa slid home inside me. California was not a fluke, and it made this sharing of bodies even better. Our chemistry and passion hadn't dwindled. I lowered myself onto my elbows and stretched my back like a cat, taking all Danuwoa was giving me.

He was giving more than just himself physically. I could feel in his touch that the connection we had ran deeper than just carnal urges. His fervent attention was driving me closer to the precipice. It was more intense than in California, and I knew it was because Danuwoa and I made sense. I never believed in love at first sight or soulmates, but this chemistry between us almost made me a believer.

When I was pushed over the edge, I saw stars. Afterward, we cuddled together, bare skin and all, with our legs entwined. He played with my fingers, and I listened to the steady drum of his heartbeat. Never in my life had I felt so at peace. There were no constant worries swimming around my head. It was just Danuwoa and me in that moment, and it was so simple and so beautiful.

SOMETHING LANDED ON MY FACE IN THE MIDDLE OF THE NIGHT. I shot up from the bed, disoriented for a second from the unfamiliarity of the room. To my left lay Danuwoa, shirtless and on his stomach. I couldn't even remember falling asleep. Between our epic lovemaking and eating dinner, I must have passed out cold from the children's Benadryl.

Patches! The damn cat had pounced on my face and was now kneading my pillow, her eyes glowing in the dark. My nose was runny again, and my eyes itched like crazy. Sharing a pillow with a cat was not my definition of a peaceful night's sleep. I scooted farther down the mattress, giving the entitled cat as much of the pillow as possible.

As I lay there trying to get back to sleep, her black tail kept brushing my nose.

Twenty-Nine

WAKING UP IN DANUWOA'S BED WAS A SIN. A DELICIOUS SIN I wanted to repeat every morning. Who needed an alarm when I had Danuwoa kissing me awake with a trail of kisses along the back of my neck?

I turned over to give him better access and felt him abruptly pull away.

"What the fuck happened to your face?" he asked, horrified.

"What do you mean?" I was squinting my eyes in the morning light and tried to open them further and couldn't. I patted my eyes with my fingers and felt the swollen skin. "Oh my god! My face! Is it bad?"

"It's not great, but you're still beautiful to me," Danuwoa said.

What kind of response was that? That sounded like something a man married for over a decade said to his wife when she made the unfortunate choice to cut her hair and give herself the "Karen," all short and angled with the flat-ironed bangs. Not what you told your new girlfriend after banging her brains out the night before and waking up to her face looking like molten lava.

That. Damn. Cat.

"Great." I scooted out of bed, but my clothes were scattered on the floor, so I wrapped myself in the blanket.

"Ember." He paused, waiting for me to look at him.

"Yeah?" I tried to hide my face. I wanted to assess the damage in the bathroom and figure out a game plan.

"Are you allergic to cats?"

"No," I said with a laugh. "Why would you say that? I love cats. This is just hay fever."

"Mm-hmm. It's okay if you're allergic to cats. I won't like you any less."

"Well, I'm not." I got up, taking the covers with me to the bathroom. End of that discussion. I just needed to invest in some heavy-duty antihistamines that were nondrowsy, and everything would be fine with Danuwoa and me and that damn fucking cat.

My face was swollen, and my nose was leaking. What a great first impression to make sleeping at Danuwoa's house. Maybe I should just cop to being allergic to the cat and ask for him to run out and get me something for this.

I started the shower, hoping it would clear my face and my mind, and I took a little longer than I intended to. The steam made my eyes feel better, and I was away from the cat, so I could breathe.

When I came out, Danuwoa had McDonald's coffee and Mc-Muffins on the bed waiting for me.

"You ran out to get me food?" Was this my love language?

"Yeah, and this." He tossed a bottle of Zyrtec at me.

"Thank you!" I squealed while swallowing a pill dry. I was desperate.

Patches sat on the bed, looking smug and content to have ruined my face. This pill had better work before I had to go into the office.

"Would you want to go to the jewelry fair with me this weekend?" I asked him, taking the coffee from the cardboard carrier and sipping the drink.

"Are there some pretty gems you want to buy me?" He was unwrapping his sandwich.

"Ha ha, very funny. Joanna is showing her work, and it's something to do." I took another sip to stop talking.

"You sure your boyfriend . . . Ron, was it? You sure Ron wouldn't mind?" He lifted his eyebrow.

Wow, he couldn't let that go.

"I panicked! Phoebe was asking me about you, saying we looked close, so I tried to get her off our trail. Besides, shouldn't you want it to look like we aren't together so we can keep our jobs?"

"Ember, Technix is a tech startup. I don't know anyone who has actually followed that company rule. I know people who hook up all the time."

"Does upper management know about it?"

"No, but—"

"Exactly. I work directly for the CEO. I need to keep this job, and you need to keep yours."

"Yeah, I really do," he conceded. "I got this mortgage at the beginning of the year." He took another bite of food. I could almost see the gears turning in his head while he thought all this over.

"This is why we can't show affection at the office anymore. We were almost caught yesterday."

He leaned back on the bed, folding his leg so that his sneaker-clad foot rested on top of his knee. "That kind of adds to the thrill of it, don't you think?"

"Danuwoa," I warned.

He rolled his eyes. "I don't want to hide you or us. That makes me feel dirty."

"We aren't hiding, just protecting this and our jobs."

"Howa." He blew out a breath. *Fine*, his eyes said.

"All right, tonight at the bowling alley we are just friends, got it?"

"Oh, I definitely do. Wouldn't want old-ass Ron to get jealous."

"We don't have to worry about that. The Little Big Horns don't play on Wednesdays, and I have an idea. Make sure you bring an extra shirt tonight."

I WALKED INTO BOBBY DEAN'S AND WAS COMFORTED BY THE FA-miliar sound of bowling balls crashing into pins and the smell of cheap beer and floor wax. I missed this place. Not the being-paid-crap part, but I missed how this bowling alley felt like home and all my friends were there.

Joanna was squirting nacho cheese on chips for the early evening rush. I led Danuwoa and Phoebe to the register to rent shoes, and we got two lanes next to each other.

"This place is perfect! Three-dollar beer? How did you hear about this place, Dan?" Phoebe asked while we tied the laces of our bowling shoes.

"I took my sister here before."

Phoebe nodded at him in understanding. He didn't look at me and was sitting next to Phoebe on the other side of my lane. It was my rule, but I missed him being close to me.

"Everyone should be getting here in a few minutes," she said, and got up to test her shoes.

"You have that extra shirt?" I asked Danuwoa.

"Yeah, you gonna wear it?" His voice was laced with promise, and I hated to disappoint him, but for my plan to work, I needed the shirt.

"Nope, I am gonna borrow it for a few hours."

"Hey, hey, hey!" Kyle called out, walking toward us, the accounting bros on his heels.

"Where's everyone else?" Ryan asked, slapping a high five with Danuwoa.

"On their way. You promised our first round, Kyle," Phoebe said, standing with her hands on her hips.

Kyle had just plopped on the bench, spread out, and taken up as much room as he could. "I did, I did, point the way to the bar." He got up and followed Phoebe.

Martin scooted next to me on the bench, changing his shoes. "You know, I'm pretty good at bowling."

"Is that so?" I could feel Danuwoa's eyes on me, but they didn't feel jealous, they felt curious and amused at Martin's attempt to flirt with me. "How about the first one to make a strike doesn't have to pay for a single drink?"

"If you wanted to buy me a drink, all you had to do was ask," he said with a wink. He sprang up and started groping the balls, measuring their finger holes and weights.

"Careful, Ember. Martin plays a lot of virtual bowling on his Switch," Nick warned as he leaned back next to Danuwoa.

"Not virtual bowling!" I put my hands against my cheeks, feigning distress. "What's a girl to do against virtual bowling?"

"Hell," Martin muttered and rolled his eyes.

"Let's get our names in." Danuwoa went up to the scoring system and programmed *Bucky* in the first slot using the toggle.

"Who's Bucky?" Nick asked.

"That's me." I fake giggled and gave Danuwoa my crazy *WTF?* eyes. "It's a childhood nickname."

He put in all our names and left Kyle in the last slot. If more people from Technix showed up, they could get another lane or just drink and mill about. We got the game going, and since I was first, I rolled and got a strike. Danuwoa hooted and hollered, still standing behind the automatic scorer. I gave a silly bow to Martin, as he was up next and owed me a drink. He rolled a gutter ball, and on his spare, he hit two pins.

"So much for virtual bowling," I teased, laughing.

Martin waved me away and sat down on the bench.

"You can go get me that drink now," I said, my voice dripping with honey.

"Oh! Shit's embarrassing. Sorry, man." Nick got up for his turn.

I sidled over to Danuwoa, who was standing with his arms crossed in front of him. He looked a little like he was sulking. "Having fun?" I bumped his shoulder.

"Careful, I thought we were keeping our distance," he muttered.

"We can be friendly as friends."

"Here we are!" Phoebe announced as she and Kyle both carried a pitcher of beer in each hand. Phoebe nudged me with her elbow to get the stack of plastic cups from under her arm. "Thanks!"

I started passing out cups while Phoebe filled them with beer.

"Cheers!" she yelled.

"Yeah! Whoop! Whoop! Whoop!" Kyle and the bros chugged their beer, quickly refilling.

"Who's up next?" Kyle asked, shaking his golden locks from his eyes.

"Phoebe." Danuwoa pointed with his chin at the scoreboard.

"Okay!" Phoebe took a big sip of her beer and set the cup down on the side table. She picked the pink sparkly ball; it was my personal favorite to use and the lightest weight. She ran up to the line and chucked the ball in the air. It landed hard and bounced once before it rolled into the six and ten pins, knocking them down and leaving the remaining eight untouched. "Poo! Kyle, help me knock the others down," she said, pouting.

Kyle picked up the black bowling ball with his right hand and strutted to the line, all while drinking his beer with his left. He threw the ball out on a spin, and it went wide and into the gutter.

"Kyle! You said you were good at bowling!"

"Better luck next time," Danuwoa said. He left my side and picked up a green ball. He was purposeful in his movements, confident. When he brushed past Phoebe, he whispered in her ear, and she turned bright red.

I locked my spine. I had no reason to be jealous of Phoebe and Danuwoa. I was in Danuwoa's bed last night, and he made it very clear where he stood with our relationship. But he had always been comfortable with Phoebe, and he had known her for far longer. Whatever this feeling was, I hated it.

Danuwoa quickened his steps, stopping at the line with a flourish of his back leg, bending and releasing the ball, his arm staying straight as if it were a compass directing the ball to aim straight and true.

It did. He got a strike.

I clapped. I was enthusiastic but not overly so. I clapped how one would for a coworker who just got a strike. But my smile and my eyes said, *I know what your penis looks like.*

His said, *You know what my penis tastes like.*

I gulped and bit my lip. Nope, I had nothing to worry about with Phoebe. It was just Danuwoa and me in that bowling alley now.

"Ember, where's this boyfriend of yours?" Phoebe's question yanked me from my lusty eye-fucking with Danuwoa.

"Yeah, where's your boyfriend?" Danuwoa asked, smirking.

"He'll be here soon."

"Really?" Danuwoa's smile was incredulous.

"Yep, let's drink." I reached for the beer pitcher.

"How's it going over here?"

Right on time.

"Joanna! Everyone, meet my best friend, Joanna. Joanna, this is everyone." We went through the introductions. Nick, Ryan, and Martin were smitten.

"Wanna drink?" Ryan asked.

"Nah, I'm working."

"You work *here*?" Ryan said "here" like it was gross.

"Yes, proudly." She bit her lip. I pulled her aside, giving her Danuwoa's shirt.

"Tito's game?" I asked.

"Yeah, promised him twenty bucks and a pack of smokes, and he said he'd pretend to be your boyfriend."

"He has to answer to Ron," I whispered.

"You know, this is getting weird, Ember."

"I know. I'll fix it. I just need tonight to go well."

From the corner of my eye, I spotted Tito carrying the wooden handle of the infamous plunger, the bottom rubber part wrapped in a black plastic trash bag.

Oh no.

"Joanna, you gotta get Tito changed quick and make sure no one here notices him."

She turned to where I was looking. "Ugh, the nasty plunger. You owe me so big for this."

"Put it on my tab." I shooed her away. This plan had to work, and after tonight, I'd tell everyone we had a bad breakup and never have to mention my fake boyfriend, Ron, ever again. In theory, this was brilliant. In execution . . . it had a high probability of being shit.

"What's good, *babe!*" Tito, doubling as my fake boyfriend, Ron, yelled over the crashing balls and accounting bros chanting for Kyle to chug his beer.

He had quickly put on Danuwoa's shirt, and he was swimming in it.

"Hey there, *babe.*" I cringed at saying something like this to my brother's best friend. "Come meet everyone."

"This is Ron?" Phoebe beamed, shuffling over.

"Yes, *Ron*, these are my coworkers."

"You look so young!" Phoebe laughed as she shook Tito's offered hand.

"I am young—"

"At heart! He is young at heart. Isn't that right, *babe?*"

"Yeah, just a young rez kid at heart."

"Oh, you're Native American too?" she asked and looked at Danuwoa.

"Yeah, we all are. Me, Ember, her brother, Joanna." He was listing us all casually like it was no big deal—and it wouldn't be, if I hadn't gotten myself in this lying mess. Luckily no one here knew I lied on my job application about that.

"Yup, I bet we all have Native roots here in Oklahoma," I said quickly, trying to change the subject. My fake-ass laugh was starting to sound desperate.

Danuwoa stood there nursing his beer. His eyes were highly entertained, and I refused to meet them, or else I'd break.

Bowling shouldn't be this stressful.

"We're out of beer!" Kyle's voice broke through our conversation.

"Oh, I'll get some," Phoebe called over her shoulder.

I pulled Tito a little away from our group. "Thank you for doing me this favor."

"Twenty bucks and smokes, remember?"

"Yeah, you'll get it. Do not mention any personal information. Just keep this super light and casual, okay?"

"I can be a great pretend boyfriend. I know how you're always single. I feel bad for you." He wrapped his arm around my shoulder. I tried to wiggle away, and he held me tighter. "We are a happy couple, remember?" he whispered in my ear, and it made me want to gag.

"Get off, I'm not a charity case—this is just so people leave me alone at work."

"Everything good over here?" Danuwoa asked, towering half a foot over Tito.

"We're great, man, just boyfriend-girlfriend stuff." Tito smiled at me like he was my knight in shining armor.

"Let's just bowl, okay?" I slithered out of Tito's hold and looked into Danuwoa's eyes, pleading for him to drop this.

"Nice shirt," he said to Tito.

I wanted to die. I created this mess, and hindsight was always twenty-twenty. If I could go back in time, I would have chosen much differently.

"You got something to say to me?" Tito got in Danuwoa's face.

"Okay, let's drop this. Don't you have somewhere to be?" I whispered into Tito's ear.

"I'm watching you, Kronk," Tito said as he pointed his fingers to his eyes and then to Danuwoa's.

Once he disappeared into the crowded bowling alley, I let out a breath. What. A. Night.

"Did he just call me the henchman from *The Emperor's New Groove*?"

"Did he? I need a drink." I tried to go around Danuwoa to the beer pitcher. It was sitting on the small table, and it was empty. Damn.

"What's going on? Who was that guy, and why did you give him my shirt?"

"He's a family friend who works here. It's not a big deal."

"You know, Ember, I'm starting to feel like maybe it is. Why not tell people you are single or, better yet, that we're together?"

"Shh!" I looked around, but Phoebe and Kyle were still at the bar, and the accounting bros were swiping right and left on Tinder together, our bowling game completely forgotten. "We talked about this," I pleaded.

"This is starting to get really fucking weird. I don't like it." He stomped to the seats and sat down.

"We're back!" Phoebe called. Kyle was looking a little worse for wear. I think we were all drinking too much of this cheap beer.

"Yo, Ember, take care of these receipts for me." Kyle handed me a soggy wet wad of paper. Gross.

"Kyle, I don't think this counts as a work expense."

He ignored me.

The night needed to end. Danuwoa refused to look at me, and this was *so* not how I wanted tonight to go.

Things finally wound down. Outside in the parking lot, as everyone was saying their goodbyes, I approached Kyle.

"Hey, I don't think I can expense this stuff. This wasn't work-related."

Kyle looked up and around, then took me by the arm away from everyone else. "What?"

"You gave me all the receipts from tonight. It goes against company policy. This wasn't a preapproved work function," I explained.

"Did I ask you for your opinion?" he snapped. He had sobered right up.

"Well . . . no."

"I told you to expense the receipts, so expense them. That's all you have to do."

"But—"

"No buts. Do you think my uncle will take kindly to the news that his new assistant was fucking the IT guy while at a work event?"

The air left my lungs as if Kyle's words were a punch to my gut. I was no prude, but the way he said that made me feel cheap and vulgar.

"We only kissed!" That he knew of.

"And who do you think he is going to believe? Family or the help?"

Did he just *threaten* me?

"I . . ." I couldn't finish the sentence. I looked down at the ground, truly afraid. "I'm sorry." In my experience with angry men, a demure apology usually cooled them off. The cheap beer was curdling in my stomach, and I wanted to be anywhere but here. All the lies, getting Tito's help, offending Danuwoa. It was all pointless, because I was trapped being Kyle's bitch, and to protect Danuwoa, I'd do anything.

"Good. I don't want to hear about it again." Kyle walked away.

Ubers were called, and our small happy hour crew dispersed. It was just Danuwoa and me left in the parking lot. He walked me to my car silently.

"What was that?"

"I'm sorry, Tito is my brother's friend, and I didn't think it through."

"No, what was that just now with Kyle?"

I leaned against the driver's side door. "Nothing, he was just asking me about a project at work."

"Really? Asking about work while drunk in the parking lot?"

"Uh-huh."

"He looked pissed." Danuwoa crossed his arms, staring me down.

He didn't know the half of it.

"Nope, everything's good. Are we good?" I smiled into his dark eyes.

He shook his head. "I don't know. I really like you, Ember. But I think maybe you need to get your priorities straight." He started to walk away.

"What do you mean?" My voice stopped him, and he turned to look at me. I continued, "My priority is keeping my job and dating you."

"We can just tell HR we're together. There doesn't have to be all this secrecy."

I replayed what Kyle said only a few minutes ago. *Do you think my uncle will take kindly to the news that his new assistant was fucking the IT guy while at a work event?* It was too late. Kyle already knew about us and was making big threats. I couldn't risk it. Maybe once Natalie was back from maternity leave, then we could come clean, but it was too much of a gamble right now.

"Can I think about it?" I tried to compromise.

He let out a sigh and looked so disappointed in me. I went home alone.

Thirty

I WENT INTO THE OFFICE WITH A FEELING OF TREPIDATION. I hadn't heard from Danuwoa since we parted ways in the parking lot last night. No "good night" text. No "good morning" text. Absolute radio silence.

I wasn't sure if we were still going to the jewelry fair this weekend or if Danuwoa had dropped me to spare himself the headache. I wouldn't blame him.

I missed the country and my former life. I didn't miss being poor, but I missed the simplicity of my life before all this. Before all of my lies. Home was only thirty minutes away, but since that dinner at my aunt's, I hadn't been back. I needed to walk around the creek barefoot to ground myself and relax. Could I? No. It was barely nine thirty in the morning and Mr. Stevenson was in a terrible mood.

It started with Mr. Stevenson barking as soon as he walked in, "Get me the Indian now!"

Danuwoa. He meant Danuwoa.

It scared me. I shouldn't have lied about not being Native, but people like Mr. Stevenson wouldn't care if I was. He wouldn't censor his speech. He would still shout about getting the "Indian" to help.

The thing was . . . we had a few actual Indian people in the company, and I mean those whose families originated from India, and who worked in finance. Danuwoa happened to be the only Native American in IT and the only Native in the company who looked like he would beat the shit out of Kevin Costner in *Dances with Wolves*. But just saying, "Get the Indian," was confusing. Which was why I emailed Sumit Patel, who was presently sitting on the couch in the waiting area, to come to our office.

I knocked on Mr. Stevenson's opaque glass door.

"Come in."

"Sumit is here," I told him, poking my head through the cracked door.

"Who?"

"Sumit Patel." The last name clearly didn't help place him. "From finance? You said to get you the Indian," I whispered.

Mr. Stevenson's face went white, and he floundered, opening and closing his mouth to try to find something to say.

"Should I send him in?" I asked with a saccharine smile. I was fucking with my racist boss, but he didn't know that. Well . . . he couldn't prove it.

"Yes, please send him in."

"Great." I closed the door and went to grab Sumit.

"Any idea what this meeting is about?" the poor guy asked me, nervously combing his hair with his hand. "I've never had a meeting with him."

"No idea," I said with a shrug.

Sumit walked in the opaque office, and the walls went clear. Mr. Stevenson mustered a smile and handshake for Sumit, and they talked for a few minutes before he was dismissed.

Sumit left with a huge smile plastered on his face. When the elevator doors closed, Mr. Stevenson walked to my desk and sat on the edge, perched with his hands clasped in his lap.

"We have a problem," he said solemnly.

"We do?"

"I was in a temper earlier and was not clear with my instructions. I typically always mean Dan Colson from IT. He is Indian from some local tribe, if the braid didn't give it away to you."

"Native American, yes. When people say Indian, I assume they mean from India."

"You put me in a really uncomfortable and awkward position just now. I'm not a racist man. I am what some might call a *woke* man. I believe women should have all the same rights as men and no one should be treated differently based on their race."

Believing in basic human decency was not being "woke," but I bet he thought that. Yelling things like what he did stripped someone of their humanity and replaced it with a stereotype. It was vile, and I felt like I was making dirty money working for this man.

"I'm of the generation where we played cowboys and Indians, and as we live in the South, I figured you understood my meaning. I just had to lie about liking Sumit's work and give him a raise to avoid an HR headache."

"That's so kind of you to give him a raise," I said, and gave him a sheepish smile.

"This cannot happen again, am I clear?" He waited for my nod of understanding before continuing, "My laptop is frozen on one Excel sheet, and I need Dan from IT here immediately."

"It's crystal clear. I'll see about getting Dan here as soon as possible."

He knocked his knuckles on my desk three times and went back into his office.

EMBER CARDINAL: Emergency, needed with boss ASAP.

DAN COLSON: What's wrong?

EMBER CARDINAL: He said he needed you immediately.

DAN COLSON: Any hint for what he needs?

EMBER CARDINAL: His spreadsheet is frozen.

DAN COLSON: Be there in a few.

EMBER CARDINAL: Brace yourself x

Danuwoa's face as he pushed the IT cart was impossible to read. He was usually so happy and smiley. I really hated that his cold demeanor was all my fault, and now he was walking into Mr. Stevenson's sour mood.

He stopped in front of my desk. "Hey."

"Hey," I returned. It was so painfully awkward, and I didn't know how to fix it. Where Danuwoa was concerned, he made me stupid dumb. I really liked him, and I was fighting so hard to protect us. I didn't know why he couldn't agree with me.

"Colson!" Mr. Stevenson's gruff bark made me jump.

Danuwoa's shoulders tensed before nodding to me in farewell and wheeling his cart into the office. Once the walls went opaque, I sent a small prayer to Creator. Poor Danuwoa was in for it.

I had things to busy myself with and take my mind off the doom and gloom of my short relationship with Danuwoa—like submitting Mr. Stevenson's expense reports from the conference and Kyle's receipts from last night. I printed the reports and felt a disgusting sense of dread as I submitted and approved the expenses with Mr. Stevenson's signature stamp.

It felt like with each slam of the stamp on my desk, my heart skipped a beat. Stamp. Stamp. Stamp. I was in some deep shit, and I was out of ideas for how to explain my way out of all this and fix things with Danuwoa. In a few months, maybe I'd have enough experience to apply for jobs somewhere else. Just forget all about this mess with Technix. Natalie would be back, and there was no way in hell I could return to working for Gary. I pissed too many people off here. A clean slate might be what I needed.

I loved numbers, and the pseudo-power the EA to the CEO had was cool and all, but it wasn't really me. I didn't know how to schmooze and rub elbows on behalf of the CEO. Managing relationships at this level was exhausting. I stopped feeling like myself the moment I accepted the promotion. I rubbed my temples before I scanned and attached the reports and sent them to accounting.

The ding of a new email hit my inbox, and I groaned at the name that appeared.

SENDER: Kyle Matthews
SUBJECT: Update—Call me

Ember,

Give me a call when you have a moment.

Kyle

If I wasn't in the office, I would have screamed. I had just sent his receipts from last night—what more did he want from me? I replayed what he told me. What he called me. *The help.* Basically insinuated I was a whore sleeping with Danuwoa on the job. It left such a bad taste in my mouth I wanted to "accidentally" delete the email and wash my hands of everything, pretend like my life was manageable.

I took several calming breaths.

Mr. Stevenson's office was still opaque, and I had to protect Danuwoa. Which was why I dialed Kyle's extension.

"*Ember*, what up?" He made his voice sound high and sang my name in a weird attempt to be friendly.

"You asked me to call you . . ."

"Not one for small talk. Okay. Is my uncle here?"

"Yeah, but he's with someone right now."

"Don't bother him. Call me back when he leaves the office."

The line went dead. I did not like the sound of that but quickly pushed it to the back of my mind when Danuwoa came out of the office, pushing his cart like he had a fire under his butt. I got up to follow him to the elevator.

"Hey, Danuwoa."

He looked at me expectantly.

"Is everything okay?"

"Just great. Do you have an IT problem?" He crossed his arms while he waited for the elevator.

"Yeah, I'm about to, if that's the only way you'll talk to me."

"I can't talk about this now. Especially not here, remember? We have to stay a secret." Danuwoa grabbed the cart handles as the elevator dinged its arrival.

"But you are willing to talk to me . . . eventually?"

His eyes said, *What do you think?*

And then the doors closed him in.

That was the problem. I didn't know what to think. I'd never had a relationship like this before. Were we over? Was this just a minor bump?

I sat back at my desk, head in my hands. I didn't know how long I sat like that, spiraling, when Mr. Stevenson breezed past me.

"Going to lunch. I'll be back in a bit."

Lunch. Danuwoa. My legs itched to get up and run to the break room, but I had to call Kyle back.

He picked up on the first ring. "Is he gone?"

"Yes."

"Great, I need you to go into his office and check his email for me."

Sirens rang in my ears.

"You want me to do what?" I had to have misheard him.

"Open his email, and I need you to look in his 'Sent' folder and delete the email he sent me at ten o'clock this morning."

"That's crossing the line, Kyle. I can't do that."

"It's fine." His tone was placating, like he was calming down a spooked horse. I *was* spooked. This was unethical and would most assuredly get me fired. "It's just a stupid email to me. It's not even a big deal."

"If it's not a big deal, then why do I have to delete it?"

He didn't say anything for a moment, and I thought the line went dead. Then he took a deep breath and said, "Do you know what happened to the last female assistant we had in finance?"

"No." I gulped.

"She was caught having an affair with Todd, our vice president of sales from Austin. Yeah, it was really embarrassing for them, since they were both married. Mr. Stevenson had her escorted out of the building."

The pregnant pause was begging me to ask, so I did. "And what happened to Todd?"

"Todd was in Santa Barbara, at the conference. You see, Ember, when 'president' is in your executive title, the company has invested a lot of resources in that person and won't waste the money or potential legal headache getting rid of them. Now, titles with the word 'assistant' or 'IT technician' are cheap and easy to replace. No one gives a shit about you. I'm sure you know it's hard out there trying to find a job, and even harder with no reference."

I was past caring about myself, but I couldn't let Danuwoa lose his job over this bullshit. "All right."

"Great. After you delete the email from ten a.m., I need you to go to his inbox and respond to the email from me at nine fifty-three a.m. Just write back 'Approved.'"

"Okay."

"Then delete that email. Got it?"

"Ye-yeah."

"Amazing."

He hung up, and I was sweating profusely. I felt like I'd agreed to rob a bank. This was so wrong. I knew it was wrong. Warning bells were going off in my head, but I knew things would be much worse if Danuwoa and I got fired. My car would get repossessed. School would never happen for me. I wouldn't be able to afford rent, leaving Joanna in the lurch. Danuwoa would go into foreclosure on his house. We would all end up homeless. Joanna and I had been in pretty bad straits, so we would figure it out, but Danuwoa needed that stability for Walela. And what kind of relationship would survive this level of destruction?

It was all too much, and the only way I could save us all was to help Kyle. Just this one email, and I'd never have to think about it again. Our jobs, our homes, our relationship would be safe. I was feeling dizzy.

This was all so fucked up and not what I signed up for. Why

couldn't I have gotten an accounting job like you see on TV, with a cute little old lady coworker who wears cat sweaters?

I tiptoed into Mr. Stevenson's office. It was unnecessary since I was the only one on the floor, but I did it anyway. His laptop was open on his desk. He hated when his computer timed out and shut down to save power, so he had Danuwoa set it up to never go to sleep. I didn't need a password or to click around. It was open on his Outlook.

I quickly found the email to delete. Kyle had asked for a raise, and Mr. Stevenson told him no. Literally it only said No.

I deleted it and sent the approval and wanted to shrivel up and die, because my integrity was compromised in a way I feared would never recover. I helped some spoiled brat get more money and was ensnared even more under Kyle's thumb. This whole situation was fucked.

I GOT HOME TO AN EMPTY APARTMENT. I HADN'T SEEN DANUWOA again at work, so I sent him a text asking if he would like to come over for dinner tonight. He said yes, so here I was hiding my brother's boxers and clothes under a blanket in the corner of the tiny living room and double-checking to make sure Sage had flushed the toilet before he left.

The minutes passed by too fast and too slow at the same time. My stomach was in knots from conjuring every possible scenario when Danuwoa knocked on my door.

He had one hand in his jean pocket, while the other scratched behind his head. He looked nervous and gave me a sheepish grin, then winked. The butterflies in my stomach woke up and stretched their wings.

"Hi," I said.

"Hi," he returned.

I opened my door wider, inviting him inside. "I hope you're hungry."

"What's on the menu? You need any help?"

"Ramen, and no, I have everything ready."

I put the steaming hot bowls on the tiny table and pointed to the chair for Danuwoa to join me. He sat down, and his frame dwarfed my tiny, cheap furniture.

It was comical. Choking on a laugh, I gave all my attention to my ramen.

"I like that you added fresh veggies and an egg to this," he said with a slurp.

"It's nothing like your homemade corn chowder." I still couldn't meet his eyes.

His hand covered mine, stilling my fork. "Look at me," he said softly.

I closed my eyes, savoring the feel of his hand on mine and the way his voice caressed me. Once I had fully braced myself for his rejection, I looked up into his warm eyes.

"What's really going on, Ember?"

"Nothing, I just made a few dumb mistakes, but I promise I'm through with all that. I won't ever make up a fake boyfriend again."

"So you want to come clean and tell people we're dating?"

"Everyone important to me knows we're a thing. I don't want to tell people at work that we are dating until Natalie comes back from maternity leave. Then I'll figure out my next move. I think maybe applying somewhere else, where we never have to hide our relationship." That thought made me smile.

"And what if Natalie doesn't come back?"

I hadn't even considered that possibility. My hope deflated.

"Have you heard anything to suggest she won't?"

"No, but a lot of people want to stay home longer with their newborns. It's something to consider."

"She's supposed to return in a couple weeks. We can cross that bridge when we come to it. Can you live with keeping our relationship under wraps at work until she's back?"

"Being discreet isn't the problem, Ember. It's the lying and weird behavior that is a red flag for me."

"That's fair. I won't lie anymore, and I'll stop acting weird and treating you like a dirty secret. I really like you, Danuwoa."

"I really, *really* like you too."

We sat at my silly little table, our bowls of ramen getting cold, holding hands and staring into each other's eyes. It was starting to feel a whole lot more than just "like" for me too. I didn't hate it.

"Do you still want to meet me at the jewelry fair this weekend?" I asked.

"I do. I'm bringing Walela."

I smiled. "It's a date."

Thirty-One

THE SCENT OF BURNING SAGE MIXED WITH SWEETGRASS FROM several stalls tickled my nose as we walked down aisles of vendors peddling beads, crystals, and jewelry. It was a dazzling maze on the fairgrounds inside the expo hall. It had been raining when we arrived, and Danuwoa's shirt was clinging to his muscles. I didn't mind it, even if my hair was heavy and frizzy.

It was Saturday, and I didn't have a care in the world. After I'd done what Kyle told me to do, I hadn't heard from him the rest of the week. I hoped his requests for "favors" had come to an end. Danuwoa and I were back to being happy and lusty. Things were really looking up.

Living with Sage was still weird. I hadn't really talked to him. We called a silent truce. He knew how I felt about him and the letter. He also knew there was nothing he could immediately do to fix what was broken between us besides showing up and following through with his promises. All I had to do was wait and hope he did.

Danuwoa and I walked hand in hand down the aisle with

Walela stopping at every vendor on our way to Joanna's. Her sign was the prettiest. It was hand-drawn on a poster board, and I could spot Sage's art anywhere. He was always great at drawing, and the vibrant yellow sunflowers around Joanna's name on the sign looked so detailed you could almost mistake them for being real ones glued on.

"Hi, Sage." Walela sallied right next to him at the table. Joanna nodded a greeting and went back to helping a couple of women pick out some of her foot jewelry. Some people loved beads around their toes. I was not one of those people.

"Hey there, Your Highness, are you here on official Indian princess business?" he asked. I missed his shoulder-length wavy hair, but with his buzz cut, he couldn't hide behind it. A few freckles dotted the bridge of his nose on his sun-kissed face. His crooked smile made Walela blush and giggle.

"Nope, I'm looking for some new jewelry. Do you recommend anything?"

"This bracelet is very cute. The blue would match the dress you wore when I first met you." His suggestion was genuine, and I was shocked my careless and self-absorbed brother bothered to remember such a detail. Perhaps he really was changing?

The bracelet he held up was pretty and delicate, the turquoise seed beads were woven with a loom and crisscrossed with tiny lapis and gold beads throughout.

"Wanna try it on?" Sage asked.

"Yes!" Walela extended her arm, and Sage clasped the bracelet around it. Once it was on there, she wiggled it around to get the feel of it on her wrist. "Can we buy this?" she asked and showed off the bracelet to Danuwoa.

"If that's the one you want, then yes."

"I *have* to have it."

"Anything else?" he asked his sister. Danuwoa squeezed my hand at the cuteness of watching Walela tap her chin as she considered the other possibilities.

Joanna's creations were all beautiful, even the weird, funky ones. She had a small following of people on social media who loved her outrageous beaded collections. It took a certain kind of person to walk around with a beaded boob that read FREE THE NIP on the center of their chest. Those people paid her good money, but the pieces took a long time for her to do.

A queue started to form to get a look at the necklace stand showcasing a green dragon spitting flames. The piece boasted a $500 price tag. It was worth it.

"We're gonna do another loop—you coming, Walela?" I asked.

"No, I think I'll stay for a minute."

"You can be our live model and show off some pieces," Sage offered.

We walked around the other aisles, stopping if something caught our eye.

"This is nice," Danuwoa told me, lifting our laced fingers to kiss the back of my hand.

And it was. We were free to walk around and explore without the threat of our coworkers or boss spotting us.

That was until, in this crowded public place, I spotted Gary freaking Horowitz. I pushed Danuwoa away from me and yanked my hand back.

"What the . . . ?" He sounded appalled, and rightfully so.

I shushed him and ducked behind a huge geode. He stood, arms crossed, looking down at me.

"Get down! You'll draw attention to us," I hissed.

"I thought you promised we were past this."

"Gary is down there," I said and pointed. "We said we would stay discreet at work."

"This isn't work."

"Gary is work," I pleaded.

Danuwoa shook his head and walked away. I put my head in my hands. I royally, massively fucked up. Again.

"Ember?" Gary's voice was behind me.

I looked up at him in my crouched position. "Gary, hi. What are you doing here?" I stood up. "I dropped my hair tie, was looking for it." I waved my hand around, like it explained why he found me crouched on the dirty floor of the expo hall.

"Right . . . I'm just here adding to my crystal collection."

"Nice. I like crystals too."

We stood there awkwardly. I started craning my neck looking for any sign of Danuwoa.

"Looking for someone?"

"What? No," I said, letting out a nervous giggle. "I'm just seeing what stall to hit next. I'll see you around the office." I darted away, flitting around the stalls like a madwoman looking for Danuwoa.

I retreated to Joanna's stall.

"What happened between you and Danuwoa?" Sage asked me.

"Nothing. Everything's fine. Why? What did he say?"

"He just looked pissed and told Walela they had to go."

"Oh."

"Wanna talk about it?"

"Not with you." I looked past Sage to try to catch Joanna's eye. She was busy with customers. She didn't need to be bothered with my bullshit. I had to find a way to fix this . . . again. The only thing was, I didn't think I could.

Thirty-Two

ONDAY, I WENT STRAIGHT TO THE BATHROOM AS SOON AS I got into the office. My nerves and all the caffeine I drank in the morning had me feeling sick. It was over with Danuwoa. It had to be. He didn't respond to a single text message after the jewelry fair incident, and I really couldn't blame him.

"Ember!" Mr. Stevenson boomed as he stormed from the elevator.

"Yes, sir?"

"I need you to come with me to take notes during my next meeting. We're going downstairs in five."

"You got it." I scooped up my laptop and waited for Mr. Stevenson to put down his briefcase. The elevator ride down was quiet and awkward. I had yet to crack the small talk code with him and have an easy conversation.

I'd been in a few meetings with him since I'd taken over for Natalie. Nothing too serious, and he never actually asked for those notes. We filed into the Chuck Norris conference room, where finance and human resources were setting up the presentation on the screen.

I opened my document to start taking notes and got so far as today's date when I was immediately bored. On autopilot, I minimized the document and opened Teams, clicking on my chat thread with Danuwoa.

EMBER CARDINAL: Hey!

Mr. Adams opened the meeting with an agenda slide and all the topics that would be covered and by who. I wrote the names and topics down and tapped my fingers, waiting hopefully for the gray dots to show up in the chat window to show that Danuwoa was typing back. Instead, I got an open eyeball icon.

He read the message. That was a start.

Minutes went by. Nothing.

EMBER CARDINAL: Hi, quick question.

It was wrong to bait him as if there was an IT issue, but I was desperate.

DAN COLSON: If you are having computer issues, you can fill out a help desk ticket.

He followed up with the link. It couldn't get any worse. My mind went blank, and my heart was racing. I couldn't think of a way to fix this, and I stopped paying attention to whoever had been talking for a while.

"Ember."

I heard a noise that sounded vaguely like my name, but my

mind was going a mile a minute. There had to be something I could do. Some way to apologize. How was I supposed to know Gary was obsessed with crystals? It wasn't like we would run into coworkers every time we went out.

"Ember!" Mr. Stevenson's shout ripped me out of my panicking spiral.

"Yes?"

"Read back the action items for finance."

"Uh, right." Shit! I hadn't been taking notes and honestly couldn't say how much time had passed. "I'm sorry . . ." I discreetly pressed the power button and my laptop shut down. "I'm having technical problems. My computer crashed. I need to take it to IT. Sorry." I grabbed my computer and booked it out of the room.

I hurried through the cubicles until I reached Danuwoa's desk. He did not look pleased in the least to see me standing before him.

"My computer crashed." I shoved it at him. "I can't fill out a ticket with a dead computer. Sorry."

He silently took my laptop and plugged it into his charger. He held the power button down and it turned on in seconds. A message window popped up on the screen that said the computer had been improperly shut down. He shot me a look. *It just crashed?*

Yup. Gulp.

"Well, everything seems to be working fine. I have a bunch to catch up on this morning."

"Danuwoa, I—"

"I can't do this with you, Ember," he whispered. His eyes looked so hurt. I had done that. I put that look on his face.

"I'm sorry," I whispered back, extending my hand to rub his back and quickly snatching it away. I wasn't sure I still had the privilege to touch Danuwoa with such familiarity.

"I know you are, but I can't do this anymore."

I nodded, looking away so he wouldn't see the tears burning in my eyes. Grabbing the laptop, I escaped back to floor seventeen.

Things went from bad to really fucking bad. There was an email in my inbox from Gary.

SENDER: Gary Horowitz
SUBJECT: Request for Meeting with Mr. Stevenson—Urgent

His name filled me with dread. The cc line had every C-level executive, including Kyle and Monica from HR. It couldn't have anything to do with me, right? I hadn't done anything wrong. I mean, I totally did but at the direction of Kyle. Surely, he wouldn't let anything bad happen to me, as it would expose him. My stomach turned to lead as I opened the message.

Ember,

Please schedule me on Mr. Stevenson's calendar before the end of the day. It is an urgent confidential matter.

—GH

Mr. Stevenson had a thirty-minute window after lunch. I set up the meeting invite, including all the cc'd parties, and urgently ran to the bathroom for the fifth time this morning. There was no reason I should think it was about me. I was being paranoid.

My sixth sense was telling me this was about me though, and my body could not handle the additional stress. I stayed in the bathroom stall for a few minutes to breathe. When I went back to my desk, Mr. Stevenson had accepted the calendar invite.

Did I eat lunch? I remember sitting there putting food in my mouth as I sat alone at the table I usually shared with Danuwoa and Phoebe. Both were absent from the break room. I was in a haze of pure panic, spiraling about the meeting and about my breakup with Danuwoa.

I did everything Natalie told me to do. I did all the work required of me and then some, like navigating legitimate blackmail to help Kyle get even further ahead. I protected my and Danuwoa's jobs. Why was I always being punished for just trying to do the right thing, no matter what fucked-up way I had achieved it?

Back upstairs I went through the motions, and when it was time, the elevators opened and Gary Horowitz, Kyle Matthews, and Monica Lewis stepped out to the sound of "The Imperial March," which played in my head. They stepped in time with the horns.

Monica gave me a warm smile, but Kyle refused to meet my eyes. Gary did not acknowledge my existence. It was like I was part of the furniture.

They entered Mr. Stevenson's office, and I wanted to flee.

I picked at my nails, willing myself not to turn around and try to hear what I could through the glass. Then Monica popped her head out of the door.

"Ember, could you join us inside for a moment?" she asked.

"Sure." I stood and adjusted my button-up cuffs and walked in, looking at the ground. Then, as I sat down and met the eyes of those in the room, judging me, I painted a smile on my face as if nothing was wrong, because nothing *was* wrong. I did everything I could as correctly as possible with the limited options I had.

"Sit," Mr. Stevenson commanded, sounding bored. He leaned

back in his chair, hands crossed over his stomach. "Care to explain why I recently approved almost ten thousand dollars of expenses?"

I looked at Kyle, who subtly shook his head.

"I submitted expense reports like I was told to do?" It sounded like a question, because I was walking on thin ice and didn't know which words would make me fall through and drown under all my lies.

"Who told you to approve them using my signature stamp?"

"Er . . . Kyle?" I wasn't going down for something I was told to do! I wished I had sounded more confident, but I had four sets of eyes on me. Gary just sat there with a smug smile on his face.

"I asked you to have Mr. Stevenson approve the expenses, Ember," Kyle admonished me, and looked to Mr. Stevenson. "I would never assume authority over someone, especially your assistant, to abuse your signature stamp."

Mr. Stevenson waved his hand away and asked me, "Didn't you learn proper GAAP rules in your accounting program?"

"Of course," I said. I mean, I learned some from Google in my brief time working under Gary. I did ask Kyle if it was okay, and now he was totally throwing me under the bus. If I could make someone explode with my eyes, it would be him.

A chuckle from Gary stole all our attention.

"What accounting program?" he asked. My stomach bottomed out.

"I told you I attended the accounting program at Oklahoma City Community College," I said, choosing my words carefully.

"You attended some classes, but I called my buddy who works over there, and there's no record of you completing or graduating from that program."

Fuck. Fuckity fuck's sake.

"I . . . well . . . er . . ." I had to say something. Anything. To explain I wasn't some pathological liar. I wanted to do the right thing and not live with this anxiety.

Gary flipped through the folder in his hand. I saw my name clearly at the top of the page: EMBER CARDINAL. My doctored résumé and application.

"I also went ahead and called the phone number listed here for Joanna Gates. Your best friend, right?"

"She is, but I do her taxes for her small business too," I squeaked out.

"What about bookkeeping for Bobby Dean's Bowling Alley?" Gary asked, and Kyle looked surprised.

"I did work there."

"Not as an accountant."

"What does that have to do with anything? I balanced the registers." The emotion in my throat was like acid, and I hated that my eyes burned with tears I refused to shed.

"Absolutely nothing, but adds to the entire story that, Ember Cardinal, you are a liar. You have no experience that would have qualified you for this job, and you exercised poor judgment with submitting and approving these expense reports."

A single tear popped out of my eye. I slapped it away.

"What about him?" I pointed to Kyle. "He threatened me and blackmailed me to submit these things for him. I didn't want to lie on my résumé, but I needed a good job, and I *am* a hard worker. Do you know how hard it is as a Native American to get the necessary job experience? Like, so what if I'm Native American? My racial background has nothing to do with my ability to work." I pushed through, looking right at our CEO, admitting to everything. "I didn't want to go into your email, Mr. Stevenson, but Kyle threatened to get my coworker fired, and I was just trying to protect them."

Kyle spoke up, his voice loud. "She's crazy. I mean, listen to her. You can't believe this? Gary has just proved that this woman is a pathological liar."

"All right, that's enough." It was Monica who cut in.

"I may have lied to get this job, but I will not lie to cover for you. What do I have to lose? There's no way I can stay here after this."

"Honey, don't cry. We want to understand this. Right, Mr. Stevenson?" Monica asked.

I looked at Monica's kind face and was hopeful, until I looked at Mr. Stevenson, who kept staring at his desk, his position unchanged.

I hunched and stripped myself bare, laying all the parts of me that I had hidden away. "I am Chickasaw and Choctaw. I grew up in Ada with my aunt. Every time I put 'American Indian' on an application, I got a rejection. My dad is white, so it's not a full-out lie."

When no one said anything, I continued, "I went to Oklahoma City Community College and am several classes away from graduating that program with my associate's degree in accounting. My brother got into trouble, and I used my school money for his bail, which he skipped, and I lost it all. I was tired of working at a bowling alley and barely getting by. I thought if I could get my foot in the door as an accounting assistant, then I could make enough to go to night school and graduate. I never wanted to be the executive assistant to the CEO. It was Natalie who put me here. I won't sit here like I stole it or something. Kyle asked me on the flight back here from California to submit expenses and said that Natalie approved with Mr. Stevenson's stamp all the time and not to bother him to ask—"

"You aren't going to entertain this, right? She's crazy!" Kyle interrupted me again.

"Let her talk, Kyle," Mr. Stevenson said.

"I'm really sorry. Kyle then started demanding more from me and told me to go into your email to delete your rejection of his raise and draft a new email to approve it."

"I can't listen to this bullshit." Kyle stood up.

"Sit your ass down. Is this true?" Mr. Stevenson asked. As soon as Kyle went to open his mouth, Mr. Stevenson added, "Cut the shit."

"I just asked for some help with expenses. I have no idea what she's talking about with the emails. This is stupid. Just fire her and hire someone else. This role is easily replaceable."

"Shut up." Mr. Stevenson rolled his eyes and blew out a breath.

Monica solemnly spoke up. "We did receive an email from you forwarded by Kyle to payroll to initiate a newly approved raise."

Mr. Stevenson gave Kyle a death glare, then got his cell phone out and called someone. "Come up to my office, now," he barked his order to whoever was on the other line. Probably security to escort me out of here.

The wind in my sails left me. I sat hunched in my chair, defeated. Gary sat with his chest puffed up like he just solved some crime that had people puzzled for years. Kyle sat with his leg bouncing at supersonic speed. Monica looked like she wanted to be anywhere but here. I kept eyeing the door to see who Mr. Stevenson invited up here.

My heart sank as Danuwoa stepped through the door. "You need something?" he asked, glancing at the rest of us in the room.

"I need you to recover some emails for me. What date was this?" Mr. Stevenson asked me.

"Last Thursday," I mumbled.

"Look up all my deleted and sent emails from last Thursday," he directed Danuwoa.

Seconds, then minutes had ticked by when finally, Danuwoa angled Mr. Stevenson's laptop screen back to him.

"I see. You're clever, boy. I'll give you that," he said, raising an eyebrow to his nephew.

"This is all ridiculous. She's fucking the IT guy! He is obviously trying to save her ass."

"That is enough!" Mr. Stevenson's voice bellowed. "That language and accusation is enough for me to dismiss you right here and now."

"I saw them kiss in California!" Kyle's face was flaming red as he spewed his venom.

"Kyle, you're dismissed. I'll deal with you later."

Kyle rose from his seat, his nostrils flaring as he glared daggers at me, and he stomped from the office.

I watched as Mr. Stevenson rubbed his eye sockets and sighed. "This is quite a mess. I don't care if you're an American Indian and lied about it to get the job. I honestly don't even care that you made up a fake résumé to get this job. You're talented and bright and have been doing fine."

"Hardly," Gary muttered under his breath.

"Thank you, Gary. I think Monica and I can take it from here," Mr. Stevenson said.

"Good luck," Gary said with derision as he set his file full of all my lies on top of Mr. Stevenson's desk.

I looked at Danuwoa. Now he knew everything. I was a liar. He didn't meet my eyes.

"I think this thing with the expenses is truly my nephew's

fault, and this email . . . well, that is what I do care about—integrity. I can't have someone working for me in such a trusted position, handling such sensitive material, who wouldn't even think to ask me about Kyle's requests."

"I understand." I hung my head. This was my penance. Danuwoa deserved to know everything about the woman who shared his bed. He was so open with his heart, and I returned his affection with lies and secrecy.

"This thing my nephew said about you and Dan . . ." Mr. Stevenson let the sentence trail off.

"We are not together," I answered truthfully, refusing so much as a glance at Danuwoa.

Mr. Stevenson nodded his head. "Right, right. Well, it's of no consequence now. Monica, if you can wrap this up and see Ember out."

"Yes, sir." She rose from her seat and motioned for me to lead the way out of the room. Her smile was strained and awkward.

As I stood to go, Mr. Stevenson held up his hand for me to pause.

"I'm sorry it didn't work out. Take care," he said.

"Thank you for the opportunity."

He nodded his head to himself, then immediately got out his cell phone. That was my final dismissal. I left the office without looking at Danuwoa, but with the office wall clear as day, I could feel his eyes boring into my back.

Monica hovered next to me as I gathered my few things into my Technix-branded backpack, which made me hesitate.

"Do I have to return this?" I asked Monica and pointed to the backpack.

"Oh, no, it's yours to keep."

I made the situation even more uncomfortable for us both, but how was I to know? Once I got home, I'd never look at the thing again, let alone use it.

Clearing out my desk took less than a minute, since I never had the time to add any personalized touches. I left my computer on the desk along with my notebook. I hiked my backpack over my shoulder and headed to the elevator just as Danuwoa was excused from Mr. Stevenson's office.

The shit was really piling up.

I found myself sandwiched between Monica and Danuwoa in the elevator, and the only button pushed was twelve. Monica saw me eyeing the lit-up floor number.

"I have to have you fill out standard exit paperwork, then you can be on your way."

"Okay." I'd never heard my voice sound so small.

I couldn't tell if Danuwoa was trying to be polite and give me space in this humiliation, or if he was so disgusted with me that he couldn't bear to acknowledge me in the elevator.

The ding chimed our arrival to floor twelve before I had any more time to ruminate about it. His quick exit made it clear where we stood.

We were nothing.

Phoebe was behind the reception desk, and she looked shocked to see me. Kyle probably told her what happened when he came back down here. I'm sure the whole floor knew now too. I watched my feet take one step after another in Monica's wake, avoiding all eye contact.

I sat in her friendly and cozy little cubicle, wanting to bolt out of the building. Monica was printing forms, two copies of everything. She didn't even try to talk to me. What would be the point?

"Okay, here we go. So, I've printed out the confidentiality

agreement you signed when you started, for your records. Now, this separation agreement you should have a lawyer look over before you sign."

"What is it for? Y'all fired me."

She gave me a tight smile. "Yes, well, it's pretty standard for those working so closely with a CEO—this has more extensive language limiting what you can say about Technix, Mr. Stevenson, and your time working here."

"Do I have to sign this?" I was flabbergasted. I was just fired, and now they wanted me to essentially sign a gag order. I guess it wouldn't look too good to have a former assistant telling people what assholes the executives were. Who would listen anyway?

"Well, no. That's why you should have a lawyer look it over. If you sign it, then I am sure I can help you with a reference to assist you in finding something else."

"So, I'll only be able to use Technix as a reference on my résumé if I sign this?"

"We don't really like to say that." Monica placed the documents in a manila folder and handed them to me. "I think you have a bright future ahead of you. You've got a strong head on your shoulders; I'm not worried about you for a minute."

That made one of us. I was very worried about myself and how I'd pay rent and the car loan and the insurance. Shit. I was worse off than I ever was working at Bobby Dean's.

I took the manila folder and shoved it in my dumb backpack and got up to go.

"Wait!" Monica shot up and walked around her desk. "Sorry, it's protocol. I have to escort you out. It's nothing personal."

All of this felt extremely personal. As we walked through the HR department and then through finance, I saw Kyle walk down the hallway. He approached us with an empty Technix coffee mug and winked and smiled at me, obviously very amused with himself and my demise.

Monica kept trudging on ahead to the elevator, but I stopped and planted my feet on the ground. Kyle looked taken aback. Good. It was all out in the open and over for me. I didn't have to play nice and pacify him. I could finally stick up for myself, and I was gonna rip him a new one.

"Fuck you," I said. I wasn't brave enough to get in his face, but I said it all with my chin.

"Excuse me?" He looked around for witnesses.

"You heard me. You are an entitled ass with an overinflated ego. If your uncle wasn't the CEO, there is no way in hell you would have the title you do."

"Okay, that's enough. I'm pretty sure you're being escorted out for being a fraud and a whore. Did you fuck all the guys in IT?"

"I did get fired for doing what you *made* me do." The hairs on my arms rose with goose bumps, and I could feel eyes all over me. I looked around, and the accounting bros and Lisa were standing and watching my confrontation with slack jaws. "Take it from me, do not do anything this man tells you to. He is a pathetic user." I started to go catch up with Monica; I'd made enough of a scene.

"Says the girl who couldn't even go to community college," Kyle called after me and laughed. It stopped me in my tracks. I was so done being belittled, being mocked for not having one-tenth of the opportunities he had for being born rich, white, and with a dick.

"I feel sorry for you, Kyle. Even with your fancy education, your money, and your connections, no one genuinely likes you. Even though I haven't graduated from community college—yet— when I finally get to where I am headed, it's going to mean something to everyone around me. *I* will be something. You will just fade away, blending into the sea of mediocre men who have come before you."

I laughed and kept going, hearing a "whoop!" from accounting. I caught up to Monica, who looked either scared of me or in awe.

"Sorry about that," I mumbled.

Phoebe kept looking at me and then back to Kyle like her head was about to explode.

"There is an opening for executive assistant to the CEO. You should definitely apply," I said, smiling at her.

"Thanks," she said with a bewildered stare. I had wanted to be real friends with Phoebe, but we just didn't click. She was nice when I started, but sometimes just because you worked in an office with someone, it didn't mean you had to become friends if you didn't connect. And that was okay.

"Ember, it's time to go. Everyone has to get back to work." Monica ushered me into the waiting elevator.

I made such a mess of everything, and even my leaving couldn't be done on the down-low.

The ride to the lobby was the longest of my life. I had to share the elevator with Monica in shame, and to make it worse, she walked me out onto the curb to make sure I was really gone and not going to cause any more trouble.

I left Technix and the First National Center behind me forever.

What hurt the most was leaving Danuwoa in my wake of shame and embarrassment.

Thirty-Three

I SAT CRYING IN MY CAR OUTSIDE MY APARTMENT BUILDING, DE-pleted from the shock, stress, and emotional confrontation. I was trying to muster the courage to face Joanna in the middle of the day. What I needed was a corn burrito and a hug before I let my misery swallow me whole. The only thought racing through my mind over and over again was *YOU'RE AN IDIOT!* What the hell had I been thinking?

No one will know. We had laughed when I came up with this harebrained scheme. Well, they all knew now. Bobby Dean had replaced me at the bowling alley, so I had absolutely nothing to fall back on. I needed Joanna to help me come up with ideas for how to get me back on my feet. Not that I really deserved it. I fucked things up so royally with Danuwoa that I doubted I'd ever get a decent night's sleep again. I just knew that as I was about to fall asleep, the scene of me getting fired in front of him would play back on a loop—probably for the rest of my life—keeping me awake as I cringed into my pillow, begging for it to swallow me whole.

I screamed and hit the steering wheel. Our older neighbor, Suzy, was staring at me, horrified, holding her trash on her way to the dumpster. I mumbled an apology as I got out of the car and went inside.

Joanna wasn't even freaking home.

It had been weeks of my brother greeting me on the couch, but today it was empty. He must have been at his new high-paying job or whatever. I had no one to turn to, and all I wanted to do was run away and hide.

Run away! That was it. I'd go home to Auntie. She would know what to do.

I began packing my pink duffel bag, throwing in whatever I touched in my closet. Then I took out a handful of socks and undies from my drawer to throw in too. My father's letter fluttered on top of my bag.

Was I looking for more disappointment? There was no way I could possibly feel any worse than this—I was at rock bottom. I ripped open the letter and laughed out loud. To say it was brief was an understatement. I hadn't heard from this man in decades, and his all-caps handwritten apology barely took up half a page of college-ruled composition paper.

EMBER TIMBER.

REMEMBER WHEN I USED TO PUSH YOU ONTO THE BED YELLING "TIMBER!"?

I did. He was the only one to have ever called me Ember Timber, and it made my heart clench. So much I had blocked out because it was easier. I never thought I'd ever hear—well, read—that nickname again in my life.

WE HAD A LOT OF FUN WHEN YOU AND YOUR BROTHER
WERE LITTLE. THERE WERE A LOT OF GOOD TIMES. I'M
REALLY SORRY FOR THE BAD ONES. YOUR MOM AND I
FOUGHT A LOT AND YOU WERE OLD ENOUGH TO KNOW
WHAT WAS GOING ON. I WAS IN A BAD PLACE, AND SINCE
I'M WRITING TO YOU FROM JAIL. I'M STILL IN A BAD PLACE.
I KNOW THERE ISN'T ANYTHING I CAN SAY THAT WILL
MAKE IT BETTER. I DOUBT YOU WANT A RELATIONSHIP WITH
ME. I CAN'T OFFER MUCH OF ANYTHING EXCEPT TO SAY
THAT I'M SORRY. I'M SORRY EMBER THAT I LEFT YOU AND
SAGE. I'M SORRY I NEVER CALLED. I FIGURED YOU WERE
BETTER OFF WITHOUT ME. I WASN'T MEANT TO BE A DAD.
BUT THAT IS NO EXCUSE. IT'S NOT MUCH. BUT I'M SORRY.

~~DAD~~ MITCH

I cried. I told myself I had no expectations, that I didn't want
to read his letter. That I didn't need his words. But I was a lost
little girl alone in a shitty apartment with no job and no boyfriend
and no future because I had just majorly fucked up my life. I was
old enough to remember the day my dad left and never came back.
I watched him walk out that door with the innocent hope of a little
girl who only wanted her family to stay together. My parents had
an explosive fight, and Sage was crying, and it was too much for
Mitch. He never even looked back at me to say goodbye, but he
knew he was never going to return. Our mother cried in bed that
night, and I picked up a crying Sage and opened a can of Spaghet-
tiOs. That was when I started taking care of everyone.

I crumpled the letter. I had no emotional capacity to go down
this road, trapped in the past and crying over a childhood I never
had and a life I never would. I had to focus on today and now. He

was right—an apology acknowledging he was a screwup didn't fix anything, but it was more than other people got. He was alive. He was in jail. He remembered me. It was going to have to be enough.

I didn't want a relationship with my dad, but I did want one with Sage. I heard the front door open and close, then a loud clang as something heavy dropped on the floor. I went out to the living room.

Sage was standing there in a white shirt, jeans, and work boots. He was covered in some sort of dust. I ran and wrapped him in a bear hug. He was my baby brother. He made stupid mistakes, but he wasn't my dad.

I was going to make sure he didn't end up like him either.

"Whoa, what's wrong? Why are you crying? Did Dan do something? Do I gotta grab Tito and we go and beat the shit out of him for you?"

"No." I sniffed a giggle. "I love you."

He awkwardly patted my back. "I love you too."

I pulled away to get a good look at him. "You're working construction then?"

"Yeah, it's good money. It's dumb how good it is. And look, one of the guys gave me some old tools." Sage started showing me his tool belt and the hammer and work gloves. I smiled, because he reminded me of six-year-old Sage at Christmas again. When he was done showing me his tools, he dug through his backpack. "I gotta shower and get this dust off me. It was windy at the site."

"Yeah, go ahead."

"You sure you're okay?"

I hadn't realized I was a leaking faucet with more tears in my eyes. "Yeah, I read Dad's letter." I waved my hands around like the idea of reading it was no big deal.

"What did he say?"

"He just said he was sorry," I said, shrugging.

Sage nodded. "Good. He needed to."

"I still don't want a relationship with him. What you do is your business, but if and when he gets out of jail, I don't want him around me."

"That's fine. I don't expect he will be dad of the year, but it would be nice to have someone besides Auntie."

"We have each other and Joanna and Tito." Even if Tito pissed me off. My heart was pretty full of people who gave a shit about me.

Sage leaned his shoulder against the hall wall, his clean clothes crumpled in a ball in his hand. "Are you and Dan okay?" he asked.

"No. I lost my job today."

"What?"

I threw myself on the couch, facedown. "Because I've been lying," I said into the cushion.

"That doesn't sound like you."

"I've been lying to you and Auntie too."

"About what?"

"I lied to get my job. I said I had a degree, and I don't. I lied to Danuwoa. I have lied to everyone."

"Shit . . ."

"Yeah . . . I didn't want anyone to know, especially Auntie."

He pushed off the wall and knelt in front of me on the floor. "I'm sorry, E. I told you I'm gonna work to pay you back. When I get you the money, you can go back to school and not have to lie anymore and find another job."

"I don't think I can use them as a reference to get another office job. I can't even go back to the bowling alley."

"You can keep applying for entry-level jobs in an office, if that's your dream."

"For now, I just need a job."

"You'll get one."

"I'm going home for a bit to clear my mind."

Sage bent his head. "Why don't you try talking to Danuwoa? He is practically in love with you."

"I can't. I really hurt him with my lies. He witnessed it all go down with my boss. He has his life together, and I'm a train wreck. He deserves someone better."

"Shut up," he said, getting up from the floor and heading to the bathroom.

"What do you mean?"

"Let the man decide that for himself. Why do you make everything so hard on yourself?"

"I do not!"

"Do too! Call the guy and tell him the truth, and if he's an idiot and doesn't want to be with you, then Tito and I will still jump him in a parking lot somewhere." Sage disappeared, and I heard the shower start running.

I was a notorious overthinker, but it was what I did. If I anticipated the worst, then when it happened, I was prepared for it. Except I was never actually prepared for any of this. Not for getting fired and certainly not for falling for Danuwoa.

I loaded up my little SUV that was now too expensive for my unemployed lifestyle. That was a worry for tomorrow. I had to get out of the city and away from the shitstorm I had created. Sometimes lying was easier, but shit got a lot harder when the truths started hammering down.

Breaking bad news to Auntie was always easier when I came bearing gifts. I hoped she was hungry for burgers for dinner.

Thirty-Four

AUNTIE SAT DOWN ON THE COUCH NEXT TO ME WITH A GROAN. "Ugh, my knees ain't what they used to be."

I blew on the mug of hot tea she made me after we finished dinner, already feeling a little better being home.

"So, you ready to talk about it?" she asked.

"Oh, it's so bad," I groaned, and sank farther into the couch.

"I figured, seeing as you haven't said anything except 'I brought dinner' since you showed up."

She was going to be so disappointed in me. I just knew it. Sage was the fuckup, not me. I was the dependable one. I was, if you could believe it, the honest one.

I set my mug of tea down on the worn but loved coffee table and opened my mouth, but no words came.

"Just let it out. Rip it off like a Band-Aid." She patted my knee, lending me her strength with her kind heart and gentle soul. I really did not want to tell her and have her worry about me too. The seconds ticked by, and I picked my tea back up, slurping to stall the inevitable. I couldn't look at her face as I told her what happened.

"I told a lot of lies and made a huge mistake at work—well, quite a few huge mistakes—and was fired. Because of my lies, Danuwoa also dumped me." I stared at a stain on the brown carpet, bracing myself for her censure and judgment.

She gasped.

"Ahhhyyy! That does sound like you fucked up bad." Her eyebrows reached her hairline in shock. Okay, I wasn't expecting her to say that. I thought she would provide a little comfort at least, then launch into a lecture.

"Auntie!"

"I'm here to tell you the hard truth."

"I already know I fucked up. I need help fixing this mess."

"How am I supposed to fix it? This is why I chose never to leave the country. The city is too complicated."

"Auntie," I groaned, setting my hot mug down again. Where was the elder wisdom to fix the situation when I desperately needed it?

"Relax, you're young. Have you learned from these mistakes?"

"I know I'll never tell another lie again so long as I live." I threw my head back into the couch cushion, my arm coming up to shield my eyes.

"See, there you go. Learning life's lessons. It's normal."

"None of this is normal. And I can get over losing the job—I was overpaid and underqualified—but I can't get over losing Danuwoa. He was nothing but good to me."

"Do you love him?" Her voice dropped to a whisper.

"I . . ." Yes. Deep down I somehow knew that I loved him the moment he changed his name in the company chat to Native

Daddy. As crazy as that sounded. That humor was once in a lifetime. His smile, his kindness, and his kisses were all exceptional, all Danuwoa. He deserved someone far better than me. I couldn't say any of this out loud, but with my auntie I didn't have to. She already knew.

And just like that, I was going to cry again.

"Oh, sweet girl, don't cry." She wrapped her arms around me to hug me, rocking us both from side to side. "This is new. I've never had to nurse a broken heart for you. What you need is a distraction."

"What I need is a job," I sobbed into her shoulder.

"C'mon. Up." Auntie slowly pushed herself off the couch.

"Why?" I was really enjoying that hug.

"I've never known you to be a quitter, Ember. I'll allow you to be sad tonight, but tomorrow we're going to see about how we can get you back on your feet."

"That's it?" I swear when Sage was upset about anything, she would go and get Neapolitan ice cream and let him watch *Tomb Raider* on repeat. All I got was a short hug and a dismissal.

"You need more help than I can give, and the employment office and higher education center are closed now."

I wiped the tears and snot from my face. "You're just gonna drop me off at the employment center?"

"Ember, you're twenty-five now. I know you and Joanna couldn't wait to move to the city and away from here, but there is a whole community who loves and supports you."

"I don't know, Auntie. Every time I go to the store or an event here, there's always someone who likes to ask about Mom or Dad and bring up stories about 'the good ol' days,' and I just can't stand to sit there and smile at the same stories I have heard all my life. Especially when I never had any 'good ol' days' with my parents."

"Our people have long memories; no one means anything bad by it. I love you, but you have an avoidance problem. Have you ever asked anyone to stop mentioning your mom and dad to you?" Auntie asked.

I answered her with silence, because, no, I had not. I never wanted to make anyone uncomfortable around me. It was just easier moving to the city to distance myself. Home was still close, but not too close. I could still get lost among the people in OKC, but a short drive and I could be home to have dinner with Auntie and check in. It seemed like the best solution. Also, there was just so much more to do in OKC than in Ada or Sulphur. More bars, more movie theaters, and a larger dating pool that I never really tapped into. It was just more fun.

Auntie put her hands on her hips, her patience at my non-answer running thin.

"You never ask for help, Ember, so I am proud of you for coming here and asking for it. But I don't have any power or money to help you. You're lucky, you're a part of something much bigger than yourself, and you have a history that goes back beyond this country. You were born into it."

Auntie had said stuff like this to Sage and me all the time before, but right now was the first moment I actually really heard her. I was part of something greater, and I tried to get ahead on my own. I tried to work and go to school and not inconvenience anyone by asking for help. And where did that get me? Nowhere. I was worse off than I ever was and back home with nothing to show for all my hard work.

"You're right," I said.

"I'm sorry, what? Did those words just come out of Ember Lee Cardinal's mouth?" she teased.

"Shut up."

"No, I don't think I heard you right. Can you repeat that?"

"You're right!" I threw my hands up. "I need major help. I need to go back to school and maybe get a job that is a bit less ambitious for the time being."

"You can get a job with the tribe. I was talking to Nancy down at the casino, and her son was like you and wanted to get away, except he went off to California. It's so expensive there, so he came back and got a whole certificate with the tribe's help."

"You can't tell Nancy or Fran about any of this. They are the worst gossips." I leaned back on the couch. They were Auntie's best friends and had nothing better to do than be in everybody's business.

She leveled me a look that said, *Have you learned nothing in the last few minutes?*

"Fine, point taken."

"Great, now off with ya. *Wheel* is about to start, and I don't want you killing my vibe. I got three phrases right yesterday."

I rose and gave Auntie a hug and went to my old room I shared with Sage. I wasn't in the mood for *Wheel of Fortune* anyway. Solving those phrases wasn't going to help me.

Thirty-Five

"THANKS FOR STOPPING IN. YOU KNOW, EMBER, I HAVEN'T SEEN you or Sage in years. Gosh! You look so much like your mama," said Mabel, the education specialist. Her face was kind and her smile genuine. She wore thick red glasses that gloriously clashed with her bright blue dress.

"Thanks," I mumbled.

"Her mom and dad are sore subjects," Auntie interjected, giving me major side-eye. It was a missed opportunity for me to practice setting some needed boundaries. I was grateful to Auntie for stepping in for me.

"Oh, sorry about that. Well, it's great to see you. How can I help you today?"

"I want to go to school to become an accountant. I've taken a few classes, but with work and rent, school is just too expensive." I picked at a hangnail on my pinkie.

"Congratulations! We can always use more accountants, what with commerce, the bank, and the casinos. You'd have no issues finding employment. Are you currently enrolled?"

Mabel made it all sound so easy. Nothing about my life had been easy.

"No, I had to drop out to work."

Mabel nodded her head in sympathy. "Yeah, I talk to so many people every day with the same story. The good news is that all you have to do is enroll and get your transcript from high school and the classes you did take, then fill out this application, and we can process your grant for the fall semester."

She handed me a two-page application. Just a quick scan revealed I'd need to attach other documentation too, but it was all easy enough.

"That's it?" I asked, because it seemed too good to be true, and the last time something seemed too good to be true . . . it was. And now I was here.

"That's it. You have to make sure you get passing grades to keep the grant, but after your first approval, all you have to do is fill out the renewal application until you finish your program. We want to help our citizens achieve their dreams. The world is hard enough as it is." Mabel smiled.

"Do you know of anyone hiring in OKC?" I asked, hope bubbling out of me, despite myself.

"You can go to this link. It's our job board. I know they were hiring tellers at the community bank downtown." Mabel handed me a card.

Being a bank teller sounded perfect—at least for now. I couldn't wait to get home and apply.

Now all I had to do was figure out . . . everything else.

PROGRESS WAS SLOW GOING, AND IT FELT LIKE I WAS IN SUS-pended reality. I was taking action to change my life, but at this point it was such a waiting game. Waiting for my transcript, for enrollment to open, for application processing, et cetera, et cetera. But today that all changed. I finally got confirmation that I was officially enrolled back in the community college, and classes started in a few weeks—August 22 couldn't come fast enough. My grant application had been approved, and it covered the entire tuition cost. I cried when the email from Mabel came in with the grant amount. I had a little left over to pay for any incidentals I'd need . . . like a new laptop. After using the one at Technix, there was just no way I could go back to the brick I had before. It was old, loud, and slow.

So that was a lot to happen in two weeks. I'd been back to the city a couple times to fill out applications at a few banks, just entry-level teller positions, and that was fine by me. I had two things left on my list of tasks to handle before classes started: finding a cheaper car and reaching out to Danuwoa.

I was sitting in my little SUV for the last time, back in the parking lot where everything started for me—Bobby Dean's Bowling Alley and Bar.

"You were the nicest thing I ever owned and did me good," I said as I patted the steering wheel. With my job situation still up in the air, it was better to eliminate all car-related expenses: the payment, insurance, and the gas. I had to cut costs, and it was the smart thing to do, but it hurt. It felt like I was going backward a bit. At seventeen, I really thought I'd have it all together by the time I was twenty-five. If teenage Ember could see me now.

A gray Toyota Camry pulled up next to me. It was the buyer, Peter. I'd listed the SUV for sale on Craigslist two days ago, even saying I'd accept cash and a trade of an older car, and Peter made the only legitimate offer I received. His mother had an unused car sitting around. I picked Bobby Dean's parking lot in the middle of the day to reduce the chances of getting murdered. Joanna stood outside the front entrance to keep an eye on me.

A man in his forties got out of the driver's side door. He had sunglasses on but looked like his photo. A little old lady exited the passenger door and came around to the back of my car to wait for me.

This was it.

"Hello," I said and waved in greeting as I walked around to the back.

"It looks as good as the photos," Peter said.

"Yeah, I haven't really been able to drive it much."

"What's wrong with it?" the old lady asked me in a husky smoker's voice.

"Mom," Peter chastised. "Sorry, she's getting more blunt in her old age."

"It's okay." I laughed the question off. "Nothing is wrong with it. I'm going back to school and trying to cut costs."

"Oh, good for you," Peter's mother said.

I talked them through all the details about the car, reiterating what I wrote online. My list price was $2,000 higher than what I owed on the car loan because I hoped after negotiation, I could sell it for enough to pay off the loan in its entirety. It would be nice if Peter paid the list price, and I could go buy something with cash.

We all hopped in the car so Peter could test-drive it. After a few blocks, we went back to Bobby Dean's.

"I'll take it."

Thank fuck! Peter's offer was enticing online, because he mentioned his mother couldn't drive anymore and had an old sedan that was taking up space in the garage. So I was a bit shocked when he offered only $500 below my asking price and the 2006

Toyota Camry. It had more miles than my old Ford Contour, but Toyotas could run forever.

We shook hands. He gave me a cashier's check and the keys and title to the Camry and was off. I ran to Joanna, who was diligently still watching over me from the entrance, and nearly knocked her down when I wrapped her in a bear hug.

Creator was really looking out for me. I still had all the administrative stuff to do, like contact the dealership loan provider and the insurance company, but none of that mattered to me. It would get me to school. Would I miss the SUV? Definitely. But now I could afford to stay in the city.

Joanna was jumping up and down. "You're gonna stay! There was no way I wanted to find a new roommate," she joked.

"That's all you care about?" I asked.

"Duh, no stranger on the internet would make me fried corn burritos whenever I ask."

I rolled my eyes, and she led me inside my old second home.

"Don't be mad, but I called in some reinforcements to help you with your other problem," Joanna said, looking out at the bar.

My stomach dropped, fearing the worst. I followed her line of sight, and waiting there were Sage, Tito, and Walela. I wanted to cry.

"Hi," I said when we approached the bar. "What are you all doing here? Sage, don't you have to work? And Walela, does Danuwoa know you're here?"

"I have the afternoon off. Joanna said you're still sad and we have to come up with a plan to get your boyfriend back," Sage said.

"I took an Uber to get here. Danuwoa thinks I'm at the mall," said Walela.

I slapped my forehead. "No more lying to Danuwoa! Walela,

I appreciate you wanting to help, but lying is what got me in this mess. We gotta get you home."

"Shut up," Tito said, groaning.

"What the fuck are you doing here?" I asked Tito icily.

"Be nice," Joanna warned in my ear. I shrugged her off.

"Whoa, you're family. I know I really fucked Sage over, but I'm turning over a new leaf. I don't want to be that guy anymore."

"And you think helping me get my boyfriend back is enough?" I deadpanned.

"Well . . . no. That's why I'm helping Sage earn money to pay you back, so you get it faster."

This was the first and last time I would ever say it, but Tito stole my breath. It was so kind and unexpected. He still pissed me off, but that was the first reasonable thing I had ever heard come out of his mouth.

"Plus, I still have his shirt you had me wear. I kind of feel bad about that." Tito rubbed the back of his neck.

Nothing like Tito unintentionally bringing up another reason why Danuwoa wanted nothing to do with me in the first place.

"Danuwoa is really sad too. He doesn't really laugh anymore, and he forgot to feed Patches a few times. We are all miserable."

"Walela, if you knew fully what I did, you wouldn't be here," I said with a sigh.

"Danuwoa tells me everything. You lied about work stuff and were blackmailed by Kyle. Danuwoa was really mad when he came home. I've never seen him pace so much. You two love each other, and I think you both need to get over yourselves."

"Shit, no holding back punches. Mad respect," Joanna said as she laughed at my expense.

"Yeah, I'm well aware there are a number of issues, most of my own creation, that we have to get over. Y'all clearly coordinated this, so did you have a plan in mind?"

"Okay, so picture this," Sage started. "We arrange an event here that Walela needs to attend in an official capacity. So, Dan's gotta bring her here, and Tito and I will wait by the door, and once he is in, we will throw a sack over his head and take him to the break room, where you will be waiting. We'll lock the door from the outside so he can't get away and is forced to hear you out. Then you can knock on the door three times to let us know you made up, and we will let you out." He finally stopped for a breath.

"And you agreed to this?" I asked Walela, bewildered. This was crazier than every stunt I'd pulled in the last two months.

"It will be fun, and after you make up, I don't think he will be too mad," Walela said as she laughed and pushed her glasses up her nose.

"If we can get him here between three and three fifteen when Bobby Dean is out back having his smoke, then we should really have no issues," Joanna offered.

"Joanna! Throwing a sack over his head and locking him in a room with me? That's your big plan?"

"Forced proximity works, I read about it all the time." She shrugged.

"In romance novels! This is the real world." How was I the only one seeing a problem with this plan? I could almost hear Danuwoa's voice now: *You don't call but kidnap me instead?* No. This would not do.

"I think it's a great idea," Tito said.

"Yeah, it would be fun, and everything would be better after that," Sage said.

"Look, I really appreciate all the effort you put into this . . ."

plan. I don't even want to get into the criminal undertones this whole idea has, but I can't do this to Danuwoa. He deserves an honest conversation from me and a chance for me to apologize and prove that I've changed. It does mean a lot that I can count on you all to have my back."

"We love you," Joanna said.

Their hearts were in the right place, and it did inspire me to come up with a plan of my own.

"Walela, I think I'll still need your help. If you're up for it."

Her smile was answer enough. It was time for Operation Get Danuwoa Colson Back. If he would have me.

Thirty-Six

M Y NEW CAR REEKED OF STALE CIGARETTES, AND I SNIFFED myself to make sure it hadn't rubbed off on me.

It had.

This wasn't a great start to my plan, which had taken a full week to put into motion. Walela had to wait until she knew for sure there was a day when Danuwoa was planning to stay home on a weekend. The text came last night, and she was babysitting for a neighbor now, so it was just going to be Danuwoa and me in the house when I hoped to lay it all out on the table. I'd taken two allergy pills before heading over to make sure nothing got in the way of this conversation.

I mustered up the courage to get out of the car and knock on his door. The last time I'd been here, I was an invited guest—now I wasn't sure if he would even let me in.

I knocked and waited.

And waited.

I knocked again and said, "Danuwoa, I know you're home.

Please open the door. You deserve an apology and more, and you deserve to have it said to your face."

I heard a faint meow on the other side and waited with my heart in my throat for minutes or hours, I couldn't tell.

Finally, I heard the lock click, and the door opened. I gasped. My soul had been parched from Danuwoa's absence in my life for the past few weeks. He stood in the doorway with his gorgeous hair flowing down, wearing his old Peter Gabriel T-shirt and a pair of jeans, barefoot. Patches wove around his ankles in support.

"Osiyo," he said curtly and nodded his head.

"Chokma," I said with an awkward wave.

Now that I was standing in front of him, like with Auntie, the ability to communicate left me entirely.

"What do you want?" Danuwoa crossed his arms over Peter Gabriel's face in front of his chest.

"Danuwoa . . . I'm so sorry about everything."

He just stared at me, his face hard and unyielding. I deserved it.

"I don't even know what to say . . ." I faltered but plowed ahead. "I'm so embarrassed. I hurt you and I told so many lies."

"Why did you do it?"

"I could never have gotten a job like that just being me. The Ember who unclogged toilets at Bobby Dean's. I had to drop out of school, and I was embarrassed by being . . . well . . . just me. I wanted to be someone more, someone better."

"I don't give a shit that you lied to get the job, I care that you lied to me even after I asked you not to. You never told me anything *real*. I can't trust that anything you say to me is the truth. I wanted to *know* you." His voice was raw with emotion.

"Everything that mattered between us was real, and you do know me," I offered weakly. God, I cringed hearing myself.

His disappointed stare pierced me.

"Goodbye, Ember."

He slammed the door in my face.

I ripped my hands through my hair. This went south so fast, but I couldn't end it like this. Before I knew it, I was pacing in front of his town house, trying to think of a way to fix this situation I kept messing up.

I ran back to the door and knocked, pleading for him to open it again.

"Danuwoa, I'm so sorry. Please just talk to me."

"Go away, Ember," he said through the door.

"Wait!" I placed my palm on the door as if I could still Danuwoa from moving away on the other side. "I have been an idiot. I made so many terrible decisions, and the worst was never trusting you. I was so scared I'd ruin your life and make you lose your job that I ended up losing you instead. You have every right to be angry with me."

I was met with silence, but I could feel Danuwoa still there, waiting. I had to do something to get him to talk to me. This couldn't be it.

I had made many dumb decisions in the last couple of months, but what I did next might take the cake. I started singing Peter Gabriel's "In Your Eyes" like in the movie *Say Anything*. I had no boom box, but I had a man who loved Peter Gabriel on the other side of the door, and I had to get him to talk to me.

I was not a talented singer at all, but I kept going, singing the only part of the song I knew, which was the chorus. I repeated the part about the light and the heat four times before he opened the door again, this time laughing, giving me the first sliver of hope.

"I'm so sorry. I'm not a good singer, and all I do is screw things up where you're concerned, and you deserved so much better than how I treated you. You're the best person I have ever known, and I know I don't deserve a second chance, but I just wanted to apologize to your face."

"Did you really just screech a botched version of the chorus over and over again?" He was still laughing.

"I don't think I've ever heard that song all the way through."

It was stupid, but at least he answered the door. A fact I was starting to regret, since he was now laughing in my face.

Danuwoa snorted.

My eyes watered because I deserved this hell. I started backing away because that sliver of hope I saw was shriveling. I only humiliated myself more, and my fight-or-flight response was kicking in.

"No, wait—" He choked on more laughter. "Come in, we can talk."

The way he said that reminded me of when that man in *Ever After* said, "I'll give you a horse," after Danielle de Barbarac carried Prince Henry on her shoulders—completely ridiculous. But still, I felt a small victory.

He stepped aside to let me in and shut the door to the outside world. We stood there staring at each other.

"You can sit," he said, using his chin to point at the sofa.

I didn't need to be told twice; I rushed to sit before he could throw me out.

"I never thought I'd have a woman trying to serenade me through my windows," he said, laughing again as he joined me on the couch.

I gave him a wobbly smile. "I promise that was a onetime thing."

"It better be! I can't have you embarrassing me in front of all my neighbors like that. Patches was horrified, she ran upstairs. And, god, what's that smell?"

The cigarette car!

"My new car needs some airing out. And my singing wasn't *that* bad."

"No, you were worse. I've never heard someone do such a disservice to Peter Gabriel before."

I should not have been laughing, because this was a serious conversation, but I missed Danuwoa and his humor. He could probably make those British guards with the funny hats break character.

"I'm sorry!" I threw my hands up.

It took a few moments for our laughter to die down, and once it did, a somber silence fell over the room.

"I missed you," I whispered.

"I missed you too," he whispered back. "Do you know what it was like standing behind Mr. Stevenson and not being able to say or do anything to help you?"

I hung my head and wrung my fingers.

"You lied so much, and I thought it was all just stupid stuff because you were embarrassed about not having money. I felt like I knew you."

"You do know me. Let me clear some things up." I took a deep breath and then started unraveling my lies. "I never played in a bowling league."

"I never believed that one," he said.

"I never lived in Bricktown."

"That one you gave away pretty quickly when I brought the printer home for you."

"Yeah . . . and I'm allergic to cats. They freak me out, honestly."

Danuwoa threw his head back and laughed. "I knew it."

"You guessed it. It's not the same as knowing."

"Nah, when you lie, your nostril does this cute flaring thing. Every single time."

"It does not!"

"There it goes flaring again."

I rolled my eyes. "Well, no one at Technix noticed it."

Dropping Technix into the conversation brought the levity down.

"It wasn't that I wanted to hide us. Kyle was blackmailing me. I didn't want you to lose your job. There was so much at risk."

"Kyle is an ass, and he was fired. Escorted out shortly after you were. Everyone still talks about you telling him off."

"So there is some justice in the world."

"I wish you had come to talk to me about it. I'm a grown man, and I don't need protecting. We are supposed to be partners and face these things together. You never should have been put in a compromising situation. It makes me so angry that you went through all that alone, pushing me away. We could have kept our relationship on the down-low and figured out how to stop Kyle together."

"I'm . . . not the best at asking for help. I've had to really work on that the past few weeks and lean on my community back home. I'm going back to school."

"That's great! Where?"

"Oh, just the city community college. Maybe I'll get a bachelor's, but one day at a time."

"I went to community college before I transferred to state university."

"I didn't know that." I smiled, more amazed by this man and how much we had in common.

"You never asked. It makes sense why you never asked, since you were making up a degree and everything."

"I didn't want to lie about myself to you." I looked down at my hands. "That was what I hated the most, telling you a single lie. I want you to have all my ugly truths."

"I want them."

I looked into his beautiful dark eyes, making sure I could believe what I was hearing. But this was Danuwoa, and all he ever spoke was the truth. He was earnest and kind and steadfast. He was the rock that tethered me to reality.

"Would you maybe want to start over?"

It was more than I dared to hope when I showed up. I thought I would have been lucky with an *I'll think about it* before he sent me on my way.

"Danuwoa," I whispered, "I'm a mess and you deserve so much better."

"Bullshit. Gvgeyui, I love you. You made mistakes, but that doesn't change how I feel about you."

"You love me?"

"I've been in love with you for a while, haven't you noticed?"

"No," I breathed.

"You are such a liar."

"I had hoped you felt the same way about me, but that is not the same as knowing."

"And how do you feel about me?"

"I still can't speak Cherokee," I said, tears starting to stream down my face. "But gvgeyui." My emotional tongue butchered the pronunciation. "I really love you."

He grabbed my face, pulling me in for a salty kiss. The best kiss of my life. It was full of forgiveness, grace, and love. We were sitting on his couch, but I still felt weak in the knees. All our pent-up longing and passion was in that kiss. He pulled me closer to his chest and I lost my hands in his long hair.

When we finally came up for breath, we fell back on the couch cushions, and Danuwoa wrapped me in the crook of his arm. We stayed like that, cuddled there for a few minutes.

I listened to his steady heartbeat and said, "I don't have a job yet."

"So?"

"I have a lot of work to do on myself. And I want us to start off on the right foot, one hundred percent transparency."

"That's okay. I'll be here, supporting you. You know, I've had a lot of practice packing lunches."

"Does nothing scare you?" I huffed.

"Only being without you. These have been the worst three weeks."

"For me too." Then this time I grabbed his face and kissed him. He shattered my walls. Every defense mechanism was no match for Danuwoa Colson, the sweetest man I'd ever come across.

"I love you," I whispered against his lips and leaned back a little. "Did my nose do the flare thing?"

"I don't know," he said, smiling. "Tell me again."

"I love you!" I laughed.

"No nose flare."

"See, I'm not lying, and I promise going forward, I'll never lie to you again."

"Wait, your nose just flared."

I bit my lip. "If I tell a lie, I promise it will only be a teensy-tiny little white lie. And it will be the last resort to spare your feelings."

"I think with us starting over, we start with absolutely no lies."

"I don't want to have to tell you that I hate your cat."

"Okay, you'll need to work on that because no one hates Patches."

I sighed. "I promise I'll try to love your demon cat."

He took my hand in his, stroking his thumb back and forth. I was the happiest I had ever felt in my life because, finally, things were working out for me, and it was all done the right way. No lies. No pretending to be someone I wasn't. Whatever the future held for me with school, work, and my ridiculous family, I knew that I—Ember Lee Cardinal, a sometimes liar but overall good person—would be okay.

Epilogue

FRY BREAD WAS SIZZLING ON THE STOVE, AND THE POTATO casserole in the oven was making Danuwoa's whole town house smell divine. My stomach rumbled, anticipating the delicious feast Auntie was cooking up with Danuwoa in the kitchen.

I felt a little guilty that I hadn't been able to help cook at all, but I had to study for my midterms. I didn't want to take any chances with my grades—I wanted them to be the best they could be to keep my grant, but also make the Chickasaw Nation proud. I went my whole adult life avoiding asking for help, and now that they generously bestowed it upon me, I wanted to do right by them.

Working for the community bank was also the best thing to happen to me. I got all the bank holidays off, and with bank hours, I could easily make it to my evening classes.

I looked up from my textbook to give my eyes a break before

they glazed over. Accounting was not the most interesting topic, but there were set rules that didn't change much, except for the tax stuff. I hated the tax code. Joanna and Walela were sitting on the floor in front of the TV, beading. Joanna was showing Walela how to make a beaded collar.

Months ago, I couldn't fathom having a wholesome holiday at home with my entire family. Now, I knew it would be like this every year.

"Brain food incoming," Danuwoa said as he placed a cinnamon-sugar piece of fry bread on top of my work. "Auntie Ruthie wants you to check and make sure the dough turned out right." He winked.

"Always happy to taste test," I said with a salute. Then I took a huge, fat bite. It was perfect. I licked the cinnamon sugar off my lips, watching Danuwoa's eyes heat.

"Not in front of the family," he whispered in my ear, before he kissed my temple.

I gave him my most mischievous smile and suggestively took another bite.

"Hello!" Sage burst through the front door.

The sound made me jump and bump my head into Danuwoa's face.

Danuwoa straightened to his full height, rubbing his forehead. "Welcome, Sage."

"Sup." Sage lifted his chin in greeting. "I brought the pumpkin pie."

"Sweet, let me take that to the kitchen. Make yourself at home," Danuwoa said.

"He always does," I mumbled under my breath and went back to work. I didn't get very far into the next paragraph when Sage scooted into the chair opposite me.

"You're not busy, right?" he asked.

"I'm doing homework," I deadpanned.

"Great, so I wanted to give this to you." Sage reached into his pocket and started placing wads of crumpled bills and quarters on the table.

I pushed my school stuff to the side. "What is all this?"

"Start counting, Miss Accountant. What's all that school for if you can't count?"

"Is this . . . ?" I let the sentence trail off, because I couldn't believe my eyes.

"Your money. All of it I owe you."

Joanna and Walela got up from the floor and came around the table, their smiles big.

"You did it, Sage!" Walela high-fived him.

"I'm proud of you," Joanna said as she socked him in the shoulder.

"What's this?" Auntie came in, drying her hands with a kitchen towel, flour sprinkled all over her apron.

"Everything I owe her. Down to the last quarter," Sage said with a wink.

I started smoothing out the crumpled bills, stacking the ones together, then the fives, tens, and twenties. There was one lone hundred-dollar bill. Then I started stacking the quarters, making piles, counting along the way until I got to $1,000.

"You really did it," I whispered, because the emotion caught my voice in a viselike grip. I was going to cry. I reached my hand across the dining table, grasping Sage's in mine and squeezing.

We never had it easy, but it was our upbringing that made us so close. He was my baby brother, and I was a proud big sister.

I felt a hand squeeze my shoulder and looked up to see Danuwoa smiling proudly in support.

"I'm really sorry for everything I put you both through," Sage said, looking to both Auntie and me.

Auntie was blotting her eyes on the kitchen towel, and Joanna turned away so no one would see her tearing up too. Walela was the first to embrace Sage, and then we all gathered in a group hug.

I loved this big family we were able to find. We chose each other and would always be there for one another. This was what I was most thankful for and would be celebrating today. On the day we Indians saved the pilgrims.

Dear Reader,

Thank you for taking a chance on this story. My dream is that in the coming years, there will be as many love stories written by Indigenous authors and starring Indigenous characters as there are federally recognized tribes within the United States.

I would not be where I am today without the support of my community and the Chickasaw Nation. The resilience of my tribe continues to inspire me every day. We are unconquered and unconquerable, and my small contribution is writing a story that would reach readers and show that we are here, in the modern context, thriving. Chokma'shki'. Thank you, Chickasaw Nation.

I set out to write the goofy, heartfelt Native American romantic comedy between an accountant and the IT guy that I'd had in my mind for years, but I couldn't get it right. It wasn't until I was a new mother, working full-time in an unfulfilling job and attending school full-time to pursue my MBA at night, that I finally "had the time" to figure this story out. It was the most sleep-deprived I have ever been, but I had to make this dream a reality.

I would be sitting in finance and accounting lectures, and in the margins of my notes would be witty banter or meet-cute ideas. These experiences colored Ember and Danuwoa's story. Like Ember, I had difficulties getting an office job after I finished my undergrad degree. I filled out applications in the masses, and there was (and still is to this day) the ethnicity question—check one box and tell us who you are. I could select "American Indian / Alaskan Native," but then I would not be able to select "Hispanic/ Latino" or "Caucasian." I am many things, so which part of myself do I deny to get this job?

But I was on fire; I finally had my degree after seven years of working and going to three different community colleges before transferring to university. It was only possible because of the grants I received from the Chickasaw Nation and the state of California. Corporate America had to know that this was a Chickasaw woman doing this. I selected "American Indian," and rejections rolled in while many other applications simply went unanswered. This happened to me throughout California and during the two years I spent in Chicago. I grew so desperate that I started filling out applications and selecting only "Caucasian" with the same résumé.

Then I started getting interviews and landing the coveted jobs I had dreamed about: executive assistant to the CEO of a company making billions of dollars. Only, once I got there, the sexism, microaggressions, and blatant racism ran rampant. You see, this older generation of executives, in my experience, loved to ask me how I paid for college, with a twinkle in their eyes and a distorted sense of glee—probably because they knew they ruined the cost of education for all generations after them. When I mentioned I received help from my tribe, weird things started happening. Stories of great-grandma Cherokee princesses I could handle, but not other things, like a former executive asking me if my grandmother was a derogatory slur referring to Native American women.

So this silly story of Ember and Danuwoa grew into something more than I initially intended. I wanted to read a story where there were characters who identify as I do, and that inadvertently is a political statement. To write *us* in the pages of a love story, where we have never been allowed to be—except as caricatures or stereotypes to help non-Natives along their journeys—is powerful.

This story started as a question: Why are there no Native American rom-coms? And then was fueled by my resentment toward this world where white supremacy categorizes us by skin tone and blood quantum. And somehow this arbitrary categorization determines what stories are worth telling and reading.

I hope, reader, that you found this story funny, but I also hope you feel empowered by Ember. She, like so many, fought for her happily ever after, and what seems so simple as a stable job really changed her life. Stability and visibility are what give us the confidence to live full, authentic lives.

Warm regards,
Danica Nava

Acknowledgments

I've spent decades reading stories and acknowledgments and dreaming that one day someone would be reading mine. So many acknowledgments mention the solitary act of writing a book, but that was not the case for me. While, yes, it was me typing away and dreaming up this story, the entire way I carried the weight of my ancestors who came before me and an entire demographic of people who rarely see themselves in mainstream media. It is with love and humility that I put this piece of work out into the world. There are 574 federally recognized tribes within the United States of America alone, and so many more that cannot be legally recognized. No two people within the same community share identical experiences, but I hope readers, Indigenous or not, can see themselves in this story and these characters.

It is with so much gratitude that I start my acknowledgments by thanking my wonderful agent, Laura Bradford. Laura, your immediate enthusiasm for Ember and Danuwoa's story made my heart sing, and I just knew you were the right champion for me and my stories. Thank you for your constant advocacy and support; I couldn't ask for a better partner in this. Thank you to my foreign rights agent, Taryn Fagerness, for advocating for my story in foreign markets across the world. To my incredible editor, Angela Kim: You have connected with the story more than I thought possible. You saw Ember and all her flaws and saw the girl just trying to do the right thing. You are patient, kind, understanding, and have a wicked sense of humor. Thank you for taking my words and making them so much more than I ever thought they could be. To the rest of the team at Berkley who have championed this book: Cindy Hwang, Liz Gluck, copyeditor Angelina Krahn, proofreaders Will Tyler and Lindsey Tulloch, publicists Dache' Rogers and Tara O'Connor, and marketers Kim Salina-I and Hannah Engler. To the team who has made this book more beautiful than I dreamed: art director Colleen Reinhart, cover illustrator Britt Newton, and book designer Daniel Brount.

I was encouraged and embraced by so many wonderful people who cheered me on to finish Ember's story and who read earlier drafts while I worked to get it right. I hope I have remembered every single name. My amazing critique partner, LE Todd—I love our writing process and sending long deranged voice notes back and forth about things as small as a piece of dialogue to large sweeping plotting questions and ideas. Erin Dixon, you were my first Bookstagram friend, and I am so blessed to know you and your friendship. I love all your book recommendations and feel your love and support from across the country. Alexis Richoux, thank you from the bottom of my heart for reading that first draft that was barely over fifty thousand words and for hopping on video calls to help me make the manuscript query ready for agents. I loved all your comments and notes throughout every page. To the best beta reader and friend a girl could ask for, Elizabeth Schultz, thank you so much for your thoughtful feedback. To my friends who helped me when I first started writing: BJ Bentley, Dr. Rebecca Sharp, and Stephanie Hotz. This story and my writing would not be what it is without all of you.

To my amazing Indigenous online writing community, I love you and am so proud to know you and read your works. Cynthia Leitich Smith, thank you for reviewing my querying materials and for all your advice about navigating this opaque industry. Erika T. Wurth, thank you so much for your friendship and for amplifying my work. Byron Graves, you are a talent, and I am so grateful to be your friend. AJ Eversole, thank you so much for your constant support and answering my Cherokee-related questions. I can't wait for your works to be published. Thank you to my fellow Chickasaw friend Kate Heart for answering all my publishing questions and giving sage advice.

Chokma'shki' to the Chickasaw Nation for your support. I really would not be where I am at all without this community.

Without the support of my cohort at USC, I would never have been able to write this book. I survived business school with the help, love, and encouragement from my OMBA family: Eugena Yu, Emilio Vela Alvarenga, Sandra Vazquez, Lloyd Magpantay, Brock Nakashima, Miguel Prado, Ada Thu Le, Sneha Mathew, Lavi Kachurik, Jennifer Chen, Parham Paydar, Santoshi Reddy, Prair Tapvong, and Will Muniz. Thank you to my favorite USC Marshall School of Business professors who loved that I was writing a novel while in the program and asked why I would want to study business when I was an author (valid question): Professor Nandini Rajagopalan, Professor Ayse Imrohoroglu, Professor Kerry Fields, and Professor Carl Voigt. Thank you to all the program staff at USC Marshall for supporting me while I started the program five months pregnant: Brittany Hawkins, Keturah Prowell, and Kristen Chen.

My fellow debuts: Ellie Palmer, Naina Kumar, Myah Ariel, and Mallory Marlowe. I know we will be friends for years to come. I am in complete awe that I am in your company and will be next to you on shelves.

Thank you to my Berkley family, also known as the Berkletes, for their shouts of support and answering all my questions as I've navigated the publishing waters: Emily Henry, Ali Hazelwood, Sarah Adler, Sarah Hawley, Isabel Cañas, Vanessa Lillie, Nikki Payne, Jo Segura, Katie Shepard, Tiana Smith, Jenna Levine, Jackie Lau, Sajni Patel, Taleen Voskuni, Elise Bryant, Sarah Zacgrich Jeng, Eve Chung, Olivia Blacke, Mia Manansala, Chloe Liese, Nekesa Afia, Jessica Joyce, India Holton, Tori Martin, Jesse Q. Sutanto, Kristina Forest, Sarah Grunder Ruiz, and Liana De la Rosa.

My comedy friends, who helped me play, explore, and grow as a comedian, thank you. Thank you to my Conejo Improv Players Troupe family: Jon Rowsey, Jeremy Zeller, Shelby Fry, Christopher Carlson, Alexandra Menna, Frank Bonoff, Scott Shrum, Cindy Harris, Kevin Schultz, and Allie Leslie. I do think these jokes are slammin' because of the years of fun we have had together.

In my professional life, there have been coworkers who have cheered me on with my writing and also guided me in my career. Thank you to Edona Kurtolli, Timmy Lau, Carolyn Brandwajn, David Richards, Nichole Bartlett, Cari Shyiak, Katariina Kujala, Gabriella Sanzo, and Sujal Shah. There were no better people to push paper with.

Thank you to all the English teachers who have shaped me and my writing: Mrs. Wantz, Mrs. Powers, Ms. Tomb, Mr. Slade, Mr. Dickey, and Mr. Andrews.

Kimberly A. Fouche', your years of counseling and therapy saved my life. Thank you for helping me heal.

George Lucas, you will never see this, but I have to thank you and all your brilliant work. I love *Star Wars*, so much so that I started my writing journey by writing prequel fan fiction. Killing Cordé off in the first few minutes of *Attack of the Clones* made me want to give that poor woman a backstory that was thrilling and exciting so she didn't just apologize for dying. It was called *Decoy* and it was not very good, but look, I found my own original stories because of your genius. Thank you.

Thank you to my mother, grandmother, sisters, stepfather, and late father for raising me. Thank you to my mother-in-law, Anna Thomas, for reading the first couple of chapters and proof-reading all my querying materials and believing in this story.

Chris, the thanks and love I have for you could fill an entire book. Thank you for your unconditional love, for inspiring me every day to be the best version of myself. Thank you for sitting in the office late at night while I read to you the freshly drafted chapters of this book to see if my jokes were landing. Thank you for believing in me when I forget to believe in myself. Your love has made me a writer of truth within my fiction. You are the love of my life, and I am blessed to walk in this journey with you.

And lastly, thank you to my daughter, Isme. This whole journey has been for you. I hope you never read this novel, but when you are fifty and really want to, I will give you a heavily redacted version. I love you forever, my tenacious, silly, brilliant little girl. You were the catalyst to get me to write again. It took me writing about a girl who was a liar to rediscover my truth as a writer.

Glossary

chokma—Chikashshanompa' for hello, pronounced chuk-mah

chokma'shki'—Chikashshanompa' for thank you, pronounced chuk-mah-sh-ki

Danuwoa—Name derived from the Cherokee word for warrior, dahnawa ditihi, pronounced dah-nu-wah

gvgeyui—Cherokee for I love you, pronounced guh-geh-yu-ee

gvlielitseha—Cherokee for you're welcome, pronounced guh-li-eh-li-che-hah

howa—Cherokee for okay or all right, pronounced ho-wah

kawolade'dv—Cherokee for breathe, pronounced ka-wol-eh-dey-a

osiyo—Cherokee for hello, pronounced oh-si-yu

Walela—Name derived from the Cherokee word for hummingbird, pronounced wa-ley-lah

THE TRUTH ACCORDING TO EMBER

DANICA NAVA

READERS GUIDE

Discussion Questions

1. Have you ever lied about your qualifications to achieve something?

2. Do you think telling white lies is okay? In what situations do you consider it appropriate to lie?

3. Do you think Ember ultimately deserved to get fired for her lies and actions, or do you think the company should have taken the circumstances into consideration?

4. What is your dream job? Would you ever pursue it?

5. Have you ever faced microaggressions in a public setting, like at work or school? How did you confront them?

6. Do you think employers discriminate against applicants based on the ethnicity question on job applications?

7. We generally have not had accurate Native American representation in media, whether it be in film or even news

sources. With that in mind, how was your experience reading about Chickasaws and Cherokees in Oklahoma?

8. Ember's final confrontation with Kyle is very heated. Do you feel like she was vindicated in that moment? What would you have done in that situation?

9. Danuwoa also had to abide by the no-dating policy at the office, but he seemed almost careless in his pursuit of Ember. Do you think he was right to want to be honest about the relationship, or was Ember right to keep up the charade at work?

10. Technix is a satirical representation of tech companies at large. If Ember were in the real world, do you think there would have been any protection for her within the company to keep her from being coerced into spending her own money for work-related tasks or being blackmailed by Kyle?

11. Sage skipping bail and losing Ember's savings is the catalyst for Ember to lie about her work experience and ethnicity. Do you think Ember forgives Sage too easily? Why or why not?

12. Ember is able to rebuild her goals with the help of her community. Often in this modern, capitalist culture, we are expected to suffer in silence and resolve things on our own, but Native culture is not that way. When everyone is working together, lending helping hands to those who need them, we thrive. What lessons in community do you take away from Ember and her story?

*Keep reading for an excerpt from
the next romantic comedy by Danica Nava*

I WAVED TO MY MOTHER AND CHELSEA THROUGH THE GREY-
hound bus window. The polyester seat smelled of stinky feet
and old cheese. Their send-off was rather unceremonious. My
mother decided it was safer to ride on a bus than risk being seen at
an airport and someone catching wind of this plan to go to Oklahoma and win over the tribe. I looked down at my bus ticket stub.

NAME: AVERY FOX
FROM: DALLAS, TX
TO: TULSA, OK
CONNECTION: OKLAHOMA CITY, OK

That line made my heart stop. A connection! That couldn't be
right. I shot up to ask the driver just as the bus started rolling, the
momentum pushing me back into my seat.

"Um, excuse me! Sir?" I shouted to the bus driver.

Everyone was looking at me, and not happily either. I guess I
broke some unwritten rule of silence. But I had to get off this

thing. I had four suitcases under the bus. I couldn't move all those by myself.

"Sir!" I called again, running to the front of the bus as the driver cruised down the street. He stopped at a red light.

"What?" he asked.

"I was unaware that this bus has a connection. I thought this was a straight shot to Tulsa."

"Nope, only one nonstop and you missed it."

The light turned green, and I grabbed his seat to steady myself.

"Are there attendants to help transfer bags to the next bus?"

"Attendants?" He cackled. "Ma'am, this is the Greyhound. Attendants . . ." He laughed again. "G'on back and sit down now. Next stop Oklahoma City."

I walked back to my seat using the tops of the headrests of the aisle seats to stabilize myself, keeping my head down to avoid the snickers from the fellow passengers. My mother was right about one thing. No one recognized me or cared who I was.

I wasn't a famous pop singer and child star to them—I was just a nobody.

I shoved my ticket into my pocket, took my satchel bag off over my head, put it in my lap, and crossed my arms.

I closed my eyes. The last few nights had been an emotional roller coaster, and I got next to no sleep. The bus bumped along the highway as we went north.

Something smelled foul, and I heard laughing from an older lady, and then a baby started screaming and crying.

This was *so* not first class.

I took in everyone around me: a young mother with a shrieking baby, two old ladies traveling together, and a young guy who looked like he walked straight out of a Fall Out Boy music video circa 2006. Flat-ironed bangs and all. He flashed me a smile and

I gave him the smallest grin I could muster back. I didn't want to be rude, but I also did not want to encourage conversation just in case I was recognized easily again, like last night.

I pulled my hood farther down my face and tried to meditate and block out my surroundings. In my mind's eye, I pictured myself in Costa Rica in a cabana drinking a margarita. Before long I'd convinced myself to relax and was startled awake when the bus stopped. I wiped drool from my mouth and looked out the window. The bus station sign read OKLAHOMA CITY.

I'd slept for hours.

Great. Now I had to get all my stuff to the next bus. I filed in line to get out and stopped next to the driver, feeling my side for my purse to tip him, and my hand brushed air. I rubbed both hands all over my sides and looked for my purse, spinning in a circle.

Where. Was. My. Bag?!

I pushed past the people behind me to get back to my seat. My bag wasn't there. I dropped to my knees and felt around the grimy floor to see if it fell.

Empty.

Someone swiped my purse! Who would do that?

No, no, *no*. My money and my phone were in there. What would I do in a world without a phone? It was definitely an example of a first-world problem, but I couldn't help it. I cried. And it wasn't the pretty, dainty cry I learned to do at Disney. No, this was the full-on snotty hyperventilating cry.

Three pieces of my matching luggage were lined up outside the bus and the driver was wheeling the fourth to join the group. Shit. I sprinted to get them before someone else tried to take my possessions away from me. All that was in there were clothes, shoes, and makeup, but they were *mine*.

"Sleeping Beauty finally wakes up," the bus driver said. His look was one of pure judgment and disappointment as he crossed his arms and shook his head at me.

"Sorry."

"Attendant," he said under his breath, and walked away, without looking at me again.

One by one I wheeled my suitcases to bus sixteen, where the new driver helped me load them. At least I had my ticket stub in my pocket. That was the only smart thing I did.

I chose a seat right in front this time, hoping that being close to the driver would mean I was safer and less susceptible to theft; granted, all I had on me was my sweater.

My stomach rumbled. I had no money for food and no phone to update my mother or Chelsea. I stared out the window, and Fall Out Boy walked into the bus station with a black quilted Gucci cross-body bag. He had nice taste. I had a bag just like that.

"Wait!" I yelled. The driver, a friendly older lady, clutched her chest.

"What, child?"

"That guy stole my purse!" I pointed out the window.

"What guy?" she asked.

I looked at her and said, "The one in the plaid super-skinny jeans." I looked back out the window and he was gone.

No!

I cried for the first fifteen minutes of the drive. Then I sat in self-pity for the remainder of the journey to Tulsa, watching the flat scenery with dead, tired eyes, thinking to myself that I deserved this. This was my hell. I did that stupid photo shoot and now I was paying dearly.

Tulsa was a big city. So was Oklahoma City, but I didn't

bother to pay attention since it was a mad dash to load my stuff, but now, sitting on my largest white RIMOWA trunk by the curb waiting for my grandmother, I took it in. There were lots of buses and cars. Some trees, *I guess*. It was whatever.

Where was my grandmother? I had no phone or watch, but I'd guess I'd been sitting here for twenty minutes.

I started kicking a pebble between my feet like a super low-stakes foosball game to pass the time. I needed food and water so bad; when I used the station bathroom—not an easy feat with all my luggage stacked in a stall—I cupped my hands and gulped down as much water from the faucet as I could.

As the day wore on, I was reduced lower and lower. Now, to add insult to injury, I had been stood up.

I looked up to the parking lot again, and the clouds parted, and the setting sun's rays shone down on a cute little old lady wearing cowboy boots and decked out in silver and turquoise jewelry. I jumped up and ran to her, wrapping my arms around her neck.

"Grandma!"

The lady froze; her arms did not wrap around me. I pulled back to look at her face to see if I could find a family resemblance.

I found none.

"Grandma?" I asked with less confidence.

"Get off me, you crazy bum!" She pushed me away. "I got a gun in my purse."

"It's me, Avery?"

"I don't care if you're Mother Teresa, you don't just grab people. This generation." The lady grumbled as she stalked away and into the bus station.

I hated today.

A thick and throaty laugh hummed around me.

Great. I had an audience. That was the final straw. I whipped around to meet the owner of the laugh and my breath left me. The man laughing at my misfortune was tall, dark, and handsome.

Just what I needed.

I rolled my eyes and walked back to my bags. I was covered in grime from the floor of the bus and running on empty. Flirty Avery was dead.

"You doin' all right there?" he asked in a voice as rich as leather.

"Yeah, great." I raised my voice but didn't bother to look at him again, I just threw a thumbs-up over my shoulder.

At least when I did meet my grandma, it couldn't be worse than getting threatened with a weapon. So there was that for a silver lining. I sat back down on my trunk and stared at my feet. I was wearing Golden Goose sneakers and was disgusted with myself. I had spent six hundred dollars on a pair of artificially distressed shoes to make them look like used street wear. Now they were indeed dirty, with real dirt and grime and a piece of an old gummy bear stuck to the bottom of one.

The tabloids were right. I was a fake. Everything about me was curated, even down to my fake-dirty, now real-dirty shoes.

A pair of dusty cowboy boots entered my field of vision. Covering the tops of the boots were a pair of light-wash boot-cut jeans also covered in dust. My eyes followed the toned line up to an equally dust-speckled black T-shirt, then up to the tanned face of a god.

It was the handsome man who'd laughed at me.

"What can I do for you?" I asked.

"You Avery Fox?" he asked, his voice gruff, with a slight twang.

Oh shit. He recognized me. I'd been found out.

"Who's asking?"

"Lottie Fox sent me." At my blank stare he added, "Your grandmother."

"Oh, right. Yes, Lottie." I said her name like I said it all the time, letting it roll off my tongue. I knew her name was Loretta. I had no idea Lottie was short for Loretta, though I couldn't say I knew anyone with either of those names.

"Is she in the car waiting?" Hope filled me as I looked over his shoulder, trying to guess which car was his.

"Nope, just me. Gotta get going if you want to make it back for food. With our luck, Red and Davey won't save nothin'."

I watched in stunned silence as this man took the handle of my biggest suitcase and one of the smaller ones and began wheeling them to an old white truck.

I grabbed my remaining two bags and quickly followed him. He walked with such authority, it was like I was on autopilot. I really tried not to look at his ass, but the denim fit him perfectly. Then I had a very worried thought.

"Are we . . . related?" I asked.

He huffed a laugh and threw over his shoulder, "No," and kept walking.

Phew. I did not want to be having any of those types of thoughts about a potential cousin or something. Now I could say as an impartial party that his guy had a fine ass.

He pushed the handle down into the suitcase, then his tan, corded muscles flexed as he lifted the hefty thing and threw it into the bed of his filthy truck.

"Hey! Don't do that!"

He stopped to give me a strange look. "I have rope to tie them down."

"Okay, but don't throw them. These are really nice, and you're gonna scuff them all up and get them dirty."

"It's luggage." He said it simply and gave me a blank stare. "So?"

"Luggage is meant to get chucked around. Will they crack open and ruin your clothes if they are tossed a bit?"

"No, these are, like, top of the line, really high quality."

"All right then," he said with a grunt as he chucked the other one in.

"They're RIMOWA!" I gripped the edge of the truck, looked in, and could see scuffs already. I hadn't even taken the brand deal photos with them yet. Now I was going to have to pay for these.

"You!" I turned on him. "I don't know who you think you are, but today is not the day to try me. I've been on a bus for four hours with no food, and I had to drink water from the faucet in the disgusting bathroom! I've been threatened by an old lady with a gun, my purse and phone were stolen, and this has gone too far! My own grandmother couldn't even be bothered to pick me up herself! Instead she sends some . . . some . . . dirty cowboy in her stead, and you're ruining all I have left."

Tears started falling down my face, and honestly, I was a little impressed. If I still wanted to act, I now knew I could literally cry for hours on end with no problem. All I had to do was be pushed past my limits, humiliated on a global scale, have nothing left to my name, and be at the mercy of an Oklahoma cowboy.

"Lucas," he said. He just stood there weathering all I unleashed on him, barely batting an eye. "I work for your grandmother."

"And how can I verify that? You could be some obsessed fan."

This got a reaction out of him. He snickered and said, "Not a fan, trust me."

"What's that supposed to mean?" I crossed my arms.

"I live on a ranch, not under a rock, lady." He brushed past me and got the other bags and threw them in. "You're welcome to stay here. But if you want to come to the ranch, then get in."

He walked to the driver's-side door, disappearing inside.

I ran to the passenger window, which was rolled down. "You said you had rope!"

"That was before you called me a 'dirty cowboy.'" He turned the key in the ignition and nodded with his chin to the passenger seat. "Get in."

I threw open the door and plopped down with a huff.

"How far away is the ranch?"

"'Bout twenty minutes or so."

"Great."

"There's a power bar in the glove compartment." All I could do was stare at him, which was a mistake, because I noticed his dark thick brows, and his nose hooked a little in a hot, hawkish way. "You said you were hungry."

Then he shifted his truck into drive and drove out of the city. I'm ashamed to say I ate that power bar in three bites.

Photo by Cindy Pitou Burton

Danica Nava is an enrolled citizen of the Chickasaw Nation and works as an executive assistant in the tech industry. She has an MBA from USC Marshall School of Business. She currently lives in Southern California with her husband and daughter. *The Truth According to Ember* is her debut novel.

VISIT DANICA NAVA ONLINE

Danica_Nava

Ready to find
your next great read?

Let us help.

Visit prh.com/nextread

Penguin
Random
House